THE BEST OF
SHADOW LANE

THE BEST OF
SHADOW LANE

EVE HOWARD

BLUE MOON BOOKS
NEW YORK

THE BEST OF SHADOW LANE

Published by
Blue Moon Books
An Imprint of Avalon Publishing Group Incorporated
161 William St., 16th Floor
New York, NY 10038

The selections from Shadow Lane and the chapters "Jealousy" and "The Attempted Taming of Marguerite Alexander" first appeared in episodic form in the publications Shadow Lane and Stand Corrected, printed between 1987 and 1990 by Shadow Lane. "Michael and Patricia" was originally published in The Shadow Lane Unbound Library Series. "Susan's Senior Year," "Ambition," "Marguerite and Malcolm," and "How Cute is That" originally appeared, respectively, in Scene One #6 (August, 1994), Scene One #11 (October, 1995), Scene One #12 (January, 1996), and Scene One (May, 1997).

ISBN 1-56201-296-7

9 8 7 6 5 4 3 2 1

Printed in the United States of America
Distributed by Publishers Group West

CONTENTS

SHADOW LANE

RETURN TO RANDOM POINT

HUGO SANDS WAS certain that Marguerite and Laura would return from their antics in Manhattan for his party, an annual event for which he had this year rented a mansion called The Cliffs.

He was still vaguely irritated with his favorite pet/victim, Marguerite, for departing from town so abruptly, without even bothering to ask whether her absence would be convenient at this time. He was particularly irked at her for not calling to let him know where she had gone until three days in New York had elapsed.

However, he understood the redhead's motives well enough. And while she did deserve to be publicly whipped for her arrogance, he couldn't help but feel a certain thrill of pride when she described how many sessions she was doing with Laura, with some of Hugo's most important clients, how much allowance the girls were racking up and how perverse their Laura could be. That was the part that most interested Hugo Sands.

Hugo threw a good party, with a full bar, amply furnished buffet tables and continuous atonal music that no one could understand. Everyone important in Random Point showed up. The remainder of the guests were divided equally between Hugo's associates in the legitimate antique business and his numerous colorful and bizarre connections in the B&D publications, entertainment and personal services. It made for a compatible mix. There were even crossovers. Why shouldn't a collector of Sevres china also have a collection of riding crops?

Marguerite and Laura sauntered in through the front door at ten. The milling throng of revelers crowding the foyer and staircase swallowed them up almost at once. A number of other guests wore leather, like the girls, also glove-tight latex and shiny PVC. Mixed in with these creatures of the night, who all seemed to be looking for Hollywood Boulevard, was a traditional selection of pirates, cowboys, clowns, belly dancers and Southern belles. There was also the small creative fringe, mostly Hugo's snotty writer friends, who dressed like pieces of sushi, or in another case, a couple that came as a plug and socket.

"I see Marguerite's gotten Laura into her first pair of 5" high heels," Hugo remarked to William Random, who stood beside him on the gallery above the choked hall and staircase. William made a splendid barbarian in a leather torso harness that displayed his impressive muscularity dramatically. Studded gauntlets garnished his forearms and lacing sandals latticed his massive calves. His full leather face mask might have been as menacing as its designer had intended if it were not for the new eye glasses, which perched so incongruously on the bridge of his nose.

"Do you think Laura will recognize me?" William queried his companion, leaning his rock-hard abdomen against the railing. "I mean, this mask is pretty effective, don't you think?"

"Since you have no clothes on, she's bound to recognize you," said Hugo patiently, while inwardly observing that the absence of pussy, for even a short amount of time, could turn an intelligent man into a babbling chucklehead.

Hugo, who considered fancy dress appropriate for everyone but himself, wore his usual well tailored evening clothes. Like William's, his gaze followed the delectable leather-sheathed forms of Marguerite and Laura, wriggling through the crowd in the foyer.

"Your wife looks even cockier than Marguerite tonight," Hugo observed at the moment eye contact was fixed between themselves and the girls. But Laura's mien of careless defiance melted at the sight of her husband.

"Marguerite, let's go up!" Laura touched an elbow-gloved hand to her friend's luminous white shoulder.

"Ouch!" her red-headed friend cried suddenly. Looking back over one bare shoulder she saw she had been struck upon the right cheek of her large, luscious bottom with a toy arrow, which actually adhered to the surface it had struck, by means of a suction cup tip. She yanked it from her leather covered rear end with a snarl, as she raked the press of guests surrounding her with a glare.

"Did you see that?" Hugo laughed.

"That was priceless," William agreed, of the insult to the haughty Marguerite.

"No it wasn't, look over there," Hugo pointed to the doorway of the cloakroom, where a tall, ruddy blonde with a thick ponytail, dressed as Robin Hood, stood laughing behind her hand.

"Who's she?" William asked, admiring the robust good looks of the flaxen haired imp, who even now was reloading her bow from the quiver of arrows slung across her back.

"That's Marnie Price, your arch enemy's little sister."

"Why haven't I noticed her before?"

"She's been keeping busy since puberty getting expelled from every prep school in New England."

"She looks like a real New England girl." William said with approval.

"Drinks like one too."

"Doesn't seem to impair her aim though."

"You'd have to be legally blind to miss a target that large," Hugo remarked ungallantly.

"Good point," his companion agreed, while still admiring the voluptuous posterior of Marguerite, who now gave it a brief rub, after breaking the arrow in half with a toss of her glorious mane.

As the girls filtered up through the crowd on the stairs, the ear-splitting roar of a Harley skidding to a stop outside let everybody know that Randy Price had arrived.

Price enjoyed making an entrance. He was twenty-eight, tall, lean and swaggering. He wore a black bomber jacket, ripped T-shirt and black jeans. From his left ear an inverted cross dangled and his skull had been completely shaved, the first sight of which caused not only Laura and Marguerite, but every other woman in the room who now recognized Randy and remembered having last seen him with hair, to gasp.

The manipulative C.E.O. of Price Enterprises was William

Random's most serious competitor. He was a Harvard Business School dropout, but this had not stopped him from pulling his family's floundering land development company out of the red several years before and building it into a corporation with wide holdings all over New England and twenty-five million in liquid assets.

With his uncanny business acumen and total lack of ethics to guide him, Randy's deals seldom blew up in his face. The incident with Damaris Perez was not typical. Price didn't like getting burned, and he was eager to transfer the sting to Damaris, should he find her mixed in with the natives attending Hugo's annual party.

He scanned the halls and stairs impatiently, ignoring all who greeted him, but acknowledging Laura Random with a smirk. Laura turned and fled up the stairs. Her violent reaction was noted by William, who now folded his arms belligerently, as he considered the growing annoyance Randall Price had become in his life.

Even as William confronted the fact that Laura had cheated on him with his most dangerous and unscrupulous competitor, he found his wife especially appealing in the cherry red leather dress that clove to her buttocks, sleek thighs and firm bosom so excitingly.

"Why does Randall keep following Laura?" William suddenly demanded of Hugo. But Laura was with them before Hugo could answer, throwing her arms about William's neck. He embraced her without hesitation, locking his arms about her so tightly that she squealed as he lifted her off the ground and swung her around.

"Well?" he demanded. "Have you decided to come home?"

"Yes," Laura said shyly, hiding her face against his chest.

"Good!" Nothing could have been more emphatic than this pronouncement.

Laura had expected him to be stern and remote. The quality of warmth did not often emanate from William Random, but it was one which she could easily get used to. Then suddenly Randy was upon them.

"Hi Laura! Like my haircut? Hey, Billy, how's it going? Hugo, no costume?" Randy was bubbling with abrasive energy. William's hands balled into fists as he let Laura go.

"Even a good haircut is no substitute for the frontal lobe job you really need," William pointed out.

Before Randy could snarl a response, Laura asked Hugo to take her to the bar.

"Don't go, baby," Randy said, touching Laura's bare shoulder. "There's so much I want to say."

"Leave my wife alone," William told him.

"She's got a mouth," said Randy. "And we both know she can use it. Why doesn't she tell me herself?"

"She asked me to deliver the message, so you'd read it loud and clear," William said, stepping aggressively in front of Laura, who took the opportunity to seize Hugo's hand and scurry away with the amused voyeur in tow.

"If I stay they'll come to blows for sure," Laura explained to Hugo, who seemed a bit reluctant to leave.

"I should have thought you'd enjoy that," Hugo remarked, allowing himself to be dragged down the stairs by his pretty companion. "Marguerite would be selling tickets."

"Gee, she's pretty," Randy sighed, like a moonstruck kid, to taunt William.

"Randall, let's go outside," William suggested.

"Why? All the chicks are in here. Listen, we'll do lunch, okay? Later." Randy had spotted Damaris Perez and the next instant he was gone.

"Believe it, asshole," William muttered, as he too caught a glimpse of his ex-secretary, encased in a PVC jumper that glittered like black ink, clinging crustacean-like to Lt. Michael Flagg's brawny arm.

"I'm glad you've left your husband," Hugo said, when she'd had her first drink. "That means we can finally play."

For the first time since he'd known her, Laura looked Hugo boldly in the eye.

"I haven't left my husband. But yes, we can finally play."

"In that case, come with me. I have everything arranged," Hugo said, and took her by the hand. He led Laura up to the attic, where he knew there was a private little room. Earlier that day he had fitted it out with a padded leather bench and a mirror opposite. It was here that he'd intended to take her, and now it would happen for sure.

"Nervous?" he asked her, leading her in.

"Not at all," she lied, tossing back her mane of soft brown hair.

"Yes you are. Come here and sit next to me," he told her, pulling her down on the bench. "And tell me why you've been so naughty lately. It really isn't like you."

"Hugo, I didn't come with you to be treated like a child," she protested.

But Hugo hadn't waited patiently for eighteen months to treat her like an adult.

"If by that you mean I'm not supposed to spank you, you should know better, Laura."

"But why?" she cried, pulling off the domino that had covered her eyes.

"Because," he said, putting his arm around her shoulder and drawing her to him, "that's what I'm into."

"But I don't want you to!"

"Look, let me explain something to you, little one, there are all sorts of spankings. Some of them hurt a lot and some hardly hurt at all. I happen to be an expert in administering what are called erotic spankings. Now if I give you my word that I'll only spank you in a way that will arouse you without making you kick, scream or cry, will you trust me enough to submit?"

The concept was a new one on Laura, but she liked the way Hugo's arms felt about her. She liked the way he smelled and the comforting firmness of his chest to lean upon. He had always been rather sarcastic with her, when he was not being overtly wolfish. This was a different Hugo and she was in fact, inspired to trust him.

"Okay," she told him.

"There's a good girl," said Hugo. "Now stand up. Right here," he pointed to the floor in front of him. Laura obeyed after some slight hesitation. He raised her arms, which she held stiffly at her sides until one hand rested on each of his shoulders. Then, using both hands, he pushed the hobbling skirt of her expensive leather dress up, from the backs of her knees to her waist. It slid very slowly upward, and as he pushed, his fingertips caressed the backs of her thighs and the curves of her buttocks, which were finally revealed, after considerable effort. The skirt, with its leather laces going up the back, was exceedingly tight, and Laura's bottom was nothing if not round.

Finally the dress was pushed up to her waist and Hugo confronted a ravishing black satin garter belt, with silk-satin bikinis to match, the suspenders holding up sheer nylon stockings, tinted black, with seams up the back. He dropped his hands to trace her stocking seams, from ankle to thigh top and back, with a whispery touch. Laura shivered, not prepared for tenderness.

"All right," he said, "come here," and pulled her down across his lap. Her sharp little intake of breath as he did was enough to let him know that nothing had changed with the doe-eyed brunette; she was as susceptible as ever to the position in which she'd been placed.

She kept her legs straight and together, with the toes of her shoes on the floor.

"You mustn't be tense," he told her, running his palm, for the first time, across the lovely contours of her bottom, through the clinging satin of her panties. Even in the low light of the little attic room, the expanse of exposed thigh she displayed above her stocking tops gleamed as white as moonlight. They were silken to the touch. He could not remember ever touching anything so smooth or so soft as the insides of Laura's thighs.

She shivered at his light caresses, not knowing what would come next, but felt herself relaxing more each moment that she lay across his lap. With one hand on her waist, he drew her closer. With the other, he continued to stoke her round buttocks and shapely thighs.

"Let's pretend you're five again," said Hugo. "You're just a little girl."

"Pretend I'm five?" she echoed with surprise.

"Only five," he told her, bringing his palm to rest on the rise of one firm cheek. Suddenly the party seemed very far away. It was so quiet in the attic that Laura could hear his watch tick.

"And you're my little girl," he continued. "My very little girl." He paused without moving his hand, to let the notion germinate. Then he went on speaking in a hushed, almost hypnotic tone of voice.

"Most of the time you're a good little girl. I hardly ever have to punish you. But today you were very naughty. You brought your kitten into the shop. You had a ball of yarn tucked in your apron pocket. You took it out and trailed it on the floor. The kitty saw the bright blue string and leaped on it. You laughed and dragged the string away from him. Again it jumped and pounced. Again you dragged the yarn away, and ran behind a corner with the string whipping after you fast. You continued to play with the kitty. Faster and faster you ran. You became so excited while playing that you completely forgot my rule about running in the shop. At last you were totally breathless. You'd run until your little legs felt weak. No wonder you lost your balance and knocked over the lamp."

At this pronouncement Laura, utterly caught up in the story, gasped in guilty astonishment.

"Yes, little girl, it's very sad. You broke the frosted glass shade of the lamp. It was one of those fluted monstrosities with flowers, fruit and birds worked in relief. No one with taste would have bought it, but I'd have sold it for a profit all the same. So naturally your naughtiness has made me very cross."

Hardly conscious of what she was doing, Laura ground against his lap. Her heart was fairly pounding and the power of suggestion had planted a lump in her throat.

"After you heard the lamp crash to the ground and you saw the kitty scamper away, terrorized by the noise, you knew you were in trouble. So you came up here to hide. But the blue ball of yarn left a trail plain as day, and I followed it. I found you crouched behind a dusty old trunk, pulled you straight out and gave you a shake!"

Laura actually sobbed aloud.

"I gave you a very stern scolding. And two big tears rolled down your face. That's because you knew that you deserved a spanking. And that was what you were going to get!"

"No! Please!" she whimpered, putting her hand back to shield her upturned bottom.

"Don't you dare, young lady," he told her, pinning her wrist to her side. "You've been a very naughty little girl!"

He raised his hand and started the spanking, over her black satin underpants. But each spank was no more than a sharp, little slap, the sort that one would give a child of five. He alternated cheeks and skipped two beats between each swat, to draw out this quaint punishment. When he'd given her precisely fifty of these baby smacks, he stopped to tug her pretty panties down.

He'd been spanking her so lightly, her behind was barely pink, and yet it felt quite warm beneath his hand. Again he commenced the spanking, a fraction more sharply this time, but pausing as long between smacks.

To Laura, all this was so poignant and sweet that she felt she might well really cry. She was overwhelmed by Hugo's affection. In a strange way, being spanked softly and slowly like this was much more humiliating than being spanked quickly and hard. Because without the distraction of genuine pain to make the experience inescapably immediate and real, the childishly light little paddling ignited a lush and voluptuous shame, hitherto confined to savored threats and fantasies.

She had no way of knowing just how long he spanked her like that. She only knew that it went on for a very long time, but she still didn't want it to stop. Hugo also wanted to continue with their charming make-believe game, but the wet spot she was leaving on his trouser leg was already huge and his cock was threatening to explode.

"Now, I know my little girl has learned her lesson," he told Laura, setting her on her feet, "but here's nothing like driving the point home. Step out of those panties."

When Laura had stumblingly done this, slightly dizzy from the excitement, and still unused to 5" high heels, he stood up and placed her face down on the bench, so she lay upon it, legs together, with her dress still hiked up to her waist.

She heard him yank his zipper down then felt Hugo straddle her ass. He parted her thighs with his hand just a bit before guiding his cock into her.

She rejoiced as she felt there was more than enough of Hugo to fill her in this or any other position. Some instinct told him Laura was a grinder, and that she'd cum while humping the bench. In any case, he liked the warm feel of her spanked bottom under his groin.

As a rule, she was not highly orgasmic. But in this case she came with two dozen thrusts.

When she came with William, it was always by accident. It happened two times out of ten. Her husband never gave his adorable wife a half hour of relentless foreplay.

As her spasms subsided Laura felt she understood Hugo's genius for the first time. When he was ready to burst in a moment or two and could not prolong his pleasure even for a second longer Hugo pulled out of her snug sheath and shot his load all over her ass. For Laura this was the perfect ending.

Leaning up on her elbows, Laura ruefully looked over her shoulder and rubbed the thick puddles of cream in circles with the heel of her hand, until they disappeared into her skin.

"Now you're a good girl again," Hugo said, zipping up his trousers.

"And you are a good man," said Laura. "Maybe even the best."

After returning Laura to the bar Hugo had little desire to remain at his own party, which now seemed to him one giant distraction.

And Hugo hated being distracted when he wanted to think.

He wanted Laura Random on a regular basis. Two to three times a week sounded right. But would this be possible without jeopardizing her brilliant marriage?

Hugo knew that Laura would not be turning these thoughts over in her beautiful willful head for a week or so. But sooner or later she would remember the chemistry of their encounter and seek to repeat the experience. They'd start meeting whenever they could. The more they saw each other, the greater their need for each other would grow. Finally the night would come when she would want to stay with him until the following morning, regardless of consequences. And how was William going to take that?

While traversing the teeming corridor between the bar and ballroom, the solution to Hugo's potential problem appeared. Glamorous, radiant, sexy Marguerite came toward him now, in sections, with her flame colored hair on her shoulders and her glorious curves packed into that smart leather dress.

Marguerite owed him one. Not only had she run off to New York without even saying good-bye, but what with her airs, pretensions and recent infatuation with Michael Flagg, she'd been a general pain in the ass for the last six weeks.

She embraced him, pressing her smooth cheek to his face. He breathed in her costly perfume.

"Are you angry with me?" she broke the embrace. Hugo crossed his arms.

"What do you think?"

"Oh Hugo, you don't know what it's been like! Have you ever been rejected for someone half your height?"

"It must be very humiliating," he was sympathetic.

"It's hideous!"

"I should probably let Lt. Flagg know that there are better ways of humiliating you, but why help him?" said Hugo, leading Marguerite into the ballroom at the end of the hall.

Without noticing Hugo and Marguerite, Michael Flagg had preceded them into the rotunda, escorting both Damaris Perez and a beautiful young dominatrix from New York named Isabel Bruno.

"You see!" said Marguerite to Hugo before they went in. "I can't take a step without being reminded of my improbable defeat! Do we have to go in there now?" She turned from the door.

"Listen, I want to talk to you in private. Go get a coat from the cloakroom and meet me upstairs on the cat walk in fifteen minutes."

Marguerite went off to borrow the lushest fur she could find and grab a bottle of champagne while Hugo caught up with Michael, Damaris and Isabel Bruno, who were standing on the edge of the strobe-lit ballroom, arguing.

Michael had come as The Spirit and was wearing a zoot-suit and spats. A domino masked his eyes.

Isabel, a leggy beauty in her middle twenties, with jet black hair and a slender torso, was as graceful as a lily in a black strapless gown with a bell shaped skirt of sequined chiffon. It was a dress to kill for, and Marguerite wanted to the moment she saw it.

Damaris shared this sentiment. Isabel looked like a lady. While she, Damaris, in her polyvinyl mini dress, looked like a tart from the Combat Zone.

"Every dominant goes submissive occasionally," Isabel insisted, as Hugo joined them, coming up being her and locking his arms around her small waist.

"Isabel, what did I tell you about spreading subversive theories?" He gave her a smack which was barely felt through her crinoline petticoat and billowing skirt.

Isabel turned her head for a kiss, grinding back against him and deliberately tightening his hold on her waist.

"Hugo, I love your party. Thank you for inviting me!" Isabel told him after nibbling on his ear long enough to give him a wicked hard-on. He let go of Isabel and shook hands with Flagg. Michael introduced him to Damaris. Hugo also shook her hand. And a pretty hand it was. He had heard about Damaris Perez, but this was the first time they had met.

It occurred to Hugo that this half pint had taken both Laura's and Marguerite's men. It was interesting. Tonight she seemed so shy. She clung to Lt. Flagg like a shivering sparrow.

"I want to whip Michael. I think we'd both enjoy it," Isabel explained to Hugo.

"Hey, you couldn't whip my little sister!" Damaris declared, the sparrow becoming a bird of prey rather quickly. She couldn't believe that this bitch, who obviously was born in the Bronx, and never even finished high school, was flirting with Mickey, right in front of her face!

"You should teach your wife some manners," Isabel remarked. "Or let me."

"You wish, you bitch!" Damaris nearly sprang at Isabel then, though from the look of them they might have been sisters, each with their jet black hair, white skin and pouting red mouths.

Beholding Damaris with pride, Michael thought: "Truly there is joy in going Latin."

"I'm taller than you," Isabel told Damaris. Then she was suddenly distracted when a missile struck her beautiful back.

"What the . . ." Isabel's gloved hand went back to pull the rubber tipped arrow free, "Some coward shot me in the back!" she cried indignantly.

Hugo excused himself and strode off in pursuit of Marnie Price.

Tall and beautifully proportioned, with straight features, thick, long blonde hair and a wide, sensuous mouth, twenty-year-old Marnie Price had the sort of looks Hugo was partial to.

As William had observed, she was a real New England girl. Her four favorite things were skiing, drinking, football and hard sex. She had recently begun her junior year at the same Boston art college that Laura's younger sister Susan was attending. But no one expected her to even finish out the year, no less graduate. Academia had never been a strong point of Marnie's.

After darting around the rotunda, Marnie led Hugo out and back down the hall to the bar, where the buffet tables attracted her attention. Manned by a corps of caterers, they offered all a hungry archer could desire for her repast. Hugo stole up behind her as the ruddy blonde began to pile her plate with roast beef, potatoes, pickled peppers and bread.

"I've seen you make seven direct hits so far, and all of your victims have been female," Hugo said.

"Oh, hi Mr. Sands," said Marnie. "Really? I hadn't even noticed." She began to eat with a ravenous appetite.

"Are you hostile towards women—or just afraid of irritating men?"

"I'm not afraid of irritating anyone!" Marnie asserted between gulps. "I need some beer."

Together they strolled over to the bar.

"I'll prove it too," said Marnie, after swallowing a tumbler full of ale. "From now on I'm going after only guys!"

"Great. Why don't you start with that one over there." Hugo pointed at William Random, who was leaning morosely on the bar, nursing a Perrier and glowering at Randy Price, who was attempting to flirt with Jane Eliot at the other end of the room, in front of the large blazing hearth.

"That muscular guy with the glasses in the leather mask? You want me to nail him?"

"Yeah. Nail him," Hugo advised.

"Consider it done," Marnie assured him, abandoning her plate and mug to put a good amount of distance between herself and her target before drawing a bead on William.

Hugo strode off to meet Marguerite, satisfied that Marnie Price would receive her just desserts before much more time had elapsed.

Marnie launched her arrow at William while he was in the midst of tearing off the mask, which had become suffocating and was starting to make him dizzy. While he didn't see his assailant, he felt her dart smack into his rib cage and this did not amuse him.

By the time William got the mask off and his glasses back on Marnie had sped away. He decided to pursue her and an epic chase began. It was a very large house with attics, wings and numerous stairwells, dozens of rooms, garages, gardens, tennis courts and grounds.

Marnie did not expect to be chased through more than a couple of rooms, but William was obviously determined to run her to ground no matter how many times she scampered up the stairs and down the stairs in her efforts to evade him. She was in athletic shape. But William was a runner. This was sport to him. By the time Marnie herself began to get winded, William was just warming up. If it weren't for the masses of guests lining the stairwells and halls, he would have caught her long before. Meanwhile, he was having a great time, and looked forward to an even better one once she was over his knee.

Swathed in furs and armed with her bottle of champagne, Marguerite welcomed Hugo to the cat walk. The roof gave a view of the cliffs and the sea. It was a clear, starry night. The inky tide lapping the beach far below could easily mesmerize one.

"There's my favorite little slut," Hugo commented, joining Marguerite as she leaned against the rail. As if the smells of a crisp Autumn evening weren't ravishing enough, now there was the scent of Marguerite to further tantalize him. Life was good.

"Am I still?" Marguerite asked hopefully, and was gratified when he slipped his arm about her as they stood side by side looking down on the cliffs.

"Of course you are."

"Because you seemed fed up with me last time we met," Marguerite felt bound to point out.

"Marguerite, you can be a very trying girl. But I don't suppose that you can really help it. However, I want to see some model behavior between now and Christmas."

"You will!" vowed Marguerite.

"Good, because I have a job for you."

"Yes?" She was eager to please.

"I remember once hearing you brag that you could make any man fall in love with you."

"Did I say that?" Marguerite became instantly wary. This could mean trouble.

"You know you did. Do you still think you can?"

"No," she said hastily, as though this feeble tactic would save her. "I really don't know what gets into me sometimes, making remarks like that. Ha! Ha!"

"Come off it. What you said was true. You can do it, and you're going to do it. For me."

"You want me to seduce someone?"

"Yes, but I'm not talking about a one night stand."

"What are you talking about?"

"A full-scale affair. I'd like it to last for a couple of months. At the minimum."

"Months?" She stared at him in wonder.

"At least through the New Year."

"Hugo, who is this person?" Marguerite broke away from him.

"Don't panic."

"But you did say months?"

"What's the problem? I have confidence in your ability to keep the gentleman interested that long."

"I must confess I wasn't thinking about him staying interested," Marguerite said. "Well, don't keep me on tenterhooks, who is it?"

"Are you being impatient with me?"

Marguerite bit her lip.

"No."

"You think I've chosen someone who isn't to your taste."

"Have you?"

"You ought to know me better than that."

"You mean it's someone I'll like?" The storm clouds disappeared from over her head.

"You like William Random, don't you?"

Upon momentarily losing sight of Marnie Price, still fleeing his relentless pursuit, William crossed paths with Damaris Perez.

She was in the picture gallery, admiring a portrait of a lady in a striking gown, when he came running through.

When he stopped short at the sight of her, Damaris pulled back, all but plastering herself against the wall.

"Well! Look who's here!" said William. "Don't worry, I'm not going to hit you."

"Oh boss—I mean William, I can't tell you how sorry I am for what I did. And after you were so good to me . . ."

"What a touching speech!" said a voice from behind William, then Randy Price stepped into view. "But I was also good to you," he told Damaris menacingly. "And how did you repay me?"

Instinctively choosing the lesser of two evils, Damaris shrunk closer to William.

"I'll tell you how, you little cunt, you set me up!" Randy snarled.

"Leave her alone," said William, putting Damaris to one side.

"Stay out of this," Randy told William.

"I don't want to stay out of it."

"You'd better make restitution, Chiquita," Price warned Damaris.

"I will!" she promised feverishly.

"Shut up," William told her. "You'll do no such thing. And you," he said to Randy, "had better let the whole incident rest. You ought to be grateful I'm not taking you to court."

"I love going to court."

"How much would it take to square it with you?" Damaris stepped out from behind William's shoulder to ask.

"A grand would do it. But if you can't raise the cash, don't worry. I'd almost rather let you work it off in trade."

"Randall, you fucking maggot, leave the girl alone," William was not liking Randy Price more and more. Veins were starting to pop in his head.

"I'll be expecting to hear from you, Chiquita." Randy had already begun walking away. "You can't find the cash, you come to my office. Don't forget."

Marguerite wandered through the strobe-lit ballroom in a preoccupied daze. Hugo wanted her to make love to the man who was married to her best and only girlfriend.

Hugo had been right, she could and would do it. But Laura would never forgive her. Of this Marguerite was convinced.

"Marguerite!" A familiar, deep, voice startled her back to reality, as the tall, broad-shouldered form of Michael Flagg blocked her path. She aborted the embrace he attempted, swiftly brushing his face with her cheek, then pulling back at once.

"Michael, your costume is perfect. The Spirit, right?" Her heart seemed to twist when he touched her, but she flashed him a charming smile.

"I like your costume too."

"Thank you." Marguerite, fully out of her trance, scanned the room for topics of frivolous conversation.

"I left some messages on your machine last week. How come you never called me back?"

"I've been out of town. Just got back this evening," she explained.

"We need to talk," he said.

"Sure Michael. Anytime. Stop by the shop," she said casually.

"I'll do that."

Marguerite was glad to jump on the distraction of a handsome couple waltzing by.

"Look at that Isabel Bruno," she said. "That tall Swedish boy is her foot-slave. Would you believe it? What a build! Isn't it astonishing at times the people who turn out to be submissive?"

"I've met that girl," said Michael. "And she's a boring little snit."

Marguerite adjusted her eye glasses in surprise, beholding Isabel anew.

"You didn't find her appealing?"

"I found her shallow, affected and egocentric," reported Michael.

"She happens to be a world class Mistress," Marguerite pointed out.

"Give me a break. She's no more dominant than you."

This cool remark made Marguerite wonder why she was being so nice to this insulting man.

"You've become quite the judge of submissives lately, haven't you?" she charged.

"I can spot a phony," he returned, of the flawlessly draped Isabel.

"Well, you are a detective," Marguerite observed, before excusing herself and rushing away. She had no heart to be nasty to him, no matter what he'd said. Besides there was a lump in her throat.

• • •

"God! What an incredible asshole!" Jane Eliot almost screamed, taking refuge in the powder room from the oppressive attentions of a half drunk Randy Price.

The two girls in front of the mirror looked up. Laura leaned against the vanity console, smoking a cigarette. Marguerite paused in brushing her hair with a silver-backed brush.

"I'll bet it's someone we know," the redhead said to Laura.

"Which asshole was it?" Laura asked the attractive brunette.

"I don't know the idiot's name, but he's got to be the most chauvinistic male I've ever met!" Jane disclosed, sinking into an elegant arm chair, glad to get off her heels.

"Oh, you must have met my husband," Laura said, exhaling streams of smoke through her nose.

"Aren't you Hugo Sands' new assistant?" asked Marguerite, suddenly recognizing the ex-social worker in the stunningly costumed young beauty who now lounged in the chair. She was wearing a black beaded cocktail dress that clung lovingly to her curves. Hugo had rented her jewels for the night and her legs looked superb in her sheer hose and heels.

"Yes, I am," said Jane, trying to place Marguerite.

"I'm Marguerite. We've met before. You came into my shop with Michael Flagg. Remember?"

Jane did. Because that was the night he had broken their engagement. Jane even recalled thinking at the time that the witchy redhead both of them had words with in the bookshop had been some sort of catalyst to Michael's ending their relationship so abruptly that day.

"Yes. I remember," said Jane, not meeting Marguerite's eyes.

"You looked very different then," said Marguerite. Jane self-consciously fingered the gems at her throat.

"I know," said Jane. "But I'm in a different phase now."

("Yeah," thought Marguerite, "Varga gatefold!")

"Hugo wants me to project a certain image to his clientele," Jane explained.

"Don't worry, you are," commented Laura, admiring the chic cocktail dress.

"Oh excuse me," said Marguerite, "This is my friend Laura Random. Laura, this is Jane Eliot."

"Nice to meet you," Jane said politely to Laura. Then she turned to Marguerite again. "How did you know my name?"

"Hugo told me."

"Oh," said Jane, relieved to hear it hadn't been Michael.

"How do you like working for Hugo?" Laura asked, rolling a joint.

"Do you think you ought to do that in here?" Jane questioned disapprovingly.

"Oh, Hugo won't mind," said Marguerite. "He's tolerant of other people's vices."

"Because he has so many himself," Laura remarked.

"I guess you know him better than I do," admitted Jane.

"You didn't answer my question," Laura persisted.

"Oh, I'm sorry. I'm enjoying working for Hugo very much."

"You aren't finding him to be a hard boss?" Laura asked. Marguerite gave her friend a look, which Laura ignored.

"Not at all," Jane replied. "He's really amazingly patient, considering how ignorant I am." At this remark Laura and Marguerite again exchanged looks. "Hugo's making her feel humble already!" they thought simultaneously.

Marguerite offered Jane some champagne, which the sleek brunette accepted as they spoke.

"To tell you the truth," added Jane, who was not used to drinking, "I'm beginning to develop quite a crush on my boss."

"We'll never tell," promised Laura.

"Thanks," Jane replied, smiling shyly, and making both of them like her at once.

"By the way," said Marguerite, "that is a striking dress."

"Yes," Laura agreed. "I love the way it clings. Did Hugo choose that dress?"

Jane blushed. "He did, actually."

"Stand up and turn around," commanded Marguerite. "We want to see how it drapes in back." To their amusement, she obeyed at once.

During the instant Jane's back was turned, both women appraised the classic proportions of her waist, legs and ass. Marguerite drew the shape of an inverted heart in the air, in imitation of Jane's perfect behind, which swelled so firmly underneath the shiny jet skirt. Laura nodded at the outline in agreement. Hugo had apparently unearthed another gem.

"It's a brilliant dress," Marguerite concluded, when Jane turned to face them again. "And you're a dreamboat in it."

"You're very kind," said Jane, surprised by this.

"Has Michael seen you since the, uh, transformation?" Marguerite asked.

"Michael? Michael Flagg? You know him well, don't you?" Jane put out her empty glass for a refill from Marguerite's bottle.

"I wouldn't say that," Marguerite replied.

"Are you two seeing each other?" Jane asked, as though it meant nothing to her.

"No," Marguerite reported truthfully. "We went out together a few times. That's all."

"Is he here tonight?" Jane asked.

"Yes."

"No, he hasn't seen me since I became Hugo's protégée," Jane said coyly; "nor do I care to see him." She gulped almost a full glass of champagne at once.

"Did you used to date Lt. Flagg?" Laura asked, beginning to smoke her joint.

"We were engaged," Jane said. "Then he broke it off. Because of her," she added, pointing at Marguerite. Jane was becoming drunk. "No offense," she said to Marguerite. "I just remembered that 5 hours before it happened we were in your bookshop. That seemed more than coincidental."

"Do you wish you had him back?" asked Laura.

"I'd never give a man a second chance to hurt me," said Jane emphatically, presenting her empty glass for another refill.

"Really? I would," said Laura. Jane stared at the other brunette.

"Don't pay any attention to Laura," explained Marguerite. "She's not very bright."

"So, you think that Michael would be surprised to see me like this?" Jane asked Marguerite, after putting down her glass in mid-air.

"I think he'd be astonished," replied the redhead.

"Well frankly I couldn't care less," asserted Jane.

"Is that so?" Laura doubted Jane's veracity.

"To me, he's just a well endowed form of pond scum who I happened to be engaged to."

"Listen Jane," said Marguerite, "I'm starting to like you, so tell me one thing—are you really off Michael?"

"I wouldn't give him the time of day," Jane declared.

At that point the door opened and Damaris Perez walked in. She stopped short on seeing Laura, not knowing quite how to behave. Finally she made a nervous greeting, then found a place in front of the mirror to fix her lipstick.

"Oh hi!" said Laura." We were just talking about you!" Since Laura had slept with 10 different men since last seeing Damaris, her attitude toward the girl who'd had a brief office affair with her husband had changed radically. Laura offered Damaris a hit off her joint.

"About me? Thanks," she accepted the cigarette and smoked. "As you can imagine, I haven't gotten high in some time."

"No, I wouldn't think Lt. Flagg would let you," Laura said.

"Oh," said Jane, with interest, "Are you the one who's going with Michael now?"

Marguerite began to brush her hair again. Damaris looked from Jane to Laura.

"This is Jane Eliot," Laura explained. "And my friend Marguerite Alexander. J and M, this is Damaris Perez."

Damaris did not feel as though either of the women Laura had just introduced her to were strangers. Jane she'd hear about from Michael, while she recognized the perfume she now smelled on Marguerite as the same scent which lingered about the cashmere bathrobe she'd found in Lt. Flagg's closet. Not many women wore Joy. She was certain that the robe belonged to this redhead.

"Actually, Michael and I aren't really going out," Damaris said. "We're married."

She extended her hand to show Laura a modest gold wedding band.

"When?" Laura cried, seizing the tiny hand.

"2 days ago," said Damaris, devastating Marguerite.

Jane was drunk and went looking for Michael. The news had amazed but not hurt her, and she wished to congratulate him. The girl was very pretty. But so was Jane. And she had her mind on another man now.

Damaris could see that Laura had forgiven her. She also noticed, shortly after her announcement, the gorgeous redhead's fine green eyes filling up with tears.

Marguerite excused herself and hurried from the room.

"There went your husband's two ex-girlfriends," Laura observed. "Wanna smoke another joint? Is that your wedding ring? Tell me everything!"

Jane found Michael in the bar, where he had been for some time. But unlike her, he could hold his liquor.

"Well! If it isn't the man whose name is on everyone's lips!" she declared, stepping up to the bar beside him.

"Jane?" Michael was stunned by her appearance.

"Champagne please," Jane told the bartender.

"I understand congratulations are in order, Michael."

"Uh, yes, I . . ."

"I know, I met your wife. She's adorable."

"You met . . .?"

"Just now, in the powder room. Also the tall, redheaded woman who owns the bookshop. She'd just heard about your marriage too, and I must say, she didn't take it well," Jane reported.

"Damn it. I wanted to tell her myself," Michael swore. "Well, never mind that. Tell me what's happened to you?"

"What do you mean, happened to me?" Jane drained her glass of champagne as soon as it was served and for a moment slightly swayed.

"I've never seen you wear heels, or such a sexy dress, or even lipstick, come to think of it." He lifted one of her manicured hands. "Red fingernails too! What's come over you? I thought you despised all that stuff."

"I thought I despised you, but instead I just feel numb," said Jane dramatically. "Another please," she added to the waiter.

"That's probably because you're so drunk."

"I am not drunk."

"Yes you are."

The waiter brought a new glass to Jane, but Michael took it out of her hand.

"What are you doing?"

"Sweetheart, you've had enough. Do you want to become violently ill? How many of these have you had?"

"Waiter, another drink please," Jane sweetly asked, adding, "Some goon took that last one."

Michael sighed. He watched her down yet another glass of champagne.

"You're going to regret this tomorrow," he warned.

"Butt out, copper!" Jane told him, and tossing her hair over one creamy shoulder, began to march away. The high heels gave her a cute, sexy walk, especially in the tightly skirted dress. And he could not recall ever having seen her toss her hair that way before.

She'd taken her precious time about it, but Jane had finally turned into a woman. His dull and dedicated plain Jane had been transformed into a pin-up girl by someone and she was apparently beginning to realize the mayhem she might be capable of wrecking on mankind.

"Ha!" said Michael aloud. He had a good mind to go after the little minx and repay her for two tiresome years of consciousness raising with two minutes of skirt raising.

Somehow it had never seemed appropriate to spank Jane. Until tonight. Even at her most irritatingly self-righteous, she had always been a sensible and responsible adult. But there was nothing adult about the cute little pout she threw him over one beautiful, bare shoulder before melting into the crowd.

Long after she had gone, the hard-on she'd given him lingered on.

Marguerite was about to leave. But Hugo intercepted her as she strode through the picture gallery.

"I've been looking for you, come with me." He took her by the hand to drag her after him.

"Hugo, I have to go home," she said, stopping him before he could pull her out of the room.

"Home? Why? What's the matter?" He scrutinized her face. After having broken down once already in the powder room, Marguerite thought she was under control. But when he lifted her chin and made her look at him, fresh tears began to well in her eyes. "Baby, what's wrong? Come over here and sit down." He led her to an upholstered bench. "Now tell me what's upset you."

"Michael's married," she sobbed, accepting Hugo's handkerchief to mop her wet eyes.

"H'm," said Hugo, who had taken her hand.

"Oh Hugo, I wanted him so badly," she confessed.

"Don't worry, you'll have him again. Haven't you been reading the statistics? One out of two marriages ends in divorce you know.

Now, if anyone could break up a happy home, it's you, Marguerite."

"You're just trying to cheer me up," she said with a sniffle.

"Listen, my little sweetheart, I've got something to take your mind off all this. That's why I was looking for you. Who do you think just showed up? Anthony Newton!"

"Anthony Newton?" Marguerite looked blank.

"Anthony Newton. The composer. You must have heard the name. Every show he writes is a hit. He's got one on Broadway right now."

"Oh. That Anthony Newton," said Marguerite.

"He happens to be a collector. He's been one of my best customers for years. He's got a huge collection of vintage instruments."

"Really? That's nice," she replied dully, her eyes glazing again.

"Yes, it's very nice," Hugo agreed, "because I have a seventy-five-thousand-dollar piano in the music room which I fully intend to sell Anthony Newton tonight, and you're going to help me."

"Me?"

"Yes, you're going to play piano and sing for us right now."

"What?"

"To help me sell the piano."

"Sing? And play? For a professional? Haven't I been humiliated enough tonight?"

"Marguerite," said Hugo sternly, "You can play by ear, I've heard you."

"Oh god!" Marguerite cried with anguish.

"It's true your keyboard style is somewhat halting . . ."

"Hugo, you know I play piano like an ungifted eight-year-old," Marguerite protested.

"That can be charming," her companion pointed out. "Besides, with that ravishing cleavage, nobody's going to notice."

"Please Hugo, don't make me do this."

"Now as to the program—I'd suggest Rodgers and Hart."

"Hugo, please, I'm really not up to this."

"Marguerite, you're not going to let me down," he declared. "I just don't ask you to do that many things for me."

"Are you kidding? You just asked me to have an affair with my best friend's husband for 3 months! Not an hour ago you asked me that!"

"That's true, but I didn't tell you to start tonight."

"No. It's just impossible!" she stood up.

"Help me sell the concert grand and I'll give you a 10% commission on what I realize."

Marguerite sat back down. But momentarily she rose again.

"No. I can't. Honestly, Hugo, I'm too upset to sing. You see . . . my heart's been broken."

"Oh brother."

"It's true!"

"Are you deliberately trying to irritate me, Marguerite? I offer you a chance to be the focus of attention, which you love, meet a Broadway luminary and go home with five grand and all you can do is whimper!"

"I'm sorry," she whimpered.

"Not as sorry as you're going to be unless you decide to entertain my guest. I didn't think I'd have to threaten you before you would obey me anymore, but I guess some things never change."

Marguerite came out of her reverie.

"Would you like to know how I first met Anthony Newton?"

"If you'd like to tell me," she replied cautiously, again sensing trouble.

"Well, it wasn't at the Antique Guild. He only started buying antiques later. He started out as one of my *New Rod* subscribers. He's in the scene, Marguerite."

"Oh really? What's his orientation?"

"I don't think I'm going to tell you. You ought to be able to figure out for yourself whether a man is dominant or submissive by now. I will say this, he isn't a switch."

"I'll bet he's submissive," said Marguerite. "These high powered types usually are."

"Dominant or submissive, he's going to watch me spank you."

Marguerite sprang up, as though to run, but Hugo caught her by the wrists and pulled her back down.

"That's right, Marguerite, since you've refused to entertain, I'm going to have to. I'll probably use your birthday as a pretext."

"My birthday isn't till December."

"So what? I still owe you one from last year. And thirty is a nice, round number. The more I think of it, I almost prefer this solution. You've had a good one coming for awhile."

"Hugo, please don't do this to me!" She actually put her hands together in a gesture of supplication.

"Think of it Marguerite, being spanked in front of all those people who must be in the music room right now, along with Anthony Newton. Normally, in such a situation I wouldn't raise your skirt, but trying to spank you through that leather one would be pointless."

"This is a nightmare and soon I'll wake up," thought Marguerite hopefully.

"Poor Marguerite," lamented Hugo. "To be ridiculous when she might have been sublime! Too bad she turned out to be such a sniveling coward."

Marguerite thought, "What if Michael comes in?" That she could never survive.

"Okay I'll sing and play piano," she said.

"Are you sure?" Hugo tried not to smile. Marguerite jumped up and took his hand. "Come on, let's get this over with."

As Marguerite and Hugo approached the music room, lush swells of piano music cascaded out the opened double doors.

"What did you do, Hugo? Resurrect Oscar Levant for the party?"

"Sounds like Tony's found the piano," Hugo told her. "You're saved, Marguerite."

They entered the large, balconied room, where several dozen guests had already entrenched themselves. A few were still sober.

Their celebrity guest motioned them over to the piano. He stood up to shake Hugo's hand and Marguerite thought, "He's not very tall."

"Hugo, this has to be the piano you were telling me about. You're right, I've got to have it."

"Couldn't you have waited 5 minutes to say that? You owe me five thousand dollars," thought Marguerite.

"Anthony, this is my protégée, Marguerite. She's a writer."

Anthony shook Marguerite's hand.

"Have I read anything you've written?" asked the musical composer from New York. Marguerite was thinking, "At least he has a good tailor. If only he weren't of medium height. He's really very good looking otherwise."

– 28 –

"She writes under the name Alma for me," said Hugo. "And I imagine you've read just about everything she's written."

"Really!" Anthony Newton gave Marguerite an even more thorough once over than initially. "I'm one of your biggest fans."

"How nice," she replied, forgetting to add that she was also one of his. Politeness was not one of her strong points that night.

"So, Marguerite, sit down here next to me and tell me all your fantasies. Alma, huh?"

"I told her if she didn't sing for my guests I'd have to spank her in front of them," reported Hugo, to Marguerite's chagrin.

"Really! We can't let that happen, can we, Marguerite?"

"No," declared Marguerite, "Absolutely not!" She thought, "He must be submissive."

So Anthony Newton accompanied her, as Marguerite sang for Hugo's guests, and was allowed to be sublime instead of ridiculous after all.

Damaris and Michael, attracted to the sound of Marguerite's lovely contralto voice, were drawn through the double doors.

"It looks like La Marguerita is feeling better," Damaris thought. She felt like watching Michael, as he watched Marguerite, but was too proud to do this.

"Of course they were in love," thought Damaris, "She's so tall!"

The sight of Marguerite, so perfect and poised, began to make Damaris fret. How could he prefer her to this goddess? Ultimately the redhead would get him back.

Meanwhile, Michael's thoughts were quite the opposite. He'd just spent two years with one stubborn pain in the ass. Now that he realized what a prima donna Marguerite truly was, he felt almost relieved to have escaped a more entangled relationship with her.

Fortunately, Marguerite could not read minds, because the casualness of Michael's thoughts would have thoroughly twisted the knife.

William was finally able to pounce on Marnie Price in The Rose Parlor.

"Got you!" William snatched her by the wrist and dragged her over to a Victorian settee, whereupon he sat down and yanked her across his lap. "Now you're going to get it!" he promised, deftly unstrapping the quiver on her back, which still contained two arrows, and tossed it aside, while restraining Marnie with his other hand.

And Marnie was not a girl to be easily restrained. From the moment he had touched her she'd resisted with all of her considerable strength. Now that she was pinned across his knees, she struggled heroically to free herself from his leaden grip.

"Give up," he told her. "You can't get away from me." Her full but extremely firm buttocks, so snugly encased in the nubby green tights, were ideally formed. He raised his arm to give them the attention they deserved.

But this was not a spanking that was meant to occur. Before he could bring his palm crashing down even once on her beautiful behind, the gods intervened for Marnie, in the form of her brother, who all but began to foam at the mouth when he passed the open doorway and observed what William Random was about to do.

"Get your hands off my sister!" he demanded, charging into the room. William pushed Marnie off his lap so that she fell to the rug with a thud. Then William got to his feet.

Marnie saw what happened next in a blur. Undeniably, Randy threw the first punch. That was very like her brother, especially when he'd had a few drinks. But anyone could see that it was not a fair fight. This asshole who had tried to spank her was obviously an athlete, while her brother was a dissipated punk. Randy had initiated hundreds of fist fights in his life; most resulting in him being knocked down. This had not ever deterred him, however, from making a career out of baiting people to the point of violence.

The fight happened so quickly that Marnie barely had scrambled to her feet before it was over, and her brother was lying on the floor not moving.

Yes, Randy had thrown the first punch—but it never connected with her assailant's face. The guy had punched Randy's face back anyway. And Randy had gone right down. The alcohol might have had something to do with Randy's becoming unconscious as the back of his head impacted against the thinly carpeted floor, but somehow Marnie doubted it.

It was not the first time Marnie had seen Randy get knocked out, but usually he regained consciousness in a couple of seconds. Randy wasn't moving.

Marnie checked her brother out. She looked up at William.

"He's never been out cold for this long. We should call an ambulance."

William looked at Randy, to make sure he wasn't faking. He hadn't hit him very hard.

No, he wasn't faking, William thought as he got to his feet. He also did not appear to be breathing.

Since only the good die young, Randy Price awoke seconds later. An awestruck Laura let her husband take her home; and Marguerite enchanted the composer from New York, who began to fall in love with Random Point.

WARMEST WISHES

MICHAEL FLAGG HAD no idea that it was Marguerite Alexander's birthday on the day that he entered her shop in the middle of Christmas week, to purchase some books on addiction for dealing with his irresponsible young wife.

There were more than the usual amount of browsers in the shop that afternoon, due to the Christmas returns. Assisting Random Point's most glamorous redhead in waiting on customers was Marguerite's friend, Laura Random, a sleek brunette who was a good deal more mischievous than her composed and graceful demeanor implied.

For instance, once she spotted Lt. Flagg, a tall and powerfully attractive young man, who had a brief but passionate affair with her leggy russet haired friend back in the Autumn, Laura could not take him aside quickly enough to let him know that she would very much enjoy watching Michael give Marguerite "31."

Marguerite, who was chatting with a customer in front of the shop's newest ornament, an enormous antique Swedish stove covered in blue and white tiles, did not fail to notice, with a spasm of shameless infatuation, that Michael was in her shop again, that Laura was talking to him in a disturbingly conspiratorial manner, that they were now looking at her, and that Michael had started to smile.

"I dare you," Laura challenged, her demure facade dropping away.

"You lascivious little minx!" Michael accused. "I think you're the one who needs the spanking."

Laura blushed in a way that implied she could imagine more dreadful things than being put across the knee of Lt. Flagg.

"But it isn't my birthday," said Laura.

"So what? I missed your last one, didn't I?"

"But what about Marguerite?" Laura pressed him.

"She'd hate what you're suggesting, you know," he pointed out.

"Why do you say that? I've known Marguerite since college. She's into it."

"Giving, maybe."

"Who told you that?" Laura demanded.

"She did."

"You must not be a very swift detective if you can't figure out when a simple girl like Marguerite is lying," Laura declared, in such a way that made Michael Flagg once again consider the idea of spanking Laura Random, whose husband had almost killed one of his wife's admirers on Halloween, instead of Marguerite.

"You know, I don't think I'm going to gratify your voyeurism, Mrs. Random. Because I think it would be a much better birthday spanking for Marguerite if you unselfishly volunteered to take it for her. Come on, let's go over and tell Marguerite." Michael took Laura out from behind the counter and led her by the arm across the room to Marguerite.

Marguerite abandoned her customer. She didn't have much to say, but she liked looking at Michael, and it showed. When he wished her a happy birthday and kissed her face she almost purred. One could see that she had the catlike urge to rub up against him, for 3-5 hours.

"Your little friend here is quite an instigator," Michael reported to Marguerite, catching Laura's wrist in a hard grip as she tried to inch away.

"Oh? Well, I must say that doesn't surprise me," replied Marguerite tartly. "Ever since she lost her angel wings she's been a real little terror."

"Really? How did she do that?" Michael kept a tight grip on Laura, who was trying to bolt and failing.

"She cheated on her husband and got away with it—so now she thinks she can get away with anything."

"Let her get away with it, did he? Now that surprises me," Michael observed.

"My husband doesn't feel threatened by any man!" Laura returned with positive arrogance.

"H'm, I suppose that's one way of looking at it," reflected Michael. (But if he ever caught Damaris fooling around . . .!)

"Don't tell us you're expecting your wife to be faithful to you, Lt. Flagg!" Laura baited him, for she was in a very wicked mood that day and was enjoying this immensely.

"And what's that supposed to mean? Why shouldn't I expect exactly that?"

"Well, Damaris isn't exactly the strongest willed person . . ." Laura said, indicating the book on quitting smoking that Michael was holding under one arm. "And of course we know she didn't scruple to sleep with her boss, who was also another woman's husband," the brunette concluded, referring to her own husband.

"I assure you that Damaris has been totally reformed and now holds the sacred marriage vows in high esteem," reported Flagg.

Laura chuckled.

"So what was Laura trying to instigate?" Marguerite asked.

"I was only teasing Lt. Flagg," said Laura, still trying to wrench her arm away.

"She wanted to watch me spank you," said Michael.

"Oh, did she?" Marguerite was clearly not amused.

"So I told her that I thought she ought to be the one getting spanked, as a special entertainment for your birthday," Michael told Marguerite, and in so saying, took a seat on one of the low wooden stools which flanked the old fashioned stove, and turned Laura over his knees.

Marguerite, who noticed several customers pause with books held in midair to watch this extraordinary event, casually announced to the dozen or so people in immediate earshot, that it was her birthday and her best friend had generously offered to take her spanking for her, from Random Point's own Lt. Michael Flagg. Everyone seemed to think this was cute and stopped what they were doing to watch.

"Shall we have Mrs. Random count, or do you want to count?" Michael asked Marguerite, pausing, with his large, heavy palm resting squarely on the luscious curve of pretty Laura's right cheek, snugly wrapped in a wool flannel skirt.

"I'll count," said Marguerite, folding her arms and leaning back against a counter to watch.

Michael's hand descended with a swift report, drawing a shocked gasp from Laura upon impact. Marguerite said, "One."

"It's fitting that you take your best friend's spanking," Michael told Laura, bringing his hand down again. Marguerite said, "Two." "Because," Michael continued, "you are obviously the naughtier, and if I may observe, the more childish of the two."

Now Michael administered ten medium hard smacks to alternate cheeks, and these were duly counted aloud by Marguerite, who was, in fact, becoming quite transfixed by the spectacle of her traitorous friend being chastised like an irritating child by her ex-lover.

Marguerite thought, "Better you than me," and yet it almost pained her to watch another woman being held and handled and thoroughly controlled by the man she still wanted more violently than any other who had crossed paths with her since she'd first started playing in the scene. Was she jealous or thrilled as she watched that uncompromising hand come down?

After the 12th smack fell smartly upon Laura's shapely bottom, which was perfectly rounded, though slim, Michael said, "She isn't even feeling this," as a preamble to raising her skirt.

"Lt. Flagg!" cried Laura, shocked, trying to fight him and hold down her skirt. He ended by pinning both skirt and wrist to the small of her back with one hand. This procedure revealed the lower half of a silk crepe teddy, in a spotted print of red, orange and gold, trimmed with Calais lace. Except for Marguerite, no one watching, from the adolescent boy with the raging erection to the most sophisticated gift book browser, had ever beheld such a lavish undergarment before, and a couple of low whistles went around the room. The teddy, which displayed virtually the entire lower half of Laura's perfect bottom in this position, was also off-set by a black satin garter belt, the suspenders of which were attached to sheer, black, seamed stockings. The picture of the pin-up was completed by a pair of 4" heels. Taking all of this in, the adolescent boy was not the only male to suddenly find himself with a hard-on in

Marguerite's cozy, overheated bookshop. Even those who weren't into spanking, which most of them weren't, as most people aren't in this world, could not fail to be charmed by this beauty's nearly bare bottom presented for view so elegantly.

"Lt. Flagg, how could you!!!" cried Laura, still struggling. "Marguerite, don't let him do this to me!"

"I believe we were at 12," said Marguerite to Michael coolly.

"Right," said Michael, tightening his grip on Laura and starting to spank her again, this time a bit more slowly, and a little harder, so that the numbers seemed more significant as Marguerite said them aloud.

Each time Michael's hand came down, the force of the blow, which was still in the realm of medium-hard, caused the restrained brunette to kick. However, she'd decided she wasn't going to give any of these horrible people the satisfaction of hearing her cry out any more! At any rate, she thought, this couldn't last much longer. He now was at twenty. Eleven more to go, or twelve at most.

Laura would just have to get through this as she got through every other ordeal as a submissive, like a good sport. It didn't really bother her to have a whole roomful of strangers watch her get a spanking. She knew how she looked and she knew how men felt looking at her. When she was released she would be able to look any one of them in the face and say, "So what?" She didn't really care what any of them thought of her. The only one she wouldn't be able to look in the face was Lt. Flagg.

"Now, Michael," said Marguerite, "I feel that you should give Laura something to show her husband tonight."

Michael stayed his hand a moment to give Marguerite a quizzical look.

"William may not feel threatened by other men," said Marguerite, "but I seriously doubt he'd be amused to learn that his wife's flirting had become outrageous enough to provoke a public spanking."

"No! Don't you dare mark me!" Laura cried, horrified by the idea of having to explain any of this to William. Laura forgot about being a good sport.

Michael of course had no intention of marking Laura and was

amazed at the manipulativeness these two girls were capable of. The problem with the two of them was that they were a couple of jaded, spoiled brats. Though maybe that was more of a pleasure than a problem, considering you could treat them like this and get away with it. They wouldn't hold it against you—not really—and probably you could make love to them as well. Still, Michael was heartily glad that his own little beauty, whom he could also spank and make love to, with all of her faults, was nowhere near as diabolical as this scheming pair.

"I think Laura's had enough," Michael said, letting the brunette up. "Now it's your turn," he told Marguerite, taking her by the arm and leading her back to her office.

Setting herself to rights, Laura realized that she had no choice but to return to her duties at the cash register. But at least she'd escaped being marked. What a relief! Now William would never have to know about the mischief she'd gotten up to today. (She was certain Lt. Flagg could have marked her with the greatest of ease.) As it was, the pinkness would fade long before the evening. It was probably already no more than a blush. But Laura had learned something very valuable just then. And it was that she wanted Michael Flagg.

Such is the power that a good spanking, affectionately given, may have upon a woman. Many times that afternoon and evening and in the weeks to come, Laura would relive various aspects of her experience that day in Marguerite's shop. The elements of the spectators, even Marguerite, would melt away in Laura's memory, and what would be left would be the actual feel of being held down across those muscle corded thighs, the sensation of being firmly taken in hand by a powerful man in a controlled manner. Also, Laura's heart thrilled to the compassion he'd shown her in the end, in not marking her as Marguerite had so vindictively suggested. Yes, Lt. Flagg was superb. She could understand now why Marguerite had been so devastated to hear he'd married.

Michael shut the door behind them. Marguerite retreated behind her desk.

"That was a very irresponsible suggestion you just made about me marking your friend," Michael told her.

"I notice you didn't do it," Marguerite replied crossly. She never seemed to get her own way!

"Come here, you," he said, crossing to her and taking her in his arms. "You're not getting spanked, but you are getting something for your birthday!" he promised. Then he bent her over her own desk, pulled up her skirt and unzipped his trousers.

"You stop!" cried Marguerite. "How dare you? You may not!" She was outraged but if he would have obeyed her just then she would have wreaked mayhem on him. "You . . . you wolf!" she accused as he pulled her black silk panties down to her creamy white thighs.

"I'm sorry, but you brought this on yourself," he told her.

And when he took her by the waist and drove into her to the hilt, she was very glad that she had.

"Why, you naughty girl," he said. "You're soaking wet! I believe you enjoyed watching me spank your girl friend." As he had begun to thrust into her slow, hard and deep with all 7 ½" of his cock, Marguerite could only whimper in response. If only he did this a little more often, not just on her birthday, Marguerite might be able to forgive him for marrying someone else.

Michael gave Marguerite the rest of the spanking that Laura had escaped, while he was driving into her, and Marguerite liked it. A well placed slap could be a stimulating thing, when one was in the appropriate mood to receive it and the one giving it was charming.

Twenty minutes later, when Michael walked back out into the shop, of the people who had witnessed Laura's spanking, only the adolescent boy remained milling around the area in front of Marguerite's new stove, unwilling or unable to remove his eyes from the girl who was now so calmly ringing up sales.

As Michael went by her counter he leveled a stern glance at Laura and told her to behave. The sweet blush and rueful smile with which she answered this injunction let him know that she was not upset with him. And the seductive look she flashed him from beneath her long lashes as he went out the door with the tinkling bell was easily understood as an invitation to punish her again whenever he liked.

He'd never bought the book on quitting smoking for Damaris after all, but that was just as well. How many girls could he reasonably hope to correct in one day? He had all the time in the world to straighten his pretty wife out. Meanwhile, he truly loved this town.

The Honeymoon is Over

"I WANT YOU to quit smoking," Michael Flagg told Damaris, on the first day he began working nights. His pretty, black-haired wife of one season paled and crushed out her cigarette.

"I don't know if I can quit," she protested, then quailed when he narrowed his eyes.

"I did it and so can you," he told her, rising from the table, where he'd just consumed one of her excellent suppers.

"I'm too nervous," she maintained, watching him strap on his shoulder holster and insert his service revolver.

"Then you're going to have to get a grip on yourself, aren't you?" he suggested without sympathy.

"But what if I can't?"

"You can and you will," Michael said, putting on his jacket. "Because the stress of quitting smoking will be nothing compared with the impact a good strapping will have on your nervous system if I catch you backsliding." He pocketed her Luckys. "Understand me, young lady?"

Damaris flushed and bit her lip, but meekly said, "Yes, Michael."

Unconvinced, he gave her a cynical smile. "Yeah, I'll bet," he said before going out the door. But he promised himself that before he was through with his shockingly self-indulgent young wife that she would understand.

As adorably petite and delightfully submissive as she was, there was never a more willful girl than Damaris. She had no more impulse to blindly obey her husband's rules than any non-submissive, self-respecting feminist might have, probably less, since she was of such a totally decadent breed of modern girl. Being given the virtue-vs-corporal punishment ultimatum by Lt. Flagg, this eternal culprit's first and only impulse was to continue sinning, only more slyly than before.

The incident occurred several nights later, at the off-color hour of 2 a.m. Damaris, who had also been working nights lately, had finished her shift at the type house and had gotten home moments before her husband arrived. He was only halfway through his own shift, but had taken a break to stop home, mainly to make sure that his wife had returned without mishap.

Lt. Flagg was irritable to begin with, as a result of readjusting to the night schedule, so when he smelled the telltale odor of grass on her, it was enough to make him lose his temper for the first time with his wife.

"So! This is how you keep your word," he charged, while unbuckling his belt. "Well let me demonstrate how I keep mine!"

"No, Mickey, don't!" she cried, backing away from her angry man.

"Come over here!" he took her by the elbow. "You're going to get a good licking!" Then he bent her over the back of the tufted leather sofa in their sitting room.

Damaris had never received a strapping before. This one was sharp and shocking, briskly applied to her little bare behind. His fashionably slim leather belt snapped across her smooth, hitherto unmarked bottom a total of 15 times that felt more like 50 to her. How they stung—for each stroke penetrated deeply, so that the after-smart was even more dramatic than the initial pain of impact. This harshness alarmed her to such a degree that the psychological effect blended with the physical to produce hot tears before the 4th lash fell. And they fell very quickly.

He pinned her to the sofa with one hand in the small of her back, pushing up her skirt while firmly holding her in place for the discipline. The other hand rapidly wielded the strap, hard enough to make her scream with childish anguish each time it cracked smartly against her pale, smooth, pearly flesh.

"You're going to stay clean," he told her, as she buried her face in her hands and her thin shoulders shook with her sobs. "If I have to make you cry before you understand I'm serious, so be it, but you're going to stay clean."

To make all of this even worse, Michael neither soothed or caressed his fallen angel after releasing her, but instead coolly put on his topcoat and left to complete his shift without a backward glance. He was extremely disappointed with Damaris for disobeying him about the drugs.

Damaris traveled through several zones of emotion that night, trying to figure out whether the harsh treatment she'd been given qualified as discipline or abuse. Had he comforted her after the strapping, which left her bottom purple, black and blue for 4 days, there would have been no question in her passionate, fiercely devoted mind. But his indifference left her feeling dejected, betrayed and a little afraid.

She wondered, as she wept, how far he might go in his efforts to make her behave. Damaris Perez Flagg associated the strap with the depressing and violent New York tenements in which she had grown up.

At dawn she was shocked to discover that her bottom was still latticed with smears of black and blue. As often as he'd spanked her with his heavy hand, Flagg had never marked his bride, nor had anyone else. She had no way of knowing how long the marks might last.

She didn't sleep and he didn't call. This hurt Damaris very much. She knew his schedule, his shift would end at seven; after this he would go to the gym before coming home for the rest of the day.

Their large, handsome apartment was already immaculate, but Damaris cleaned for hours while she pondered her situation and waited for her husband to get home. She was aching for a smoke now, but for once, she didn't dare.

That morning it was blustery and raining; still she showered, changed her clothes and went out. Had it been a normal day she would have gone to the bakery for fresh bread or rolls for Michael's breakfast. As it was, she didn't know where to go. Rather than wander around aimlessly she decided to go back to the type house and work a half shift. But she couldn't concentrate on her word processing tasks and after an hour she claimed a headache and left. Several minutes after Damaris walked out of the typing bureau, her husband called for her.

Damaris got into her canary VW bug with the cartoon eyes on the roof, and drove around Random Point environs for several hours that afternoon.

The beach was completely deserted, for it was windy and raining and cold. But here it was exhilarating to watch the choppy grey waves pitch and toss. And here she could smoke as much as she liked. The moody and beautiful sea lifted her spirits. To a girl who'd grown up on the unloving streets of New York, Random Point was a village from a fairy tale. Damaris began to feel better, but still not enough to go home.

She decided to visit Laura, her friend, who lived at the edge of the woods beyond the beach. Twenty minutes later she was pulling up her skirt and lowering her black wool tights to show Laura the purple marks Michael's belt had left upon her perfect ass.

"He did that to me just for smoking a joint with a buddy on my break at work!" Damaris complained, setting her clothes to rights.

"That must have really stung!" Laura said with feeling.

"Did William ever use his belt on you?"

"Not like that," replied Laura, trying to imagine how it might have felt to be punished so severely by Lt. Flagg.

"It's your own fault for getting caught," Laura observed. "You're going to have to learn how to cover your tracks. If William found out every time I do something he doesn't approve of, I'd be permanently marked. But watch me sneak!" And in fact, Laura now snuck a cigarette out of Damaris' pack and enjoyed an illicit smoke with her husband's ex-secretary.

"Yeah, well it's easy with William. He's self-absorbed. Mickey's different. He watches me like a hawk all the time now— and don't forget, he is a detective."

"So what? He's only a man, which means he can still be deceived."

However, when her husband walked in on the two girls drinking coffee in the front parlor a half hour later, he gave Laura such a look and slapped his folded *Wall Street Journal* against his thigh in such a way that her cockiness completely disappeared.

"Get over here," he told Laura from the doorway, while giving Damaris a cool nod.

As soon as Laura emerged into the hall William flung down his paper and briefcase and dragged his wife out into the kitchen.

"What do you think, you can do whatever you like now?" William demanded, pulling a straight backed chair into the middle of the floor and taking Laura straight across his lap. "Didn't I tell you to stay away from that girl?" Smack! "Was I talking to myself?" Smack! Smack! Smack! The palm of his hand came down hard on Laura's bottom through her wool challis skirt. Each spank made her kick up her legs, which were shod in dainty little Victorian boots that laced tightly to the ankle. "This is my house," William told her. "See that you don't forget it again!"

William pushed the bell-shaped paisley skirt up to her waist to finish spanking Laura on the seat of her cranberry silk-satin bikinis. He did not need to lower these luxurious underpinnings to make his displeasure felt.

"So tell me," William demanded, of Laura, who'd been gasping between wallops, "Why did you disregard my specific request that you not mix with Damaris anymore? If you've got even a remotely acceptable reason I might see fit to return you to your guest instead of going for a wooden ladle."

"Damaris was upset—" Laura began to explain, twisting around on his lap to eyeball him with her most appealing doe-eyed gaze.

"Talk fast, I'm getting bored," William said, pushing her head back down and tightening his grip on her slender waist before delivering a brisk, measured volley of half a dozen smacks.

"Oh William, stop! I'll tell you if you'll let me!" Laura twisted again and put back her hand to protect her satin-wrapped oval cheeks. "He gave her a terrible strapping! She's never been marked before. She didn't know what to think!" Laura blurted out dramatically.

"Ha!" William snorted. "The both of you girls should be permanently marked with the mischief you get up to!"

Laura was relieved to be set back on her feet. She meekly followed William back into the sitting room, giving her bottom a rub through her skirt.

– 43 –

"I'm intrigued," William said to Damaris, who was blushing with embarrassment at what she had just overheard. "Let me see the damage." He folded his arms and waited.

"Go on, Damaris," Laura urged, "Show William. He'll tell you whether Michael went too far." William gave Laura a look, as much to say that such a thing was hardly possible.

Damaris pulled her skirt up and lowered her tights a second time that morning.

"Very sexy," William commented, without hesitation, for he was a connoisseur. Then he added, for the sake of her dignity, "Looks like you took a pretty good strapping, young lady."

Damaris dropped her skirt again but her blush was slow to fade.

"He'd never used a strap on her before," Laura helpfully put in, by way of explaining the emergency nature of the visit and hence her decision to override his rule against fraternizing with an employee he'd had to dismiss as a result of her criminal conduct.

"Let's hope it's the beginning of a trend," said William. "I can't think of a more deserving recipient." And yet he was becoming tired of staying angry with this excitingly submissive ex-secretary of his, who seemed so ideally suited to be his wife's comrade in misbehavior.

"So . . . you don't think what he gave me was so bad?" Damaris asked William, hesitantly, even while knowing he'd be bound to take her husband's side. And yet she thought of William as being kind and fair. In this matter she felt she could trust his judgment.

"Whatever it was you did, you got off easy," William said. "And you ought to be glad you've got a man who cares enough about you to accept the Herculean labor of correcting your faults."

"I would be glad if I did think he cared, but I know he doesn't like me now at all!" Damaris said, then she let it spill out all at once in a flurry of sobs, how he had simply walked out after punishing her—how he'd been a block of ice!

As Damaris dissolved into a bundle of tears, Laura said, "You see!"

"Now look here, Damaris, you're all wrong about your guy," William said.

"He only married me because he felt sorry for me," she whimpered, also feeling sorry for herself. "He hates me for being weak.

I'm a grave disappointment to him," Damaris was careful to articulate between sobs. "He really loves that tall, athletic redhead, Marguerite. I'm sure of it!"

"All men love Marguerite," Laura said. "That doesn't mean a thing. He married you. Right William?"

"That's right, you can't go by Marguerite," William agreed. "She even flirts with me."

"For that matter, she sometimes flirts with me!" Laura pointed out, while noting her husband's last comment with interest. Marguerite had been flirting with William lately—she'd noticed it herself but had not paid much attention to it, then. A warning alarm was now going off in her head.

"So you don't think Michael cares about you, huh?" William took Damaris by the hand. "Come with me. I don't ordinarily take it upon myself to discuss my clients' projects, but I think if this particular client knew how much a young lady who is very dear to him needs reassurance just now, I don't think he'd mind my violating his confidence."

They went into William's study, where he selected a blueprint from a long, flat wooden drawer and spread it out on his drawing board.

"If you mention a word of having seen this to Michael that strapping you got today will be nothing to what you'll get from me, understand?"

Damaris nodded that she did, mystified.

"These are the plans to your new house."

"Michael's having you build a house for him?"

"For you, you silly girl. Look, it's even going to have a cozy little dungeon for your punishments."

Damaris was overwhelmed. Michael was building a house for them! For her!

"See here? It's even got a nursery," William said.

"Oh, we don't want to have children," Damaris told him.

"It's for you," William replied. "For when you need that sort of therapy. It's the first house I've ever designed for a client in the scene and it's going to be really special."

Damaris was touched. She thanked William and hastened to her car.

"Don't forget to act surprised when he tells you," William warned, hoping he had done the right thing.

• • •

When Damaris got home she found that her husband had fallen asleep, fully dressed on the four-poster in the little back room with the window on the woods, the room they both considered her room. He awoke at the sound of her footfall in the doorway.

"Come over here, you brat. Where have you been?" He wrapped his arms around her when she came to him, making her sit in his lap. He seemed very glad to see her and kiss her full red lips. "I was beginning to wonder if you'd left me," he told her, reluctant to break the embrace. She shook her head but couldn't speak. She was embarrassed.

"Did you think about leaving me?"

"No!" Damaris lied.

"Let me see your bottom."

Damaris shook her head again and tried to resist, but he easily turned her over on his lap, pulled up her skirt and rolled down her tights to reveal his handy work, her round, lovely, thoroughly marked bare behind. He stroked her gently now and kissed the punished flesh.

"Poor baby," Michael said softly, and Damaris knew this was as close as he was going to get to an apology. He righted her once more on his lap and crushed her to his chest.

"You feel sorry for me?" she asked.

"Not nearly as sorry as you feel for yourself," he replied.

"But you're certainly not sorry that you . . . thrashed me!" she accused, looking into his cool, pale eyes with her enormous, glittering black ones. As she began to complain of her whipping, she felt something throb under her. (Oh, The Beast! Damaris thought. He's getting turned on!)

"I'm as sorry for having given you a good licking as you are for disobeying me."

"It's true, I'm only sorry I got caught," Damaris declared, with some spirit.

"I know. That's why I'm not sorry I thrashed you. If I don't show you the respect you seem to feel you deserve it's because you behave like an irresponsible child."

"I'm afraid of you now, you know that?" A defiant accusation that made him throb again. They were flirting now.

"You'd better be afraid of me," he told her sternly. Instantly, a blush suffused her cheeks and Damaris hid her face between his shoulder and throat. Flagg's raging hard-on sent an urgent message to his brain, but he decided to ignore it for the moment and continued to cuddle his resentful, embarrassed and enthralled little girl.

"It isn't going to be easy," Michael told her. "The odds are against you. You're a genuinely bad girl and I genuinely like to spank you. Hard. Even if you tried to be good, you'd slip up constantly. Since you won't even try to be good, but merely avoid getting caught you're bound to slip up even more. So any way you look at it, you're in for some trips to the woodshed in the months and years to come."

"Happily, we don't have a woodshed," Damaris murmured, enjoying the feel of his tightening arms, in spite of his threatening words—or maybe because of them.

"Don't you worry, we will," Flagg promised.

SHADOW LANE II
RETURN TO RANDOM POINT

New Talent

Jane Eliot was a lovely young woman, yet even after watching her trim bottom wiggle around his shop for 5 months, Hugo Sands still was not inspired to seduce her. The first time she had bluntly approached him about sleeping together, he had wanted to want her, but the attraction wasn't there.

Jane had been shocked to be refused by a man. Was he offended by a sexually aggressive woman? Hugo explained that she was anything but sexually aggressive.

"An aggressive woman would have touched, not asked," Hugo had informed her; "I've known a lot of them and they go for the crotch without hesitation."

Jane had blushed, paralyzed by the thought of reaching out and touching him first. "Is that what I should have done?"

"I don't know. You'd have to weigh the risk of getting your hand slapped." Somehow Jane guessed that he did not mean this figuratively either.

So far she had never risked it and that conversation had taken place several months before. Yet she had approached him, several more times about taking their relationship to a more intimate level.

Each time she seemed to want it more sincerely. Each time she brought it up, she was shyer than before. Finally, this new and appealing shyness began to penetrate Hugo's defenses. However, he felt bound to inform her that she still wasn't ready for him.

"When will I be ready?" Jane demanded, just that afternoon, as they were arranging the table for the hard cider party he was giving that evening at the shop to show some new pieces that had just arrived from Italy to a selection of his choicest local clients.

"Jane, this is not the time to discuss this. We have a lot of details to take care of before Mrs. Granville Reagle and her friends arrive."

Jane knew better than to argue with him, but brooded the entire afternoon while assisting in the preparations. Then at the party, after only two drinks, Jane completely forgot where she was and why. She walked straight up to Hugo, taking him away from Mrs. Duncan Blandings, who was Hugo's best customer in Random Point, and who was becoming extremely interested in a rosewood writing desk from Tuscany, to drag him into his office and brazenly state her desires afresh. She had never encountered an elusive man before and kept feeling there must be some mistake, something he was failing to grasp about her intentions.

"Jane, what the hell do you think you think you're doing? I have 25 customers out there and no one is on the floor. You're supposed to be working and you're half looped. I was talking to Mrs. Duncan Blandings, who routinely spends five to ten thousand dollars on a visit to my shop. Are you mad to interrupt me like this?" And with that Hugo stormed back out into the shop.

But when he got there, Mrs. Duncan Blandings had departed, as well as Mrs. Granville Regale. Hugo was angry then. It was uncanny the way Jane picked that particular moment to pester him. When Jane reemerged he gave her a look that froze her. She looked around and noticed that the society matrons had gone. Jane felt suddenly weak with dread. Hugo's plump turtledoves had taken wing without spending any money and it was Jane's fault.

Jane found it hard to concentrate for the rest of the party, which didn't help her case with Hugo. In fact, she wrote no sales. Hugo, on the other hand, could always move something, and was mollified when he managed to persuade William Random to buy a black lacquer Art Deco mirror for his wife. There were also some less significant sales. These items soothed Hugo's temper somewhat, but when the last patron had finally departed, he locked the door with some relish.

Jane's heart was beating like a drum when Hugo crossed the room to seize her by her wrist and drag her back into his office. "Come with me, young lady!"

"Oh, Hugo, I'm so sorry about ruining the sale!" she exclaimed.

"Not nearly as sorry as you're going to be!" he promised, pulling her into his office and pointing her at a leather sofa under windows looking out on the rocky shoreline that edged the village. "Sit down," he told her, while he himself went behind his imposing desk, sat in his chair, irritably lit a cigarette and glared at Jane through the smoke for a long minute. Presently he spoke coldly.

"I'd just like to know what you were thinking about to interrupt an important discussion between me and my most valuable client to deal with your personal sexual frustrations,"

"I . . . wasn't thinking," Jane replied weakly.

"Do you think that was businesslike?"

"No," Jane meekly said. "And I'm terribly sorry. I feel horrible."

"I'm not impressed. And furthermore," he crushed his cigarette out violently, "I would like you to give me one good reason why I shouldn't put you over my knee and spank some common sense into you."

Jane, who had never been quite so much in the wrong before, did not know what to say. If only she herself had not behaved in such a highly unprofessional manner, she might have had some reasonable objection to his proposal; but as the thought of why she'd pulled him off the floor returned to her she blushed with the shame of her foolishness.

"Well, can you think of a single good reason why I shouldn't paddle you right now?" he demanded, getting up out of his chair and coming to sit beside her. "Haven't you been childish?"

"Yes," Jane admitted, feeling her face growing very warm as she unconsciously shifted away from him on the leather couch.

"Haven't you been completely thoughtless and totally unprofessional in your comportment?"

"Yes, Hugo," Jane agreed, staring down at the shiny hardwood floor. She'd begun to twist her hands in her lap like a nervous little girl.

"Why do I go to considerable expense and trouble to throw wine parties and teas, Jane?"

"To sell," Jane replied, feeling more guilty by the moment.

"And who is my best regular in town, Jane?"

"Mrs. Duncan Blandings," Jane whispered.

"And who distracted me from giving that gracious lady the attention she has come to expect from Sands' Antiques?"

". . . me," Jane almost sobbed with remorse.

"And exactly why did you feel it necessary to call me away from the floor?"

"Oh Hugo, do we have to talk about this now?"

"Why so reticent, Jane? You had no problem discussing your sexual needs while a ten-thousand-dollar customer was cooling her heels out on the floor. Isn't it as exciting after hours? Or do you crave the extra thrill of bankrupting me?"

"Hugo, please, I never meant to do that. I simply didn't think."

"Jane, you're getting a spanking," he told her, pulling her easily across his lap. She was a lithe, slim waisted girl, of medium height, with adorable curves and shapely legs. That day she was wearing a two-piece tweed dress with smart high heeled pumps. At first he did not pull up her full skirt, but applied his palm as firmly as he knew how to the seat of it for two to three minutes without saying a word.

Jane made a number of protesting sounds, none of which could have been termed an actual word. Mostly she just took what she had coming, thinking that this wasn't so bad. Over her skirt it did sting, but apart from the humiliation of being in this position, she couldn't say that she found being treated like this unpleasant. In a way, it felt sexy being held across his lap, after dreaming about being with him for so many nights. This was the first physical contact they had ever had.

"Are you learning a lesson?" he demanded, tightening his grip on her waist while smoothing her skirt down over her firm, oval buttocks.

"Yes," Jane choked on being spoken to like this, and yet she'd brought it on herself.

"You know, Jane, you think you're a grown up, but you're really just an impatient little girl," declared Hugo, just before lifting her skirt to reveal her athletic legs and buttocks, snugly encased in a pair of sheer, seamed, black tinted tights, the kind with a fancy lace panty built in. Jane's bottom filled the seat to perfection. When he stroked her through her designer pantyhose she shuddered. She made no move, he noticed, to free herself. "However," he ventured, "You're taking your discipline very well, so far. I may even forgive you."

"I hope you do," she said, venturing a look over one shoulder.

"First you have to be punished."

Jane bit her lip.

"Tearful supplications will get you nowhere," he informed her, gently pushing her head down and taking a fresh hold on her waist. "Jane, how much money did I spend on refreshments for this evening's entertainment? You filed the receipt from the wine shop today, I believe?"

"It was about a hundred and eighty dollars," Jane replied, with trepidation. She was suddenly feeling very exposed.

"Then why don't I give you about a hundred and eighty smacks. That way I'll be able to feel I've gotten my money's worth."

"Oh!" cried Jane, as the spanking commenced, a bit sharper than before. In fact, the smacks grew somewhat harder with each short volley of five or six, until each one that fell began to impart a real sting.

"I hope you realize you're getting off lightly," Hugo informed her as she whimpered and squirmed across his lap to try to avoid getting smacked on the same spot too many times. "Better learn to get used to this," he advised. "If you stay on as my assistant after tonight's performance, it's going to be on my terms. That means you'll be getting spanked whenever you annoy me; figure on an average of once a day."

Hugo went on spanking her while waiting for the protest that didn't come. One thing he had to admit, and it surprised him, was that Jane seemed fully and cheerfully capable of taking a damn good spanking.

"Are we up to 180 yet?" he suddenly asked.

"That was 187," she replied, timidly, looking over her shoulder at him again.

"Counting, were you?" he pushed her head down again. Then he rolled down her pantyhose panties and exposed her rose-tinted oval backside. It felt warm and was deeply infused with color from the protracted spanking. He rubbed her bottom in circles with the palm of his hand. She relaxed across his knees, making no move to escape.

Now he began to smack her bare behind.

"Are you ever going to behave so immaturely during work hours again, Jane?"

"No, Hugo. I mean, that is, I'll try not to!"

"What do you mean, try? Is that the best you can do?"

"It's just that I've been so distracted lately."

"You mean you've been restless, don't you?"

A few more smacks prompted her embarrassed reply.

"Yes, I've been restless!"

"Lie still," Hugo ordered, inserting one finger into her throbbing little sex, only to pull it out soaked with her fluids. "Look at that!" he held his hand in front of her face. "That came out of you. Aren't you ashamed of yourself, getting turned on from a spanking?" He resumed masturbating her quite slowly.

"I did not!" she protested. "It's just because of you."

Hugo noticed an interesting reaction after he inserted his middle finger into her bottom instead of her pussy. Jane had been purring, now she began to moan, nor did she pull away, as many women might have done when probed in this manner. The second he slipped his finger in between her luscious cheeks Jane went into a whole different gear.

"Tell me, Jane, did your ex-fiancé ever go in the back door?"

Jane took such a long time to answer that he pulled his finger out of her snug little ring to give her a few hard smacks.

"I asked you a question, young lady," he snapped. "Did Detective Flagg ever fuck you in the ass?"

"He did," admitted Jane.

"Really?" Hugo carefully reinserted his finger into her bottom. "Why have you been keeping this interesting secret to yourself?"

"I didn't think it would make any difference. Does it?"

"Happens to be one of my favorite things to do with a lady."

"Please do it with me! I want it so badly with you. I think about it every night."

"What I should do is hold you down and force you to climax like this, then fuck you in the ass."

"I couldn't!"

"Couldn't what?"

"I could never come like this!" Jane protested.

"Want to bet?" Hugo withdrew his finger again to spank her six or seven times. "You doubt my ability to get a simple little girl like

- 56 -

you to climax?" More smacks. Jane twisted on his lap and tried to cover herself with her hand. He caught it and pinned her wrist to her waist. "Lie still!" he ordered. "It's your horniness that's been causing all the problems around here, and I intend to relieve you of it, my way."

Once Jane realized she wasn't going anywhere until Hugo got her off it didn't take long, particularly as he continued to methodically switch back and forth between spanking and masturbating her bottom with equal firmness. The way she responded simply to being held in place indicated to Hugo the potential for a variety of bondage and discipline adventures with Jane Eliot. And her reaction to the careful anal stimulation left no doubt in Hugo's mind that she could be taught to associate and enjoy spanking with the anal orgasms she obviously craved. There was obviously a whole world of untapped response in Jane and she was offering it to him to explore without restraint.

After that distinctive shudder which Hugo knew so well, he ceased his rude attentions to her bottom and assisted her in putting her clothes to rights then took her on his lap the right way up. She seemed content to be held like a child and breathed a heartfelt sigh.

"I spanked you," Hugo said.

"Yes," Jane replied.

"Gonna quit?"

"No."

"Gonna sue me?"

"No."

"You did have it coming."

"I know."

"You don't feel politically compromised?"

"Somehow, no."

"If you stay on, I'll certainly spank you again," he warned.

"I understand," Jane agreed, with a shiver.

"Not just because it turns me on. You need it," Hugo told her.

Jane felt a strange thrill at being told she needed it, which overthrew all prior political commitments. She had formerly thought of self-styled "dominant" males as abusive, sexist swine; but Hugo wasn't that. He'd called it punishment, but she felt as though she'd just been made love to.

When Jane didn't argue about needing to be spanked and forced to climax across Hugo's lap, he knew he'd found a new submissive. He wondered if she'd go for an official debut. His small circle of intimate friends in the scene would appreciate this wonderous transformation each in their own way. Hugo was particularly interested in observing Detective Flagg's reaction to Jane, his ex-fiancée, submitting to corporal punishment, from him or possibly even Marguerite! In Hugo's conservative estimate, he was perhaps a month away from Jane's readily agreeing to make such a spectacle of herself. What he'd observed of Jane that night convinced him that she was not averse to becoming the center of attention.

Hugo laughed aloud at the thought of showing Jane off to his friends, while she powdered her nose. Tonight he'd take her home with him for the first time. Possibly he would give her another spanking before bedtime, if only to bring back that adorable blush and confusion to her face. Then he'd take her upstairs and slowly sodomize her, as requested. He imagined she'd fall asleep softly. It was pleasant prospect to contemplate Jane's being his, so long as she continued to behave as beautifully as she'd done tonight.

Of course, he'd have to quit smoking, thought Hugo crossly. One couldn't dominate a morally superior woman. This would make him cranky and she would suffer for it, but if she introduced a note of wholesomeness into his life and he injected a dose of perversity into hers, then it wasn't a bad exchange.

THE PRIVATE LIFE OF
MARGUERITE ALEXANDER

WINTER STILL CLUNG about the cape like a wet and icy glove on a late afternoon in March when Marguerite Alexander, knowing that Detective Flagg's little chili pepper was out of town, dialed the Random Point police station house.

Flagg was at his desk puzzling over a forged check case when the redhead's call came through.

"Have I reached Detective Flagg?"

"Marguerite. Nice to hear your voice."

"Skip that," she said impatiently.

"What's on your mind?"

"You don't seem to have any compunction about strolling into my shop or my house whenever you please to . . . take me . . . do I have the same right to your attentions when I want them?" Marguerite demanded.

"Marguerite, are you propositioning me?" Flagg threw down his pen and closed his fraud folder. He suddenly felt glad that his partner was on nights all that week.

"Maybe," she replied coolly. "That depends on whether you're prepared to do things my way this time."

"Your way?" he was intrigued. "I didn't know you had one."

"A slap and a tickle is fine now and then, but I want real B&D. I want a scene."

"Seems little enough to ask," he commented, while he wondered what it was the redhead meant.

"Shall I expect you this evening?"

"Yes." Flagg hung up thoughtfully.

After showering and dressing in his nattiest double breasted wool suit, Michael sat down with a shot of whiskey to read his back issues of the *New Rod*, Hugo Sands' spanking quarterly, for which Marguerite often wrote. After reading all her stories he felt so warm that he finally understood the meaning of having to take a cold shower. He couldn't go over to Marguerite's like this, with a savage boner threatening to explode out of his trousers at any moment. In a state like this the whisper of her mouth on his cheek would be enough to make him come. Flagg felt he had no choice but to masturbate. He owed it to Marguerite, who had demanded a full-scale scene.

On his stroll to Marguerite's house on the beach, which was at the very tip of Random Point, Flagg barely felt the bitter wind. He knew very well that willful submissives like Marguerite expected men to read their minds, but having reread her voluptuous stories, he felt he had a plan. It was really quite a challenge, when he thought about it, attempting to devastate a sophisticated beauty like Marguerite with the complex rituals of B&D seduction.

A light snow had begun to fall as he knocked on Marguerite's door. She answered at once, as she'd been listening for his step. When the door swung open he beheld her in a black velvet bustier dress, with a cameo on a black velvet choker around her throat. Her shoulders and full cleavage were smooth and white while her russet hair tumbled luxuriantly to them.

"Michael!" she drew him inside and closed the door. "I was dreadful on the phone, wasn't I?"

Her large green eyes were grave. And for once she wasn't wearing her glasses. She seemed shy for the first time with him and he realized she had been working herself up just as much as he had for this encounter. Having taken the edge off his own lust himself, just before coming over, he felt that he had a distinct advantage over her, in spite of a freshly awakened erection which reared up the instant she pressed her voluptuous yet feline torso up against his in the foyer.

"I'll admit it isn't like you to demand attention," Michael said, pointedly removing her hands from around his waist and crossing her wrists behind her back as he held her. "But that doesn't makes you dreadful, just sadly neglected." He felt her tremble. "I want you in gloves," he told her. "Bring me a whiskey when you've put them on. I'll be upstairs." Then he went straight up to her attic dungeon. It had porthole windows looking out on the ocean, a hard wood floor, a whipping post, mirrors, a padded leather trestle bench and a leather bondage bed. This was Marguerite's playroom. It also contained free standing wardrobes with her fetish clothes and boots; and there was a wooden cabinet full of her toys. A tilting cheval mirror faced the whipping post and a skylight let in the moon until the snow covered it.

When Marguerite reappeared she'd donned black satin opera gloves and bore his drink.

"What have you got on under that dress?"

"A corset."

"Come over here. Turn around." He put his drink down to unzip her gown. "Step out of it and put it away."

The gown fell to reveal an exquisitely dainty and richly brocaded black satin corselet, with garters attached. Her black tinted stockings had seams up the back and her heels were 5" high. The corset displayed her ravishing bosom and womanly hips to perfection. A black satin G-string gave her some modesty, while baring her large, luscious bottom to Michael's appreciative gaze.

"Very pretty. No wonder you're so spoiled," said Michael, much understating his feelings about Marguerite's appearance at that particular moment. He turned her around and looked at her from every angle. She did not dare meet his eyes. When he touched her to make her turn she felt the blush that suffused her face travel up and down the entire length of her body.

"Poor baby. You don't know what's going to happen, do you?" he lifted her chin. When he kissed her he pulled her against him, with one hand on her waist and the other on her bare bottom. "You haven't the slightest idea what you're in for, do you?"

"No, but—"

"But what? Never mind. You just say yes or no. Understand?"

"Yes."

"Yes, what?"

"Yes . . . sir?" Marguerite ventured hesitantly.

"That'll do," Michael said. He liked that. "Now turn around. Back to me." He produced a clean white handkerchief from his pocket and blindfolded Marguerite. This took the leggy redhead by surprise and changed the balance of the entire situation. Now she felt intensely vulnerable and twice as aroused as the moment before. He was gratified by her blind trust. She'd allowed him the liberty of blindfolding her without the slightest protest. Now she stood with head slightly bowed, a helpless Aphrodite caught in a web of her own design.

"Come over here," he said, scooping her up and carrying her over to the bondage bed, where he sat down to put her over his knee. "You need a lesson." He then proceeded to spank her rather lightly at first and then a bit harder, until it stung and tinged her white cheeks pink.

"Don't fuss," he said, when she whimpered a bit. "You can get a spanking once in a while you know." Michael had never had her over his knee properly before and he liked the feel of her weight across his thighs and the way her lovely legs looked from the back. "This is for being a bossy brat on the phone," he informed her, continuing to smack her firm, toned buttocks with a rhythm that was neither too fast or too slow.

Marguerite gasped as the warms waves of excitement rippled through her torso, from her tender pounding heart to the very core of her sex. The way he curved his hand around her slender waist to hold her felt right. The tempo of the spanking and the force of it felt right. He was always the man that she wanted. She felt she belonged in his hands.

"I could keep you in this position all night and not get bored, but you're probably ready for something a little more grown up," he announced, lifting her up off his lap and setting her feet on the floor.

"Michael?" she was breathless.

"What?"

Locating him by voice she threw her arms around his neck.

"What do you think you're doing?" he disengaged her arms. "You stand still and don't move an inch until I give you leave. Understand?" He punctuated this command with a sharp smack on each buttock.

"Oh!" cried Marguerite. "I only wanted to hug you."

"You do as you're told and nothing else. And what did I tell you about speaking?"

"Yes and no?" she replied with trepidation, rubbing her bottom a bit with one hand.

"That's right. And did I tell you you could rub? That's it. I'm going to have to tie your hands. Put your wrists in front of you. Now!" He produced a length of soft nylon cord from one jacket pocket and tied her wrists snugly over the gloves.

Now that he had her on a lead he could pull his blindfolded beauty anywhere he wanted in the loft.

"Young lady, you are going to get the cropping of your life!" he promised, leading Marguerite behind the leather upholstered trestle horse and then gently bending her over it, so that she straddled it with her legs and her tummy and upper body pressed against its length.

"Put your hands in front of you and rest your pretty head," Michael said, gently pushing her head down and pausing to make sure the blindfold was still snug. While there, he brushed her hair away from one ear and kissed her behind it, then took her earlobe between his teeth for a nibble, but a tiny pearl stud got in the way, so he tongued her ear for a moment or two instead.

"Why are you wearing earrings?"

"I . . . you didn't tell me not to," she replied softly.

"I'm taking them out," he informed her, and then did so with some delicacy. "I might have to pull you by your ear like the naughty little girl that you are and I don't want these in the way." He put her precious earrings into a cabinet drawer and gave her a half dozen stinging spanks to communicate his annoyance with her lack of clairvoyance on this issue. Marguerite caught her breath with shock each time his palm connected with her fully exposed backside.

"Michael, it's not fair, you didn't tell me what to wear!" she protested, craning her head around to peek at him from under the blindfold.

"What did I say about talking? Head down," he ordered, giving her a few more smacks for emphasis. "I shouldn't have to tell you. You should know these things. Now where is your crop? I want that nice, white English one you showed me once but I didn't get to use . . ."

"It's in the armoire," she answered meekly, while lowering her head, but still tracking him around the room from under the blindfold.

"Why haven't you laid out your favorite toys? That's another thing you should have known. If I have to spend a lot of time playing hunt the slipper I might use one on you."

"No!"

"Wouldn't like that, huh? Well, let's hope that your toys are accessible."

Michael retrieved the British made crop with the white handle and small, square, black leather slapper at the end and returned to Marguerite, who was visibly trembling as she waited. He paced around and swished it in the air, which made her start. Then he lay it down for a moment and proceeded to fasten her down to the trestle horse by means of an attached leather strap around her waist and leather ankle cuffs attached to D-rings at the base of the horse.

As Flagg tightened each strap or closure he came close enough to kiss her, which he did, and this made her heart pound violently.

"Damn!" he suddenly swore.

"What?" she would have jumped if she hadn't been tied down at this exclamation.

"Forgot to take your G-string off."

"Oh!"

"I don't feel like redoing your ankles. Look, I'm just going to cut it off. I'll buy you a new one."

"Oh!"

He got out his pocket knife, matter of factly jerked the string out of her crack and rended the scrap of lace with one swipe. Then he cut the string around her waist to completely free her from the triangle of satin which had been shielding her reddish brown muff. Marguerite felt the all over blush once more. She had expected Flagg to be awkward at this game; now it appeared he'd been studying the art in some depth.

"Do you know what I did just before coming over here, dear girl?" Michael asked, gently stroking her bare bottom while letting the crop rest across it.

"No . . ."

"I sat down and read all of your stories."

"Oh my god!"

"Yes, they are shockingly perverse. But you wrote them so they must reflect at least some of your fantasies."

"They were written purely for the entertainment of men!" Marguerite protested.

"Just a modern day Sheherazade, are you?"

"In a way, I suppose," she replied warily.

"That's charming. Too bad it won't save you from a cropping," he observed, letting his caressing fingers stray from the voluptuous contours of her hips, to creep between her satiny inner thighs, and then just one of them, into her creamy, glove tight little slit. Flagg was agreeably surprised by her wetness. She was almost dripping with excitement.

"You little slut!" he accused. "Look at this! Aren't you ashamed of yourself?" he soaked two fingers in her sopping snug velvet pussy for a moment, then inserted the same fingers into her own mouth. Her lips, already moist and parted with her excitement slowly closed around his fingers, which were coated with her own juices. "That's you," he told her. "You must have gotten turned on by the spanking." He pulled his fingers from her trembling lips and took up the crop. "In spite of the indignity of being across my knee. Am I right?"

"No!" Marguerite cried, wriggling against the snug bonds that held her down over the horse. This outburst was rewarded with a smart tap with the square slapper at the end of the crop, really a spanking device. "Ouch!" she cried.

"Before I'm through with you, young lady, you'll wish you were back over my knee getting an ordinary spanking, unless you moderate that tone when I ask you a question!" Michael warned, giving her a half dozen medium hard strokes with the crop on alternate cheeks. As before, she gasped with each fresh smack; he waited several beats between striking, so that she could react to each, one at a time.

"You're making too much noise," he declared, in responses to her shocked little cries of inarticulate protest each time the spanker came down. "Am I going to have to gag you?"

"No!" she replied vehemently, so there would be no misunderstanding with regard to gags.

"Let's try that response again, a bit more respectfully," Michael said, giving her two more strokes with the crop, only this time they were serious and sent two jolts of searing pain through her lushly padded bottom and brought tears to her eyes instantly.

"No, Sir!" she cried, reeling in disbelief at the impact of those two hard strokes. Before the pain of these two blows had seeped in fully, Marguerite began to sob. In moments the handkerchief that bound her eyes was soaked, for Flagg laid on six more hard strokes, each of equal intensity to the first two shocking ones before throwing down the crop.

"What's this?" He went around in front of her and pulled her blindfold down. Her beautiful green eyes were overspilling with tears. Her full red lips were trembling and she tried to turn away. "I thought you could take it. You're not supposed to start sobbing twenty minutes into the session you know," Michael said, quickly undoing the fastenings which bound her to the horse. She let him take her off it and sit her on his lap, then hold tightly while she finished her cry.

"You baby!" he accused her. "Don't you ever get spanked hard?"

"Not very often," she replied. She let him kiss her tears away.

When she'd calmed down sufficiently he took her to her own whipping post and put her back against it, then cuffed her wrists to it above her head.

"What are you going to do?" she fretted, every fiber athrill, as Flagg gently but firmly released her ravishing bosom from the confines of the corset and began to softly stroke and knead it with his hands. He buried his face between them and tasted each perfect rosy nipple in turn.

"Work on your thighs for awhile with the crop," he said, as he went to get it. "I know that might sound a bit harsh, but I just remembered how much it annoyed me to see you rubbing up and down against William Random the other day at the gym. I can't help but thinking that part of that particular show was put on for my benefit. Am I right?"

Marguerite bit her lip and could not meet his eyes.

"Were you showing off to attract my attention, Marguerite?" he asked, flicking at one of her smooth, soft, creamy white inner thighs with the slapper of the British riding crop. She caught her breath but did not cry out, as he now used the crop much more gently than before.

"No," she replied.

"You're lying."

"I'm not!"

"What did I tell you about a disrespectful tone? Remember what happened the last time?" he ran his hand across her thighs.

"Oh please! I'm sorry! Not as hard as before!" Marguerite arched back against the whipping post.

"Sorry, but you have to be punished for that. All I ask is a civil response and you seem to find that impossible."

"Oh god!" Marguerite trembled and her tears began to flow freely once again the instant he began to wield the crop. This time he struck quite deliberately, taking care to make each stroke sting. She continued to sob, like a little girl getting the first whipping of her life.

"All right, young lady," he said. "Turn around and hide your face." He turned her to face the whipping post and changed the position of her arms from above her head to around the post in front of her. He also spied an iron leg spreader on the floor. Attached to it were rings which attached in turn to her leather ankle cuffs.

"It's time for your whipping," Flagg informed her.

She turned her head to look at him appealingly.

"Not hard," she pleaded softly.

"Yes, hard," he replied pleasantly, shaking out the lashes of the small martinet he'd found in the armoire.

"Better get more comfortable for this," Michael said, pausing to finally remove his jacket and tie, unbutton his collar and roll his sleeves up. The glimpse of Flagg's lean, broad shouldered torso that Marguerite got as he passed by her to get his drink raised her temperature yet a few more degrees.

After draining his glass he picked up the martinet again and went behind Marguerite to commence the whipping. But no sooner had he raised that mighty arm then the delectable redhead simultaneously shrieked and cringed.

"No, don't!" she cried.

"Why the devil not?" he lowered the whip.

"I'm . . . afraid."

"I thought you loved whipping."

"I do, but—"

"Well?"

"I don't think you've ever used a whip before . . ." she suggested timidly.

"Well!" He flung the martinet down hard enough to make her jump. "It's nice to know you have so much confidence in me."

"Michael, it's not that—but the way you raised your arm just now, if you followed through on that swing I'd be lacerated!"

"Oh, stop," said he skeptically.

"Well at the very least marked for a month."

"I'm sure you're exaggerating."

"You should practice on Damaris."

"Don't get smart," he warned.

She looked at him over her shoulder. "I didn't mean to insult you," she said softly. He coolly met her gaze, deliberately unbuckling his belt.

"You'll be happy to know that I've used a strap before," Michael said, jerking his leather belt off with a snap and wrapping the buckle and a good length of the belt around his hand to create a single thonged lash with the end. Then he slipped an arm around her waist from below to hold her in place and close to him while raising the other to strike.

She gasped on being seized in this way and on lifting her head saw herself and Michael in the mirror which faced the whipping post; she with her bottom jutting out, her ankles spread by the bar, her wrists cuffed to the post, resting in the cradle of his arm as he pulled back the other to administer the strap to her satin framed behind.

He brought the strap down once, then twice, then again and again, alternating between right and left, and then across both plump half moons. She gasped afresh each time the end of Michael's belt stung her.

"You know why you're getting a strapping?" he demanded, pausing to let her catch her breath.

"No," she whimpered, dizzy with excitement.

"Because you've been bad!" he said, bringing the strap down again, and then a half dozen more times. Each time time leather impacted against her bare flesh a hot rush flooded through her. The strap was Michael's instrument. He had practiced quite a bit with it on his wife since the first time he had used it on her too hard, and now knew how to make a strapping an erotic experience for a submissive woman.

"Oh Michael, please . . ." Marguerite seemed to want something.

"What?" he stayed his hand and examined her satiny buttocks, which were beginning to become lightly imprinted with red strap lines.

"Could you do something for me before you go on?" she pleaded prettily.

"What do you want?" he pretended impatience. "And this better be good to interrupt me for."

"Could you take your shirt off?" she asked, with the first naughty smile he'd seen from her all evening. He put the belt down. He saw her view of them in the mirror. "Yes," she said, "I want to see your handsome back while you . . . strap me." This last statement brought the blood rushing to her cheeks, for although he was arousing womanly feelings, he was still treating her like a child, and she was hesitant to reveal the full extent of her arousal at that precise moment to him, for fear of being put in the corner by her new found disciplinarian.

"You little tease flirt!" Michael accused cynically, while blushing a little himself and quickly removing his shirt. Before picking up the strap again he came around in front of Marguerite to kiss her her full on the mouth. "You're trying to get out of the real thrashing you have coming with cheap flattery," he told her, cupping one beautiful breast in his hand while raking her throat with his lips.

"I love your body," she confessed.

Michael pulled away and straightened up, feeling himself about to become sentimental while gazing into her wonderful eyes.

"You know there is a reason for the strapping you're about to get," he told her, loosening the ankle cuffs to free her from the leg spreader. "There, I want your legs together for the rest." He worried that he'd left her too long with her legs spread apart and massaged each one from ankle to thigh for what seemed to Marguerite to be an achingly long time before standing up again.

"Reason?" She was in a glowing daze from his attentions, which seemed to be assaulting her in increasingly delightful waves.

"As a matter of fact, I'm angry with you, Marguerite," Michael declared.

"Why?" It was hard for Marguerite to pretend that spasms weren't surging through her, particularly when he touched her. Now that her ankles were free she leaned comfortably against the post to which her wrists were still cuffed, almost hugging it as she watched him pace a bit around her attic dungeon, with folded arms and stern demeanor.

"You haven't been up front with me about your true nature. If I'd known what you were really like back in October I wouldn't have married Damaris," he bluntly admitted.

Marguerite felt hot tears prick the backs of her eyes.

"Would you have married me?"

"I would have asked you but I didn't think you were the marrying kind. You always seemed so aggressively independent."

"My mistake," Marguerite admitted, two tears rolling down her face.

"Don't you dare start crying, young lady. What's done is done and we'll just have to work around it. Right?"

"Right, Michael," she agreed, cheered by the implications of this remark.

"Meanwhile you've got a good licking coming to you, don't you?"

"I do?"

"Haven't you been ridiculously proud? Don't you regret your comportment? Isn't this all your fault?"

Marguerite shook her head no.

"What? Are you saying it's my fault?"

"You could have read my mind," she said.

"Don't be flippant. You're already in enough trouble," he warned her, wrapping the belt around his hand again. The he took her around the waist. In the mirror she saw her face peeking round the whipping post, his back, with its spectacular musculature, his mighty arm, holding the belt, raised to strike. She felt his hard torso against hers, and was deliriously happy to be close enough to breathe in the smell of his male flesh.

"Now you'll learn a lesson," he promised. Then he began to snap the strap crisply across either cheek. He skipped a few beats between each application, maintaining a steady tempo that was neither too fast or too slow. There was enough time between strokes for each swat to penetrate deeply, to be fully felt and reacted to, before the next one fell.

Marguerite at first watched his arm fall and rise, but this proved almost too exciting, combined with the feel of the strap impacting firmly, though not cruelly on her tender backside; she felt the rushes almost too strongly when she watched that splendid arm come down and felt the follow through. She thought she'd understood in the past what it meant to "melt" with pleasure or to feel "dizzy" with desire, but her former enjoyments had been nothing to what she was experiencing that moment, which was the thrill of being seriously disciplined by the one man she truly adored.

"You were bad, weren't you?" he said, pausing. Marguerite sobbed. "Answer me!" he snapped, strapping her hard once. She cried out and for the first time tried to jerk away from him. "Stand still while I'm strapping you," he ordered, "unless you want to be more tightly restrained."

"Oh no!" she cried. "I'll be still."

"You'd better."

"Oh, Michael, I . . ."

"You what?" he stayed his hand and rubbed her, also letting a finger slip into her sopping wet slit. If a woman was ever about to climax, it was this one.

"I love you!"

Michael turned her head to kiss her glowing face. "I love you too," he told her, reaching around to undo her wristlets. Having freed her from the post he turned her around and took her in his arms. "And in spite of what I said, the fact that we're not together is as much my fault as yours. I was too stupid to realize what a jewel you are."

"In that case can I whip you?" Marguerite said, with a twinkle. "Teach you how to use it!"

"Do you want another spanking, so soon?" He picked her up in his arms and carried her over to the leather upholstered bondage bed, then he gently lay her down on her back and straddled her. "Unzip my trousers, get out my cock and put it in you," he instructed. Marguerite needed no further encouragement to free his large, throbbing cock and guide it in. "Now, you know what you're going to do while I fuck you?"

"What?" She strained upwards to meet his first hard thrusts with joyous energy.

"You're going to tell me exactly what it takes to get you off."

Marguerite stopped grinding up against him and looked surprised.

"But Michael, I'm having a wonderful time . . ."

"I want to know what it takes to really make you come," he insisted, with some determination.

"But, I don't want to come and I don't have to come and I don't enjoy being pressured about it!" she declared, almost petulantly. He pulled out of her abruptly.

"I want an answer to my question, Marguerite." All at once he was standing over her, zipping his trousers back up and then he started hunting for the cuffs for her wrists and ankles. "If you don't tell me straight off I'll have to interrogate you in the traditional style," Michael advised her, while strapping her wrists into the fleece lined leather cuffs. "I'll have to strap you till you tell me."

"But why is it so important that I come?" she pouted as she held her hands in front of her and watched him tightened the wristlets.

"I've done it 10 times with you, so you can do it this once with me. Or don't you think I'm worthy of giving it up to? On your tummy. Right now!"

"But this isn't nice!" she protested. "You can't force me to have a climax!"

"Want to bet?" He pushed her down on the bench and bent to fasten one wrist cuff to a D-ring at the head of the bondage bed.

"What are you going to do?" She hesitated before giving him her other hand.

"Don't you dare," he warned, holding out his hand for hers. She quickly gave it to him and he fastened that wrist cuff as well. "Head down," he told her, pushing her head gently down to rest against the bench. Then he went down to the foot of the bench to fasten her ankles similarly, effectively spread-eagling her face down on the leather couch. "Now where's that belt of mine," he wondered, standing up.

"Please don't," she begged, craning her head around to watch him return with the belt.

"You're not too good to come. You just think you are," he informed her, leaning down over her, and pressing his left hand firmly down on the small of her back. "You're a superior little bitch, aren't you?" Michael brought the strap down with medium force across both luscious buttocks at once. Marguerite cried out. He struck again. Again she sobbed. She tried to turn her head to look at him but he pushed her head back down. "Head down. I don't want to have to tell you again," he told her sternly. She hid her face and abandoned herself to the bittersweet seduction of her lover's strap. Finally, it was the strapping combined with grinding her sopping wet pussy against the leather bondage bed that caused her to have a delirious climax that left her breathless, spent and satisfied.

They spent the night together in her bedroom with its windows on the beach. He made love to her three times. Between bouts he kept her beside him in bondage, mostly on her side, with her lush bottom turned toward him, wrapped in a satin nightgown that he put her into himself. That night belonged to Marguerite and she loved it.

So Young, So Bad

SUSAN ROSS HAD been attempting to seduce Sherman Cooper, the young but stuffy lawyer who was administering her late father's estate, for over a year. Cooper lived in the Majestic Apartments on West 72nd Street, over-looking Central Park. It was an overcast afternoon in April when the doorman called up to announce Susan's arrival there.

The tall, fair, bespectacled attorney was never completely comfortable in dealing with the charming little person to whom he opened his door several minutes later. He acknowledged that encounters with the pretty minx always left him restless and the moment he saw her cute pony tail he realized that his resolve not touch her was about to be tested again.

Susan was a petite and well proportioned blonde, with a complexion quick to blush. She was dressed in a short, plaid, pleated skirt of black and yellow, a black V-neck vest, a white blouse with a Peter Pan collar, bobby sox and black penny loafers. The fragrance of carnations wafted from her hair as she smiled up at him.

"Susan. What are you doing here?"

"I know our appointment was for Monday at your office, but I just couldn't wait. May I come in?" She spoke without faltering and seemed confident.

"If you promise to behave yourself," he said doubtfully, ushering her into the green sitting room, where he'd been having tea. Susan studied him as she followed, admiring his slimness in his well cut khaki trousers and plain blue cotton shirt. There was a degree of sobriety in Cooper's demeanor that had long beguiled her.

"What fun would that be?" Susan murmured.

Vaguely disconcerted, he invited her to sit down and took a seat in a leather wing chair opposite her.

"Did you read my letter?" she came to the point as soon as she was settled.

"I read your letter," Sherman replied.

"So? Will you okay the transfer?"

"Look . . . would you like a cup of tea?"

"Oh, yes! It's a bit chilly out and I've been riding through the park on my bike," Susan admitted. At that moment thunder struck and it started to rain. Susan rushed to one of the windows. The expensive new bike which Anthony had given her was chained to a post on the street seven floors below. She fretted momentarily about leaving it out in the rain while Sherman disappeared to get her tea. On his return he also brought a tin of cookies. He had Susan sit opposite him on the bottle green leather love seat.

"Susan, I'm not sure your father would have approved of you leaving a perfectly respectable art school to come and live in New York."

"My father was an iron-minded fuck," Susan rejoined.

"Is that the sort of language they're speaking in Boston these days?" Sherman frowned.

"My father didn't approve of anything, you know that," Susan ignored the censor.

"Never the less, I've studied the provisions of his will and I think I understand what he envisioned as the firm's role in administering your finances during your college years."

"You know, Sherman, I'm really glad that your uncle retired and you're the one who's handling my affairs now," Susan remarked.

"You mean you'll be glad if I give you what you want," he observed cynically.

"I want a cookie," Susan said.

"Susan, I'm not sold on the notion of you moving to New York," said the serious young man, pushing the tin across the coffee table to her. "Although you did say in your letter that you'd been accepted at an exceptional school, there's the matter of your residence to be considered."

"I explained that I'd been invited to live with a friend of the family."

"Mr. Anthony Newton?"

"That's right."

"You say he's a friend of the family, but I rather suspect he's your particular friend, and not a very wholesome one at that."

"How can you say such a thing?" Susan jumped to her feet. "He's a Broadway luminary!"

"A theatrical person, a man twice your age, who's been married five times . . . are you telling me that his interest in you is purely avuncular?" Sherman did not bestir himself, but kept to his chair in a dignified manner while she began to pace.

"Well, certainly, why shouldn't it be?" she demanded.

"You're not being totally frank with me Susan. In fact, I have a very strong notion that Newton is your only reason for wanting to come to New York."

"Mr. Newton has an entire apartment in his house that he's willing to set aside for me," Susan pointed out.

"It seems to me, Susan, that if you did transfer to school in New York, it might be more prudent for you live in a dorm. It would be more wholesome for you to live with girls your own age rather than with an older man."

"You know, Sherman, only a hard-core pervert would be as fixated on wholesomeness as you seem to be," Susan observed.

"I beg your pardon?" Sherman started because he was a hard-core pervert. Was it that obvious? Susan seemed to grow more adept at rattling his composure every time they met. As little as she was and as young as she was, she was in control.

"I'll bet that beneath that bland, myopic exterior you're completely depraved," Susan declared sensationally.

"Really! And what leads you to that fantastic conclusion?"

"I happen to know that all lawyers are kinky. Besides, I can see that you admire my ankle sox," she smiled mischievously as he involuntarily focused his gaze on her smoothly shaved bare legs.

"I'm sure I don't know what you're talking about!" he returned, rather grimly.

"Sherman, think of it, if I were in New York, you could offer me the guidance a wayward orphan needs, even take me in hand when necessary. Doesn't that idea appeal to you?"

"I'm not sure I understand what you're talking about, but it sounds as though you're trying influence peddling with the firm, using yourself as a bargaining chip," he replied stiffly.

"Well, what's wrong with that."

"Susan, you just can't go around offering people your sexual favors whenever you want something from them," Sherman told her.

"Why?"

"Don't be ridiculous, you know perfectly well why. Furthermore, if you don't stop coming on to me I will certainly put you over my knee!"

"Oh, you will not!" Susan scoffed, wandering over to the window again. "Look, Sherman, it's really coming down. Can I stay here til the rain stops?"

"I suppose that you'd better," he said, his heart beginning to pound. Although he didn't normally smoke, he now fumbled a cigarette out of an enameled box on the table. Susan grabbed the matching lighter and lit it for him.

"Thanks," he muttered.

"I didn't know you smoked, Shermy," she commented.

"Don't call me that," he snapped.

"Irritable, aren't we?" she grinned.

"Who wouldn't be with you around? Now let's get back to this business of you moving to New York. I suppose that your life will be over if the firm refuses to approve the transfer?"

"One way or other I am coming to New York," Susan firmly declared.

"Oh?" Sherman bristled, "And what is that supposed to mean?"

"It means that if I have to give up my inheritance in order to do what I want then I will."

"Really? And how would you manage after that brilliant move? Barnard isn't exactly a budget school."

"My sister's husband will pay my tuition," Susan opined decisively.

"Is that so? Well, why don't I get him on the phone right now and ask him about that?" Sherman went to the phone on a desk across the room.

"No!" Susan cried.

"No? Why not?"

"I . . . haven't exactly asked him yet, but I'm certain he'd agree."

"As I said, we can ask him now," Sherman told her, dialing Massachusetts information. Susan sprang up and raced across the room to prevent this rash act.

"I'd rather ask him myself, if you don't mind," she said.

"But I do mind," he told her and proceeded to ask the long distance operator for the number of Random Construction. "And I don't mind telling you that I've met your brother-in-law and I don't think he's going to go for it," Sherman confided, the moment before he began speaking with William Random. Susan paced in front of the desk as Sherman quickly told William that he had just been nominated Susan's benefactor in the event that she flaunted the provisions of her father's will and thereby became disinherited.

". . . What's that you say, Mr. Random? You have no intention of paying Susan's tuition at Barnard this year? . . . Oh yes, I quite agree. She's being a very naughty girl . . . You suggest I do what? . . . Well, I can't say the thought hadn't occurred to me . . . ." It was at this juncture in the conversation that Susan noticed Sherman holding one finger down on the phone button and realized that he was only pretending to be speaking with her brother-in-law! "All right," continued Sherman gravely, "I'll keep you posted. Thank you, Mr. Random. Good-bye."

Susan intuitively backed away from Sherman as he came around the desk.

"What? What did he suggest?"

"He suggested I give you a good spanking, which is exactly what I intend to do! Come over here!" Sherman caught Susan's slender wrist and pulled her over to the love seat she'd vacated in a couple of strides.

"Stop!" Susan tried to pull away. "I saw you holding that button down; you didn't even talk to William!"

"I decided to save the toll by speaking with him telepathically. Don't worry, he told me exactly what to do," Sherman confessed.

"No, Sherman, No!" she cried as he sat down and put her over his knee.

"I'm going to spank some sense into you!" he told her, holding her in place with one hand on her waist while the other one flipped up her pleated wool skirt. Snugly encased in sheer, white, nylon bikini panties, Susan's bottom looked like Valentine's Day. After ten hard smacks the color began to suffuse her fair skin to the degree that the pinkness of it could be seen even through her panties.

"You stop that!" she insisted, simultaneously attempting to cover her bottom with her small white hands and kick him in the head with her tiny feet.

"You need a lesson in circumspection!" Sherman said, pushing her feet back down, pinning both her wrists to her back and continuing to smack her bottom sharply through her panties.

"Ow! That's enough!" protested Susan. "I've learned my lesson. Please!" She craned her head around to fix him with a beseeching gaze.

"Oh no, you haven't yet," he told her firmly, pushing her head back down, then pausing in the spanking to pull her panties down to her knees.

"Ooooh! How dare you!!!" Susan squealed, trying to wrench herself off his lap as her bottom was bared.

"How quickly you've colored up!" Sherman said, giving her a few light, admiring pats before continuing with a volley of stinging smacks. Alternating from side to side, he delivered perhaps 30 hard swats to each cheek before stopping to survey his work.

"Wah!" Susan wailed. "Let me go! You're mean! You're hurting me!"

"You deserve a painful punishment for even thinking about throwing over your inheritance!" More smacks. "And don't you think it's a bit selfish of you to plan on freeloading off your brother?" More smacks. "Now, young lady, I would like to think that you're beginning to be sorry for behaving like a thoughtless, (Smack!) forward, (Smack!) arrogant, (Smack!) brat!" Smack! Smack! Smack!

"Why should I be sorry? You're the one who's going to be sorry!" she threatened, trying once more to separate his head from his shoulders with her dangerous elfin feet.

"Don't you dare try to kick me," he warned her sternly. "Put your feet down. Right now. Or I'll take my belt off and continue with it instead of my hand."

"Sherman, please, let's talk!" Susan tried a new tack.

"Alright, what's on your mind?" Sherman paused, clasping her left wrist in his right hand and resting his forearms on the small of her back.

"Sherman, did you know you have a large erection?" Susan asked, gazing back at him again. She immediately observed a deep flush spread from his throat to his brow. He pushed her off his lap and jumped up to his feet.

"My god, you're fresh!" he charged, completely flustered.

"Gee, Sherman, you have a really big one, don't you?" Susan remarked, pulling up her panties while keeping her eyes riveted on the crotch of Lawyer Cooper's pleated poplin trousers, which were currently tented around an impressive hard-on. "Did spanking me do that to you?" she queried innocently.

"Stop it!" he ordered, putting several lengths of carpet between them as she looked in danger of reaching out to caress the obvious protrusion.

"But why, Sherman? Why fight it? I'm here, you're hard. I'm willing, you're able. Let's make love!" And before he could stop her she had crossed the room to fling herself into his arms. He found her pressed against him, her tawny head nuzzling his chest, her arms tightly hugging his waist and her limber little torso grinding ever so softly against his treacherous zipper. He looked down helplessly to meet her melting blue eyed gaze. Her full red lips were parted in a naughty smile.

"Please?" she added, unnecessarily.

Sherman had always wanted to scoop a girl up in his arms, the way they did in old movies, but he'd never encountered one to whom such a gesture would seem appropriate before. Susan was so small and light that she was easily swept off her feet and up into the air. Once she was at eye level she wrapped her arms around his neck and pressed her pretty mouth to his throat. She purred for she had won.

He carried her into the master bedroom and sat down on the enormous white four poster with Susan in his lap. She fastened her lips to his mouth and opened them to his invading tongue. They French kissed so long and so deeply that Sherman felt slightly dizzy when she finally pulled her mouth away. He took her down to the bed and covered her small body with the length of his long one. Then, fearing to crush her slim little frame, he moved off to one side and slid a hand up under skirt until he reached her moist panty crotch with his fingertips. He pressed his palm upon her pubic mound through the nylon panties. She stretched and sighed and turned toward him with her entire torso, to press the length of her warm little body against his lean one. Her arms went around his neck again and she clung to him. He continued to probe her through her panties, kneading her muff and palming her sex until her panties became completely soaked with her excitement. It only took a minute. Finally he slipped one finger in under one of the panty legs and worked it up into her creamy slit.

"Oh! I ache between my legs," she whimpered, clinging to him harder and twisting her hips so as to take as much of his finger up her throbbing pussy as possible. "Don't torture me like this!" she insisted, now thrusting her well rounded bosom against his chest, then hiding her face against his chest and finally maneuvering her entire torso into the face down position, so that she lay stretched on her tummy beside him, with her pert bottom arching invitingly as he continued to probe her hot and lightly clenching little glove.

Sherman sensed that she was trying to tell him something with her body language and withdrew his finger from her pulsating sex to push her skirt up to her waist and stroke her luscious buttocks through her panties. From her faint corresponding moans of pleasure he divined that he was on the right track.

"I don't think I spanked you nearly enough," he commented, slowly pulling her silky panties down and off. On the way he also removed her tiny shoes, caressing every satiny inch of her thighs, knees and calves as he did so. When she remained face down on the bed, slightly grinding her blonde fuzzed muff against the counterpane, he became firmly convinced that she craved more attention to her bottom.

"Come on, back over my lap," he said, gently repositioning her across his knees. "Since you've had this spanking coming for a year, it might as well be a thorough one."

"Oh, not too hard! Please!" she cried, almost swooning with the thrill of being placed in the time honored position again.

"Not too hard," he promised, bending to kiss the back of her neck. Then, placing one hand on the small of her back, he started to spank her again, rather lightly this time, alternating smacks from cheek to cheek and pausing after every set of ten or twelve to finger her sopping wet pussy. This combination of spanking and finger fucking soon had her squirming on his lap in a frenzy of excitement. Her clitoris swelled hugely and prompted her to cry, "Oh Sherman, please, do something!"

"All right." He paused in the spanking and finger fucking to try something new. Dividing her lightly pinkened cheeks with one hand, he slowly inserted his well lubricated middle finger into her tiny bottomhole. Once he'd buried it as deeply as it would go and she'd started to whimper delightfully, he resumed spanking her with his other hand.

"Oh no! No!" she cried, writhing with pleasure and shame all at once. In less that fifteen seconds he felt her tight anal ring begin to spasm wildly around his finger as she ground against his lap in a delirious climax.

When Sherman lay her back down on the bed there was a large wet spot on his trouser leg and Susan was sobbing with embarrassed emotion.

"There, there, little kitty cat, there's nothing to be upset about," he told her, brushing some stray damp blond hair from her brow. He leaned down to kiss her on the mouth. Then he gathered her into his arms and held her until she calmed down.

In a couple of minutes, after she had regained her composure, she began to pull off various items of apparel, the better to grind against his lean, hard body. She disposed of her skirt and her vest and began to wriggle around on the bed in just her white blouse and white ankle socks, inviting him to join her.

"Please, Sherman, let's do it!" she begged, undoing his belt for him and starting to work on his zipper.

"I'm not sure I ought to," he replied, while allowing her to pull the belt free from the loops of his trousers. "You're really too young to take advantage of like this!" he declared.

"Maybe you should punish me some more. It might put you in the mood," she suggested, handing the belt to him and assuming the all-fours position on the bed while casting him the most inviting look imaginable over her shoulder.

"The mood to take you in the bottom, I'm afraid!" Sherman warned her, coiling the belt around his hand to hide the buckle under several leather wrap arounds and ending up with a thin strap 8" in length.

"I've never had that done to me before," she murmured.

Sherman stood up beside the bed and placing one hand in the small of her back, gave her a few light, experimental licks with the end of the belt. Susan caught her breath each time the leather connected with her bare bottom. The feel of his hand pressed down on her back, the kiss of the strap, the sound of it impacting, the nearness of his hard, masculine body all combined to start the freshet of excitement coursing through her again. He inwardly rejoiced on observing her response. Clearly, domination aroused this little darling and she was obviously anal to the core.

"All right, you're going to get a good strapping, and then I'm going to sodomize you. Does that sound like something you think you deserve?" he demanded in his characteristically soft spoken style, so that the words, although forceful, were also caressing.

"Yes!" she accepted the sentence with trembling anticipation, removing one palm from the bed momentarily to free her pony tail and allow her long hair to spill down her back and around her flushed face.

"Lie down," he told her, pushing her down so that she lay on her tummy. Then, placing one knee on the bed he raised his arm and began the strapping, which was slightly sharp and caused Susan to gasp with shock each time the belt struck her adorable bottom. He placed the strokes evenly, administering about two dozen across both blushing cheeks and taking care not to strike the same area twice in a row. He worked his way up and then down her bottom six times, giving her the strokes in groups of four and scoring her buttocks with light red lines which were perfectly even and precisely measured. Sherman had a very steady hand and knew how to make the lashes sting without cutting, tingle without burning, punish, but ever so lightly.

When he tossed the belt aside and went off to his dressing room in search of a good lubricant, Susan shuddered with excitement. Her bottom felt radiant. She fancied she could feel each individual stroke and relived each one of them as she breathlessly awaited his return. The strapping had been so exquisite that a shadow orgasm rippled through her while she contemplated it.

Then Sherman was back beside her, unzipping his trousers, dropping them to the floor and getting up on the bed beside her, with something very wet and sheer and sticky on his fingers.

"Don't move a muscle, young lady," he warned her, working the wetness up and down her bottom crack with one hand while shoving a pillow under her belly with the other. "I want you to relax. Completely. Understand?"

"Yes," she whispered, and groaned a little as he inserted a finger into her bottom.

"You're not nearly relaxed enough, Susan," he told her, withdrawing his finger and spreading her cheeks with both hands so that she was utterly open to his gaze. This had the effect of making her whimper and grind against the pillow in a spasm of embarrassed desire.

"No, hold still," he told her. "If you come right away you'll lose interest and tighten up."

"I can't help being excited," she protested weakly.

"You'd better help it unless you want another spanking," he warned her, placing his large, faintly throbbing cock between her buttocks and pressing the knob lightly against her anus. "Now lie perfectly still and don't move," he said.

"I'm scared, it feels so big!" she cried.

"There's nothing to be afraid of. I know what I'm doing. I've done this a hundred times before," he assured her.

"But it will hurt!"

"What did I tell you?" he paused to smack her bottom rather smartly three or four times.

"Ow! All right, I'll be good!" she promised.

"You had better be a little angel," he told her, rubbing his cock up and down her crack, which was by now well lubricated with the sheer, sticky liquid he'd produced for this purpose. "Perfectly still, remember," he whispered, once again taking hold of both her cheeks and pulling them apart. This time he also nudged his penis through the rim of her lightly stretched bottom hole and began to insert it into her hot, tight rectal canal a half inch at a time.

"You know, Susan, I could play with your bottom all day and never get bored," Sherman told her, "I could spank it and finger it and plug it til you came a dozen times." Susan groaned at this as inch after bone-hard inch of his thick, seven and a half inch cock disappeared into her spread bottom crack. He continued to hold her cheeks well apart to ease the entry of his penis into her and this had the dual effect of embarrassing her to the point of sobs and allowing her to absorb the entire length of organ painlessly.

Once he was all the way in, he let go of her cheeks and allowed her bottom to close around his cock.

"Now lie perfectly still and get used to it inside you. Don't move an inch unless you want the thrashing of your life!" he warned her, mainly to distract her from the frightening reality of having a large cock up her bottom for the first time. Panic and fear at a moment like this could ruin everything.

"Oh!" Susan cried, wriggling ever so slightly under the exquisite impalement, flexing her bottom around his hard cock in spite of his warning to hold still and relishing the tiniest throb of his penis with her tight sheath.

"What else?" she moaned cryptically.

"What else what, sweetheart?"

"What else would you like to do to my bottom?" she shyly asked. She craved the raunchy details while he fucked her in the ass and arched her bottom up to prove her need.

Seeing that she was relaxed, ready and receptive, he began to slowly thrust, first with shallow strokes, then with deeper ones, reaming her with his steel rod, between the cheeks that he had soundly strapped.

"What else would I do? I'm so happy you asked! I'd have a special butt plug made just for you and I'd insert it in to your behind every time I fucked your adorable little pussy, just so you'd remember what a naughty girl you are."

"Oh Sherman!" Susan cried, unable to stop herself from grinding against the pillow as he plunged ever harder and deeper into her bottomhole.

"What's more, the next time I put you over my knee for a spanking, I'm going to put a vibrator into your bottom first and turn it on. I might even buy a nice little leather paddle to paddle it til you come," he mused.

The notion of this, combined with the plunging in and out of Sherman's dick inside her bottom was too much for Susan's engorged clit to withstand an instant longer. With a shudder and a groan that seemed to emanate from her tender little heart, she gave up another girlish orgasm to him then, which caused her tiny anal ring to clench so hard and fast that he felt he might be in danger of having his penis sheared off at the base.

Realizing she would be feeling too tender for further play the moment her climax had subsided, Sherman took the opportunity presented by her shudders to shoot an ecstatic load of hot cream into her bottom at that very moment. In this manner their orgasms exploded and subsided at just about the same time and in a minute or two after Susan's bottom had ceased to spasm, he gently pulled his penis free of it, managing to do so without causing Susan discomfort or pain.

While the rain beat on the window they climbed under the counterpane and blanket. Sherman took Susan in his arms and cuddled her until she fell asleep for a little nap on that chilly spring afternoon.

In about a half hour she awoke with a start, feeling suddenly guilty, worrying about her bike, about the time, about what Anthony would say when she confessed what had passed between Lawyer Cooper and herself that day.

She hurriedly pulled on her clothes and dragged a comb through her tangled hair. Sherman was sad to see her go but did not press her about calling on him again. He was prepared to look upon the afternoon's delights as a gift and had no intention of making his approval of her transfer of schools from Boston to New York in any way conditional. He didn't like to let her go out in the rain, especially to ride her bike all the way back to the Village, but saw that she was determined to have her way about it. He did make her take a rain slicker and hat, which he buttoned up for her himself, as though she were his own little girl. When he kissed her good-bye in the lobby downstairs he told her that if Newton ever evicted her she could always bunk in the Majestic Apartments with him. Susan reflected on her way back to Anthony Newton's house that she might have to take Sherman up on his offer after she told Anthony about what she'd been up to that afternoon.

Laura Random

Late that November, Laura Random gave a dinner for her friends. As she greeted her guests in a dress of golden velvet, it was clear that she had mischief on her mind. Her husband had departed that morning for a climbing trip in the Andes and would not return for a fortnight. The significance of this announcement was not lost on any of her guests.

Michael Flagg, who arrived alone, said his wife was also out of town. The truth was, she had left him. Damaris had been gone for a week. He had an idea that she had gone to L.A. to immerse herself in drugs and vice.

Marguerite Alexander, looking very Rhonda Fleming in a blue suede bustier gown, bristled at the warmth with which Laura greeted Michael. Marguerite had known for months that Laura coveted Detective Flagg and could have thrashed her best girlfriend for this.

Hugo Sands' companion, Jane Eliot, was similarly distressed by the affection with which Laura greeted Hugo. Hugo and Jane had been intimate for some months, but now, as pretty but pedestrian Jane beheld the soft manner in which Hugo embraced Laura, it gave her a sinking feeling. How could she ever hope to compete with a siren like Laura for Hugo's limited affections?

Naturally, Hugo was interested to hear that William Random was currently roped to a small climbing team on a windy Peruvian peak. Although it had been over a year since Hugo had made love to Laura at his Halloween party, the enigmatic brunette had never been far from his mind. With her husband out of town, Hugo's path was clear, providing Flagg didn't block his campaign.

When, toward the end of dinner, Laura casually announced that Michael's absent wife Damaris had called her from California that afternoon, the handsome ex-Boston detective went red in the face the way only a fair haired man can.

"She's working at a B&D club," Laura went on to reveal sensationally. "In Hollywood!"

For seven seconds no one spoke. Then Michael, who was furious at Laura for bringing up this awkward subject in company, forced himself to reply with a conversational, "She's just saying that to get attention."

"You think so?" Laura rejoined.

"I'm certain of it," Michael replied firmly, intimidating Laura into lowering her eyes.

"Michael, has Damaris left you? Already?" Jane was jubilant, as she had not yet forgiven Michael Flagg for breaking their engagement the previous year.

"No!" Michael snapped.

"What's a B&D club?" Jane wanted to know.

"You don't need to know that," Michael replied, so overbearingly that even Marguerite, who unequivocally adored the tall detective, raised her sculpted eyebrows.

"I need to know whatever I want to know!" Jane returned indignantly.

"Jane, I hope you're not driving tonight because you're well over the legal limit and I might have to arrest you," Flagg informed her.

"You go to hell!" Jane advised her ex-fiancé and tossed back the contents of her wine goblet in a couple of gulps. After an initial blue spark exchange, Michael smiled. Jane had turned into a real little bitch and she suddenly seemed very sexy.

"Just don't let me catch you on the road, young lady," he warned her, throwing down his napkin and getting to his feet. It was time to leave for his shift at the police station anyway. Jane made an obscene gesture at Flagg's retreating figure, for which Hugo slapped her hand at the table.

"Ow!" she cried. "How dare he talk to me like that!"

"Behave yourself," Hugo told her, in spite of his amusement.

Uncomfortable about the scene which her ill-advised remarks had given rise to, Laura walked Michael outside to his car. It was a very brisk autumn evening on the Cape and a crisp wind was blowing through the spruce and pine trees which thickly overhung Shadow Lane.

"Laura," he said coldly, "I didn't appreciate your throwing a spotlight on my personal life tonight."

Laura blushed guiltily. Knowing that she had irritated Michael rather excited her, yet she didn't like to be thought badly of.

"I'm sorry. I spoke without thinking," she admitted with a shiver.

"Get in the car for a minute," he told her. Laura entered from the passenger's side while he turned on both the motor and the heat. "So she called you, did she?" he asked quietly.

"She really has been working at a club," Laura said. "Shall I give you the name and the number?"

Michael scowled and snapped, "What for?"

"In case you want to call her . . . or go after her," Laura explained, puzzled by his indifference.

"I'm not going after her," he replied.

"You aren't?"

"Of course not. Why should I? She left of her own accord. I didn't throw her out. On the contrary, I've gone to considerable expense to build a beautiful home for that ungrateful little slut."

"Michael, don't call her that!" Laura was shocked by the harshness of his face in the moonlight.

"What would you call a girl who'd rather let a succession of strangers tie her up and whip her than behave like a proper wife?"

"Oh Michael, she didn't want to leave. But she has her pride. She doesn't think you love her."

"Oh, baloney," Michael rejoined. "Just because I'm not slobberingly sentimental . . ."

"You know it's not that," Laura said softly.

"What then?"

"The way you carry on with Marguerite."

The color rushed to Michael's face for the second time that night.

"Michael," Laura went on, "Damaris wanted you to know what her situation is."

– 89 –

"Why? What does she expect me to do about it?"

"She wants to be rescued," Laura patiently explained.

"She'll need to be rescued from my strap if I find her turning tricks in some B&D bordello!"

Laura's tummy clenched at this grim pronouncement, but she managed to murmur, "I think she'd be enchanted to take a good licking from you if you cared enough to go after her and bring her home."

"Sorry if I'm skeptical, but in my opinion, Damaris has been secretly yearning to escape her straight life with me and get back into drugs. This jealousy bit about Marguerite is just a red herring. She's simply run away to be bad."

"That only goes to show how little you know your own wife," said Laura.

"She's made her choice, now she can live with it," he stubbornly insisted, adding, "And dragging her back home like some outraged Victorian husband just doesn't go in this day and age."

"Excuse me if I chuckle, but since when did you become liberated?"

"I beg your pardon, Mrs. Random, but I went out with an ardent feminist for two years without commiting a single sexist gaffe."

"If you don't count breaking your engagement. Michael, be honest, doesn't the idea of recapturing Damaris appeal to you on a erotic level?"

"I suppose that it does, but it seems an awfully expensive and inconvenient way to get a thrill," Michael stated with a good deal more detachment than he felt.

"Well, you know best," Laura sighed, ready to give up. She saw that he was a very hard man, even more inflexible than her husband. However, when she chanced to meet his eyes she was startled by the sudden look of warmth with which he now regarded her.

"What are you up to, Mrs. Random?" Michael demanded. "Earlier in the evening you appeared to be giving me a signal that you were available, now you want me to jump on the next plane for the coast. What's going on in your head?"

Laura paused a moment then said recklessly, "Michael, you must know I have a crush on you."

Michael was taken aback but charmed. "I'd better go," said

Laura, opening the car door with a pounding heart. "Do you accept my apology?"

"For a forfeit," said Michael, impulsively taking her in his arms and kissing her full on the mouth. The wide bench seat of the old sedan made it possible for Flagg to fully embrace her and he crushed her slender torso to his chest throughout the long, deep kiss. Once he had her close to him he was reluctant to let her go and began to fondle her delightful bosom, dainty waist and firm thighs through the voluptuous nap of her golden velvet gown.

Laura was thrilled but terrified. This was happening too fast and she knew that the moment was wrong. She broke from the embrace and told him firmly, "I should go," and instantly slipped out the door. Michael watched her run back to the house with her long skirt lifted above her slim ankles and wondered what had gotten into him just now. And he had called Damaris a slut!

Hugo, who'd remained remarkably sober throughout the evening, was making arrangements to drive Jane and Marguerite home when Laura returned to the house with a racing pulse, flushed cheeks and tingling lips. Her over excited demeanor was duly noted by each of her departing guests with varying degrees of disapproval. That something had gone on between herself and Flagg just now was patently obvious to Marguerite, Hugo and Jane.

When Hugo stopped to let Marguerite off at her house on the rim of the village, the tall redhead invited Jane to come in for a nightcap. Hugo was pointedly excluded from the invitation. One of Marguerite's shining talents was her ability to deftly arrange complicated seductions. In this case, she knew very well that Hugo would wish to return to Laura as soon as possible. Offering herself as a distraction to Jane seemed both humane and politic to Marguerite, who was always interested in making points with her influential patron.

"Michael is right, you girls are drinking too much," Hugo observed gravely. "I think you've both had enough. I know I certainly have." The fact that these remarks were wholly out of character for Hugo, did not occur to Jane.

"I'll decide when I've had enough to drink!" Jane retorted predictably.

"Oh you will, will you?" Hugo exchanged glances with Marguerite, who was beaming at her own cleverness. "Jane, you're going to have an awful head tomorrow as it is," Hugo warned. But Jane was already getting out of the car.

"That's my business," Jane told him airily and followed Marguerite through the picket gate into the garden. Hugo got out of the car, folded his arms and waited until Jane gave him a pert backward glance.

"Jane, you're being a bad girl. Let me take you home," Hugo coaxed her, rather gently, for him.

"No!" Jane actually stamped her foot before marching over Marguerite's threshold.

Marguerite waved to Hugo from her door, secure in the knowledge that her good deed would also keep Laura from pursuing Michael Flagg any further that night. Meanwhile, it would be interesting to study the woman Michael had almost married at that jaded hour of a full moon autumn night.

When Hugo returned to Laura's house some fifteen minutes later he found her releasing her two tabby cats into her leaf strewn back yard.

"Hugo, what are you doing back here?" She was all innocence, with soft golden light surrounding her in the doorway.

"Someone has to teach you a lesson," he told her, entering her home and locking the door behind him.

"Is that what you're really doing here?" She hooked her hands into his lapels and looked up at him so appealingly that it was hard for the besotted antique dealer to resist kissing her.

"It is," he replied, cooly disengaging her hands and retaining only one of them, to lead Laura out of the pantry, through the kitchen and down the wood paneled hall. "We're going to have a nice long talk first, you and I," Hugo told her, pulling her behind him into the room where Laura had served coffee to her guests an hour before. He deposited her on a sofa and sat down beside her.

"Cigarette?" Laura proffered a painted box deliberately.

"You know I've quit smoking," Hugo replied indignantly, though he lingered over lighting one for her.

"Hugo, was I awful tonight?" Laura's plaintive query disarmed him. The last thing Hugo expected any woman to do was admit she'd been bad.

"Well, let's see," Hugo said, "you upset Marguerite by making advances to Michael; you infuriated him by telling everyone his wife had run away; you annoyed the hell out of Jane by coming on to me; and frankly, I'm a bit put out with you myself."

"Why shouldn't I be friends with Michael?" Laura demanded. "Didn't his wife have an affair with my husband?"

"Really, Laura, that's crude for you," Hugo chided her.

"I don't care. I've always felt that Michael and I should sleep together at least once, for balance."

"Is that how you see your marriage to William, like a ledger sheet of infidelities?"

"What if I do?" she replied carelessly.

"What about Marguerite? Don't you owe her better loyalty than that? She didn't enjoy watching you come on to Flagg tonight," Hugo pointed out.

"She gets to play with him all the time," Laura returned, quite the petulant child.

"Whereas you only get to play when your husband's out of town, right?" Hugo noted with growing irritation Laura's perverse attachment to Flagg. "You're a selfish little opportunist, do you know that?"

"I just want to cut loose for a couple of days," Laura replied, resentfully. "And as for Michael being peeved at me for bringing up Damaris, well, if he'd been paying enough attention to her she never would have run away. It's appalling the way he takes her for granted."

"If he's as callous as you say, then why are you bothering to pursue him?"

"On a purely physical level he's just my type," Laura replied coolly. "Although I do have more than one type," she favored Hugo with an honest smile.

"I'm heartened by that news flash, but don't you think you might have been a bit more circumspect about broadcasting it in front of Jane? She is the jealous type, you know."

"I should think you'd know how to deal with a tantrum by now, Hugo," Laura replied smartly. "Besides, if you didn't think it was worth it, you wouldn't be here."

"You're pretty sure that you've got all the answers tonight, aren't you, young lady? You know, Laura, you're very much mistaken if you think I appreciate being kept on ice for a year then summoned to perform for you the first time your husband is well away," Hugo said, taking her cigarette away, crushing it out and in one rather suave movement, pulling her over his lap.

"I am seriously annoyed!" A flurry of sharp smacks followed this pronouncement and Laura reacted to each with a squeak of surprise.

"You've been asking for a spanking all evening," Hugo remarked, smoothing her luxurious golden velvet skirt down over her perfect oval cheeks before initiating a second volley of hard smacks. "Isn't that so, you brat?" Smack!

"It might be so," Laura responded softly, inwardly melting as her gripped her slender waist. Ten or twelve harder spanks followed.

"You've become spoiled rotten," Hugo declared, continuing to vigorously spank the seat of her skirt, which molded to her buttocks so flatteringly. She turned to look at him with her soft brown eyes and was electrified by the stern frown in his blue ones.

"You seem to think you're entitled to whatever you want," he charged, spanking her quite soundly now at a very brisk pace.

"Well, aren't I?" she dared to rejoin, attempting to stay his hand.

"You're certainly entitled to the full effect of this spanking," Hugo said, putting her hand aside, then pushing the lavish yards of velvet up to her waist to reveal a perfect bottom, gleamingly encased in ivory satin tap pants, trimmed with beige lace. Laura's slim legs were showcased by seamed stockings and a satin garter belt.

"Laura, I hope you don't think I enjoy punishing you. I'd much rather spank you nicely. But someone has to set you straight," Hugo intoned, stroking her adorable bottom through the exquisite material of her panties gently for a moment, then delivering a series of a dozen, sudden, stinging smacks which took Laura's breath away.

"Yes, I thought that would get your attention," Hugo observed.

"Ow! Why so hard?" she protested, rather squeakily for her.

"So you'll realize I'm serious," Hugo told her, while lowering her pearly knickers to reveal her delightfully rounded bare bottom, now tinged a deep, dusky rose by the palm of his hand. "We're going to get something settled tonight, Laura," he punctuated this declaration with another ten or twelve smacks, first striking her right, then her left cheek, first reddening the outer contours of her bottom, then striking closer to the center, first slapping high up on the hips, then down low upon the silken crease which divided buttock from thigh, repeating this outer to inner, upper to lower path until he had darkened the entire surface of her ravishing bottom with the imprint of his hand.

"Hugo, please!" Laura cried.

"Please nothing, you have this coming," Hugo informed her, while continuing to thoroughly redden her bottom. "I never thought I'd have to punish you, Laura, but your behavior tonight warrants correction."

Laura fretted over this injunction in silence for several difficult minutes across Hugo's knees before bursting into sobs. It was the shame much more than the pain of the spanking that made her begin to cry, for the seductive rhythm of the smacks had begun to transport her beyond the pain and into another realm of sensation much more subtle and moving. The sense that she was being punished for having behaved dreadfully was somehow thrilling and somehow awful to Laura, especially since the punishment was being administered by Hugo Sands, whom Laura considered a discerning and elegant man.

Gradually, as the spanking progressed, the pain was replaced by a pervasive warmth which washed through her like liquid light. Now each time his palm came down upon her bare bottom, she felt impelled by its relentless impact to grind her pubic mound against his thighs. An ache of longing pierced and inflamed her. She was lubricating copiously now.

She was now overwhelmed by a feeling of dizzying helplessness. This sensation of acute vulnerability sprang from the position in which she had been placed and the way in which he held her there, with his hand lightly pressed upon her waist, as though he were confident that she would put up no more resistance than a blushing little girl when put across a grown man's knee.

"You can cry all you like, but you need this," he told her firmly, continuing to spank her for a minute or two before pausing to lean forward and scrutinize her face, which was flushed, wet with tears and very sweet. Laura's emotionalism touched Hugo. He turned her over on his lap and embraced her, kissing her mouth first, then lingering about her soft throat and velvety ear lobes. When he pushed her gown aside to nuzzle and lightly bite her smooth, white shoulders Laura whimpered.

"Get up," Hugo told her and stood up as well. He took her by the shoulders and made her kneel on the sofa with her bottom to him and her arms leaning on the back of it. "Face that way," he said, pushing her down with a gentle hand on the small of her back, so that she was ideally positioned to be taken from behind. He raised her skirt to her waist and pulled her panties off.

"Don't move, young lady," he told Laura, removing his finely tailored suit jacket. She turned around to look and was promptly rewarded with a smart slap on the upper thigh. "Eyes front," Hugo told her, unbuckling and snapping off his belt. He doubled it and cracked it a few times for effect. Laura flinched each time he did this but could not resist craning her neck around to measure the length of the strap just once before turning away. This act of shy defiance earned her one sharp stroke of the belt, which made her cry aloud and called forth a fresh torrent of tears.

"I don't want to have to tell you again," Hugo said cooly, but momentarily put the strap aside to come around in front of her and mop her face with a pristine handkerchief. There was also time to kiss her again, run his hands through her fine brown hair and take her ear lobes softly between his teeth. Laura sighed, sobbed, melted. This way he had of punishing then petting her kept Laura's tummy fluttering as it hadn't done since the early days of her marriage. Meanwhile Hugo was finding Laura so charmingly responsive that he was more inclined to cover her with kisses than red marks. Then he remembered how long she had made him wait for this evening, and this recollection hardened him just enough to make it exciting for Laura. He straightened up and threw the hand-kerchief aside. He showed her the belt.

"You're getting a strapping. Understand?"

"Yes," she replied meekly before lowering her expressive eyes and leaning over the sofa back with adorable resignation. "And there isn't going to be anything playful about it," he advised her, stepping behind her, placing one hand on the small of her back and delivering a sharp, stinging lick with the belt across the middle of her bottom. Laura gave a little cry and put one hand back to rub her bare behind.

"Can't stay still, can you?" Hugo picked up the discarded hand-kerchief. He went around in front of her again. "Give me your wrists, Laura," he said and when she obeyed with startled eyes, he tied them together with the handkerchief. "If you'd held your position properly I wouldn't have to do this." He gently pushed her back down so that her tummy was supported by the back of the sofa and her bound wrists were in front of her.

Hugo took up the strap again with a sigh. "Who would have thought it would have come to this, my having to resort to restraints to make you mind me," Hugo's tone conveyed profound disappointment.

"I'll mind you," Laura replied softly, while waiting with trembling for the next stroke to fall.

"Is that so? I'm pleasantly astonished, but why should I believe you?" Hugo stroked her pink tinged bottom with the palm of his hand.

"Because I say so," Laura murmured.

"Yes, well we both know that your word isn't worth the paper it's written on," he rejoined. "A true change of attitude has yet to be effected in you, princess." He clarified this point by flicking the strap across her buttocks a half dozen times, sharply and in rapid succession. Laura cried out with a startled little, "Oh!" each time the leather stung her bottom.

"So you're going to mind me, are you? That's sweet," he paused in the whipping to slip his left hand under Laura's tummy and press his palm against her silky, cream-soaked pubic curls. Tucking the strap momentarily under one arm, he used his other hand to probe her, getting each finger wet in turn inside her snug, pulsating sheath. Hugo masturbated Laura gently, but firmly for some time, slipping his middle finger into her pussy as far as it would go, then pulling it out again, then putting it back again, very slowly and carefully, until her entire muff was frothy with her juices and both his hands were dripping as well. Ten times in those ten minutes she felt herself on the brink of climax, but it always slipped away. She had the sense that he was controlling even that.

Hugo took his hands away and picked up the belt again. He said, "You're getting a dozen of the best now, Laura Random, after which you are going to pledge, in all sincerity, to forget about Michael Flagg."

The first two strokes were briskly delivered, causing Laura to cry out in pained surprise. Hugo continued, "You will stay away from Detective Flagg and not upset our dear Marguerite." Two more licks of the strap followed, falling one above the other across the upper then the lower half of her bottom. Red marks appeared immediately.

"Your disloyalty to your own sex is shocking!" Hugo scolded. Two more times the strap came down, now across her tender upper thighs, which brought fresh tears to her eyes. "And speaking of loyalty, how do you think William would feel knowing that you made blatant advances to Michael in front of the rest of us tonight?"

"Oh, he doesn't care who I sleep with!" Laura protested.

"Is that so?" Hugo paused in the strapping, but only long enough to let her catch her breath.

Two more cracks of the belt quickly followed, robbing her of it again.

"How many was that, monster?"

"Eight," Laura replied at once.

"Eight what?" Hugo sounded impatient. "Eight . . . Sir?" she ventured timidly, daring to look around at him for a moment.

"That's better. You know, I like a bit of formality between dominant and submissive. In your case, courtesy and respect are lessons which obviously need to be relearned." Hugo furthered the instructional process by administering two more licks with the belt.

"How many does that leave, Mrs. Random?" he demanded, rubbing his hand across the hurt part and leaving a tingling in its wake.

"Two, Sir," Laura returned, keeping her eyes properly front this time.

"Now, you're going to feel these," he warned her, before delivering two more smart whacks. Laura sobbed aloud at these, though they were only a bit harder than the others. Hugo threw down the belt.

"Knees apart and arch your bottom higher," Hugo told her, unzipping his grey flannel trousers and allowing his large, pulsating erection to escape. Guiding the knob of his cock into her snug, wet portal, Hugo smoothly and deliberately plunged all seven plus inches into her pussy at once.

"Oh!" she cried, pierced to the core. She would use the exclamation repeatedly over the next quarter hour. Fastening his hands upon her slender waist, Hugo commenced thrusting into Laura and continued with this intensely pleasurable activity for a good fifteen minutes without either of them uttering an articulate word.

The moment he began to drive into her, waves of liquid excitement began to course through Laura's body. He pinched her ear lobe smartly, then carefully freed her breasts entirely from the front of her gown to firmly handle them, never pausing in the rhythmic assault of his cock on her glistening pink glove. Everywhere he touched Laura thrilled her.

"Thirteen months you've kept me at bay," Hugo charged, pausing in his thrusting, while still buried to the hilt, to slap her right buttock hard. Laura gave a shocked cry at the unexpected resumption of her spanking, especially at that moment. "And now you admit that William doesn't even care about who you sleep with!" Hugo gave her another hard spank, this one on the opposite cheek and Laura cried out once again. "Now, I want to know exactly why you've been avoiding me all year," Hugo slapped her several more times to impress her with the extent of his curiosity.

"What's the use?" Laura wailed. "You won't believe me!"

"I will if you're telling the truth," he murmured soothingly, continuing to fuck her now without the accompaniment of smacks. She was aware of both his hands on her hips now, pushing her from him and pulling her back up against him as his engorged cock pistoned rhythmically into her wet, velvet pocket.

"I do find you very attractive," she began, haltingly, having to catch her breath every few seconds as she came closer and closer to a delirious climax while he pumped her. He slowed down his thrusting to listen.

"You've captured my attention, continue," Hugo urged, slipping one hand under Laura to press upon her flat, satiny tummy while continuing to plumb her clinging depths.

"I . . . don't know what else to say," Laura stumbled.

"Really!" Hugo snorted. "Well I don't consider that an adequate explanation. Either you're for me or you don't give a damn."

"I'm for you!" Laura cried, squeezing her pussy around his cock hard.

"And I suppose you thought that denying yourself to me for a year was a good way of expressing this fondness?" He spanked her five times in a row on her right cheek. "I don't think so!" Then he spanked her five more times on the left one and each smack was hard enough to make her give a little yip of hurt surprise. But it was enough to also send her over the edge. So intensely stimulating was his firm hand striking her bottom while his hard cock thrust inside her to the hilt that Laura enjoyed a shuddering climax before many more minutes had elapsed. Moments later Hugo joined her.

"I've been afraid of having an affair with you." Laura admitted, reclining on the sofa after having her wrists freed.

"And why is that?" Hugo demanded, standing over her to put his belt back on.

"Because I think I like you too much," she explained, every fiber of her sex still athrob. She almost came again just looking up at him, for his looks were quite appealing to her.

"If you like me that much, why be afraid?"

"It might wreck my marriage," she replied, with a sobriety which indicated that she had given this problem a great deal of thought.

"Really!" Hugo's expression was pleasant as he slipped his suit jacket back on then deftly adjusted his tie in the mirror.

"Hugo, you almost look as though you like that idea!" Laura accused, shocked by the enormity of the concept.

Hugo merely smiled at her serenely and said, "Let's just say the wrecking ball has arrived."

SHADOW LANE III
THE ROMANCE OF DISCIPLINE

Susan's Senior Year

Susan Ross began her senior year at Barnard, but after she was mugged in broad daylight on the Morningside Heights campus during the first week of October, Anthony Newton convinced her to transfer to college upstate for the remainder of the year.

At that time in their relationship, the only thing Anthony enjoyed more than seeing Susan on weekends and holidays, was receiving her letters. Susan wrote her lover continuously, with her impressions of the school, the professors, the characters in the lesbian girl gang which she had been absorbed into, and especially her fantasies.

However, Anthony, who was himself a scholar, knew Susan was not spending enough time on her studies because of their correspondence. And he took her to task accordingly on a visit to her in November.

They were leaning on the railing of the wooden bridge that spanned Vassar Lake, staring at the burnished reflection of leaves in the wind rippled water. It was about three in the afternoon, chilly and overcast.

"Susan, I love your letters, but you can't keep spending so much time writing me," he told her fondly, rubbing her small, leather gloved hand against his cheek.

"Why not?" She pulled him by the hand over the bridge and

onto the path into the woods, where they began to walk. The floor was soft with pine needles and fallen logs were everywhere.

"I'm sure you're not studying enough, Susan," he scolded. "You're spending too much time on frivolous diversions, like girl gangs and letters home. I notice you're even sending a weekly letter to Dennis!" He referred to his young English driver, who was devoted to Susan and had been heartbroken since she went away.

Susan blushed at this last remark.

"Am I not supposed to do that?" she asked.

"That's depends on what you're writing. But why you should have anything to write to my chauffeur is a mystery to me," he endeavored to sound stern.

Anthony waited until they had walked another ten minutes before stopping in the woods.

"Get over here, young lady." He took her by her arm to the perfect fallen trunk, sat down on it and turned her over his knee. "But, what did I do?" she asked as his hand came down on the seat of her tweed skirt.

"You argued about the letters," he said, giving her a brisk spanking.

"But, I can't not write you!"

"You can write shorter letters and study more," he smacked her soundly, holding her firmly across his lap by her little waist. "And you can stop flirting with my driver!" He pulled up her skirt and smacked her on the panties, which were white cotton. "What kind of letters are you writing Dennis, anyway? Mistress letters?"

"Was I not supposed to do that?" She gave him an adorable look over one shoulder.

"You're a very bad girl," he told her sternly and pulled down her panties. "I'm going to have to spank you on the bare bottom for that."

"No! It's too cold out here!" she cried, trying to pull her panties back up.

"You won't feel cold for long," he promised her and proceeded with the spanking.

The smacks sounded much louder when administered to her creamy, white, bare bottom, but they were completely alone in the woods except for the squirrels and birds and neither of them felt concerned about the noise. Anthony concluded the spanking with twelve of the best and then let her set herself to rights.

"Speaking of correspondence, Susan," he said, "that was an extremely wicked letter you wrote me the other day."

In the letter he referred to, Susan had revealed a guilty fantasy, which she had nurtured for years, but never dared try to fulfill. She looked at him, blushing and rubbing her bottom. He got up and they began to walk again.

"Do you really think it's wicked?" Susan asked him, almost dizzy with excitement from the brief spanking.

"No. It would only be wicked if I were your real life daddy. However, it's probably no accident that you only fall in love with men who are old enough to be your father."

"I guess that's true," she said. Anthony had just entered his 40s. Sherman Cooper, the executor of her estate and her uptown lover, was in his middle thirties. Hugo Sands, her mentor in the scene and occasional playmate, was in his middle forties. William Random, her brother in law and sometimes lover, was also in his middle 30s. Susan would turn 21 that year. "But I don't think of you as my father," she hastened to explain. "You're so boyish and charming. My father wasn't anything like you. They're not making older men the way they used to."

Susan had explained in her letter that she longed to experience a scene in which she was spanked like a helpless little girl.

"I'll tell you what, Susan. Tonight, at the inn, after dinner, you can bring me your report card. All right?"

Dutchess County was filled with bed and breakfast inns and Anthony Newton had booked connecting rooms for Susan and himself in one of the prettiest and oldest of them for that weekend. In her room, after dinner, Susan changed into a navy pleated skirt and white blouse, white knee sox and burgundy oxfords.

She knocked on Anthony's door timidly but slipped inside quickly, a beautiful young lady, with wavy, long, dark blonde hair. Anthony had managed to obtain a room with a piano and he was playing some delicate étude of Chopin when she entered, which gave her a thrill.

Anthony rose from the bench and managed to look very serious upon her arrival.

"Well, it's about time you got home, young lady. Did you hope that if you stayed away long enough I might forget that you were bringing your report card home today?"

Susan was speechless with embarrassment. She had never actually entered into a play acting situation with Anthony before and felt suddenly very intimidated about the whole idea. And yet, she had prepared a report card. Unable to think of what else to do, she handed it to him.

Anthony sat down in a large wing chair by the fireside. Ordering her to sit upon a hassock by his side, he consulted the paper. Susan had printed it out on the Mac in her dorm room. At the top it said: Gramercy Park Middle School. Then below that it said: Susan Ross, 7th grade. First Semester. Teacher: Mr. Elgarten. Then came her grades: Art 98%, English 92%, Social Studies 80%, General Science 74%, Music 68%, Algebra 65%, French 64%, Physical Education 66% And under the section for remarks, Mr. Elgarten had commented: *Susan is a nice girl, but she often talks in class and distracts the other children. Susan should apply herself more and bring her up grades in French and Math.*

Anthony looked up at Susan sternly. Suddenly she felt weak. These were her actual marks from her seventh grade class, first semester class, which she could never forget as it was the first time she had ever failed anything.

"Susan, this is very disappointing. Some of these grades are shocking, considering your intelligence. You've actually managed to fail French."

Susan hung her head.

"Susan, do you remember the last time you brought home a poor report card to me? We had a talk then and I told you what would happen if you continued to disgrace yourself with marks like this. Do you remember what I said?"

Susan merely shook her head.

"I said that if you didn't show an improvement by your next report card that I would give you a good spanking."

Susan looked at him with wide eyes. He got up, took her by the wrist and led her to a heavy, wooden straight backed chair which he had placed in the center of the Tudor style wood beamed room.

"Imagine a daughter of mine getting 68% in music!" said Anthony indignantly, while turning her over his knee. "You're a very bad little girl," he informed her, smacking the seat of her skirt very firmly several dozen times.

"Why are your grades so poor, Susan?" he paused in the spanking to ask her.

"I don't know," she murmured, only aware of the hot flashes of excitement which flooded her tummy.

"I'll tell you why. It's because you're an idle, spoiled brat who'd rather read *Mad* magazine than do her homework," he decided, flipping up her skirt and commencing the spanking all over again on the seat of her white nylon panties. These panties were so sheer that the pinkness of her well spanked bottom glowed through the material to entice him.

"Don't fuss," he paused in the spanking to warn her. "You're going to be punished." He pulled her panties down to mid-thigh and renewed his grip on her tiny waist before bringing his palm down vigorously on her bare bottom.

Anthony's hand descended firmly and rhythmically several dozen times, reddening both her cheeks thoroughly with inexorable determination. Susan kicked and squirmed across his lap but didn't cry out, mindful of their situation within the inn. He had to hold her little hand by the wrist to prevent it from covering her pink, vulnerable bottom towards the end of the spanking.

"Aren't you ashamed of yourself?" he demanded.

"Yes," she sobbed, on the verge of real tears from the emotion of the scene.

"Yes, what?"

"Yes, Daddy," she replied.

Anthony tucked his arm around under her waist for increased control over her lithe, little body.

"And as if the poor grades weren't bad enough, I also have to hear from Mr. Elgarten that you've been rude enough to talk in class. That makes me very angry, Susan. I thought I taught you better than that." Anthony continued to spank her slowly and firmly, alternating cheeks, until her entire bottom had been stained a deep magenta by his hand. "Lie still, young lady," he ordered when she gave a little kick at an especially hard whack. "You're not going anywhere until I'm satisfied you've been properly corrected."

Susan lay across her lover's lap and felt as much like a child as she ever needed to feel. She was aware of his hand on her waist and the clock ticking on the mantlepiece. The spanking was becoming harder and she had begun to feel uncomfortably sore, though the actual smacks were continuing to stimulate her.

Anthony soon found himself embracing the spirit of the fantasy. When he caught his own reflection in the mirror he was amused by the determined compression of his lips as he continued to sharply apply the palm of his hand to Susan's round, upturned bottom.

"I never want to see another report card like that again," he warned, finishing the licking with a hard, fast, dozen swats. Then he helped her up off his lap and pulled her panties back up. She turned away from him and hid her face. "Now go to your room," he told her sternly.

When she entered her own room she threw herself face down on the bed and attempted to still the pounding of her heart. With her bottom so warm and sore it was easy to imagine that she really was a little girl who got a spanking from her handsome, young daddy.

She lay there fantasizing until Anthony came in and slipped into the large feather bed beside her. She snuggled into his arms and lay her fair head against his chest.

"You make me so happy," she confessed. He picked up a plush brown Peter Rabbit in a blue coat she'd had in bed with her.

"Susan Ross, I've never known you to sleep with a stuffed animal," he teased her fondly, locking her in his arms from behind, so that her now cool bare bottom was pressed against his now very hard cock.

"But when I was eleven I did," she confessed, grinding back against him.

"Those were your real grades, weren't they, Susan?"

"Yes," she admitted with some embarrassment. "I failed French."

"Just be thankful I wasn't your father the day you brought home a 68 in music," Anthony sternly declared.

Susan sighed.

"When I was eleven," Anthony told her, "I greatly admired a little girl named Jill. We were part of the same after school clique and it got to the point where I walked her home from school every day and very often kissed her. She also let me put my hand into her blouse and squeeze her bottom under her skirt.

"However, Jill was a fresh little girl and one day she took it into her head to make me jealous. She let my friend David walk her home from school that day and pitched bottle caps with him all afternoon in the street.

"I was furious. I had my usual piano lesson at 4:30 and I remember that was the first day I stumbled all the way through the *Rhapsody in Blue*. At 5:30 I ran over to her block and was lucky enough to see Jill playing potsy with two or three girlfriends from our class. We all had to get home for dinner within the half hour but I was able to call Jill away from the other girls and induced her to take a walk around the block with me.

"There was a vest pocket park on the way and I stopped at our favorite bench. The one where she used to let me kiss her. We had it out then and there. I told her that she had made me angry walking home with David and spending time with him all afternoon instead of me. Then, Susan, I actually told her that I was going to spank her. She looked at me and didn't run away. Then she let me pull her across my lap and swat the seat of her skirt at least six times. When I let her up she immediately kissed me, then ran away. I think I masturbated for the first time that day. She stayed my girl friend all summer after that, though I never dared attempt another spanking."

Absence inflamed Susan's passion for Anthony. When a weekend came when they couldn't be together because of his commitments, she became cross and unreasonable. And when she was told that Anthony would be in London during Thanksgiving week, the first big school holiday of the year, she sulked and cried. Anthony was surprised, touched and annoyed. She had never taken on like this before about trips abroad, which occurred frequently in his life.

Before departing for England, Anthony made time to drive up to Poughkeepsie. He found her in the cathedral-like library. He knew her favorite spot, under the Venetian glass window, depicting the first woman receiving her degree in 15th century Florence.

Susan's heart contracted when she sensed him behind her. He never wore cologne, but she knew the scent of his soap. He sat beside her and said nothing for a moment or two, fixing her with a serious gaze that caused her tummy to fill with butterflies.

"Gather up your books, we're going for a walk," he told her.

A light snow was beginning to fall as they followed the path beside the brook. Anthony stopped as soon as they were alone in the woods and picked up a fallen branch. Susan watched with great surprise as he broke off its longest, thinnest branch and swished it through the air with a whooshing sound. He looked at her without smiling.

"What are you going to do?" she backed away but he reached out and grabbed her by the wrist, then pulled her towards him and tucked her under his left arm.

"Teach you a lesson," he replied, bringing the switch down smartly on the seat of her dark blue jeans. Susan cried out with pain and surprise. The switch hurt! He held her fast. "Don't you dare move," he told her, "and be grateful I'm not taking your pants down for this!" He applied the switch to the backs of her calves now and she sobbed at the effect. Once more he switched her bottom, then her thighs, then her calves. She caught her breath and sobbed at each cut, but did not struggle to get away. Then came six hard strokes in a row, all across her bottom at evenly spaced latitudes. These cuts brought tears to Susan's eyes.

Anthony let her go. They sank down on the bank of the stream. She wept against his jacket while he held her.

"You let me down, Susan," he told her. "We've been together almost three years now and I've never known you to behave as immaturely as you have this week."

Susan hung her head, which looked particularly sweet in a heather wool beret, which was now becoming flecked with snow flakes.

"I expect you to be self-reliant and resourceful when I can't be with you."

"I'm sorry." She accepted his handkerchief.

They walked back to the dorm called Main where Susan lived. This was the original building of the college and it dated back to the Civil War. It was a grand, imposing winged edifice, fashioned after the Tuilleries in Paris. Susan had a room in one of the fifth floor towers. She took him there.

It was a corner room with four windows, painted smoky blue with oak mouldings. Her windows displayed autumnal vistas on every side. Anthony sat in one window seat and she in another while they speculated about the long history of the room they were in and the many women who had inhabited it.

"The first girl who lived here undoubtedly wore whalebone stays and had her own maid," Susan told Anthony.

"I wonder whether that young lady ever had marks to show her lover," Anthony mused. Susan took the hint and came to him. She allowed him to unzip her jeans, pull them down and then her panties. He lay her across one knee and caressed her bare bottom, which bore several traces of the switch. She was only lightly marked. It was enough to keep the glow of this afternoon alive until he returned.

Anthony locked the door and made Susan get on her little school bed, on her hands and knees with her bottom toward him. He penetrated her quickly and smoothly from behind, fastened his hands to her small waist and began to fuck her soundly. Anthony was young enough to have enjoyed the first wave of totally permissive college campuses, with coed dorms already established at Yale when he was an undergraduate. So he thought nothing of taking his girlfriend right in her dorm room. In spite of this room's pristine innocence for the first 100 years of its existence, the last 30 had been filled with scenes like this one. An elegant hotel would have been more to his taste, but he had no time to stay the night in the Hudson Valley and hadn't come to see her just to chastise her.

He admired the curvaceous symmetry of her bare bottom between his hands as he held by the hips and drove into her creamy pussy.

"I'm bringing home a cane from England, to replace the one you put in the incinerator," he warned her.

"But you said they don't make them anymore," she turned her head and caught their reflection in the mirror over her little oak dresser.

"Don't worry, I'll find one," he promised, tracing one of the light red marks left by the switch with a fingertip.

Susan closed her eyes and pushed back against him, returning each thrust as firmly as it was given. She went into a dreamlike state of endless pleasure whenever he took her like this. Sometimes the force of a thrust would remind her so much of a slap, or the stroke of a belt, that she would feel a deep, delirious contraction in her tummy. His forceful style conformed exactly to her needs. When she had sex, she wanted to be taken, just like this. She wanted it to be almost another act of discipline, and most importantly, an expression of control.

Anthony came before her, in the usual way, outside, not inside her lovely young body. Then he lay her across his lap and forced her to have an orgasm by finger fucking her in the bottom. It didn't take very long.

Soon after that he was putting his overcoat and hat back on and preparing to depart. Susan insisted on walking him downstairs. Dennis sprang out of the Bentley to open the door for his employer and greet Susan, who favored him with an affectionate smile before being swept into her lover's arms for one final kiss.

Susan rushed back to her room, remembering as she raced up the five flights of steps, how nimbly he had taken them beside her an hour before. After locking the door she examined her marks in the mirror. They were light for the pain she had felt. Although she didn't resent the switching, Susan inwardly resolved never to earn such a punishment again. Yet his strictness seemed very sexy in retrospect.

After Anthony forbade her to write him long letters and embarrassed her about writing to Dennis, she had to find another worthy correspondent and she picked Michael Flagg. This choice was made in the spirit of sheer mischief, Susan deciding that she could not put off the pleasure of giving herself to the good-looking detective any longer.

Michael received the first letter a few days before Thanksgiving, and it was Hugo who forwarded the letter to Michael from Susan. He opened it very late one night, after coming home from his shift. It was written in precise script, on one thick, perfumed sheet of cream stationary with the initials SR embossed on the top.

Dear Michael, it began, *I hope you will remember meeting me at the impromptu auto-de-fé which Hugo Sands arranged for the betterment of my sister Laura at the beginning of September.*

I am writing to let you know how impressed I was by your restraint that evening. You alone resisted the invitation to thrash Laura, even though she would have submitted, because you instinctively felt that it was not respectful to do so. Laura and I discussed it afterwards and she also appreciated your highly developed sense of propriety. (Which I hope you will completely ignore when dealing with me.)

I enjoyed it very much when you held my hand. Why did you do that?

Best Regards,
Susan Ross

Michael's reply showed up in her mail slot the day before she left for Thanksgiving. She had it to look at in the back of the Bentley as Dennis drove her to Random Point for the holiday. She didn't even open the plain blue envelope until they were driving out of the grand, circular driveway fronting the entrance to her dorm. It began to rain as they passed through the main gate and Susan looked forward to enjoying the long drive to Massachusetts in the rain. Dennis was blissful up front, knowing he would get to talk to Susan when they stopped for a couple of meals and would be staying on the Cape the entire long weekend with Susan and her sister Laura, so he could be at her disposal and drive her back to college on Sunday night. She would be getting her license shortly and this would be the last time he would drive her to and from school.

Now Susan opened her letter and read the following lines, which were boldly scrawled on white letterhead.

Dear Susan,

Thank you for your letter. You are a thoughtful and adorable young lady, whom I would enjoy getting to know better when the time is right.

When I took your hand I hoped to distract you. You seemed disturbed by your sister's punishment. When I took your hand I forgot all about your sister.

Please feel free to call me if you'd ever care to chat at the phone number above.

Fondest regards,
Michael Flagg

Susan read the letter until she'd memorized it. Then she tried to figure out what to do next. Did she really dare to call him? Call him and chat about what? She revolved a number of scenarios in her mind and fell asleep dreaming about being in the power of Detective Flagg.

The next morning in Random Point dawned frosty cold. Susan and Laura put the turkey in the oven as soon as they could, then dressed in warm leggings and sweaters and went skating on the duck pond. Susan's heart began to pound fiercely as they glimpsed Michael Flagg already skating when they arrived.

Susan had already told Laura of her brief correspondence with Michael and had found her sister extremely sympathetic. When Michael skated over to them Laura invited him over for a turkey dinner later in the day. Gratified and slightly embarrassed by the soft attentions paid to him by the pretty sisters, Michael flushed but accepted the invitation, intending to visit the girls before beginning his shift at five.

Dennis, who was helping in the kitchen, suffered keenly at Susan's excitement over their tall, handsome guest.

Over dinner Susan and Laura begged Michael to tell them lurid police stories, which he obliged them by doing. Then it was time for him to go. Both girls insisted on kissing his cheek. He slipped his arm around Susan's small waist and gave it a firm squeeze. Their blue eyes locked when he let her go. He smiled at her, but Susan couldn't tell whether she was being encouraged or merely treated politely.

"Walk him to his car," Laura whispered. But Susan couldn't bring herself to do that, not knowing what to say.

She returned to school on Sunday night having gotten no further with Michael and unsure of how to proceed. Then on Monday afternoon she was surprised by an autumn bouquet, which had been left outside her door by a florist with a note from Michael, thanking her for the dinner. Laura also got flowers. He had also had written on the card to Susan, "I'd love to see some of your artwork and stories sometime."

Susan immediately went to the library and photocopied a comic strip she was working on and mailed it to him with a letter describing the week before her. It was the beginning of a correspondence which was characterized by long, sometimes illustrated letters from Susan, answered by friendly but circumspect letters from Michael.

After about three weeks of polite and pleasant letters back and forth, Susan decided it was time to get a rise out of him. So she wrote a long and colorful letter about a recent jaunt to West Point she had made with a carful of rowdy seniors, drinking all the way there, then picking out cadets to fuck on Flirtation Walk. Susan casually bragged about a 6'6", buzz cut blond god managing to pull out and shoot with her just like a porno star after both of them drained his hip flask of JD in the bushes. It was enough. The letter she received back was brief and to the point.

Dear Susan, it read, *Remember I mentioned I have a woodshed? One more letter like your last and you'll get to see it next time you're in Random Point.*
Michael.

Excited by the note, Susan finally decided to initiate the next phase of their affair. She'd stayed up late on whites editing the final draft of a paper that was due the next day and now intended to reward herself. Michael was on graveyard shift at the station when she called.

"Detective," he said, answering the phone, in a three a.m. voice that sent a shiver down her spine.

"Michael? This is Susan Ross," she said, thrilling to the sight of fresh snow falling against the black sky outside her window.

"Well, hello young lady. What are you doing up so late?"

"I just finished a paper and I was wondering . . ."

"Yes?" he leaned back in his chair with a smile. It had been snowing outside his windows for some time.

"Whether I'd get to see your woodshed when I come home for Christmas."

"Now, Susan," he said, in a maturely discouraging tone, "the letters and the flirting have been charming, but realistically, aren't you spoken for?"

"Anthony doesn't have to know," Susan said quickly and without a twinge of conscience.

"I see," he replied noncommittally.

"You sound hesitant." She felt her heart contract with disappointment at his lack of enthusiasm for playing with her. "I probably shouldn't have called you so late."

"That's all right."

"Do you not want me to write you anymore?" she asked.

"I didn't say that."

"Are you afraid of falling in love with me?"

Michael laughed at her audacity.

– 115 –

"Very well, young lady," he told her, giving up his feeble attempt at circumspection, "we have an appointment the next time you're in Random Point."

"In your woodshed?"

"If you have the nerve."

"Oh, I do."

For the next week Susan fantasized about Michael Flagg continuously. In her studio art class she worked on a clay bust of his head, falling deeply in love with her creation and longing to see and touch the strong, virile body which supported that noble dome. She intended to photograph the piece for her portfolio, then bring it home and present it to him the following week.

Luckily, Anthony Newton did not mean to join Susan at his house in Random Point until Christmas Eve, which was several days after Susan intended to arrive, and he therefore missed the entrance of Susan with the bust. This was fortuitous, as she had decided that her current infatuation with Michael Flagg was best kept from her lover.

As soon as she had a chance to bathe and change her clothes, Susan called the second number which Michael had given her, which was his home number. She got his message machine, which informed her that he would not be home until midnight. Susan left a message that she would be happy to meet him at midnight.

When Michael checked his machine at ten he was delighted at the sexy message little Susan had left him. He called Anthony Newton's house and she drowsily answered the phone.

"You fell asleep, didn't you?" he admonished her. "I should have known that little girls can't stay up until midnight."

"I can stay up as late as I like," Susan said defiantly.

"I'll pick you up as soon as I can," he told her and hung up.

When he arrived just after twelve he found her waiting for him dressed in a perfect tartan jumper over a cream wool turtle neck, cream cashmere argyle knee sox and little mahogany oxfords. He had called her a little girl and she wanted to be that way for him.

It was snowing outside when she opened the door to him. Tall, fair and Viking-like, Michael seemed to fill the foyer. She blushed very deeply when he took off his top coat, handed it to her and watched her as she hung it in the closet. She escorted him through the richly carpeted hallway to the downstairs drawing room and offered him his choice of nightcap. He selected Irish whiskey. She refrained from drinking but watched him shyly as he drained the shot glass.

"You must be tired after working all day," she ventured awkwardly.

"I was, until I got your message."

"I've been very forward, haven't I?" she ventured, daring to meet his eyes, but only momentarily. He was clearly amused by her shyness and confusion.

"You are bold on paper," he agreed.

"In reality too," she said bravely, while inwardly trembling at his height and apparent strength.

"That's right. You're the one who keeps cadets out past their curfew at West Point, fucking them in the bushes."

"Oh, I only said that to be sensational."

"You mean you didn't really do it?"

"I did it. But I only bragged about it to tease you."

"Susan, get your coat."

Susan got her navy reefer coat and tam and his coat out of the closet and they both bundled up. Before leaving she brought a box out of the bottom of the closet and had him help her put it on a table.

"I made something I want to show you," she said, opening the box, taking out straw and the lifting out the bust.

"You made a bust of Joel McCrea?" Michael asked, examining the finely turned head.

"No, it's you," she explained indignantly.

"Me?" Michael laughed.

"Of course it's you and I think it's an excellent likeness."

Michael studied the bust, feeling immensely flattered.

"I want you to have it," she told him.

"Thank you. I'm overwhelmed," he replied, putting it carefully back in the box. Susan glowed with pleasure at the the way her surprise made him flush.

Within ten minutes he was letting her into his refinished rustic cottage in the woods skirting Random Point. She didn't take her coat off until he'd started a large, crackling fire in the main room, which was graced by an imposing stone fireplace. The storm was whipping up thick drifts of snow about the woods and village and Susan was glad to be cozy inside.

Michael brewed her tea on a hot grate built into the hearth. She sat on an upholstered stool by the fire and drank her tea, hoping he'd leave the woodshed for an evening in summer. He came up behind her and ruffled her soft, long, wavy blonde hair. She turned to find him kneeling beside her. Unable to resist, she placed a tiny, innocent kiss on his face. Michael kissed her back, but without innocence. The next thing she knew they were both on the floor in front of the fire, she in his arms.

But as he drew her against him his hand inevitably curved around the swell of her girlish bottom and the touch of his hand on this portion of her body electrified them both. Michael pulled away, then let her go.

"No," he said, "this is too easy."

She knew exactly what he meant and her heart began to pound.

"Luckily for you, snowdrifts piled up against the door preclude a trip to the woodshed tonight; however, there is still the matter of the letter to be dealt with . . ."

Michael got to his feet and pulled her up to hers, then took her by the hand and led her to his favorite heavy straight backed chair, whereupon he sat down and turned her over his knee.

"You didn't think you were going to get out of this, did you?" he asked, smoothing down her skirt over her heavenly little bottom.

"For a minute I did," she confessed, then gnawed on her knuckle and waited. Michael paused to enjoy their reflection in a full length mirror across the room. Susan looked so adorably worried.

"Now, Susan, you knew very well that if you teased me enough I would spank you."

Susan had no reply to this fact. He patted her bottom. She squirmed.

"I like this jumper," he told her, smoothing down the skirt again.

"It's my actual prep school uniform," she told him pertly, over her shoulder.

Just when Michael thought his cock couldn't get any harder and was threatening to burst his zipper, she said something like that. Michael brought his hand down on her bottom no harder, he thought, than a boarding school girl deserved, for a minute or two, to warm her up. Susan squirmed and kicked her little shoes, but made no outcry. However, the small, breathy noises she did produce were those of startled and embarrassed pleasure. His large hand coming down so firmly on her bottom caused thrilling sensations to ripple through Susan's tummy.

"One can only imagine the sort of mischief you got up to in this," he remarked, raising the skirt to her waist to expose her cream silk panties, which clung snugly to her perfect bottom.

"I fucked my boyfriend in it constantly when I was 14," she blithely revealed.

"You know, young lady," he told her between hard, admonishing spanks, "you have an unbecoming habit of boasting about your sexual experiences that I find objectionable in one so young."

A sound spanking followed, while Susan kicked and squirmed. He easily held her firmly in placed with one large hand on her waist.

"Hold still, young lady," he told her. "I'm going to teach you a lesson about being more circumspect around people you hardly know," he scolded, pausing to lean down and look at her face.

"Ouch," said Susan, looking at him with wide eyes.

"I'm afraid I'm going to have to pull your panties down," he told her, tucking his thumbs under the waist band and lowering the briefs to mid-thigh. Susan's smooth, round bottom was already dark pink from the spanking on her panties and charmingly radiant. He pressed his lips to her bottom several times, causing her to catch her breath with surprise and look back at him. "Beautiful," he briefly explained, giving her bottom a pat.

"I'm sorry I said controversial things," said Susan with trepidation, as he raised his hand to smack her bare bottom. The flesh of her cheeks had begun to mark dramatically, but in his rapture Michael chose to ignore this warning.

"You said vulgar things," he corrected her, spanking her hard. She cried out at every swat now that they had become more severe and tried to put her hand back to protect her bottom.

"Even D.H. Lawrence used the words fuck and cunt in his novels," Susan pointed out.

"Yes, but you'll note that he put them into the mouth of an uneducated gameskeeper, not Connie Chatterley's," Michael gained his point and finished the spanking.

Susan knew that it was one of the hardest spankings she had

ever received, yet she was so aroused by being handled and controlled by Michael that she accepted it as though it had been a mild love spanking. She didn't even cry. Whereas if Anthony had spanked her that hard, she knew she would certainly cry, because he never spanked her that hard unless he was angry with her. But Michael seemed so affectionate and protective toward her and his penis was so hard the whole time that she couldn't help but feel deeply loved as he punished her. He didn't dispense many compliments, but the way he looked at her and held her communicated tender admiration.

Finally he allowed her to stand up and pull her panties back up. She turned her face away, feeling embarrassed. Then she went to the mirror to pull up her skirt and pull the panty legs to one side so she could examine the possible damage. Susan was shocked to note that her bottom had been stained dark purple highlighted by a lattice work of black and blue marks. She had taken a hard spanking! How could he have spanked her hard enough to mark her like this without causng her to scream for mercy, she wondered, touching the tender flesh, which now began to feel quite sore, with a tentative finger tip. She rubbed her bottom ruefully.

"I guess I asked for it, but . . ." Susan set her panties back to rights and let her skirt drop. ". . . I sure am marked." She frowned in consternation, walking around the room, absently rubbing her bottom while examining small objects of decorative interest.

"Is this going to cause a problem?" he asked, following her, stopping her, pulling up her skirt and pulling aside her panties to examine the damage. She looked over her shoulder with him at her thoroughly marked bottom.

"Only if you don't immediately fu—make love to me," she told him with an impudent smile.

Michael evaluated the marking in the distracted manner of a person who suddenly realizes he is guilty of a rash deed. The sight of her poor, belabored bottom, which had come to him so pristine and white, was confusing and very distressing. He had never marked anyone with his hand before. Indeed, the only marks he had ever left had been with a strap, and even then, they were lighter and less bruiselike than these. Had he really bruised this darling little girl? He knelt behind her to press his lips to her poor, punished bottom. She reached back to take him by the hair as a child grabs the mane of a favorite big dog.

"Did you hear me?" she asked.

"I want to put something on your bottom immediately," he told her, getting to his feet and disappearing into another room. Susan beheld the marks with awe, thrilled that he had spanked her severely enough to leave her this memory of him, because by now she was extremely enamored of Michael Flagg.

Michael returned with a towel and some aloe cream. He sat on the sofa by the fireside and beckoned her to him. When she came he took her across his knee again, but this time to apply the healing ointment to her bottom. He pulled down her panties and began to massage the cream into her purpling buttocks deeply and gently, still trying to sort out his feelings about what he had done. He deeply regretted placing ugly marks on her flawless bottom. But he understood from Susan's words and gestures that she had no resentment of him. She was sophisticated enough to know that marks were an occasional liability of playing and that if a girl didn't want to have to conceal them from her lover, she shouldn't let very strong men with extra large hands spank her on the bare bottom. Never the less, he worried. He ought to have stopped spanking her sooner. And he ought not to have spanked her so hard. She had done nothing to merit this sort of discipline.

"Hey!" she protested, "I think this is making it hurt worse!"

"I'm going to give you this cream to take home," he told her, "and I want you to use it at least twice a day. It should help the marks to go down. Another thing you can do is coat the area with toothpaste for about twenty minutes. It draws the bruising to the surface of the skin and makes it fade faster."

"Toothpaste?"

"Yes, my ex-wife Damaris learned about that when she worked in the B&D club."

He let her up and she set her clothes to rights again.

"Maybe we should do the toothpaste now, when it'll do the most good," Michael decided, abandoning her to go in search of toothpaste.

"No!" said Susan, rubbing her bottom. He came back with the toothpaste and sat down again.

"Come on, we're going to give this a try," he told her, pulling her back down across his lap.

"No, this is silly!" she protested, trying to pulling her skirt back down. She wriggled on his lap and tried to get away but he held her fast.

"Don't be obstinate, Susan. This is for your own good."

"I don't want you to put toothpaste on my bottom. It sounds like some old wives tale!" She thrashed against his thighs, trying to break his hold on her. "Let me go!" she said in a tone so angry that he immediately complied.

Susan jumped off his lap and then retreated to the other side of the room. Now that the clear and present danger of the toothpaste humiliation had passed, Susan calmly confronted him. Everything had changed in an instant between them. It was unfortunate that when he wanted so badly to charm her, all that he seemed to be doing was blundering. Such a look of consternation came over his face at this thought that Susan couldn't help but laugh.

"It's all right," she reassured him. "I'm not mad at you, just don't mention toothpaste again."

Michael wasn't used to being scolded by a girl, especially one almost young enough to be his daughter, and was painfully aware the fact that he was no longer in control of the situation.

"Why are you so quiet?" She came to him and sat on his lap, placing her lips against his throat between collar and ear.

"I'm just wondering what to do with you." He tightened his arms around her tiny waist and inhaled the perfume of her hair and skin. Her body was softly compliant as she put her arms around his neck.

"Why don't you let nature point the way?" She asked, bouncing impertinently on his lap, which still concealed a lead pipe she could feel through the layers of clothes between them. Michael's self-doubt did not interfere with his body's response to her dear proximity.

He carried her into his bedroom, deposited her on the big, four-poster bed, and began to undress. Susan kept her eyes on him but also slowly began to get out of her outfit. She paused now and then to examine her bottom in the mirror opposite the bed.

"I'm going to say I went skating and fell a lot," she decided. His clothes were off before hers and she made a gratifying fuss over his physique. By the time she had kissed and caressed all the handsome planes and contours of his gracefully chiseled torso,

Michael's confidence began to return. Susan didn't tell him of her fetish for bodybuilders, but her knowledgeable admiration of his major muscle groups gave her secret away. She begged him to pose for her nude.

Michael made no promises but began to unbutton her white cotton blouse, the jumper already being tossed on the floor.

"How do you like being made love to best?" he asked her, pulling off her blouse and cupping in his hands her small, rounded bosom, which was perfectly presented in a cream lace front closure décolleté bra. He gently undid the clasp and freed her breasts, which he then caressed and kissed.

"Face down and from behind, with my tummy pressed against something I can grind on," she answered in all frankness.

"Sounds easy enough," Michael said, placing a large oblong bolster cushion in the center of the bed. "Straddle that," he told her.

"Now?"

"Just to get the feel of it," he said, helping her. She was now in her pale silk panties and knee sox. She sat on the bolster and leaned forward, jutting her bottom back towards him and hugging the hard pillow with her knees on either side of it.

"Perfect," she said, leaning forward so that her lower abdomen was pressed flat against the bolster, which was richly covered in forest green damask. He got behind her and made her lean forward completely until she was face down against the pillow.

"Head down and bottom up," he told her, helping to raise her hips. He separated her knees as far as they would go and also spread her bottom. Susan gave a little cry of surprise. Then he reached between her legs to separate her labia with careful fingers. As he touched her he felt how wet she was and this brought a smile to his lips. It was a small vindication for part of his behavior, yet everytime he focused on her bottom and saw the dreadful marking he had put there, he inwardly shuddered.

"Now Susan," he said, carefully working one middle finger in and out of her velvet pussy, "we don't have to go all the way."

"Huh?" she mumbled.

"I mean, I can get you off just like this, you know."

"Mmmm, that sounds nice," she murmured, "but let's try it the normal way first, so we can come together."

Michael lubricated his painfully hard organ with her own

copious juices and slowly began the immensely satisfying task of penetrating her. He was large, but gentle and adept. Having been married to a petite woman, Michael knew that the key to fully taking a girl of Susan's size was to do it by slow degrees.

Susan closed her eyes and hugged the bolster. This was so exciting. She'd dreamed about this. She relaxed and opened herself to him. She peeked out of the corner of her eye into the mirror opposite the bed and thrilled to the sight of this extremely handsome and muscular male, invested with the authority of the state of Massachusetts, with his large hands which had subdued and disciplined her fastened to her waist and his hips thrusting forward every time he plunged inside her to the hilt. How she longed to sculpt those rock hard abs and pecs! Michael noticed her soft smile in the mirror as she shyly watched him take her and fell deeply in love. He stroked her bottom firmly while he plunged repeatedly into her delicious little pussy.

Then Michael brushed her long blonde hair away from her right ear and took her ear lobe firmly between his thumb and forefinger in the manner of a disciplinarian.

"Are you ever going to write me such a naughty letter again?" He pinched her velvety ear lobe just hard enough for her to realize that she was being scolded.

"No," she replied, experiencing a ripple through her tummy which foreshadowed the climax she had been teetering on ever since he'd achieved full and vigorous penetration. "I'll write a worse one next time!"

"Oh. I see." He let go of her ear and sharply slapped her thighs. Susan cried out in shock and pain but the sensation produced by the discipline was tremendous. She ground against the bolster when he resumed taking her forcefully and gave a little sob when she came. Michael withdrew within a split second of his own climax and ejaculated against her bottom cheeks that he himself had so sternly marked.

They stayed up most of the night talking, with her curled against him and his arms around her in the dark. He found out that Laura and Susan had different fathers, which explained why Susan was an heiress and Laura was not. Susan had had a strict, scary, dominating, older father, who had tyrannized her until his demise when Susan was in her senior year at prep school.

Michael was surprised that for all of the terror he had inspired, that Susan's father had only spanked her a couple of times, between the ages of 3 and 6.

"What do you suppose he would have done had he discovered the many uses of your school jumper?" asked Michael.

"Given me a strapping for sure," she said immediately. "And he would have pulled me out of school."

"But he never did find out about anything you did, did he?"

"No. I was a good girl."

"You mean you were a clever girl."

Michael in his turn revealed that he used to receive regular and severe strappings throughout his childhood from his ex-marine, cop father, whom he still resented greatly. Then Susan and Michael both agreed that children oughtn't to be spanked, except very occasionally.

"However, had my daddy been handsome and loveable and young, I might have enjoyed being spanked by him. I might even have been naughty on purpose, to get the attention," she mused.

"But that wouldn't have been proper," Michael pointed out.

"Why not?"

"Because then it would have been eroticizing your relationship."

"But it wouldn't have been sex, just spanking."

"I'm just telling you what I think."

"Suppose you had a little girl of five, who consciously provoked you into spanking her, would you refuse to satisfy her harmless little need?"

"It depends on how naughty she was in trying to provoke me. She might succeed."

"Sometimes when I see the cute, young daddies come to visit their daughters at school I wonder whether any of them have ever spanked any of my classmates. They're not making daddies like they used to, you know. Some of them even look like you."

"Yuppie daddies don't spank their daughters and you know it," Michael smiled at her optimism.

Susan snuggled against him and fell fast asleep.

The next morning Susan asked Michael to go skating with her at the duck pond. He had to drive her back to Anthony Newton's house so that she could change into leggings and get her skates. Michael waited in the car, reading the paper while she rushed inside.

She encountered Dennis immediately as he was in the process of taking in the milk and paper.

"Hi, Dennis," she tossed off lightly as she started up the stairs.

"Mr. Newton got in last night," Dennis quickly revealed in a hushed tone, stopping Susan cold.

"He did?" A dart of anxiety pierced her heart as she looked up towards the second floor landing. "What time?"

"About two a.m."

"Did he ask where I was?"

"Of course."

"What did you say?"

"That I didn't know."

"What happened then?"

"He went to sleep."

"Is that what he's doing now?"

"Yes."

"Okay. Thanks, Dennis," she said, and tiptoed lightly up the stairs to her room, with a racing heart, wondering whether she should lie if she ran into him now, or try to create an alibi by calling certain friends in the Village who could cover for her. With her pulse still pounding, she exchanged her a jumper for a skating skirt, turtle neck, cropped jacket and tam, all in shades of winter white and cream wool. Her leggings were flesh colored and the skates which she carried were sparkling white. Meanwhile she wore little ivory lace up boots.

She ran back downstairs in a very few minutes, highly aware of the fact that her lover was a very light sleeper. But mercifully she was allowed to escape without apprehension. However, had she looked over her shoulder and up before getting into Michael's car she would have seen Anthony Newton on his bedroom balcony, very much awake at nine a.m. and not a little curious as to who Susan was rushing off with without even coming up to see him.

As soon as Susan drove away Anthony called William Random, who was immersed in his newspapers and coffee.

"William, does anyone you know around here drive a late model Olds, navy blue?"

"Michael Flagg has an Olds Cutlass that's dark blue."

"Is that so? Thank you, William," Anthony said, hanging up, all mysteries resolved.

Susan took her time in returning home, figuring she was in for it no matter what time she got back. By now Anthony would have called around to William's and Marguerite's looking for her to no avail. So Susan spent almost two hours skating at the pond with Michael, after which they went to the Bone and Feather for a large breakfast.

"Are you going to get in trouble with Anthony for this?" Michael asked her as she prepared to get out of his car in front of the Cliff House at one.

"Maybe just a little bit," she said, playing down her anxiety.

"Don't lie about the skating. He'll know where you got the marks and if you lie it'll make it worse."

"I won't lie," she promised.

Michael took her hand and kissed it.

"Susan, if you ever decide you need a new boyfriend, I want to be first on your list."

"Thank you, but Marguerite would beat the living daylights out of me."

Michael smiled and kissed her.

"Wait til you get my next letter," Susan teased, running her hand across the bar of lead which had sprouted in his trousers at her proximity.

"Susan, behave!"

Susan hugged him and got out of the car. Taking a deep breath she entered the house. No sooner had she quietly shut the door behind her than Anthony Newton appeared on the second floor landing to frown down at her.

"Susan, come up here, I want to talk to you," he told her and then returned to his rooms. She threw her hat, jacket and skates into the closet and proceeded upstairs in the short pleated skirt and turtleneck. Anthony was dressed in a salt and pepper Donegal tweed suit that was cut perfectly for his lithe, medium frame. He wore a white shirt, no tie and had his short, dark hair slicked back. He was clean shaven and meticulous in every aspect of his appearance. Anthony's dark, cynical eyes riveted her the instant she entered the room with the trepidation of a schoolgirl who has far outstayed her curfew.

"Well?" he said, folding his arms and looking her up and down, "what have you got to say for yourself, young lady?"

"I'm sorry I wasn't here when you got in last night, but you know I wasn't expecting you for a couple of days," she explained.

"Why didn't you come up this morning when you came back to change your clothes? Dennis told you I was here."

"I . . . wanted to go skating," she replied slowly, aware of how childish this sounded.

"I see. Well, that explains this morning. What about last night? Did you spend the night with Michael Flagg?"

"Yes, sir," Susan lowered her eyes, feeling her face grow very warm.

"And how did this happen to come about? I didn't even know you two knew each other beyond meeting that once at Hugo's at the end of the summer."

"I saw him on Thanksgiving," Susan admitted. "After that, we began corresponding."

"You have, have you?" Anthony said, with a tinge of irritation, uncertain that his toleration levels would stand a strain as great as Michael Flagg.

"Well, I have to write to someone!" she protested.

"Letters are one thing, spending the night in another man's arms is quite another!" Anthony paced. Susan flushed with guilt and excitement. He seemed genuinely annoyed. If one had to put a word to it, he almost seemed jealous this time.

Anthony took up his usual position at the piano and began to play a moody, dissonant piece by Scriabin, while fixing Susan with an accusatory stare. She came over to the piano and looked contrite.

"You'd better be careful, little girl," he warned her.

"Why?"

"Two can play the same game, you know."

"What do you mean?"

"I mean that I might have other correspondents besides you as well."

"Do you?"

"What do you think?" Anthony wondered whether Susan had the vaguest idea of the type of following a composer who had had three hit Broadway shows could possess.

"I don't know. Tell me," she asked, with a pounding heart.

"There is one particular girl I could become very fond of, if I allowed myself to," he admitted, paralyzing Susan with dread.

"A girl?"

"To be quite frank, I haven't met her yet," he revealed, "And I'm not going to, until she turns eighteen."

Anthony was gratified at Susan's stricken look.

"Why? How old is she now?"

"Seventeen and a half," he replied cooly. "Shall I tell you about her?"

Susan nodded.

"She's a senior at the Julliard School. A pianist. She's got a terrible crush on me. She's been writing me for two years now. I haven't encouraged her much, though I can't help but be interested in her career. She's sent me several tapes of herself playing my music and they're quite charming. I could easily patronize her. She's been begging me to come to her recitals for years but I've steadfastly refused until now. With the slightest encouragement she'll fall helplessly in love with me. Young girls are like that. They're not all sophisticated like you, Susan."

"So, are you going to encourage her?" Susan sat down beside him on the piano bench, her eyes on his fingers on the keys.

"What would you do in my position?"

"I don't know. Is she pretty?"

"Would you like to see her photo?"

"Sure," Susan said, almost dizzy with fear. Anthony went to a secretary and came back with an 8" x 10" black and white head shot of a beautiful young lady with jet black hair, big, dark eyes, flawless skin, full red lips and a graceful nose. Susan stared at the photo a long time.

"Why haven't you met her before?" she asked, finally placing it on the piano.

"Because she adores me and she's still a minor."

"Noble of you," Susan said.

"Don't get smart. But do answer the question. What would you do about Elaine?"

"That's her name?"

"Elaine Ruskin."

"I guess that would depend on whether she was into D&S."

"D&S? Are you kidding? Who could possibly be more compliant than a protégée who is in love with her mentor? But beyond that, I do have one major proof of Elaine's potential as a future submissive. When she was fifteen she began sending me the most extravagant and fantastic letters I'd ever received. Even more shocking than yours. At the time I wrote her a brief note stating that she deserved a good spanking for spending more time writing to me than studying. Well, she never did stopped writing me letters and every letter she has written since that date is signed with some reference to the day she can look forward to receiving that spanking from me."

Susan felt ill. She got up and paced. Anthony looked serious as he began playing again.

"So, what are you going to do?" she finally asked again.

"I don't know," he shrugged. "What would you do?"

"I wish you wouldn't keep asking me that."

"Why? Because you're a slut and the answer is obvious? As I said, Susan, two can play the same game." He got up and strode into his bedroom. Susan followed. When she did he grabbed her and threw her down on the bed.

"Come here, you little slut," he said, positioning her on her back. One by one he took her little feet between his hands and unlaced her boots to pull them off. His expression was neutral but his movements deliberate. She understood that she was about to be taken and not politely. He yanked down her leggings and then her beige stretch briefs and pulled them off. Susan's bare legs were very smooth and white and she had pretty, small feet.

"I'll teach you to run around with other men on the night before I get in!" he told her, spreading her legs and unzipping his trousers. He stopped to pull his jacket off and loosen his collar, then freed his large, fully erect penis. He inserted one finger deep into her blonde fuzzed public mound. She was lubricating nicely as he did this, suddenly very excited by the aggressiveness with which he had flung her on the bed and pulled up her skating skirt. "Who are you wet from, Susan?" he asked sarcastically, "the last one in or me?"

"You . . . I think," she answered, punishing his rudeness.

In a moment or two he was penetrating Susan forcefully,

plunging in to the hilt with her bottom cheeks cupped in his hands. As he pulled her up and against him, one of his middle fingers found its way into her bottom. Susan wrapped her legs around his waist and pressed up against him until the tease became too intense to withstand and she climaxed. Anthony followed shortly thereafter, the spasms of her orgasm acting as a catalyst to his.

Susan escaped as soon as it was possible to do so and ran off to her room to lock herself in and change her clothes. As soon as he had stopped fucking her, the face of the girl in the photo came into her head and upset her. She exchanged the skating skirt and sweater for black pegged wool trousers, a grey linen shirt, black leather lug soled walking boots, a salt and pepper overcoat and a black suede cloche with gloves to match. Now that she looked more like a proper art major than a snow bunny she felt there would be less chance of people throwing her down on their beds and taking her without preamble. She headed immediately downstairs and out the door to begin a 2-hour stroll down the hill to the beach and then to Random Point.

She really had to think, though it twisted her heart to do so. Elaine Ruskin. She had looked like the young Natalie Wood. And a musical prodigy, who had adored him for years. Not yet 18! Susan felt so old at almost 21.

As she trudged down the hill, digging her little shoes into the melting snow on the gravel drive, she didn't hear Anthony come up behind her until he was at her side and this made her jump.

"Oh!" she cried.

"It's just me." He fell into step beside her, in a thick tweed overcoat and grey fedora. They walked for a few minutes without talking, enjoying the sharp, fresh, ocean air and flawless blue sky.

"Why are you so quiet?" he asked when they finally reached the rocky beach at the bottom of the cliff. "Feeling guilty about spending the night with Michael?"

"Not really," she admitted. "I was thinking about the girl."

"The girl?" He sounded puzzled.

"Elaine."

"Oh!" he smiled. "Don't worry about her."

"But everything you told me makes her sound exquisitely desirable."

"Almost like a fantasy come true?"

"Exactly."

"Elaine Ruskin is a character in a play I'm working on. The photograph is of the actress we're considering for the lead."

Susan felt her face grow very warm at this admission and she experienced one of her rare moments of anger.

"You were playing with me then?"

"Just teaching you a lesson," he replied matter of factly. They began to walk again, she trying hard to conquer her impulse to tell him off. He glanced at her to try to gauge her mood but she refused to look at him for the next hour.

They walked down into the town and Anthony told her he wanted her help with his Christmas shopping. This obviated the need for any significant conversation between them for the next several hours. By the time Anthony called the house to have Dennis pick them up he had all but forgotten the events of the morning, having spread much good cheer in the village and been fortified by strong mulled cider. But Susan hadn't forgotten and she returned to brooding as soon as they got home. Anthony noticed and pulled her into the music room as soon as she hung up her coat.

"What's going on?"

"You shouldn't have told me that horrible lie," she accused, on the verge of tears.

"Why not?"

"It upset me."

"Oh! And you don't think it upsets me to find out you're conducting intimate correspondences with other men? And then fucking them?"

"But—"

"Yes?"

Susan hung her head.

"You should be down on your knees begging my forgiveness for the disrespect you've shown me. Instead you're sulking because of a mild reproof."

"Mild reproof? You told me that story to make me violently jealous!"

"And did it?"

"It made me ill."

"Then you'd better mind your manners with me," he told her

cooly. Susan felt a dart through her stomach as she dared to meet his eyes. If there was one thing which Susan could not resist, it was a handsome man who chose to affect a stern demeanor.

"I'm not sure I understand what that means," she said.

"It means that if you keep on having affairs with other men I'm going to start having affairs with other women and there won't be any point to our cohabitation."

"But I haven't been having affairs," she protested, frightened at the finality of his statement. "I've just been getting into a little mischief now and then."

"A bit too close to home, young lady."

Susan couldn't decide whether he was really angry with her or still just trying to teach her a lesson.

"May I be excused?" she asked politely. He allowed her to leave and immediately sat down at the piano, wondering whether he'd been too harsh with her. The cohabitation line had made her tremble and he knew that she had been on the verge of tears when she left. But damn it, he thought, beginning a vigorous Rachmaninoff prelude, she had to be taught not to take him for granted.

Then he suddenly remembered how roughly and crudely he had taken her directly after she came home after being with Flagg and inwardly winced. "Did I do that?" He stopped playing, got up and paced. Perhaps her feelings had been hurt by that unromantic assault. He decided to go to her room.

He knocked and found Susan curled up in her window seat, looking out at the darkening sky as it was almost evening now.

"Susan?" He went to her and sat beside her and took her hand. "What are you doing?"

"Nothing," she replied, tears ready to fall.

"I'm sorry I was mean to you just now," he told her, kissing her hand.

"You don't love me anymore," she declared and started to cry.

"Susan, how can you say that?" he pulled her into his arms. She felt very warm against him, almost feverish. The dampness of her soft white skin against his shirt front and the smell of her hair aroused him greatly. "You know you're the love of my life," he said sincerely.

"I am?" she raised her eyes to his.

"Of course you are."

"No." She pulled away, jumped up, walked away, then shyly looked at him. "You don't love me anymore."

"Now, why do you say that?"

"Because you didn't . . ."

"Didn't what?"

"You didn't spank me when you found out I spent the night with Michael."

Anthony found it difficult not to smile at this complaint,

"I see," he replied, considering what he should do.

"I suppose I'm very simple," she said, not meeting his eyes.

"You're very naughty. Susan, come over here."

Susan went to him and he pulled her down across his lap. A breathless "Oh!" escaped her lips as she was put in this position, with her woolen trousered bottom upturned for his hand. He fastened one hand on her waist while raising the other and soon he began to bring it down, with extreme determination, on the seat of her pants. Susan was thrilled to be pulled across his lap and spontaneously spanked over her clothes. After a volley of ten smacks he stayed his hand on her bottom. She realized she'd been gasping with excitement during the last few spanks and had also begun to grind against his muscular thighs. He found this very endearing and gave her a good rub, which made her grind even harder.

"Stand up," he told her, helping her to her feet, then unbuckling her belt and pulling down her zipper. Next he yanked her pants down to mid-thigh and put her back across his lap. Her sand-colored French cut cotton briefs hugged the round cheeks of her small bottom tightly. Anthony brought the palm of his hand down vigorously ten more times on the voluptuous little seat of her panties. Again the swift volley of hard smacks took her breath away and freshets of lubrication dampened her panties. Once again he paused, this time to pull her panties down, which immediately revealed the particulars of how she had spent her evening with Michael Flagg.

"Susan, you're terribly marked," he told her, running his palm across her black and blue mottled cheeks with care. "What in the world was Michael thinking of?" The marking had already begun to fade considerably since the previous night, but the bruising was still shocking.

"It didn't seem that hard at the time," she said over her shoulder.

"You know what? I just remembered something. Get up," he tumbled her off his lap and strode into her adjoining bathroom.

"What?" She began to pull her panties back up, sorry that the spanking was over.

"Toothpaste reduces bruising!" he announced, coming back with a tube of toothpaste. Susan sighed and stretched out face down on the bed.

MICHAEL AND PATRICIA

PATRICIA FAIRSERVIS, 32, divinely fair, slim and expensively dressed, entered the taproom of the Bone and Feather Inn on an oddly balmy December afternoon and scanned the booths for the sight of a man in a khaki poplin suit with a pink carnation in his buttonhole.

The editor of *Cape Cod Style* had pinned a white flower to the lapel of her own faultlessly tailored grey wool suit. Patricia paused before the mirror, lit a cigarette and scrutinized her straight, shiny, shoulder length honey blonde hair for imperfections, before allowing her gaze to rest upon the man.

"Michael F. or Code 8C?" she referred to the designation of his personal ad. He rose and shook her beautifully manicured hand.

"Hello, Patricia," replied Michael Flagg. He possessed two short, exciting, well written letters from this woman. She'd let him know immediately that she was a very bad girl. He knew she'd be pretty, but he hadn't been expecting someone quite so gem-like.

"Well, you're an unexpected surprise," she frankly observed, though not without a blush, sliding into the booth opposite him. If he was half the ripped hunk he looked, Patricia anticipated spending the night in the charming village of Random Point, Massachusetts.

He smiled and echoed her remark, "I can't understand why you refused to exchange photos."

"I never exchange photos," Patricia revealed, requesting the wine list from the young innkeeper, Connie Barton.

"Why is that?" Michael asked.

"As I wrote you, I'm married, but my husband is unaware of my activities. I'd hate for a disgruntled playmate to embarrass me."

"Do you answer many ads?"

"I meet a new person about twice a month," she coolly admitted, then added to herself with absolute candor, "But never one who belonged on the cover of a bodice ripper!"

"Tell me all about your experiences with the ads," Michael said, lighting her newest cigarette.

"Well, I've only been playing for about six months, and it's been thrilling, in its way, but so far I haven't met a man I liked enough to have an affair with."

"You must have stringent requirements if you've managed to remain pure for 6 months," Michael observed.

"I didn't say I remained pure," she hastened to declare flirtatiously, "I only meant I haven't gone back for seconds so far." She then turned to Connie to order a very expensive bottle of wine, after which she presented the innkeeper with her card and promised to confer with her that evening about profiling the hostelry in an upcoming issue of her magazine. Michael was favorably struck by her sweetness of manner towards Connie, which indicated a pleasant disposition.

"What about you, Michael? Are you what they call an experienced player?"

"If I have any experience at all it's only due to my dumb luck in picking Random Point to move to."

"Oh? Why is that?"

"An abnormally high concentration of women in the scene live around here."

"You're married, though, right?" she asked, tasting and accepting the wine when it arrived.

"As I stated in my ad, I'm separated and seeking a compatible playmate."

"How long have you been separated?"

"Almost 4 months."

"And why did your wife leave you?"

"That would be telling. But how did you know that she was the one who left me?"

"I just knew. It wasn't because you . . . spanked her, was it?" asked Patricia in a hushed tone. Michael smiled and shook his head.

"When you say compatible, what exactly do you mean?" she asked, draining her first glass of wine.

"Well, obviously, my companion would have to enjoy discipline, as I think you do . . .?"

"I think I do also, but I'm not sure," she said. "I don't necessarily want to be punished. I merely want to feel punished," explained Patricia with care. Thick, sandy lashes fringed her blue eyes, which fixed him with a thoughtful gaze.

"I understand," said Michael. She seemed touchingly new to this and he suspected her tolerance for spanking was that of a child.

"I've met with a couple of men who misunderstood what I wanted and hurt me."

"Tell me where they live and I'll kill them."

"Thank you!"

A pleasant lunch was passed in this manner, with Michael and Patricia mildly flirting while he decided what he was going to do with her and she waited in a torment of anxiety for him to do it.

Agreeing to drive the short distance to his house in the woods, they rose to depart. At this point a small incident occurred which signalled an end to the perfect harmony which had graced the first hour of their relationship.

When Flagg asked Connie to put the bill on his tab, she informed them that the lunch and wine were presented to Mrs. Fairservis and guest, compliments of the inn. Patricia, who of course, expected this courtesy, as the editor of *Cape Cod Style*, was never the less relieved, in view of the dearness of the wine. But she was annoyed when Michael failed to leave a proper gratuity.

"Would you mind?" she asked.

"Mind?"

"Leaving the tip?"

"Oh, sure," he said and placed a five on the table.

"Could we possibly do a little better than that, sweetheart? We just consumed a $65 bottle of wine," said she, stunning Flagg.

"Don't worry about it," he told her, steering her away from the table by the elbow. "Connie will get her plug, after all. You just told her so."

"Still!" Patricia insisted, dug in her Chanel purse and added another twenty-dollar bill to the table before allowing him to lead her away. "I despise parsimony," she advised him as he handed her into the driver's seat of her late model Mercedes convertible.

"I can see that," he observed, taking in every gleaming inch of the smoky blue Germanic wonder and praying to the god he didn't believe in never to make him responsible for this woman's charge card bills. "But, sweetheart," he echoed her facile endearment with amusement, "do you really think you're fit to drive after all that wine?"

"Piece of cake," she assured him, pulling smoothly away from the curb.

He directed her to his house, via a bumpy, narrow woodland road, which the precision car rolled over smartly. At this point she pulled out the fattest joint he had ever seen and asked him if he minded if she got high.

"Not at all!" Michael was cheerfully encouraging.

"So, what do you do for a living?" she asked, casually exhaling pungent billows of smoke.

"I'm a cop," he replied, amused by the stricken look this confession inspired, until the distracted Patricia almost drove off the road.

"Maybe you'd better let me drive," he told her. She stopped the car without arguing and they switched seats. "I always wanted to drive one of these," he revealed happily. She stared at him. He patted her knee.

"It's okay," he told her, "I've never busted a girl I wanted to date."

"Is that what you want to do?"

"Sure, my favorite hobby is trying to straighten out co-dependent submissives."

"Really? What's your success rate?"

"Zero," he said, parking in front of the cottage.

Patricia was impressed by Michael's beautifully redone turn-of-the-century cottage, with its lavish wood paneling and ingenious built-ins.

"Want to buy it? You need a getaway house, Patricia," Michael suggested vigorously.

"Why would you want to sell it?"

"The payments are heavy for one person."

"You may marry again."

"I don't think so. Marriage is too restrictive."

"Now I understand," Patricia admired a beautifully framed portrait of Damaris which adorned the mantlepiece. "You were unfaithful to her once too often and she left you, right?"

Michael was amused by his sophisticated new friend. She was irritating, but likable and smart. She was also physically very appealing to him and this enhanced their first moments alone. To the limited extent that a sensible man can entertain such a notion, Michael realized that he was already in love with her.

Since Patricia was in the scene, he showed her his playroom.

"You'd be hard put to describe the uses of some of these furnishings to your readers," Michael pointed out, pulling down from a mahogany wall cabinet a spanking bench of upholstered leather, scooped in the center and the perfect height to bend a girl over. A set of leather straps were attached to hold the culprit in position.

Patricia blushed deeply as she regarded this custom built piece of equipment and was about to nervously stroll away from its proximity when Michael reached out and grasped her wrist.

"Try it," he told her, gently pushing her down across the saddle before she had a moment to protest. She noticed a mirror opposite as she went over, in which she was now able to observe the entire tableaux of which she was the focus.

Michael placed one hand on the small of her back to hold her in place then smoothed her skirt down over her trim, shapely bottom. She looked back at him.

"Perhaps this is a bit esoteric for starters," she suddenly suggested, popping up off the bench in a sprightly manner. She had either become embarrassed or taken a sudden fright, but the opportunity to utilize the spanking bench seemed to instantly pass. He folded his arms and fixed her with a look that made her tummy spasm.

"This is a bit fancy," he agreed, "when what you really deserve is a just a good, old fashioned, spanking," he told her, removing his jacket.

"But, why?"

"For making that scene about the tip at Connie's."

"But you were wrong!" asserted Patricia, stamping one small foot, which was shod in a pump costing more than a used car salesman earns in a month.

"I was not wrong, you snotty brat. I just happen to be aware of the fact that one doesn't tip the innkeeper."

"If one is a cheapskate one seizes upon every available loophole to avoid rewarding those providing goods and services," she pointed out. A champion of waitresses, shop girls and cab drivers was Patricia.

"That's your point of view, is it?"

"Your own profession, for example, is notorious for perquisite abuse, isn't it?" charged she triumphantly, slipping momentarily out of grabbing range.

"I really wouldn't know," he told her, clearly not amused. Her heart began to pound but she lit a cigarette.

"Come on, give me a break," she replied.

"Patricia, am I going to have to give you a lesson in manners so soon?"

"I suppose that's entirely up to you," Patricia ventured with a blush.

"You are a little monster," he told her. "But I think that you might benefit from correction."

"Correction from you?" said Patricia, daring to raise her eyes to the stranger who was about to become her best friend.

"I think it's the only possible way for me to address your behavior today at the Inn."

Michael strode across the room, took the cigarette away from her and took her by the arm. "Come over here, young lady," he told her, within inches of his favorite straight backed chair.

Michael noticed that she offered no resistance as he turned her over his knee and adjusted her to his satisfaction. She was very light across his lap and the tight suit skirt encased her bottom provocatively. She looked back at him and said, "Oh dear, are you really going to do this?"

Michael did not smile when he replied, "I'm afraid you need it."

Patricia dropped her head and waited, her stomach full of butterflies.

"Patricia?" he paused with his large hand resting on the curve of her girlish bottom.

"Yes?" she replied, turning her head slightly towards him.

"Do you need to be treated like a naughty little girl?"

"Yes!" she replied, dropping her head, with a tiny sob of emotion; her answer caused him to immediately tighten his grip on her waist.

"I think you need a spanking," he told her, patting her bottom lightly, then more firmly. She wriggled on his lap, still tightly wrapped in the tailored wool suit.

Then Michael began to spank this sexy, savvy, important woman just as though she were a child of six.

He administered a thorough spanking over her skirt, firmly alternating cheeks, with heavy, determined strokes of his large right hand while he held her in place with the left. Now and then the smacking caused her to kick up her heels but she made no serious attempt to escape. Each slap which fell upon her bottom sent a thrill through her slender frame and caused her sex to throb. The rock-hard penis shape which she felt through both their clothes, seemed agreeably large.

Then she was suddenly set on her feet.

"Now let that be a lesson to you," he told her sternly. Patricia melted and was speechless. She would have followed him to hell. Sensing his advantage he pulled her towards him and began to undress her. She stood still, kept quiet and let him. Patricia didn't even dare meet his eyes. She was embarrassed and afraid she might laugh.

Presently, he bent her over the spanking bench and took her from behind. Patricia couldn't resist staring in the mirror throughout this performance, particularly when he fastened his hands to her waist and drove into her like John Leslie. He even pulled out at the last moment, as an adult performer would and delivered his copious benediction all over her bare, upturned, bottom.

However, the first thing Patricia did when she regained her footing was to deal him a resounding slap across the face.

"How dare you fuck me without protection?" she charged furiously. Now it was Michael's turn to flush as only a person of Celtic ancestry can.

"I'm sorry," he stammered, sincerely.

"Oh, never mind, I'm sure you're safe." Patricia felt a pang of guilt at the red imprint of her palm on Michael's face. "I'm sorry." She kissed his face and nuzzled it.

"No." He locked his arms around her waist. "I had it coming. And I think you're wonderful."

Much later that night, after completing his shift, Michael came to

Patricia's room at the inn and she opened the door to him half drowsy, in a sleeveless surplice gown of white silk.

"Is it too late to come in?" he whispered, embracing her briefly in the doorway in defiance of all convention. She drew him inside and locked the door at once.

"Get back in bed," he ordered as it seemed chilly in the room. "Your fire's almost cold," he observed and hastened to load on logs. Patricia got back under the down comforter and gazed upon the tall, fair haired man removing his jacket and placing his valuables on the antique marble dresser top. The sight of his service revolver in its holster excited her.

"Michael, is it true that cops have groupies?" she asked, holding the coverlet up to her chin until the fire began to blaze.

"Only the ones who give out drugs." He sat on the bed beside her.

"Will you give me drugs from now on?"

"No."

"Will you come and visit me in Boston?"

"Just tell me when," he told her, pulling the top of her gown open and covering her satiny bosom with his hands. Her breasts were elegant and perfect, neither large nor small but voluptuously round and firmly upstanding.

"Michael," said Patricia, "do you see that charming little sofa by the fire? I chose this room because of it."

Michael appreciated her directness. For a spoiled brat she was thoughtful. He carried her to the sofa to administer that perfect spanking by the fireside which she had envisioned when the innkeeper Connie had shown her the room that afternoon.

After warming the seat of her silk gown for several minutes, Michael lifted the hem and bared her flawless bottom for a protracted spanking interspersed with deep caresses and a thorough finger fucking that left her soaking wet.

After the spanking, which lasted a long time and during which Patricia had her first climax ever while over the knee, they went to bed and made love.

The next day Michael began a week's vacation by driving Patricia back to Boston. They were already in love and both of them knew it. But Michael was also in love with two other women and this presented certain problems.

The first thing Patricia did when they got to Boston, after a devastatingly romantic drive, during which they had stopped several times in the woods to play, was to present Michael Flagg to her husband, Lawrence Fairservis, a Harvard professor, with whom she shared a Back Bay triple decker. She introduced Flagg as the home security expert whom she'd engaged to make the building burglar proof, a sudden inspiration, as it would mean that Michael would have a legitimate reason to visit the house more than once that winter to figure out and install a system.

Patricia's husband was a large, cheerful, robust man who was highly social and enjoyed dining out. He delivered all of Patricia's important messages succinctly, made a few cynical comments about mutual friends and actually gave his wife's bottom an affectionate but meaningless pat through her cream cashmere sweater dress. He then shook Michael's hand, wished him luck, informed Patricia of a fundraising dinner he was attending that evening and disappeared into his study.

"He's a nice man," Patricia told Michael, pulling the detective into her private dressing room for a dangerous kiss.

Later that afternoon they strolled through Back Bay, stopping in little antique and art deco shops. Patricia insisted on buying him a clock for his mantelpiece at home in Random Point.

"So you'll know it if I'm late," she informed him with a mischievous smile. Michael felt a thrill at the implications of this simple statement but he was suddenly oppressed with musings which blunted his enjoyment of her enthusiasm. Noticing a change come over her new friend's face, Patricia asked him what the matter was. Michael simply shook his head and told her he had had enough of shopping for one day.

As they walked along the Charles, with the winter wind whipping their faces, Michael told Patricia about Damaris and Marguerite.

"They sound as if they're both too good for you," the blonde girl observed at length. "You'd better start dating me instead."

As Patricia's job took her up and down the Cape on an almost daily basis, it wasn't difficult to coordinate several meetings a week between Random Point and Boston. Patricia would always book them into the choicest bed and breakfasts and more often than not they stayed free, in return for the favorable review Patricia would then write.

Michael admired his new friend greatly, in spite of the fact that Patricia was a selfish girl. She wanted everything her way, at all times, and if she didn't get it, she threw tantrums from hell. She had no fear of Michael. She had no circumspection. He was used to women like Marguerite, Damaris and Laura, who chose their words carefully, cultivated modest demeanors and let their eyes do the rest. Patricia said whatever came into her head. She was capable of the most insulting remarks and behavior. She was arrogant, opinionated and savagely jealous.

Their affair wasn't two weeks old before she began to give Michael ultimatums. He had to stop seeing Marguerite and trying to see his estranged wife. If he didn't do these two simple things she'd have to stop seeing him. She pointed out that there were multitudes of men in the scene she could date. Michael attempted to reason with her, encouraging her to date all the men she wanted, so long as she left time for him. This made her furious. Once she met Michael she had no further desire to date other men.

Accepting her faults, Michael rapidly became attached to Patricia. Her passion contented him much more than her possessiveness irritated him. It was refreshing to play with a woman who actually deserved to be spanked and spanked hard, at least once a day. The more he knew Patricia, the more he admired the subtle restraint of both his wife Damaris and his long time lover, Marguerite. These women left much unsaid. Even when they behaved in ways which could only be described as lifestyle radical, they never did so at the risk of that certain natural dignity which they both possessed. He recalled that the other two local girls in the scene he most admired, Laura Random and her sister, Susan Ross, were also exquisitely well behaved around men, except for exhibiting a bit of provocative rebellion now and then just to spark the interest. Patricia, on the other hand, embodied every negative female stereotype Michael had ever heard of, but had never encountered before, from PMS to maxxed out charge cards. Every positive about her was cancelled by a resounding negative. Patricia was angelic to shop girls and waitresses, hellish to friends and loved ones. Patricia was one of the most feminine women he had ever met, possibly because of the shocking sums she spent on maintenance. You couldn't undress her without running into a Fernando Sanchez teddy in pure silk. Naturally he liked this, but it frightened him as he wondered who had the privilege of paying for all of this.

Patricia was fascinated by everything in Michael's life, his police work, the adventures he had had and all of his ambitions. However, the more she discovered about his former relationships, each of which appeared to be on-going, the less secure she felt.

In theory, Michael was ready to give everyone else up. Until he happened to run into Marguerite Alexander in the woods, striding along in a sweater and jeans with her long red hair down her back and the most ravishing color in her face.

Nor could he help his heart from pounding uncontrollably whenever he encountered his wife in town. She made a point to avoid him whenever she could. When she did allow their eyes to meet, he felt almost physically ill at the thought of having lost her. At this point she wouldn't even favor him with a conversation beyond what was strictly necessary to tie up their affairs. She was divorcing him and he was not contesting it. Damaris was conducting herself with dignity and style. These were concepts alien to Patricia in all but matters of fashion and home decoration. That Damaris Perez Flagg should give up her magnificent, if somewhat unfaithful man so easily mystified Patricia. Particularly after the first time she beheld the Puerto Rican pocket Venus in the village while she was on the arm of Flagg. It was a horrible moment. Fortunately, for Damaris, she was herself in the company of her employer, William Random. Both girls felt dizzy and ill upon confronting each other for the first time. Patricia was astonished that Michael should have allowed such a beauty to walk out on him and feared for their eminent reunion. Damaris saw a blue eyed blonde with her blonde, blue-eyed husband and thought how well they looked together. She appealed to William to take her away he was happy to oblige her. Patricia noticed the two men, who were friends, exchange rather helpless glances at the embarrassing situation before all four parted to go their separate ways.

That night Michael and Patricia had a dreadful fight about Damaris and the fact that he was still in love with her. But this was nothing compared with the explosion which came the first time Patricia glimpsed and spoke with Marguerite.

It was Patricia who insisted on visiting Marguerite Alexander's book shop. In the middle of the visit she was to figure out that the stunning proprietress with the Julie Newmar figure was Michael's other lover. Marguerite was all charm and friendliness to both of them, though a few slightly warmer words and glances tossed in Michael's direction were quite enough to clue Patricia in as to the redhead's relationship with the good looking detective.

Patricia was thrown into a turmoil of anguish and envy contemplating Flagg alone in the village five nights out of seven with those two sirens in the closest possible proximity. To make the situation even worse, Patricia actually happened to walk in on Michael while he was entertaining another neighborhood visitor, Laura Random, the estranged wife of William Random.

Laura had dropped into Michael's one Saturday afternoon solely to flirt. In the process of this enjoyable activity, Patricia arrived and had to be introduced. Laura had been flirting with Michael for several years and had planned to lay siege to him that winter. But Patricia made it abundantly clear that Michael was hers now. Laura sensed the force of Patricia's attachment and pleasantly slipped away to wait a while longer for the perfect scene with Michael which she had been fantasizing about ever since he had given her the little birthday spanking in Marguerite's shop years ago.

Meanwhile, Michael did his best to assuage Patricia's anxieties by courting her continuously all winter. At first he didn't know how to handle their quarrels. He attempted to console her, to appease her, to prove his love through as many hours of attentive devotion as he could offer in view of their separate commitments. But nothing ever seemed to soothe her. Nor could he appeal to her powers of reason, of which she seemed woefully bereft on the subject of love. Try as he might to point out that she herself was married and slept with another man at least sometimes, she would barely acknowledge the commitment. Her marriage didn't count in the equation because Lawrence wasn't in the scene and didn't turn her on.

Once, when Michael and Patricia were spending a weekend in New York so that she could review a small hotel, they were browsing in Saks Fifth Avenue and he was recognized by little Susan Ross, looking extremely cute in wool knickers and a sweater, who blushed deeply as they chatted. When Susan told Michael she'd be visiting Random Point over the weekend and that maybe she would run into him at the skating rink, Patricia's heart contracted. She couldn't leave the subject of Susan alone for the rest of the day.

Michael described the particulars of only his first meeting with Susan in the early autumn. He did not omit the fact that he had briefly held Susan's hand while they had watched Laura Random being cropped by Marguerite. These details caused Patricia to feel ill with jealousy. Hating herself for doing so, she accused Michael of wanting Susan.

"It's only a matter of time before you fuck her," declared Patricia as they strolled through Central Park on a cool winter afternoon. It was about 3 p.m. and many of the beautiful, secluded walks were empty. "I just hope for your sake she's of age."

"Patricia, cut it out, I have no intention of fucking Susan Ross." (*"At least until the next time I have the opportunity,"* he added to himself.)

Patricia was of course very foolish to have worried about other women that day, as fetching as she looked in her buff leggings, heather beige tweed blazer and cream wool turtle neck. The little urban hiking boots, worn with rolled sox, allowed her to scrambled up the hilly paths around the park with tomboyish grace. Her thick, glossy blonde hair hung to her shoulders in a Veronica Lake finger wave that kept him hard all afternoon.

Michael added, "You're horrible."

"It's no use," she informed him, turning abruptly, "I can't go on like this. You just have too many women. You don't need me."

"Patricia, as I've told you before, those girls are just friends in the scene. You're the one I'm interested in now," he took her by the shoulders and made her look at him.

"Until you go home to Random Point," she said resentfully.

"So leave your husband and move in with me," Michael suggested.

Patricia stared at him.

"You're just saying that because you know I can't do it," she finally decided.

"Why can't you?" They began to walk again.

"I need to be in Boston for the magazine. You know the social demands I'm subject to."

"You can live on the Cape," he told her.

Patricia was impressed by his offer, which left her speechless for several moments.

"Why do you have the need to go skating with that little girl?" Patricia suddenly demanded. Michael sighed.

"Patricia," he said quietly, "didn't I just invite you to live with me?"

"Yes."

"Then what's the problem?"

"I just don't think you ought to see other women."

"I'm not seeing other women. And I'm getting tired of telling you that. Come over here," Michael said, taking Patricia by the wrist and dragging her over to a bench.

"What are you doing? No!"

Michael turned her over his knee and spanked her hard. His large hand came down rapidly on her small, round, bottom, so snugly encased in the nubby woolen leggings. She kicked her legs but didn't try to get away.

"I'm going to cure you of this ridiculous jealousy," he promised, administering several dozen smacks.

"Oh, please, Michael, don't! What if someone comes?"

"Then someone will see you getting spanked," Michael finished with half a dozen extra hard slaps, then placed her on her feet. "Now let that be a lesson to you, young lady. From now on, every time you utter an irrationally jealous remark, I'm going to paddle your bottom. Do you understand?"

"No!"

"Really? Well, let me clarify my remarks," Michael told her, and once again sat down and pulled her across his lap. But this time, just as Patricia went over, a young couple, probably lawyers, came strolling into her view, he in a black cashmere overcoat and scarf, she in a smart grey wool suit, topcoat and perfect boots. Both had white skin that never saw the sun except by accident and jet black hair. They looked at each other and smiled at the frivolous blond children they'd stumbled onto, playing spanking games in the park. Patricia was deeply humiliated and tried to jump off his lap but Michael held her fast and having ascertained that their visitors were not the type to interfere began to vigorously apply the palm of his hand to the seat of her pants as before, only more so. Patricia was speechless with indignation as Michael continued to spank her and she was forced to meet both the eyes of the girl and the man. They both seemed amused and joined hands before strolling out of sight.

"I'll scream if you don't let me go!" Patricia cried, imagining she saw a group of boys in plaid shirts and turned-around baseball caps approaching through the trees. "I mean . . . what if some unsavory persons happened by when you were taking these sorts of liberties with me . . .!" she very sensibly appealed to his protective instinct.

"Oh very well," he said, letting her up and resuming their walk.

"We don't want to get me gang banged, right?" she rubbed her bottom with both hands as they walked along.

Michael could not fail to notice that she was good for the rest of the day. He then began to realize that Patricia needed to be civilized.

Their attachment for each other grew, exacerbated by the onset of spring. Patricia's husband departed for a sabbatical in Italy, freeing her from her few domestic responsibilities for the remainder of the season. This new development naturally made Patricia more restless than ever while her longing for Detective Flagg increased.

Michael was perfectly ready to fall in love with Patricia. He enjoyed her sarcasm, even when he was the butt of it. Of course, he wasn't about to let Patricia know that. 95% of her insults Michael virtually ignored, while inwardly agreeing with her. Now and then, for the sake of his own dignity, and because she would have been disappointed otherwise, he felt compelled to punish her for her rudeness.

Patricia added a degree of glamour and excitement to his life which he allowed himself to enjoy without reserve. She also bothered to tempt him in ways which he found quite enchanting. With Damaris he was always the one to decide that they were going to play. With Marguerite he was lucky, very lucky, when he could get her to give in and play. But Patricia initiated encounters with a charming enthusiasm.

Once, for instance, when he arrived at her house in Boston during her husband's absence, he found her in the drawing room, seated at the piano and practicing scales, dressed in a fitted, full-skirted, black velvet dress, with an enormous white linen and lace collar and white cuffs, under which she wore a starched white lawn petticoat, trimmed with three rows of lace and the sheerest white cotton panties he'd ever seen. Her opaque white stockings were held up by embroidered garters and on her extremely pretty little feet she wore high heeled black patent leather mary janes. Her blonde hair was pulled back in a black velvet ribbon and she looked demure in it. Michael was touched that she'd gone shopping for the grown up little girl dress just for him. When the time came to fold back her satin lined skirt and white petticoat, he appreciated her attention to detail all the more. And he took great care to spank her only as hard as a little girl should ever be spanked, which was not very hard at all. She melted, of course, though she probably would have benefited from a sound caning even more.

Patricia was much more experimental and adventurous than the other girls he had known, or perhaps she was merely more fearless. Within knowing her two months he had received as presents: a wooden hairbrush, an ivory hairbrush, an English school cane, a razor strop, a Scottish tawse and, unbelievably, a Hermes riding crop. Due to her extremely wise choice of profession, Patricia woke up in luxury hotel suites and lavishly appointed inn cottages at least once a week. So when Michael was handed a beautiful, evocative implement with which to correct the wayward, spoiled young woman, it was often in the most romantic and rarified of settings.

Patricia had no compunction about adopting a room in Michael's house as her own private hideaway, complete with computer, Ralph Lauren daybed and hope chest filled with her own selection of diaphanous nightgowns and silk chemises. Patricia was vastly compulsive and she spent a great deal of her time organizing her wardrobe, appointments and men. Michael had no objection to her moving items into his house. It reassured him. All of Damaris' possessions had been picked up and hauled off to the cottage at Pigeon Cove, where she now resided.

It destroyed Patricia's fragile grip on reason to contemplate Michael with Marguerite on one or more of the many nights when she was not with him herself. For Michael had told her, quite firmly, that it was impossible for him to entirely avoid the occasional encounter with Marguerite. Patricia absolutely hated this. She threw horrific tantrums about it. Michael told her that she could obviate the problem by moving in with him, but Patricia did not find that a convenient option. To which Michael had pragmatically replied, "I'm not making any promises I can't keep."

"But, damn it, how many women do you need?" Patricia was working herself up into a passion, pacing across the floor of a private cabin, set up in the wooded hills of an exclusive Nantucket inn.

She strode out to the porch which overlooked a pretty patch of woods, which led down to a pristine white beach. Her fair, slender charms were set off to advantage by a luxuriously embroidered black lace over beige satin peignoir set, fitted close through the torso, with a full skirted gown and magnificently trimmed wrapper. But the pre-Raphaelite princess spoiled the romantic illusion by sulkily lighting a cigarette.

Sitting with his chin on his hand and an enormous cup of café latté before him, Michael gazed at his terrifyingly willful sweetheart and recalled a phone call he had received while at the station house earlier in the week from the Princess, which was the nickname he had given her in recent weeks to amuse himself when thinking about Patricia. She didn't know about it yet.

They'd exchanged small talk and engaged in the usual flirting when she abruptly interrupted the casual flow of the conversation to interject, "Sometimes I think I'd like to be treated . . . more harshly."

"Is that so?" Michael's tone did not betray his excitement. Patricia then pretended she had a call on the other line and broke the connection.

All week he had tossed around ideas. He wondered what she meant by the word "harsh." Did she, for instance, want him to handcuff her to a cot in one of the holding cells, thrash her and ravish her? He'd been rather careful until now in the way he played with Patricia. Was it possible that the sort treatment which his ex-wife might have considered too severe would prove perfectly suitable for Patricia?

"Patricia!" he addressed her in a commanding tone. "Come in here."

Patricia ignored him and continued to smoke, leaning on the railing with her back to Michael. Michael sighed and strode out the the balcony. He turned her around, took the cigarette away from her and crushed it out.

"Didn't I call you?"

"So?" she challenged.

Michael took her by the hand and dragged her back inside, picked her oval ebony hairbrush up off a dresser top and sat down on the bed with Patricia across his lap. Without raising her skirts he applied the back of the brush to her bottom a dozen times, hard and fast. Patricia was too conscious of her position as editor of *Cape Cod Style* to scream at the top of her lungs in a guest cabin at an exclusive Nantucket inn, but she gratified him by immediately bursting into tears. He then pushed her off his lap.

"Why did you do that?" she sobbed, with tears rolling down her face, pulling up her skirts to examine the angry red brush strokes which now decorated her pearly flesh as she knelt on the floor.

"Because you're getting on my nerves."

"I'm sorry," she whimpered. He folded his arms.

"Think your sulks are amusing?"

Patricia dashed away her tears with a petulant shrug.

"You're the most difficult woman I've ever known."

"You must know insipid women," she returned.

"If you're this insolent I must not have spanked you hard enough," Michael observed, picking up the hairbrush again.

"No, please! I'll be good!" She wrapped both arms around one of his legs and rubbed her cheek against it like an ingratiating cat, looking up at him innocently.

Michael couldn't help but laugh. However, after they had gotten dressed and gone out for a walk through the woods to the beach, he spoke his mind to Patricia, telling her that he had no intention of avoiding the occasional encounter with one or more of his few female friends in the scene, including his wife if she ever agreed to see him again. He reminded Patricia that she was married herself and had a whole separate life apart from him, therefore she had little right to restrict his contacts in the town where he lived and she did not. Michael concluded by warning Patricia that he would dissolve their relationship rather than suffer guilt and persecution under her tyranny.

"I see!" Patricia was as hurt and disappointed by Michael's statements as any spoiled child who has been denied a treat. She folded her arms as they walked along, she in a bias-cut taupe silk summer dress, he in khaki trousers and a blue chambray shirt.

"How would you feel if I knew all sorts of men in the scene and played with them?" she asked.

"For all I know, you do. Your pain tolerance certainly indicates experience."

Patricia blushed at this observation then scowled, "I keep forgetting that you're a detective."

"But getting back to your question, I wouldn't mind at all if you played with other men. In fact, I think it would help you to feel less insecure about us. I'd be happy to introduce you to some trustworthy players the next time you're in Random Point."

"Fine! So I'm to be passed around among your Castle Roissy buddies, now, am I?"

"Patricia, you know damn well I'm not into a Master trip," he told her, losing patience.

"I don't know any such thing."

"Patricia, you're being willfully obtuse," he declared, stopping in his tracks.

"I am not."

"Suppose I was able to introduce you to a couple of possible playmates for you, without letting them know you're in the scene?"

"I don't understand. To what end?"

"If you liked one you could make the advance yourself at the proper time and place. I wouldn't have to be involved at all."

"But, what would you get out of that?"

"Possibly a more relaxed girlfriend," Michael replied.

"And you wouldn't be jealous?"

"No. And I think it would help our relationship."

"You just want an excuse for your own catting around," she accused.

Michael sighed, "I guess I was dreaming expecting a woman to be rational."

"That's exactly right!" Patricia concurred and no more was said on the subject of new contacts in the scene for the moment.

The next time they met, however, in Random Point the following Friday, Patricia asked Michael to describe the various persons he had in mind to introduce her to. Michael bluntly refused, telling her she was wasting his time, then immediately suggested going antique shopping that afternoon instead. Piqued at having her curiosity denied when she'd been thinking of nothing but Michael's dangerous friends in the scene all week, she assented to the shopping trip in a distracted mood.

Michael was pleased to find Hugo Sands manning his shop when he arrived with Patricia. Hugo was naturally beside himself with joy at the unexpected visit of this important personage in his shop and took some pains to show her his most interesting recent acquisitions.

The editor of *Cape Cod Style* browsed through the shop with Michael in tow, only subliminally aware that the highly educated proprietor was a good looking man. Thrilled to distraction by Mrs. Fairservis' visit to his establishment, with visions of full color magazine spreads revolving in his practical brain, Hugo barely noticed how beautiful his important guest was, nor did it even remotely occur to him that this media goddess was also an available submissive. Meanwhile, Michael was enjoying his friends' nonreaction to each other and trying to decide who to tell first about the other.

"Hugo, why don't you tempt Mrs. Fairservis with your collection of antique riding crops?" Michael finally said, causing both Hugo and Patricia stop and stare at each other.

"I'd love to, but they're at my house," said Hugo, searching Michael's face for more information. The tall detective simply stared guilelessly back at Hugo. But the remark, after all, had been enough to clue the antique dealer in.

Suddenly realizing that this natty gentleman with the elegant shop and charming manners was one of Michael's friends in the local scene, the blonde girl blushed from brow to throat. She stammered a thank you as Hugo handed her his card, on the back of which he wrote his home phone number.

A few days later Michael got a call at the station while he manned the desk on the late shift.

"Thank you for introducing me to Mrs. Fairservis," Hugo said. "But what's the policy on her?"

"What do you mean?"

"Well, she's made an appointment to come and see the riding crops."

Michael inwardly rejoiced at these words.

"Patricia is my new sweetheart," said Michael.

"Congratulations," said Hugo sincerely, marveling at Michael's good fortune. To get that lucky that fast after losing the divine Damaris was indeed remarkable. Nor did Hugo forget that his adorable ex-assistant, Jane Elliot, with whom he'd had so much fun a few seasons ago, had also come to him through Michael Flagg. He made a note to send Flagg a good bottle of brandy.

"Yes, thank you, and for the most part, it's working out well. She's married, as you know, but so far that hasn't interfered with any of our plans. No, the problem is that for all of her sterling qualities, Patricia is a bit possessive, and I thought that by introducing her to a few local people in the scene it would distract her from fixating on me."

"Good thinking," said Hugo, "and thanks!"

After an appropriate amount of time had elasped, Michael asked Patricia whether she had seen Hugo yet. They were lying under a large leafy Elm in the long, soft grass of his unweeded back garden which was ringed by the enclosing woods. Patricia was in a full skirted navy halter dress and ankle strap sandals and gold jewelry at her ears, throat and wrists.

"No," she replied, blowing away dandelions.

"Tell me the truth, Patricia." He sat up beside her. Patricia blushed and sat up.

"I said no," she stammered, regretting horribly that she'd begun the lie.

"Patricia, do you want me to turn you over my knee?"

"No!" She sprung to her feet but he captured her wrist before she had a chance to flee and pulled her back down on the grass.

"I think you need a good spanking for lying to me," he told her, pulling her across his lap and bringing his palm down on the seat of her skirt hard and fast several dozen times before pausing to question her again. Patricia, feeling no constraint about noise in their secluded retreat, gave voice to her injured feelings as he spanked her soundly.

"Now, tell me the truth," he ordered.

"Okay, I saw him. I went to his house."

"And did you play?"

"No."

"You're lying," he declared, pulling up her skirt and beginning the spanking all over again, only this time on the seat of her white silk panties. This time he spanked her slower, but harder, until he could see her fair skin color up pink under the sheer briefs.

"All right, we played!" she finally admitted. Michael was pleased to hear this and gently smoothed her skirt back down. He pulled her up and kissed her.

"Don't lie to me again, young lady," he told her sternly. Her lip quivered and she almost cried. He took her down to the grass, pulled her panties off and penetrated her quickly. Face to face, within the first dozen thrusts, Patricia had an orgasm.

For days the thrill of the spontaneous spanking he had given her, and the firmness of the sex which had followed, caused spasms of pleasure to ripple through her flat little tummy. Patricia adored Michael. He was everything she had always looked for in a man. He looked the right way and said the right things. And he punished her so beautifully. So correctly. Patricia was in love.

Patricia was so extraordinarily compulsive that Michael dared hope she was anal, though at first she would only admit to entertaining vague fantasies. She seemed afraid of anal sex with him because of the size of his cock. However, the first time he inserted a finger into her bottom while she lay across his lap, Patricia ground against his trousered thigh until she came, and this didn't take long.

Encouraged, he became more inventive.

One Friday night, when Michael found it impossible to drive into Boston to be with her, he'd had a terrible argument with Patricia over the phone. She'd thrown one of her usual tantrums and he'd responded by hanging up. For an hour or two he was fed up with Patricia and vowed not to call her again for a week. However, when she phoned him at the station house at midnight to tearfully apologize, he felt touched by her childish needs.

"If I drive into the city tomorrow," he told her sternly, "it will only be to punish you."

"I understand," she sighed, ashamed of her own immaturity, yet perversely excited by the concept of really being punished.

When Michael arrived at Patricia's house in Back Bay the following evening he curtly told her to put on a short black dress and heels. When she took too long a time in selecting her outfit,

Michael turned her under his arm and smacked her hard about a dozen times. The sharp blows brought tears to her eyes. Michael wasn't smiling when he let her go.

Patricia hastily chose a black jersey sheath, black seamed stockings, garter belt and black patent leather ankle-strap stiletto heels. While she was dressing in her large, walk in closet, Michael sat on the bed and placed his handkerchief, containing a certain object, beside him.

"Patricia," Michael said, "Don't come back in here without the KY."

Patricia shivered in fear and excitement on the other side of the door. Presently she obeyed his command, standing before him in her clinging dress, all silky blonde hair and slim legs. Michael unceremoniously pulled her down across his knees and pushed her tight dress up to her hips. Her sheer, full black briefs encased her luminous white bottom with the flawless radiance of a Varga gatefold. He eased these down at once and left them bunched around her knees. Now her garterbelt framed her bare bottom so prettily that he couldn't help but spank her.

"I'm disappointed in you, Patricia," he told her. "You should know better than to distract me with nonsense while I'm on duty."

"I'm sorry!" she vowed sincerely, since he'd begun to smack her bottom vigorously.

"You're a very bad, very spoiled little girl," he declared, separating her thighs as far as the bunched briefs would allow. "Hold your legs apart, Patricia."

Patricia gave a tiny sob and complied to the best of her ability, feeling ashamed. He reached for the lube and she placed it in his hand. Tossing the cap aside, Michael plunged the open tube between her satiny bottom cheeks and squeezed out a quantity of clear jelly. This done, he unwrapped from handkerchief a brand new 5" retention plug, cast in flesh-colored rubber.

"See this, Patricia?" He brandished it in front of her. She gasped in shame. "I'm going to insert this in your bottom and then we're going out."

"No! You can't! Please don't!" she begged and twisted on his lap. Relentlessly, Michael separated her cheeks and placed the tip of the plug in between them.

"You've been asking for some real discipline for awhile. haven't you, young lady?" He spread her open with one hand while inserting the butt plug into her, quite agonizingly slowly.

"God, no! You can't do this to me!" she protested weakly, trying to fend him off with one hand. This he grabbed and smacked as though she were a naughty child.

"Lie still. You don't need a boyfriend, you need a master."

"Oh, please, darling, stop! I can't stand it, I tell you. If you continue doing this, I'm going to come!"

"Whether you do or don't, I intend to take you out." he told her.

But Patricia didn't come. The whole experience was so humiliating that she could think of nothing but escaping it. She begged and cajoled Michael to remove the toy and let her go. Instead, he pushed it in deeper, until all but the hilt was buried in her bottom. Then he pulled her panties off.

"You know what? Just to enhance the sensation, don't you have a shiny black long line panty girdle?" Michael had a very good memory for hiding places and strode immediately to the proper dresser and even the right drawer. He soon discovered the ultra-tight, retro knickers which were trimmed with black lace at each leg hole. Once on they came to just above her knees and hugged her slender thighs and oval cheeks like latex. "They're almost a form of bondage," he declared, turning her around between his hands, and examining her lithe bottom and legs from every angle as she blushed with shame.

Simply to amuse himself he bent her over his knee again and spanked her lightly over the long line panty girdle which had become so popular with the Victoria's Secret crowd lately. She felt desperately humiliated whenever he patted the center of her bottom, exactly atop the deeply anchored retention plug.

Michael held her by her slim waist as he tormented her with a mild but embarrassing spanking.

"This is a very smart garment," he commented, "and perfect for holding your retention plug firmly in place." He punctuated this declaration with a volley of one dozen sharp smacks across the center of her upturned bottom, seeming to drive the plug in deeper with each fresh blow. As he spanked her he worked his free hand around and under her tummy to cup her throbbing pussy in the palm of his hand while spanking her with the other.

"No, please!" Patricia cried.

"Don't fight it, Patricia," he told her. "You're finally getting the attention you crave." Michael held her fast and spanked her harder. But then he quite abruptly let her up.

"I've decided to postpone your orgasm," he told her, because he wanted to keep her in the perfect dildo bondage. "Put yourself together now, we're going," Michael said.

Patricia looked momentarily mutinous, but Michael stared her down with a look that jellified her spine. Finally she turned to comply with his command, but he pulled her back around to face him.

"Were you about to rebel, Patricia?"

She lowered her eyes sullenly. Michael took her by the wrist and slapped the back of her hand, then forced him to look at him and slapped it again, harder. Tears sprang immediately to her eyes as she pressed her prettily manicured little hand to her flushed face like a four year old who has just been summarily disciplined and is about to burst into tears.

"Don't defy me," he told her sternly. Her lower lip quivered, then she tried to hide her face behind her hands. He pulled them away from her face. Seeing that she was about to cry he pulled her against him and held her. "It's all right, Patricia," he soothed her, fearing that he was breaking her down too fast.

Michael kissed her and continued doing so until the danger of her bursting into tears had passed. Then he repeated the command to get her jacket.

"I can't possibly go out like this!" she protested.

"Why not?" he stared back at her.

"I'll die of shame."

"No you won't."

"Please don't make me go out like this," she begged. Ignoring her, he himself got her short leather jacket and put her into it as he would a recalcitrant child.

"We are going out, just like this, and what's more, we're going to do some really sleazy things, starting with a trip to The Pleasure Chest to buy you a proper harness."

"No!"

"I love the way you haven't stopped blushing," he said, escorting her out into the balmy May night.

Patricia bit her lip in vexation as he refused the keys to her Mercedes and instead hailed a cab on the street.

"Public transportation will be good enough for Princess tonight," Michael informed her.

Patricia endured the reckless taxi drive downtown in humiliated silence, with eyes turned toward the window. When ever she looked at him, however, each fresh glimpse of his sternly masculine demeanor would cause her tummy to contract.

Michael insinuated his hand under her dress to caress and separate her thighs in the tight panty girdle. He pressed his palm against her lower abdomen and pubic mound through the stretch Lycra.

"Don't think you won't get another spanking once I get you home, young lady," Michael said, without paying the slightest attention to the cab driver, who appeared to have barely enough English to understand directions. However, Patricia noticed his liquid, Middle Eastern eyes perk up with interest in the mirror at the key word "spanking."

At The Pleasure Chest Michael did not consult Patricia about any of their purchases. The lady's torso harness was made of black leather, and trimmed with stainless steel studs. It was adjustible and slit at the crotch and seat in order to accomodate one or two dildos and hold them in place. The belt could be pulled tight enough to snugly fit a slender woman. Patricia stood by with burning cheeks as Michael discussed in great detail the subtleties of the device with the helpful gay male clerk. Together they chose the perfect pair of vibrators to slip into the slots of the harness and then moved on to additonal accessories. Michael summarily rejected nipple clamps, ball gags, and dilators but accepted a large, cased set of textured dildos intended for anal stimulation. He also purchased two pair of leather cuffs, suitable for binding wrists and ankles, boat hooks for fastening them, as well as two stainless steel spreader bars, designed to fully or partially spreadeagle a playmate. Next a variety of exotic lubricants were selected. A black leather blindfold and a multi-thonged flogger, which was a kind of whip with broad, supple lashes, also joined the pile of costly fittings on the counter top.

The only item which Patricia protested was a cheap French maid's outfit which Michael fingered momentarily on their way out of the shop. "No way in hell," she murmured at the cut and texture. Michael smiled at the fussy little perfectionist who would accept two dildos and a harness with very little protest but who would have thrown a ballistic tantrum had he actually tried to force her into a tacky polyester maid's outfit.

Hailing another cab, Michael then took Patricia into the seedy

Combat Zone, where strip clubs and adult bookstores and hooker hotels abounded.

"Michael, I don't like it around here," she said. He had left the bag of toys in the cab and told the driver to wait, showing him his badge to make sure that he did.

"Don't worry about it," he told her, with the confidence of a cop in the city he grew up in.

The disinterested clerk behind the high counter at the adult video and magazine store barely looked up as they entered. Michael picked out a hard S&M video from B&D Pleasures to rent and they retired together to a private viewing booth at the back of the store.

Once they got into the booth Michael sat in the chair, unzipped his trousers and released his large, throbbing erection quite casually.

"Take the knickers off now," he commanded. Eyes locked with his, she obeyed. Not wanting to put them down anywhere, she held them in one hand as he pulled her down to sit on his lap, facing away from him and towards the screen. "Lean forward," he told her, holding her around her slender waist with one hand and attempting to guide his cock into her pussy with the other. "One way or another, this is happening, so you'd better concentrate on getting it in at the right angle," he softly suggested.

Patricia was outraged and deeply aroused. She'd never had a masterful lover but her mind had thrilled to the thought of one since her very early teens. Now she was getting the attention she had craved, just as Michael had said. So naturally Patricia was wet enough to slide it in. And as it did go in, all the way in, as Patricia leaned forward against his encircling arm. The retention plug, meanwhile, was still firmly lodged in her bottom, so that when Michael's cock completely filled her, she experienced double penetration. Once she was settled snugly down on his lap, he brought his left hand around to press on her lower abdomen and pull her back against him hard each time she drifted slightly forward. His other arm, meanwhile, was still locked around her waist, to anchor her to his lap while her beautiful legs straddled his.

"Now this is what we're going to do, Patricia," he whispered in her ear. "You're going to lean back now and grind against me and your plug like the naughty girl that you are while I keep the palm of my hand flat against your clit until you come. Understand?"

"Yes, sir," she dared to breathe.

"Then, I'm going to come," he told her.

It happened just as he predicted, with a sharp little smack against her outer thigh sending her over the edge. Then, almost as soon as her spasms began to subside, Michael fastened both hands to her waist and effortlessly bounced her light body up and down on an engine that was now in danger of overheating until a large, boiling emission threatened to burst inside her clinging sheath. At the very last moment he lifted Patricia off his lap and pulling his penis free, ejaculated harmlessly against her satiny bottom cheeks as he pulled her back against him. Neither of them had bothered to glance at the screen for more than a moment or two but once they were done both of them felt as though they'd been to a hell of a movie together.

After the incident at the Combat Zone bookstore, where Michael and Patricia had rented but not watched a bondage and discipline video, Patricia became deeply infatuated with her long distance lover. The youthful detective exactly conformed to her ideal of masculine charm. Michael was not overbearing. He had no apparent interest in interfering with any portion of her life. Even his sexual dominance over her was restrained in Patricia's perception, though Flagg at first worried that he sometimes went too far.

Patricia had a large tolerance for corporal punishment. She was also a terrible brat. She knew she needed a thrashing every couple of days and went out of her way to make sure one came to her.

Patricia presented Michael with his first cane, his first tawse and his first heavy wooden paddle. And he did truly enjoy inflicting hard corporal punishment on a young lady who so desperately craved it.

But even more interesting to him was the combined effect of sound spanking and embarrassment, upon a woman of Patricia's temperment.

He had taken home the purchases from the Boston sex shop, including the harness and laid these items aside for a future significant encounter.

Ever since Michael had introduced Hugo to Patricia she had become 90% more circumspect about reproaching him for his interest in other women. Congratulating himself that he was finally able to outsmart a woman, he now enjoyed almost complete peace of mind with regard to their relationship. However, an annoying 10% of the time, Patricia continued to persecute him relentlessly about all of the Random Point girls. Except Laura.

Patricia had only run into Laura once, by accident, when Laura had decided to visit Michael's house to flirt. Naturally Patricia's alarms went off when she took in all of Laura Random's quiet charms and effectively frightened the native away with a steely glance. Laura had no wish to get into a cat fight with a jealous, high strung woman over a man who would probably live in her neighborhood all of her life. So Laura wasn't seen again in that part of the woods behind Random Point until Michael called her himself, with Patricia at his side, several weeks later, with an unusual request, especially coming from him.

Patricia was visiting for the evening and realized too late that she had left her pot in Boston. Boldly and without the slightest hesitation or shame, Patricia began to pester Michael about finding her some grass in the village. Michael immediately thought of two girls, his ex-wife and Laura.

"I could call Laura," he said casually. Normally he did not approve of drug use and shuddered at the thought of abetting it, but weighing the positve benefits of presenting Patricia with a trust-worthy girlfriend in the scene, he overcame his scruples and made the suggestion.

"Would she bring some over, do you think?" Patricia seemed to forget that she was ever jealous of Laura.

"It's a possibilty, but let me think about it for a minute. Do I really want to encourage this sort of behavior . . .?" he mused.

In the end, he called Laura and she arrived with supplies for Patricia within the half hour. The two girls went out into the woods together to smoke and since it was a warm May evening, lingered there until the sun went down. When they returned Michael threat-ened to spank them both for being so naughty, but Laura merely smiled and went home.

Patricia now had a girlfriend in the village, to bring her infor-mation and to confide in. Laura was so frank with Patricia about her admiration for Michael that Patricia no longer feared her. Laura understood and respected the fact that Patricia was now

Michael's girlfriend. As it happened, Laura was just as happy to have a new girlfriend, with whom she had so much in common.

For some time now Laura had been experiencing an urge to play games with another woman. Girls like Marguerite and Damaris were somehow too close, almost like sisters she knew them so well, but Patricia seemed just right. Her education was on a par with Laura's and Patricia had style. She also seemed very submissive and the budding imp of dominance in Laura's personality responded to that.

From the start they behaved more like playmates than regular girlfriends. Patricia would never return to Random Point without a beautiful present for Laura. And Laura would never visit Patricia without a tasty treat tucked into her pocket. One day Laura smacked Patricia on the bottom.

They were in the big, well furnished kitchen on the ground floor of Anthony Newton's Cape Cod house, where Laura had resided since leaving her husband. They had been fixing a snack and Patricia looked so cute leaning over the sink in her Guess? jeans that Laura couldn't resist.

Patricia looked at her with a rush of passion that almost frightened Laura and said, "If you're going to do it, girlfriend, do it right."

"All right," said Laura, pulling out a kitchen chair of the perfect height and stability and pulling Patricia down across her own denim thighs.

Grasping Patricia firmly about the waist Laura felt a curious thrill. So this was what it felt like to be William or Michael or Hugo or Anthony. All the men she knew and were fond of had experienced this sensation with her. They had looked down to see a slender, sweetly compliant girl stretched across their lap, with her bottom upturned for a spanking. It felt extremely satisfying to bring her hand down smartly on Patricia's slim, muscular bottom, so snugly encased in the jeans. The smacks made a luscious sound to Laura's ears and a surge of vicarious pleasure shot through the core of her sex as she remembered what she liked about being in this position and tried to provide exactly that for Patricia.

"I'm doing this," Laura advised her captive, who looked back at Laura over one bare shoulder in her red gingham halter top.

"Why do you want to?"

"I just want to," Laura explained, smoothing the seat of Patricia's jeans with her palm before bringing it down on her bottom again and continuing with the spanking.

Patricia enjoyed the spanking over her jeans for the next fifteen minutes without saying another word. When it was over and Laura let her up, Patricia could barely prevent herself from handing Laura an implement, craving more and harder spanking now from her pretty, dark haired friend. But Patricia was too embarrassed to ask for more and in fact, blushed for at least an hour following her first spanking from another girl. Also, her bottom felt warm and tingly under her jeans for what seemed like an hour after the spanking, though it hadn't seemed at all that hard at the time. Laura realized, towards the end of the spanking, that she had to bring her hand all the way up before bringing it down, in order to make a good impression on a girl who was used to being disciplined by a 6'3" man. This was invigorating.

Later, Laura told Patricia that Patricia was the first girl she had ever taken across her lap, though she admitted to having nuzzled the ears and throat of Damaris Flagg and clasped her about the waist several times when they were working together in her husband's office the previous summer. Patricia suffered whenever she heard about Damaris because she never heard anything but good of her and she knew that Michael still loved her dearly.

Patricia and Laura began to play regularly but made a compact not to let the boys know about it. To Hugo and Michael, they were simply compatible girl friends. But when Patricia and Laura were alone, Laura always wore trousers and always sought to dominate her pretty blonde friend. Laura was enthralled by Patricia's accessibility. Every time they played they went a little further. First the skirt came up. Then next time the panties came down. And the time after that, Laura's sensitive fingers sought the source of Patricia's excitement. And the time after that, Laura forced Patricia to climax.

Once Patricia had acquired Laura as a friend and playmate, her insecurities were further reduced. She had very little time to be jealous between all of these interesting new friends. When the girls were together they spent most of their time discussing the men they played with and the things they did with them.

Patricia admired Michael's coolheadedness in arranging her sex life for her so as to cancel out any playing he might do. In each of her past relationships, including her present marriage, she had always been able to easily manipulate her men. This time it was different. In many ways, Michael was more sophisticated than she and he expected her to rise to his level of understanding.

As the spring progressed, Michael began to notice an improvement in Patricia's attitude. She scarcely seemed jealous anymore. But this was mainly because she knew that Michael never saw his ex-wife.

Michael began to explore some of his more esoteric fantasies with Patricia. One afternoon, they were enjoying a full tea at a charming Vermont inn, when Patricia insisted that she had to go out into the garden and have a cigarette. Michael barely seemed to notice, as he was working the Sunday crossword, but when Patricia returned he mildly admonished her, saying, "With your toxic lifestyle, dearest, you really ought to be cleansing regularly."

Their blue eyes locked as she regained her seat, his serious gaze causing her tummy to contract. "What do you mean?" She appeared confused, but her blush indicated full comprehension of his statement.

"I'll be happy to show you. And you'll feel much better for it," Michael promised.

"Really, I could never endure it," she protested, her face flaming now.

"Why not?" he reached for her hand and enclosed it in his. "Do you think I would suggest this if I didn't know what I was doing?"

"But, what would you get out of it?"

"You always ask me that," he smiled.

"I've fantasized about it," she admitted, "but I really couldn't bear the embarrassment."

"You'd enjoy the hell out of it."

"No!"

"Never mind. I'll take care of you just fine. We'll do it in our attic room. And I checked—there's no one below us tonight. So I can probably give you a sound spanking as well."

Then Michael gaily went off to the village to purchase what he needed. Patricia spent the afternoon in an ecstasy of painful anticipation. Right before dinner they walked in the woods and Michael administered a hard spanking over her beige chiffon summer dress which clung to every elegant curve of her torso and thighs like fairy wrapping. He had found a stump to sit down on and Patricia fit across his thighs perfectly.

"I can't spank you very long or hard at the inn, Patricia, so I think I'll do both now."

Patricia always loved being over Michael's knee in the woods. A long, hard spanking over her dress, slip and panties left a subtle sting that lingered for hours.

All through the splendid gourmet dinner, which they ate in a beautiful wood beamed room overlooking a waterfall, Patricia remembered the few minutes in the woods, along with the feel of his big hand coming down on the back of her skirt. Across the table he looked handsome and mild. But when he caught her looking at him in that dreamy and distracted way she had, he frowned sternly.

"Don't drink too much wine," he warned. "You're being punished tonight."

Patricia stared at him wide-eyed.

"You do remember what we discussed earlier, don't you, Patricia?"

"No!" she lowered her eyes willfully and tossed her glass of wine down.

"You're a self-indulgent child," he told her. "You need discipline." He squeezed her thigh under the table, then reached between her thighs to lightly probe her through her panties. Her panties were already wet from the spanking over his knee in the woods. Patricia pushed his hand away with a furious blush. Michael smiled and ceased to torment her for the remainder of their meal.

After playing one game of backgammon in the parlor, Michael told Patricia it was time to go upstairs. When they reached the isolated attic suite he locked the door behind them. A skylight admitted moonlight and stars. Two low lamps had been lit but otherwise the ambiance was sleepy and intimate.

The large, adjoining bath was, of Italian design, with black marble and cherry wood furnishings and a free-standing claw-footed antique copper tub. Beside the tub stood a tall, wooden towel stand.

Michael told Patricia to take a hot bath. While Patricia was cautiously bathing, Michael entered, rolled up his sleeves and wordlessly began to bathe her, squeezing the hot sponge over her breasts and back and gently soaping her there for a long time, until her tension began to recede.

After her bath she slipped into the shower stall to rinse off. When she came out Michael helped to dry her and put her into her nightgown and robe. The tint of her skin was revealed through the gauzy material.

Michael firmly bend Patricia over the marble sink and pulled her skirts up to her waist.

"Spread your legs apart," he told her, reaching into a cabinet for a leather bag he had placed there earlier in the day. "Arch you back and present your bottom to me," he added, ready to instantly punish the slightest hesitation. Michael had positioned them opposite a full length mirror, set in the fancy wooden towel closet door. "Patricia, if you turn your head just a bit to the left you can see what I'm doing to you," he suggested while inserting his right hand into a sterile latex glove. Patricia stole one glance then turned her head away.

"Don't you want to see?"

"No!"

"Pay attention, Patricia, or I'll spank you," he advised. So she forced herself to watch as he produced a tube of lubricant and began to penetrate her bottom with the middle finger of his gloved hand. "Arch your bottom higher and don't contract," he ordered, using his free hand to divide her satiny white cheeks. He screwed his finger in and out several times before withdrawing it completely and discarding the glove. "Stand up," he told her. Patricia turned to face him, blushing deeply. Michael pulled her to him and kissed her. Then he made her look at him. "Are you embarrassed, Patricia?"

She bit her lip and turned away.

"You need to be disciplined," he reiterated. "Now fill the bathtub again with very warm water and plenty of bubbles."

After Patricia started the soft water running from the graceful antique spigots, Michael took her across his lap as he sat on a varnished wooden bench.

"What are you doing?" she trembled.

"While we're waiting for the tub to fill up I'm going to examine you and take your temperature," he informed her, separating her thighs as much as possible and gently probing her now creamy sex. "You're very wet," he told her unnecessarily. "The treatment is already conferring benefits on you."

Withdrawing two dripping fingers from her pussy, he dried them on a fluffy white towel and produced a thermometer. Still extremely well lubricated, Patricia felt no discomfort as he inserted it into her anus and then held it in place as the bath tub continued to fill.

"It's a shame that none of your many lovers ever cared enough about you to do something like this, but I'll make up for that neglect," Michael promised, patting her bare bottom kindly. Patricia groaned in a torment of excitement, fervently agreeing with his observation.

"Thank you," she murmured, a meek, little, blue-eyed lamb for once.

"My dear, you have a shockingly high temperature," he informed her presently. "I can see we're just in time here."

Once the tub was filled with creamy bubbles Michael had Patricia strip completely naked and climb back in. He then positioned her with her elbows leaning comfortably on the rim of the tub while kneeling with her upturned bottom thrusting up through the foam. Michael knelt in front of her momentarily to show her the hot water bag.

"See this, Patricia? I'm going to fill this with warm water and give you an enema. This is the nozzle." He indicated the long, multi-perforated white plastic nozzle which attached to a hose and then connected to the black rubber bag. "Do you think this will be any problem for you?"

"No," she replied, blushing again and averting her eyes while throbbing with excitement.

"You're being such a good girl about this," he complimented her, kissing her lightly on the lips before filling the bag and suspending it well above the tub on the handy wooden tallboy.

Michael told her to spread her thighs as much as possible and open her bottom to him. Patricia became painfully aroused as it penetrated her inch by inch until the entire 5-inch nozzle had disappeared into her rectum and only the hose protruded from her bottom, which tightly contracted around it.

Michael released the clamp and warm water began to flow into her, causing an intensely pleasurable yet profoundly humiliating reaction.

"We'll start with just a little at a time," he said, closing off the flow and taking a few moments to check and adjust the position of the hose as it protruded from her bare, soapy bottom and reach under the water to briefly cup her pubic mound in his hand, then pass his palm under her tummy to explore its gentle swell. Patricia moaned, half dizzy with pleasure.

Before beginning the flow again Michael administered a half dozen smacks to her vulnerable bottom. They were baby smacks, barely hard enough to sting, but in combination with the anal intrusion, the spanking made Patricia whimper.

"You see, darling? Obedient girls receive very mild spankings." He released the clamp again and the water once again began to fill her tummy. "Now, Patricia, I want you to notice the mirror above the bathtub. That's right, just raise your head and you'll see it."

Patricia couldn't avoid acknowledging the oval mirror suspended over the bath in such a way as to reveal her soapy, glistening bottom, now forced to accomodate the rubber hose. How many mirrors could one bathroom need? She couldn't look for long. It was much too intense to feel and to see at the very same time.

"Do you know why you have to be treated like this, Patricia?" Michael finished administering the enema.

"No," she whimpered.

"Because you need to learn self control. Now hold completely still while I remove the nozzle," he recommended, then adroitly withdrew the long plastic tube from her bottom. Patricia groaned.

Michael helped her out of the tub and dried her completely before wrapping her in the white gown and robe. Then he took her across his knee and bared her bottom. Producing a 6-inch rubber retention plug, he divided her cheeks and attempted to insert the well lubricated tip into her tightly contracted anus.

"Relax and let me do this," he told her.

"I'm afraid to!"

"Nonsense. I told you that you're going to learn some self control. You're going to retain your first enema for at least 15 minutes and naturally you will have a retention plug inserted into your bottom for the entire time."

"I understand," she replied, trembling at the tone in his voice.

Michael relubricated the rubber plug, separated her cheeks with his fingers and plunged the flexible dildo in between them. This time it slipped immediately up into her bottom. He held it in place with his hand for a minute while she lay across his lap, passive now as an obedient child.

Presently he began to spank her on her bare, firmly plugged bottom. Patricia felt shameful pleasure and wriggled on his lap.

"Of course you need to receive at least two enemas for the treatment to be even slightly effective," he informed her, while smacking her bottom just a bit harder. "So you're getting a second one shortly. And you'll be expected to hold that one longer, I'm afraid." The smacks fell rhythmically, on one cheek then the other, then across the middle, right atop the plug, driving it in if it ever slipped out. Once it all but popped out and Michael pretended to be angry at her lack of control. "You're not paying attention, Patricia!" he scolded, pulling it all the way out, then carefully plunging it back in to the hilt. Once more he repeated this. "Don't you dare let it slip out again," he warned, again withdrawing the retention plug completely before completely reinserting it into her tight, slippery bottom. These humiliating attentions rapidly achieved the desired effect of causing Patricia to have a long, intensely satisfying climax across his lap.

Patricia was then allowed one hour to herself before Michael promised to return and administer the second course of the treatment. He went for a walk around the grounds and found it difficult to cool off even in the brisk evening air. She was a marvellous girl.

Given such a luxurious amount of time Patricia was able to see to her most urgent bodily demands, shower and regain 90% of her dignity in a fresh pegnoir set and then was even able to get high. Michael was not happy about this when he returned.

"Patricia, haven't you learned anything? You're supposed to be undergoing a detox treatment this evening. Smoking in the middle is counterproductive."

"Damn it!" Patricia pretended to curse her own weakness.

"And I really don't know why you bothered to put a whole new outfit on," he continued to complain, summarily depriving her of a pristine blue cotton wrapper. "The other one was barely damp from

your excitement. I really don't know what I'm going to do with you."
He turned her under his arm and spanked her bottom soundly
through the light nightgown. "You have to conquer this compulsion
you have to constantly change your clothes," he told her. He finished
up with six hard smacks. "Don't make me tell you that again," he
said, setting her back on her feet, in the fresh, exquisitely fitted gown.

"You haven't learned anything at all about self control yet," he
lamented, producing the leather harness he had bought her in
Boston, along with two vibrators. "Don't be alarmed, Patricia.
This is for your own good."

"What are you going to do now?"

"Now I'm going to administer your second enema. Only this
one will be a Bardex. Leave the gown here and meet me back in
the bathroom."

While Patricia fastened the straps of the leather body harness
around her naked torso, Michael prepared her second enema with
a fuller bag. When he was ready for her, he positioned the broad
wooden bench and towel valet adjacent to each other and suspended the hot water bag from the top peg, as before. Laying out
what he needed beside him on the bench, he took Patricia across
his lap and positioned her comfortably.

"Arch up," he told her, lubricating one of the vibrators and gently
inserting it into the leather slit atop her vagina. The dildo slid up
into her creamy pussy with embarrassing ease. Patricia's face
burned with shame at Michael's laugh. He patted it into place and
anchored it there by means of a leather strap attached to the harness
and looped to the vibrator through a special hook. "The harness
should hold that in place nicely throughout the coming ordeal,"
Michael promised. "I won't turn it on just yet."

Next he showed her the Bardex nozzle.

"This is to help you retain your enema without a plug," he
explained, causing her to blush and sob. "Yes, I know it's embarrassing even to discuss such things, but please remember that if
you were a good girl I would never have to resort to such measures. I told you that you had to learn some discipline. The nozzle
goes in deeply, then the bulb inflates inside your bottom, to seal
the water in without you even thinking about it. Understand?"

Patricia nodded. Michael lubricated her anus and spread it with
his fingers. Then he inserted the nozzle slowly into her rectum. It

took a long time to go in all the way and Patricia wriggled involuntarily as the penetration continued. Once it was in completely in, he inflated the bulb inside her. She had to make her mind a blank in order not to instantly orgasm again.

He began to give her the enema a little at a time. It felt very warm as it filled her. She took the entire bag without a protest. Michael patted her bottom softly as the last few drops filtered in.

"Now, young lady, I expect you to behave yourself for a least twenty minutes this time. And I believe I promised you a sound spanking as well."

Keeping her firmly anchored across his lap, with the enema hose still protruding from her delicious white buttocks, he began to paddle Patricia with a small, oval wooden paddle he produced.

Patricia writhed with pleasure and shame across her lover's thighs, her small tummy filled with hot water and her bottom tightly plugged.

"Dearest, things are about to become a bit more extreme now," Michael warned her, before giving the top of the vibrator a twist and starting it vibrating in her pussy. He pressed down on her bottom gently as he also adjusted the hose still depending from her bottom. "You know, Patricia," he advised her, "After you're thoroughly cleaned out and fully recovered from the multiple orgasms you're about to have, sometime around dawn, when you're just waking up, I intend to slip my cock into your bottom and take you properly there."

Michael listened closely to the small inarticulate noises issuing from Patricia's parted lips and shut the vibrator off.

"Hold still," he told her, deflating the bulb and very slowly withdrawing the Bardex nozzle from her bottom. Laying this apparatus aside he showed her the other vibrator, a 7-inch model, slightly thinner around than the one he had inserted into her vagina. Lubricating the plastic dildo as well as her anus, which was accessible only through the slit in the harness, he inserted it into her bottom, slowly and as deeply as it could go. Finally only one inch of hilt protruded from the harness slit which targetted her anus so cunningly and Patricia was as completely filled as she had ever been.

Too humiliated to utter a sound, Patricia abandoned herself to the sensation of having her pussy and bottom stuffed with large dildos while her tummy was filled with warm water and her dominant lover held her firmly across his lap. She sobbed and bit her knuckle. It was really too much! If he did just one more thing she would climax immediately.

Michael held her by the waist and began to spank her soundly. "This is just what you need, young lady," he told her, bringing his palm down hard on her fully exposed buttocks until her fair complexion was tinged a dark pink. Then he paused and activated the vibrator he had inserted into her bottom. Michael held her firmly in place and resumed spanking her vigorously until she came, which happened almost immediately.

After her spasms died away, which took quite some minutes, Michael lay her down on the bench, extracted the dildo from her vagina and replaced it with his own cock. Still plugged from behind, Patricia accepted this new mode of intercourse with shy curiosity.

"But what if it slips out!" she worried as he drove in to the hilt and started to deliberately pump her.

"If it slips out you'll be severely punished," he warned, in a tone which caused her to have a third climax. Gratified at this unusual degree of responsiveness, he did not prolong his own release, which of course had been pending for the last two hours.

Later that night, as they lay in the moonlight, Michael cradled Patricia in his arms. She was very sleepy.

"You see, you do feel better now, don't you, Patricia?"

SHADOW LANE IV
THE CHRONICLES OF
RANDOM POINT

JEALOUSY

When you go to a spanking scene party, you should be on your best behavior, or someone might take you in hand . . .

In this episode, Patricia is publicly spanked by Hugo and whipped by Michael; Diana is whipped soundly by Marguerite, and later spanked with a hairbrush before having her bottom taken by Sherman; Laura is spanked and masturbated to orgasm across Michael's lap. Brief appearances are also made by the rest of the Random Point gang.

MICHAEL FLAGG FELT pleasantly excited yet profoundly uneasy about attending the first meeting of Pandora, the new B&D support group on Cape Cod. But this was only because every woman he had slept with for the past four years was going to be there, including his current sweetheart.

"Here's something unexpected," Michael tactfully forewarned his fair-haired companion on perusing the list of speakers when they stopped at an inn to dine on the way to Provincetown.

"What?" said Patricia Fairservis, the distinctive and difficult married woman Michael was in love with.

"The one who's giving the talk on *female self-pleasuring* is my

– 179 –

ex-fiancée." Michael pushed the program across the table to his suddenly tense companion. "I didn't think she even knew how to masturbate, no less talk about it," he added candidly.

"You never mentioned an ex-fiancée in the scene." Patricia scanned the program with a racing pulse.

"She wasn't in the scene when I knew her."

"Oh? You never played?"

"No way in hell. She was a real Feminazi back then."

"So, were you in love?"

"Well, she did let me sodomize her," he was compelled to admit. "But our relationship wasn't about self indulgence. It was about duty. I was the good cop. She was the idealistic social worker. We ran in 10K's together and ate whole grains. We were going to get married. We even bought a bed from Hugo Sands' antique shop. That bed I tie you up in sometimes."

"Then what happened?"

"I got transferred to Random Point and realized I'd found the Peyton Place of the Scene. Soon after that I broke off the engagement."

"And the woman you jilted will be there tonight?"

"Just thought I'd tell you so you wouldn't have to hear it from someone else."

"Thanks," said Patricia suspiciously. It had not been a comfortable afternoon for the strikingly pretty but insecure editor of *Cape Cod Style*. She and her handsome detective had almost quarreled about the party, because she was violently jealous.

Compulsive to an excruciating degree, choosing an outfit took Patricia so long that Michael finally decided for her by picking out a leather halter dress and telling her to put it on before he thrashed her.

Then their leaving was further delayed by an exhaustive search for her Armani sunglasses. When Michael reminded her that the sun would not be shining by the time they arrived, she icily informed him that she had no intention of jeopardizing her anonymity at a coven of B&D freaks.

"You know, we're two of the freaks, you arrogant brat," he reminded her, bristling.

"I meant *alternative life stylers*," she corrected herself carelessly.

"I should put you over my knee for that remark."

"Maybe so, but the sunglasses stay on," she defied him, looking very La Dolce Vita, a slender woman of fashion, about 30, with smooth, well cut, light blonde hair.

Over their coffee and liqueur, as the sun went down on the secluded cove which the inn overlooked, Michael remarked on what a pretty place it was and suggested they stay there the night instead of continuing on to Provincetown.

"Loosing your nerve?" she challenged, rising gracefully in her Charles Jourdan 4-inch pumps. He followed her out to the car and got into the driver's seat.

"Patricia, we have to have an understanding about tonight."

"Oh?" She lit a cigarette.

"You have to promise to behave yourself and not embarrass me."

"Embarrass you how?"

"By being catty to someone for instance."

"You mean one of my numerous sisters in the *I've Been Sodomized By Michael Flagg Sorority*?"

"You see how you are?"

"Well, how would you feel if I revealed those kinds of details to you?"

"You do. All the time. You've told me exactly what you do with your husband as well as the many professional associates you manipulate, and I don't find it off putting in the slightest."

"Oh, you're so insufferably secure it's nauseating," snarled Patricia, exhaling out the window.

Michael laughed, but before he started her luxurious Mercedes he took her hand. "Patricia, I have felt for some time now, that in your own horrible way, you were meant for me. Having said this, let me add that if you do anything tonight to make me regret bringing you to the orientation, I *will* use a hairbrush on you when I get you home."

"Look, I'm not a little savage. Let's just get this over with," Patricia said, inwardly aglow at his blunt declaration of love.

The orientation was given by the tall, sandy haired Hugo Sands, natty in a light linen suit, and the statuesque Marguerite Alexander, who showed spectacularly in a dress of black silk cobwebs. Hugo was in the midst of defining scene terminology when he was disturbed by the sound of Patricia Fairservis whispering to her friend, Laura Random, yummy in a snug, PVC apron dress.

Patricia was excited because she recognized the musical composer Anthony Newton sitting with Laura's little sister Susan Ross. "Goody! I finally get to meet him!" Patricia commented in a fairly audible tone to Laura, as magazine spreads of Newton's lavish homes unfolded in her mind.

Hugo looked directly at Patricia, who instantly subsided in her chair, having already been caned by Hugo on one occasion and recognizing that certain look in his eyes.

"Do you have something to contribute, Patricia?" he asked her, in a tone that put everyone in mind of their most intimidating grade school teacher.

"No," she replied, blushing.

"Disturb this meeting once more and you'll be part of the corporal punishment demonstration," he warned her. Patricia bit her lip to prevent herself from saying something she might regret and began to nonchalantly study her fellow fetishists.

William Random, whose chiseled muscularity was revealed by pegged Levi's and a rolled sleeved white shirt, locked his arms around the waist of Michael's ex-wife Damaris in a manner that indicated a solid attachment.

"My god, you left that Calvin Klein ad for craggy old Hugo Sands?" Patricia queried Laura in a barely audible whisper. Yet, when she looked up she noticed with a start that Hugo was once again provoked by the interruption. Michael smiled behind his program while everyone else stared at Patricia. Especially Michael's ex-fiancée, Jane Eliot, who was extremely curious about the woman Michael had ended up with.

During the intermission, Jane was the first to come up to them, which was exactly when Patricia noticed that the lithe brunette was wearing the same halter dress from North Beach Leather she had on. A violent color flooded Patricia's face as she remembered that Michael had picked this one of the hundred dresses in her wardrobe.

"I was amazed when I saw your name on the program," Michael told Jane, after a friendly embrace and introductions.

"You'll never believe it, but I'm living with a woman now too," Jane confided unselfconsciously. "A bisexual woman," she added, indicating a tall, lean, blonde girl dressed in black jeans and a T-shirt, drinking beer across the room and talking to Hugo Sands and William Random.

"You and Marnie Price?" Michael recognized Random Point's premiere spoiled rich girl.

Jane now turned to Patricia with interest. "Obviously, we share the same taste in a couple of things," Jane said, regarding the dress on Patricia. "I hope it looks as good on me as it does on you," she added in her pleasant, nonthreatening way. Patricia merely smiled in return, having not yet decided what her attitude towards Jane should be. She did not like the way Michael was smiling at Jane and eyeing Jane in the body sculpting dress.

"I just can't get over the fact that you feel comfortable enough with this stuff to actually lecture on the use of *vibrators*," Michael remarked, with an open admiration which annoyed Patricia.

"I was such a pill when you knew me. I don't blame you for not attempting to enlighten me. I probably would have advised you to seek counseling."

"Instantly," he agreed.

"Well, everyone isn't equally gifted with an understanding of their own sexuality. Some of us need a guide. Hugo was the one who brought me out."

"Really? I know Hugo," said Patricia, suddenly more interested in Jane. Now it seemed they had shared two men in common! That almost made her more of a sister than a rival.

"But recently," Jane went on to explain, "I realized I could better integrate my new affinity for bondage and discipline with my ardent feminism by experiencing the scene with other *women*."

Patricia noticed Marnie Price eyeing her lover jealously from across this room and this reassured her.

"How did you two meet?" Jane asked.

"After Damaris left me I placed an ad. Patricia responded to it. She's married but her husband isn't in the scene." Michael revealed. Meanwhile, Patricia had almost lost interest in Jane, whose newfound lesbianism seemed to eliminate her as a rival.

Michael couldn't fail to notice Patricia staring across the room at his ex-wife, Damaris, who had joined William, Hugo and Marnie in conversation. Damaris was tightly corseted under her full-skirted, cranberry cocktail dress. Her chin-length hair was black and geometrically cut. Her face was open and untroubled, with big, dark eyes and a wide, beautiful mouth. William reflexively slipped his arm around her 23-inch waist as she stepped into the circle. Her bosom and bottom were well rounded and womanly.

Damaris had peeked over at Patricia and Michael at least once, and of course Patricia had noticed and it had chilled her. Damaris had given a little friendly smile and a very tiny wave, to indicate that she knew who Patricia was and was prepared to be gentle about her replacement. Patricia managed a weak smile back and ran outside to smoke.

Outside the meeting hall, Susan Ross and her college friend, Diana Stratton, admired the row of motorcycles parked at the curb.

"Is the dick-of-death-detective here?" Diana begged Susan to tell her.

"Yes," replied Susan, who was 21, with long, wavy, goldenrod hair. Diana was 20, with a chestnut pageboy. Both were petite, intellectual and accessible.

Susan wore an A-line denim dress and Diana a navy gingham halter dress with a full skirt over a white petticoat. These little out-fits were drawing attention away from the leather and latex ensembles which clad the many svelte and voluptuous female forms now emerging from the hall into the balmy night air, but the girls remained oblivious of the stir they were creating as they lingered on the pavement near the bikes.

"That's Michael's girlfriend over there," Susan explained, indicating Patricia. "I've only met her once. I think she's the jealous type and I'm sure she doesn't know I've played with Michael. So don't blurt out anything inappropriate," she added.

Just as Susan said this the girls saw Hugo stroll out of the hall and pause on the front porch for a moment to light a cigarette, but when he looked up and saw Patricia smoking at the curb he threw his away and strode over to her with a purposeful look which caused her to tingle with apprehension.

"What?" she challenged, with a hostile flare to her nostrils.

"What do you think?" he asked quietly.

"Hugo, you're not spanking me in public!" she declared.

"No?" Hugo took Patricia by the earlobe, as though she were an Edwardian schoolchild and using the bumper of Anthony Newton's Bentley as a bench, turned the willowy blonde over his knee. Patricia was so shocked that she could barely speak to protest as a small circle of amused on-lookers watched Hugo bring his palm down hard on the seat of her leather dress a dozen times.

"Chairing a meeting is hard enough without having to deal with rude girls talking out of turn," said Hugo, administering another twelve forceful smacks to Patricia's well-protected bottom before letting the furious girl up.

"Wow!" said Diana to Susan, "I think I'm in love."

"With which one?"

"You're right," said Diana, longing to put her arms around the stunning blonde woman and comfort her, yet even more violently drawn to the stern Pandora coordinator.

"How dare you?" Patricia cried, as he let her up. At that moment Michael stepped up to witness the end of the confrontation.

"Excuse me," Patricia said haughtily. then strode back to the meeting hall. She had never felt so ill-used. It almost made her wish to seek revenge on Hugo Sands. She could easily undo all the good she had ever done him with one indifferent squib on his shop in her magazine. How dare he spank her in front of those two college girls, tattooed bikers and even Marguerite Alexander!

In the bathroom she lit another cigarette and swallowed a sob of anger. Laura immediately followed her in. She was Hugo's girl-friend now as well as Patricia's only female friend in the scene.

"Hey, what happened?" she scrutinized Patricia's face. "Are you upset? I heard Hugo spanked you."

"Yes, in front of twenty people. Including your sister and her friend. I thought I'd die."

"I wish I hadn't missed that!" Laura lamented rather heartlessly.

"Laura, he can't do things like that. Wasn't he just talking about consensual B&D? I didn't consent to play just now in front of two dozen people."

"You do have a point."

"How dare he lay hands on me in front of strangers? I hope Michael punched him out." Patricia folded her arms in glee at this thought.

"I guarantee that he didn't," Laura smiled.

"How *can* you deal with a man like that?" Patricia asked her, with a shiver.

"Diplomatically, I suppose."

"You mean you can never tell Hugo off? Because he's so fucking dominant?"

"You make a habit of telling Michael off?"

"No. But he doesn't need it."

"Well, at any rate, come on out so people won't think this was any big deal."

"All right, but Hugo had better apologize to me."

"Hugo never apologizes."

"Is that so? Well, Hugo Sands may soon find out that there are other forms of retribution besides physical!" Patricia threw down the dark glasses in disgust and savagely did her lipstick. Laura took a brush out of Patricia's purse and began to brush her friend's fine, blonde hair. Then Laura put the brush down and put her arms around Patricia's waist from behind. They looked at each other in the mirror and smiled.

"With that tiny little waist and gorgeous bottom, no wonder you get spanked so much," said Laura, kissing Patricia behind the ear. Patricia shivered and ground back against Laura.

Being the bad girls they were, Susan and Diana decided to cut the demonstration portion of the meeting and walk down to the edge of the village, where the water met the rocks, to smoke and discuss what they had already observed. Diana was fascinated by Hugo Sands.

"He was the first man to ever spank me," Susan told her friend as they tossed pebbles into the inky water. "He's always been in love with my sister. Now he's finally got her. But I don't think she can handle him."

"What do you mean?"

"Well, you saw how he acted tonight. He did something similar to me last year. In fact, he picked one night to humiliate both me and Laura in front of several people who are here tonight."

"What did he do?" Diana loved the idea of being punished publicly, especially by one so cool and composed,

"He spanked me for interrupting the grown-ups, much in the same way he just did to Patricia. Then he caned the hell out of Laura."

"Ooooh!" Diana shivered with excitement. "I wish he'd do that to me."

– 186 –

"No, you ridiculous girl, the way he caned my sister was excessive," Susan was surprised by her own vehemence in retrospect. "I ran and got William and he broke it up. Anthony was no help. He was enjoying the show. It took me a while to get over that."

"Hugo sounds delicious," said Diana. "Is he also the master of that ravishing redhead who's co-chairing?"

"Marguerite was a protegee of his at one time. She and my sister were at Bennington together."

"Who does Marguerite belong to now?"

"Well, she's been quietly in love with Michael Flagg for years, but I think he's only one of several."

"I think Sherman Cooper is falling in love with me," Diana wisely concluded, enraptured by the moon.

"Have you done it yet?"

"No, but tonight I may allow him to."

"Do you love him?"

"How could I not? We're the quintessential F. Scott Fitzgerald couple, he the Princeton-bred lawyer, me the perverse Vassar girl who's driving him insane. I hope we don't crash and burn."

When the meeting resumed, Marguerite Alexander gave a talk on restraints, demonstrating some simple rope ties on Laura Random. Next, Marguerite discussed the art of Victorian corseting, using as a subject the exquisite Damaris Flagg, who had removed her dress to reveal a black satin waist cinch, tightly laced. Her voluptuous bosom was enclosed in a black lace brassiere, but her round bottom was bare from mid-hip to thigh, the G-string affording her no modesty. Her beautifully turned legs were hosed in sheer black stockings, held up by the eight suspenders. Patricia could not take her eyes off the delectable creature who allowed Marguerite to fondle her slim hips and press her tiny waist in describing the virtues of corseting. How and why could Michael have abandoned this Venus? Patricia looked at her man with perplexity.

Marguerite filled Patricia with a greater fear. For as soon as she was brought to meet her, Patricia detected the faint, light perfume which she sometimes smelled in Michael's wardrobe. This confirmed Marguerite as The Other One. Tall and striking, with the body of a showgirl and glasses, this independent woman was about Patricia's age, with a similar education and sophisticated taste. "The only difference between us is that I'm married and have smaller curves," thought Patricia gloomily.

Throughout the rest of the exhibitions, on piercing, latex, tattoos, transvestites and foot slaves, Patricia studied her various rivals. Then she caught Sherman Cooper looking at her and a new idea fluttered her heart. Perhaps she was foolish to spend her time worrying about other women when she might instead be flirting with other men!

After the demonstrations were concluded, almost everyone signed up to join as members in the new group. Then Anthony Newton told Hugo and Marguerite to invite anyone they liked to his house in Random Point for a party. He sent Laura back to open the house and alert Dennis that guests would shortly follow. Meanwhile, he and Sherman went to comb the town for Susan and Diana.

Patricia was talking to architect William Random, to whom she had just been introduced, about doing a story on him for the magazine, when she noticed Hugo gazing at her thoughtfully.

"You know, I'm thinking of buying a cottage on the Cape," Patricia told William, ignoring Hugo. "Perhaps you could put me onto something good. I know you re-did Michael's place and I'm in love with it."

"I'll build you a house from scratch if you like," William said obligingly.

"I couldn't afford that."

"I own a construction company, so I can build at a very low cost. And the publicity of doing a house for Patricia Fairservis would be worth a special effort."

"You're very nice," smiled Patricia, still wondering why Laura had abandoned this beautiful, boyish young man for the distinguished yet somewhat faded Hugo Sands. Patricia, who had once admired Hugo's looks and style, could find nothing to appreciate about him that evening. She would, in fact, hate him till the day he died, she decided, turning from William to confront Hugo, who had crossed the room to stand at her elbow.

Patricia glared at him, pausing to frame a devastating set down when he astonished everyone within earshot by apologizing to her.

"Patricia, I wanted to say that I'm sorry I lost my temper with you earlier. It was totally out of line and if there's anything I can say or do to make it up to you, please tell me what it is," Hugo said with perfect sincerity. William was a witness to the seriousness with which the apology was made and was able to report on the confrontation faithfully later that night to the two or three people who asked him to confirm the event.

"Anything you can say or do, huh? You're lucky I'm not a switch," Patricia said, putting out her hand to shake his, adding, "Apology accepted." Hugo took her hand and kissed it rather nicely, thanked her and walked away.

"I wouldn't have believed that if I didn't see it," William said to Patricia, who couldn't suppress a small smirk of satisfaction herself.

"Oh, he probably overheard me say I'm moving to Random Point and wants to me to furnish my house though his shop," Patricia observed cynically.

Though in truth, it was more a matter of conscience than greed which had prompted Hugo to apologize to a lady who had never done anything but good to him in their brief relationship. Her generous spreads on his shop had greatly increased his business the previous quarter and all he'd ever given her in return was a couple of hard corporal punishment sessions which had ended with her submissively on her knees and ready to serve him. It was true that in many ways she was an impossible princess, but she was not his princess and therefore he had no right to take her in hand. Besides, he hadn't enjoyed the look of disapproval on Susan's face when he let Patricia up. Susan and her sister Laura represented the modern reform movement in the scene, compliant to a point, yet instinctively rebellious against the clumsier aspects of male chauvinism in practice. Since Laura was his hard-won girlfriend and Susan was her sister, it mattered to Hugo how both girls perceived his behavior. It was the nicety of their discernment that made the sisters so rare. An abject submissive was the easiest creature in the world to enthrall, an analytical one the most elusive. Laura had forced him to court her for years before accepting him as her dominant, thus he valued her above any other submissive he had ever loved.

Having discharged this duty, Hugo felt better and not at all compromised. Patricia softened as she watched him walk away. The fact that he had chosen to restore her dignity in front of another dominant male meant something to her. Perhaps he wasn't as much of a nightmare as she'd supposed. Tomorrow she would visit his shop and demand a present!

Diana had correctly identified the affliction of Sherman Cooper, who was now amusing Anthony Newton with his anxieties about the girls. Diana had made sure to let Sherman hear her invite Susan outside to admire the handsome Harleys.

"Perhaps some leather dykes will kidnap us and take us by force in the woods!"

Sherman was disturbed at the voicing of such dangerous wishes, though Anthony assured him that Diana had only said this to tease him. Sherman did worry about Diana constantly, because she was a thrill seeker. She would brag to him of her sexual adventures, to cause him to punish her harshly whenever they met. After he'd spanked her, she'd confess that she'd made the stories up. Sherman didn't know what to believe. He adored Diana and felt that fate had finally provided him with The One. Hadn't she let him strap her the first day they met?

"I must be mad," Sherman confided to Anthony as they walked through the quiet town towards the shore, "becoming attached to a 20-year-old!"

"She's a heartbreaker all right," Anthony agreed, not very helpfully.

"You wouldn't believe the things she's told me she's done or wants to do," Sherman said, with active worry. "And she's a profoundly bad influence on Susan as well."

"Oh, I agree. Diana is a catalyst for trouble."

The men ran into the girls walking back through the village. Sherman did not say a word to Diana, to signify his displeasure about her abandoning the meeting. He now felt foolish about being an alarmist, seeing as the girls were just strolling along, but at the same time he was angry with Diana. It was hard to know what she wanted or expected from him. She had specifically invited him for the weekend, but now that he was here, she was virtually ignoring him.

The four times he'd seen her since their first meeting with Susan, had been perfect little scene dates, each including a dinner or lunch, a diversion such as a gallery, play or concert and a brisk corporal punishment session, generally based on the degree of mischief performed by Diana during the entertainment. It was usually something cute, like attempting to unzip his trousers under their coats during a performance of *Hedda Gabler*. But tonight there were many other dominants available to fuss over Diana, so he wondered why she should need him here at all.

When it was time to get into the Bentley, Diana got in front, with Anthony behind the wheel and left Susan to sit in back with Sherman, who was distinctly brooding.

"What's the matter, Sherman?" Susan squeezed his hand and rubbed the back of it against her soft cheek.

"Is Diana deliberately trying to provoke me?"

"I don't know about that but I think she likes you very much," Susan informed him.

"She has an odd way of showing it," Sherman pointed out.

"She's a brat. As a friend I'd advise you to thrash her," Susan said. "Really make her cry. That's what she's waiting for."

"But I don't want to make her cry," Sherman protested.

"Oh, come on, every dominant wants to make his girlfriend cry at least once."

"Well, I certainly don't and I wouldn't presume to call Diana my girlfriend."

"She could be, you know. But you have to scare the hell out of her to make her respect you. Otherwise, she'll walk all over you. She'll make you *her* submissive. I can see the indications."

Since Susan was Diana's best friend and confidante, Sherman considered what she told him very seriously. However, it was difficult to adapt his own personal notions of chivalry to the needs of an insatiable and decadent young girl.

Susan Ross didn't feel that she was counseling her dear friend Sherman improperly since she herself had worn out her arm in spanking Diana without hearing a single plea for mercy.

When they reached Anthony's house on the cliffside road overlooking Random Point, Diana immediately abandoned the entire group to go and search for Marguerite Alexander. She had played with several older women, but they had been older pro doms from the city and the scenes had had a maternal feel to them which Diana didn't crave. Marguerite was just old enough to be worldly and wise, but still young enough to be dashing, a model to aspire to, a goddess to submit to. She had heard from Susan that

Marguerite was an expert whip mistress and she had longed to be whipped while lashed to a whipping post, for as long as she could remember. Marguerite was able to gratify this quaint ambition within moments of their introduction at the impromptu champagne bar which Dennis had set up. They went directly up to the small ballroom which Anthony was transforming into an airy dungeon. There they found several couples who had been at the Pandora meeting already playing, but the whipping post was unoccupied.

When Sherman wandered into the room a few minutes later he was treated to the sight of the tall, russet-haired Marguerite whipping the bare buttocks of the girl he adored. Diana's arms were fastened around the carved, light mahogany whipping post. The skirt of her dress as well as her white crinoline, had been tucked up above her waist and her white silk panties had been pulled down to her knees. By this time, her fair skin had been marked by the whip with many lashes, so that a dark pink hue suffused the entire surface of her dainty bottom. Sherman was depressed to note that the same delightful pants and groans Diana breathed while he played with her, could be extracted just as readily from his darling by Marguerite Alexander. He had no doubt, now that he thought of it, that anyone might be able to elicit a similar response from Diana, if only they knew enough to whip her.

Michael and Patricia sat on a love seat and watched the whipping of Diana with rapt attention. Her love of beauty and eroticism permitting her to forget that Marguerite was her arch rival, Patricia admired wholeheartedly the perfection with which the voluptuous redhead was teasing and tormenting her enchanting captive. Marguerite was currently using an antique riding crop to separate Diana's legs and touch up her parted bottom cheeks. But sometimes Marguerite would stop punishing Diana all together and simply make her ride the crop.

"Why don't you offer to take her place, Patricia?" Michael suggested.

"I'm sure you would enjoy that," Patricia replied.

"I feel cheated that I didn't get to see your first public spanking," said Michael, referring to the brief spectacle that Hugo Sands had made of her outside the meeting hall.

"I don't mind showing off, but I won't be whipped by anyone but you," she surprised him by replying.

No one had ever seen Michael Flagg play in public before, except for the one time Marguerite and a half dozen customers in her book shop watched Michael give Laura Random a birthday spanking several years before. So it was with a great deal of interest that such personages as Susan Ross, Damaris Flagg, Jane Eliot and Marguerite Alexander observed Michael leading his glamorous blonde companion to the whipping post when Diana had been freed from it. He removed his jacket and tie and rolled up his shirt sleeves in an unhurried manner while Patricia waited with her hands clasped behind her back. Turning her to face the several dozen observers gathered around the whipping post in the rotunda, he unzipped her leather dress and let it fall to the floor. Patricia looked down at her shoes and at nothing else as a blush tinged her cheeks.

She was clad in an exquisite black lace and brocade corset with a décolleté bra. This London-bought waist cinch gave Patricia a ravishing figure, which was the primary reason she had agreed to be exhibited. He turned her around and fastened her wrists into cuffs, which he then attached to the post above her head. Everyone admired the sight of Patricia's slim but lush bottom when it was turned towards them. Michael dispensed with her gossamer-sheer black panties immediately, pulling them down and making her step out of them. Then he knelt beside her to cuff her ankles together. As he rose to his feet he ran his hand up the backs of her long legs, hosed in sheer, black stockings.

Patricia was glad that her back was to them, but then was horrified to note that the whipping post had been positioned in front of a multi-paned mirror, in which she was able to see the reflection of almost everyone watching the exhibition. She saw Jane Eliot staring at her with great absorption and Jane's Valkyrie of a lover staring jealously at Jane. She saw little Susan Ross, impossibly fresh and dewy from her college graduation, gazing with open admiration at Michael's well defined torso as he took up a flogger to begin with. Patricia also saw Damaris, safely seated on the granite thighs of William Random, who appeared to be enjoying the view. Damaris was looking at Patricia and Michael with interest, but her head was nestled against William's throat and William's hands were locked around the Puerto Rican girl's waist. No problems foreseeable there, thought Patricia, who now found herself concentrating on everything but what was about to happen to her. Hugo and Laura were watching as well, sitting together with glasses of champagne, thighs touching, occasionally whispering to each other and laughing. Hugo wasn't so bad, thought Patricia. At least he had apologized. It took a real man to do that. And it hadn't been a terrible spanking. Very hard, of course, but she liked that. Her bottom had tingled for at least a half hour afterwards.

Everyone became riveted when the whipping began, because it was a real one.

"Pay attention, Patricia," Michael told her, lashing her smooth, white, bare bottom in a way that made her immediately cry out with shock.

"Hey! What about my warm up?" she demanded, under her breath.

"You're getting a whipping, not a warm up," he replied, lashing her hard a second time.

"Ow! You can't start out that hard!"

"Do I have your undivided attention?" Again the whip came down.

"You have it!"

"Good. Let's keep it that way," he told her, continuing to use the flogger, but more moderately, though in six or eight strokes he was back up to the same intensity that had made her cry out.

"But, what did I do?" she whimpered.

"What didn't you do? We could start with this morning, or the first day of second grade. You're just bad, Patricia."

"I don't remember being bad on the first day of second grade," she mumbled into the whipping post, hiding her face behind her arm as he laid on harder. Now she was fully focused on the whipping in front of them all. She had to show them that she could take it. It was important they realize that she was the right one for him. She certainly couldn't imagine Marguerite holding still for this kind of lashing, nor the tiny Damaris.

Marguerite was indeed shocked at the way Michael was whipping Patricia. Dark, angry, red marks were beginning to blossom all over her taut, white bottom. Damaris also watched with a pounding heart, remembering the couple of nights when she herself had received almost as hard a thrashing from Michael Flagg while his wife. But she saw no tears in Patricia's eyes or anguish on her face. Instead, she saw a concentration of the kind one observes in athletes. It was a point of pride to Patricia never to say mercy.

Hugo enjoyed the whipping very much. He liked seeing the haughty Patricia take it and greatly approved of Michael's vigorous style of application. *He* didn't think it was too hard. But Laura Random, his companion, deemed the whipping unduly harsh. She herself remember being caned to tears by Hugo the summer before in front of a group of people and how it had humiliated her. She had thought him cruel and insensitive for months. Finally, because she missed his attentions greatly, she had forgiven him and allowed him to win her back. After which it was pretty well understood between them that he would never discipline her so severely again. The punishment they now witnessed made her tremble with anxiety.

And yet, an hour or so after the whipping, when Laura ran into Michael as he leaned in the bay window of an alcove off the third floor stairwell, a painful stab of pleasure rippled through her as she recalled the severity of Patricia's whipping.

"What are you doing?" she asked, dropping down in the window seat which overlooked the cliffs and sea.

"Just getting away from the smoke," he replied.

"Don't you mean avoiding all your ex-wives, fiancées and girl-friends?"

"Come on, Laura, be nice."

"I'd much rather be naughty, *with you*," she openly flirted.

"Is that so?" He smiled.

"If not now, when?" she asked bluntly.

"Does Hugo permit you to play with other men at parties?"

"Permit?" Laura laughed.

"Oh? It's not that sort of relationship?"

"Well, didn't you just see him spank Patricia? Right outside in the street he did it!"

"Because of extenuating circumstances, that doesn't count," Michael had the conscience to inform her.

"What extenuating circumstances?"

"I asked him to do that. To distract Patricia. Do you think it worked?"

"Michael Flagg, how entirely unethical of you!" Laura cried, remembering how upset Patricia had been after the public spanking.

"Do you really think so?"

"Can I have been so mistaken in your character?" Laura stood up suddenly.

"Take it easy, Laura," Michael yanked her back down. "You don't understand what Patricia can be like. She's been torturing me all day about this party—the ex-girlfriends and all that, yet insisting on going. I merely thought that if something happened which made her the center of attention, she'd forget about being jealous of the other girls and enjoy herself more."

"Ingenious." Laura got to her feet. "But somehow it falls flat. Excuse me."

"Not so fast, Laura dear." He captured her small white hand and patted it between his large ones. "Now, we're not going to share this insignificant, little secret with my hell-cat of a girl-friend, are we?"

"Why not? I think she has a right to know what a stinker you can be," retorted Laura, trying to break away.

"I'm sorry, I was being rude. You did say you wanted to play, didn't you?" In one fluid motion, he pulled her down across his lap and imprisoned her with a heavy arm across her waist.

"No! I've changed my mind," said Laura. "Let me up!"

"Now that I've got you in this position, I don't want to." He stroked her bottom through her tight, shiny skirt. This tender attention took some of the starch out of her resistance. She had dreamed about a real spanking from Michael for years. All of her girlfriends had played with him. Even her little sister. He was so tall, so fair, so handsome, with the rock solid thighs of an athlete to rest firmly upon. His large hands melted her. "You *can* relax, you know," he told her. Then he began to spank her, long and hard on the seat of her skirt, until Laura was stirred by the heat. Before he pulled her skirt up he asked her permission. But once it was up and her bottom glowed through her sheer black panties, he assumed an authoritative tone.

"You're *not* mentioning the incident with Hugo to Patricia. Do you understand me, Laura Random?"

"Give me one good reason why I shouldn't."

"I'll give you a hundred and one," he told her and smartly began to smack her on the seat of her panties. After the full count he pulled the panties down, rubbed her bottom deeply, bent to kiss it and inhaled the heavenly perfume of her dewy Venus mound.

"Will you keep my secret?" he asked again.

"You haven't yet convinced me that it's important to do so," she challenged softly, unwilling for the punishment to end.

"It's going to feel harder on the bare," he warned her, almost regretfully. She ground against his thighs, hardly sensible of the pain in her excitement at finally being handled and manipulated by Michael. The birthday spanking in Marguerite's shop years before and the one stolen kiss in his car, while William was away for so long, had formed the sum of their physical contact. Now, for the first time she was solidly across his lap, held fast by his huge hand, for the attentions she'd longed to receive from him ever since the first day they'd met.

"Laura, knowing Patricia as you do, can you really be indignant that she got one extra licking? After all, she was being a noisy, snotty brat, disrupting the meeting like that."

"Patricia deserves to be thrashed twice a day," Laura agreed, grinding dreamily against Michael's thighs. Her bottom was turning a deep, voluptuous shade of magenta under his hand.

"And so do you," he told her, bringing his hand down hard. She almost climaxed when he deliberately spread her cheeks and smacked her in between them. Then he spread her thighs and slipping his left hand in under her tummy, inserted one long, middle finger up into her vagina.

"Oh!" she cried.

"Hush, you bad girl," he continued the spanking in this manner until she succumbed to a thrilling climax about 40 seconds later. "That'll teach you to be a tattletale," he added.

After Michael restored Laura's clothes to their proper order, she climbed back on his lap the right way around and they embraced in the alcove seat for a long time, with her head in the crook of his shoulder and his hands clasped around her taut bottom. Laura was caught, thus luxuriating in Michael's strong embrace some few seconds later by her lover, Hugo Sands, who had just dashed up the stairs on his way to the playroom.

Laura recoiled from the displeasure in Hugo's eyes and jumped off Michael's lap with a feverish blush. Hugo continued on his way to the playroom without comment. When he got there he abruptly decided to take his leave of his host and depart for the evening. Laura followed him and said, "Are we going?"

"I am," Hugo told her and went past her down the stairs. Laura ran down after him.

"Hugo, wait!" she cried.

"Well?" he turned.

"Hugo, please don't be angry. What you saw just now was no big deal," she lamely protested.

"Oh?" He folded his arms and waited for her to continue.

"It was just a little post-scene cuddle. It never occurred to me that it wouldn't be all right to play with Michael tonight, especially after I saw you spank Patricia earlier."

"I see," said Hugo, honorably refraining from revealing his pact with Michael.

"You do?"

"Good night, Laura," he said, turning to go.

"Hugo? Am I not to go home with you tonight?"

"Go home with me? As though nothing had happened?"

"But nothing did happen, Hugo. I just told you—"

"Laura, there was nothing casual about the way I saw you grinding on Michael's lap," said Hugo bluntly.

"I was not grinding!" she cried.

"Well, whatever it was you were doing, it wasn't befitting a girl-friend of mine."

"Oh, Hugo, you can't be jealous of me playing at a party!"

"Playing is one thing, necking another," he replied stiffly.

"Necking?" Laura laughed.

"Besides, I believe I've spoken to you before on the subject of Michael Flagg."

"But I didn't think it applied to party situations," she protested softly.

"Perhaps you should have asked me how I felt before deciding that."

"But Hugo, Michael's been a friend for years. We've never gotten to play and I've always been curious. We had an enjoyable session. Was it so wrong of me to feel a certain amount of affection, even tenderness towards him afterwards? Aren't those the emotions playing ought to elicit?"

"What you're saying makes perfect sense, but we both know

that it's sophistry. You've had a crush on Michael for years and I'm sure you allowed him any liberties he sought," he intuited. She dropped her eyes guiltily.

"I didn't think that it would make any difference," she offered.

"You mean so long as I didn't find out."

"Hugo?"

"What?"

"I agree that I was frivolous, but I meant no disrespect," she vowed sincerely. This simple declaration pleased Hugo but by no means satisfied him completely. Encouraged by his softened expression she pressed this small advantage to add, "Please tell me what I should do to make amends for my error." Her air was so contrite and supplicating that his irritation with her subsided.

"You should stop being so flirtatious," he suggested, in a tone that touched her conscience.

"But it's so hard to resist temptation," she explained.

"Are you saying you ever try?"

"No," she replied honestly. Her frankness brought a faint smile to his lips.

"You know, Laura, there are words for girls like you," Hugo murmured, resuming his stride.

"I remember a time you wouldn't have scrupled to use them," she observed, falling into step beside him.

"Well, love has taken its toll," he told her unselfconsciously.

She smiled and said, "Hugo, when I first met you, you were an insultingly cynical dom with ice water in your veins. But recently you've become so . . . almost human."

"Yes. It's been a real job of work."

"I understand you even apologized to Patricia tonight," Laura said as they went out to his car. "I remember the days when you'd be as likely to chug wine from a screwtop bottle as apologize to a submissive."

"Anyone can become rehabilitated, Laura."

"Hugo?"

"Yes, Laura?"

"I hope you aren't in danger of becoming *too* civilized."

Hugo gave her a look as he started his car, to which she returned such an impudent smile that he couldn't help but lean over and kiss her. "Just wait till I get you home, young lady," he warned her.

"What happens then?"

"Then you'll see how a civilized man deals with a flirtatious fiancée!"

They had driven half the way to Hugo's house in the woods before Laura had the nerve to echo, "Fiancée?"

"Don't panic, I believe in long engagements," Hugo soothed her. "However, you should know that fiancees are whipped much harder for inconstancy than mere girlfriends."

"The way Michael whipped Patricia tonight?"

"Hardly. You'd be screaming for mercy on stroke two."

"Then what kind of a whipping, Hugo?" she persisted, laying her head against his shoulder.

"Well, since you were courteous enough to assure me that you meant no disrespect, I think my belt will do."

As a grandfather clock tolled midnight in the hall, Sherman decided to retire for the evening to the well appointed bedroom Anthony had provided for him. Since his suite adjoined Diana's, he supposed he'd hear her come in and finally go to sleep just before dawn. Sherman wondered again why he had come. He could feel Anthony and Susan deftly conspiring to assist his case, but obviously Diana was a capricious child. Sometimes she seemed tantalizingly accessible, yet her sexual ambiguity restrained him. If she really preferred women, dare he ever suggest a culmination to their play more in keeping with his own ardent temperment?

Sherman emerged from the bathroom wrapped in a towel as a knock came on the door. He stumbled to the door without his glasses and opened it to admit Diana. The petite brunette, by now quite flushed with the evening's activities, slipped into the room and locked the door behind her immediately.

"Why, Sherman, is that you?" she exclaimed. "What a glorious physique you've been concealing under those baggy trousers! And I don't believe I've ever seen you without your glasses before. I suddenly feel faint."

"Hmmph!" said Sherman stiffly, stumbling back to the bathroom for his glasses. "It's a bit late for flattery," he told her, tightening his towel around his flat stomach and going to the dresser to brush back his wet blond hair. Diana came and sat down on the upholstered bench which fronted the cherry wood four poster.

"Are you angry with me, Sherman?" Diana asked, almost hopefully. When he looked at her in the mirror she returned a mischievous smile. Sherman's heart contracted but he remembered Susan's sage counsel and stared back at her coolly.

"I'm annoyed," he told her bluntly. "I came all the way from New York in response to your invitation and did not expect to spend the night being ignored."

"But, I'm here now, Sherman."

"So you are," he said, discerning an agreeable uneasiness in her countenance. Perhaps she did care how he felt.

"I'm very sorry I neglected you tonight," she said, in all humility, yet unable to keep from examining the exposed torso of her future lover for the first time. When he saw her looking at him, as a child eyes a dessert cart, he felt encouraged.

"I'm sure you're not sorry at all," he told Diana. "You just feel like playing with me now so you'll say whatever it takes."

"Well, Mr. Cooper, if you feel that way about me being here, I'll just leave you alone to brood and have Dennis massage my feet instead. I've been in these heels all night." Diana stood up suddenly and strode into her room without a backward glance.

With compressed lips and sudden determination, Sherman followed her and took the phone out of her hand, "You'll do no such thing, you selfish brat. Dennis has enough to do cleaning up after all the guests," Sherman scolded.

"I assure you, Dennis would regard the task of massaging my feet as a reward rather than a onus!" Diana declared haughtily.

"That does it. Come over here," he said, taking her by her smooth, bare upper arm and firmly turning her over his knee, using her vanity bench as a seat. "You're getting a good paddling."

Positioning her neatly and properly across his lap, he locked one arm around her waist and smoothed down her skirt over her round, little bottom. "Now obviously, you didn't need me here tonight," he said, spanking her a few times very firmly. "So why did you ask me to come?"

"Because I've missed you, Sherman," she hastened to reveal, turning to look at him.

"Oh?" This confession stayed his hand for a moment. Then

Sherman carefully folded back the skirt and white nylon petticoat and began to spank her in a measured and deliberate manner on the seat of her silk briefs.

"It was very rude of you and Susan to leave the meeting hall like that without telling anyone where you were going!" The series of hard smacks that followed emphasized his point. When he finished her bottom glowed.

"I'm sorry," she softly rejoined, grinding her silky muff against his thigh.

"I think you did that just to irritate me, Diana."

"I *was* naughty," she admitted.

"Yes," he sighed, pulling down her panties to her knees.

"Oh!" cried Diana.

"Modesty, Diana? From the girl who ground against a whipping post in front of twenty people while Marguerite Alexander flogged her?" Sherman paused to examine the condition of her luminous bottom and was satisfied to find her only lightly marked with pink stripes. "Was it at least a hard whipping, Diana?" he lay his hand upon her warm, tender bottom.

"Not excessively so," she replied.

"Well, you two did look very pretty together, but I prefer you in this position," Sherman told her and then proceeded to deeply redden her bottom with the palm of his hand. Relieving his frustration with Diana in this way excited Sherman and she soon became painfully aware of his manhood pressed against her tummy.

"Ow! Sherman, stop! Your penis is too hard and it's poking into me," she teased.

"You're going take this spanking seriously, young lady," he told her firmly, grabbing an oval wooden hair brush off the vanity with determination while at the same time shifting her weight on his lap to make her more comfortable. He then applied the back of the brush to her bottom ten times, fairly hard and fast. This shocked Diana almost to tears and she panted with emotion.

"This is what you need," he said, pressing the cool back of the brush against her warm bottom. She wriggled on his lap. "For as bad as you've been, I should spank you till you cry," he declared, remembering Susan's suggestion. Diana bit her lip and waited. As Sherman raised the brush she fantasized he was her husband. Under this illusion, the ten brush smacks that followed seemed even more poignant than the first and had an even stronger effect on Diana, whose rich imagination had transported her to her honeymoon night.

"Oh, Sherman, darling, would you like to take me?" she turned to look at him, her face aglow.

"Diana, you know I would." He turned her around on his lap and took her in his arms, forgetting all about making her cry.

"But, could you do it in the way I've dreamed about?"

"I could do it any way you like." He brushed her lips with his.

"Sherman, would you take me *forcefully*?" Diana petitioned breathlessly.

"I would, but you'll have to explain what you mean," he encouraged her.

"I want to pretend I'm being had against my will."

"But why against your will?" Sherman instinctively recoiled from the unaccustomed role of ravisher.

"Perhaps because I don't know what's good for me," Diana explained. "In my fantasy, my *husband* is determined to teach me about sex, but I resist his will. He responds by taking me by force, then forcing me to come."

"I suppose you realize that I'm not accustomed to taking women by force," Sherman said, on the verge of becoming offended.

"I promise not to struggle in the slightest," she assured him guilelessly.

"I might tie your little wrists together, just to make sure," Sherman said experimentally.

"Oh yes, please!" she murmured her assent to this plan, grinding on his lap.

"Stop that," he scolded, smacking her bottom. "I'm fed up with you."

"Because I'm so perverse?"

"Only where I'm concerned. You seem to yield to others instantly."

"Oh, no! Never instantly."

"You're a perfect kitten with Anthony Newton I notice."

"Are you jealous, Sherman?"

"Yes!"

"You needn't be. We've never made love. He's only made me come. And in the most childish way. You're the one who will have my true womanly favors.

"Your fantasies are dangerous, Diana." Sherman seemed troubled by the violent role she'd assigned him.

"Not if *you're* the only one who fulfills them."

"I should punish you severely for being such so reckless," he told her, parting her legs to insert his middle finger into her pussy up to the knuckle. He made her ride it until she almost came. However, he stopped teasing her just short of this and instead ordered her to strip naked.

"Take everything off?" she faltered. He folded his arms and nodded. Out of the dress and high heels, Diana appeared smaller, younger and much more vulnerable. "May I wear just two things?" she asked him.

"And what would they be?"

She handed him a pair of rubber-tipped, silver nipple clamps which she kept in a lacquered box at her bedside. "Susan puts them on me sometimes and I truly love them," Diana confessed.

Sherman almost flinched when he attached the clips to the fully erect, rose-hued nipples, which surmounted her firm, peach shaped bosom, but when he heard her sigh of pleasure, and observed the contented smile which then adorned her face, he knew that she had not exaggerated their power.

Now that she was naked except for her earrings, nipple clamps and the pearls around her throat he commanded her to assume the all-fours position on the bed. Piling pillows in front of her, he unceremoniously pushed her down over them, in which position her bottom was thrust uppermost.

"Put your wrists together in front of you, Diana," he ordered, taking a white tee shirt from the dresser and ripping it. Tying her wrists together with the soft, cotton shirt was the work of a moment and Diana regarded him with breathless expectation. Finally he discarded the towel which had girded his own loins and allowed her to observe, for the first time, the exact magnitude of his desire for her.

"Wondering how it's all going to fit into your tiny, little pussy, Diana?" Sherman got up behind her on the bed and casually rested his large, hard, faintly pulsing pink engine against her bottom while gently but deliberately parting her thighs, then her labia. Diana gave a little groan in response and attempted to assist him by arching her bottom even higher and spreading her legs apart wider. She wriggled and rolled her bottom under his cock until he slapped her hard and ordered her to be still. "You needn't worry," he assured her, "because I mainly intend to sodomize you."

"Oh!" she cried with genuine surprise, trying to turn around.

"Keep your head down," he ordered and insinuated the smooth, blunt head of his penis against her creamy vaginal slit until it was slick with her juices. Then spreading her labia deftly, he inched his cock inside her by slow degrees. Diana was so acquiescent, so wet and softly sighing that he nearly forgot that the objective was to convince her that she was being taken against her will. Yet he was reluctant to disappoint her in this, the only sexual request she had ever made of him. Also, there was the notion that if he let her down this evening, she might never allow him a second opportunity to impress her with his mastery.

"Four times you've put me off, Diana, but not tonight," he plunged in a little deeper with this phrase. Still she felt him holding back, even teasing her with his large cock. Pistoning in with a quick, shallow stroke, he succeeded in making her yearn for deeper penetration. He felt her open to him and attempt to engulf him more fully. In response he smacked her bottom sharply.

"You're too eager for a nice girl," he told her coolly. She sighed in such a way that he knew she liked the scolding.

"Stay loose and don't cling," he recommended. "Just let me get it wet." He injected one more inch into her velvet glove and at the same time spread her blushing bottom cheeks to completely expose her tiny rear aperture. "You'd better concentrate on getting very wet, young lady, because I can't be bothered trying to find any lube in the house at this hour and I intend to take your bottom in about three minutes."

He held her by the waist and penetrated her vagina a little more with each stroke, until he was smoothly pumping a full three quarters of his thickly veined erection into her slick canal.

"Your three minutes are up," he warned, smoothly reaching under her to press his palm up against her flat belly as he filled her gripping pussy with his cock.

"No," she protested weakly, "please don't take my bottom like that. You're much too big. I'll die. And besides, this feels wonderful!" Indeed, the smooth, firm pistoning of his cock in and out of her pussy had begun to send shocks of pure liquid excitement through her body, the likes of which she had never before experienced. She felt that she was truly being taken, and that surrender was sublime.

"I'm sorry," he said firmly, pulling free of her snug vagina and positioning his knob between her bottom cheeks, "but you need to be taken like this, to teach you humility." He pulled her apart and used his penis to lubricate her with her own copious girl juices. "And discipline," he added meaningfully, holding her open and pushing through the ring into her bottom. "No, Diana," he warned, "don't contract. I want you open. Do you understand?"

"Yes, sir."

"Resign yourself, Diana," he forced another inch of hard cock into her tight anal ring. "Before I'm done with you tonight, you're going to accommodate every inch."

"No, I couldn't possibly," she protested, only to be rewarded by a hard smack on either cheek. "Oh God!" she cried, clutching the pillows. Being spanked and sodomized at once was sexual splendor.

"Oh no?" Sherman now amused himself by alternately spreading her apart with his fingers, feeding his cock ever deeper into her bottom and spanking her cheeks hot pink. Diana pressed against the pillows in sheer abandon, tottering on the edge of climax every instant as the largest, hardest cock she could ever imagine nearly painlessly invaded her bottom.

"I'll teach you to invite me to a party then ignore me all night," he told her, beginning to pump her.

"I'm sorry!" she whimpered, scarcely able to catch her breath for panting and sobbing with emotion.

"You'd better be," he told her, giving her a smack. She was touchingly, achingly, throbbingly responsive to every dart and plunge of his cock in her bottom and small, convulsive spasms rippled through her tummy almost continuously throughout their first sex act.

"I hope you understand you're being taken," he said, causing her girlish climax to burst like the torrents of spring and bath her thighs with liquid pearls. It was all over for Sherman then too, her orgasm triggering his own.

Presently he pulled her against him on their sides and reached around to free her from the nipple clamps. Each one coming off elicited a groan which let him know how sore her nipples had become. But when he began to untie the binding on her wrists Diana pulled them against her protectively.

"No, Sherman, I want to sleep in bondage," she protested, nuzzling back against him.

"Well, that was easy," Sherman thought, his face buried in her perfumed hair. "What in the world was I worried about?"

"You see how you were worried for nothing?" Patricia chided Michael as they undressed for bed in his cottage.

"I have to admit, you mostly behaved yourself tonight," he was pleased to agree.

"Speaking of well behaved, I don't believe I've ever seen a more courteous group of ex-attachments than yours," Patricia commented thoughtfully. "None of them seemed even mildly piqued at my presence at your side."

"That's because they're all well rid of me and they probably feel sorry for you," he replied. "Of course, none of them know how diabolical you are."

"They might find out, if I moved to Random Point."

"Oh? Are you moving to Random Point?"

"I can't go back to Boston and leave you here with all these girls. You're probably an inch away from fucking Laura as it is."

Michael was grateful the lights were off when he felt the color rise in his face.

"You're wrong about that," he told her firmly, "but I wish you'd move here anyway."

"Michael?" she tucked her gossamer clad body against his nude one in the big wooden bed. "That was an awfully hard whipping you gave me." He took this as a hint to pull up her gown and stroke her bottom.

"I had to get your attention."

"I don't think any of the women approved."

"Really?" Michael seemed surprised.

"Laura said it seemed unduly stringent."

"Oh, she and her sister are famous for being cry babies,"

Michael told her, remembering Laura's delicate whimpers as he'd held her across his lap earlier that night.

"Marguerite looked shocked as well," Patricia pointed out.

"Well, that's just because she's so protective of other women."

"And your ex-wife seemed stricken with compassion for me."

"She's a baby too," he explained.

"Still, it *was* a very hard whipping," she murmured, content that she had proven her point.

"Yes, and you are the only one who could have taken it and liked it," he granted. "However, let's not forget that you're also the only one who deserves it."

"And what do you deserve, for being such an alley cat?"

"You."

Shadow Lane V
The Spanking Persuasion

AMBITION

ANTHONY NEWTON, NORMALLY the friend of every living creature, had taken a dislike to Patricia Fairservis whose best friend, Laura Random, was lodged as a perpetual guest in his house.

"I hope your friend Mrs. Fairservis is out of town," he remarked to Laura over breakfast that rainy Friday morning in early October.

Laura gave a guilty start. "Actually, she is coming by for an instant this morning," she admitted. He looked at her in exasperation. "I couldn't stop her when she found out you were in town."

"Well, never mind. I'll leave word that I can't be disturbed."

"Okay."

"You'd better see to it that I'm not disturbed either, young lady."

"Oh, Anthony, what have you got against Patricia?"

"Laura, I don't want to insult your friend, but she strikes me as someone who should be living in L.A."

"But, Anthony, doesn't the fact that Patricia's in the scene count in her favor?"

"Not unless I get to personally thrash her."

This was an unfortunate moment for Patricia to arrive, but she did so in a flurry of perfumed fur and silken, straight blonde hair the instant their exchange was concluded.

Anthony greeted her civilly, then drifted over to the piano to practice preludes while the girls chatted over coffee. Patricia's bright blue eyes kept drifting over to him, but the composer affected total absorption in the keyboard, forcing her to abandon any plan to engage him in conversation.

"Michael's going to some jackbooted, motorcycle cop convention in Boston tonight and I haven't been invited. What are you doing?" Patricia asked Laura at length.

"I'm having dinner with my ex-husband," Laura replied with a smile.

Anthony wished Laura had not said that, for it left him bufferless against an onslaught from Patricia. And sure enough when he looked up he caught the editor of *Cape Cod Style* eyeing him again. He began to pound the keyboard.

Patricia had just relocated to Random Point and was still unpacking. She would get restless alone in the lighthouse tonight and remember that he lived only a half mile up the road. Anthony sighed.

Patricia and Laura exchanged a glance. Laura shrugged and Patricia looked disappointed. It was apparent that Anthony Newton did not like her and this hurt Patricia's feelings. She prepared to depart in dejection, admonishing Laura to call her.

"Good-bye, Mr. Newton," Patricia said respectfully, having stayed a bare seven minutes.

"Oh, good-bye Patricia," he said pleasantly, suddenly stricken with guilt for not having been nicer to her.

Perversely enough, the moment Patricia left, Anthony began to miss her. All day the thought of her returned to him and he now considered what a joy it might be to feel that light, resilient girl across his lap.

By dinnertime, after Laura had left for her date and Michael had zoomed out of town on his motorcycle, Anthony began to think that if Patricia did stop by that night, he would not instruct Dennis to send her away.

When William Random placed Patricia as his tenant in the old lighthouse which surmounted Lilac Cove, she suddenly acquired the best view and most isolated playroom in all of Random Point. Especially on a stormy night.

Although she hadn't paid for any of it, Patricia's new domain was furnished with handsome pieces from Hugo Sands' shop, including a pretty little piano he'd just gotten hold of at an estate auction. Remembering the proximity of Anthony Newton, she'd begged for this particular piece.

When Hugo put pencil to paper after Patricia had ransacked his shop, he figured that *Cape Cod Style* owed him a year of full page color ads. Hugo didn't ask Patricia how she was going to explain this to her publisher, Randy Price, but knew that if her scheme backfired he could always reclaim the furniture and take the cost of his aggravation out of her hide.

The truth was that Anthony's instincts about Patricia were regrettably correct. Much that she did was in questionable taste and some downright unethical. Like promising Hugo free ads for the furniture.

Because Patricia had only ever seen her boss, Randy Price in a good mood and because he sometimes flirted with her, she felt confident of being able to get around him with sex should the need arise. Meanwhile, he liked what she was doing with the magazine, liked her, and was made of wealth, both old and new. The chances were he wouldn't even notice the free ad space going to Hugo's shop in *Cape Cod Style*.

Patricia had thought of calling Anthony Newton that evening, but the chilly reception she'd received that morning caused her to suppress the urge and organize her wardrobe instead. Anthony called her at eight-thirty.

"I just realized that you're new in the neighborhood," he confessed pleasantly, "and I was wondering whether you needed anything."

"Well," she stalled to gather her thoughts, "you might bring a corkscrew."

"That all?"

"And some computer cabling."

"How about dinner?"

"Sure. And bring that gorgeous English boy to serve it."

Anthony looked at the phone and shook his head, wondering if it was too soon to start regretting this. Nevertheless, an hour later he arrived with Dennis, dinner from the inn, wine from his cellar and all the computer cabling necessary to connect her equipment.

Meanwhile Dennis laid out dinner and spent the rest of the evening happily unpacking and putting away Patricia's things.

"How come you're being so nice to me tonight?" she asked as Anthony sat down at the fine old piano. "I thought you didn't like me."

"Who told you that?"

"I figured it out."

"I like you tonight," he candidly admitted, beginning *My Reverie*.

"But not this morning?"

"I apologize for my rudeness this morning. It's been bothering me all day." He stopped playing to give her his full attention and Patricia was shocked to realize for the first time what a really youthful millionaire he was.

"You did hurt my feelings," she reproached him. "I suppose you were afraid I was going to ask you about profiling the Cliffs again."

"Yes."

"You know, it's not easy filling a magazine every month," Patricia pointed out. Anthony sighed. "And I haven't had a really great celebrity house in three issues," Patricia continued. "Oh, please, Mr. Newton, won't you reconsider?"

Anthony started playing again. At length he coolly asked, "Besides the inconvenience, what's in it for me?"

"Free publicity," she answered lamely.

"Don't need it."

Patricia began to think that she would never gain her objective and had only succeeded in sanitizing a sexy moment when he suddenly startled her by saying, "Why don't you offer me something good?"

Taken aback she stared at him. "Okay. What did you have in mind?"

"Come over here," he said, pushing the piano bench away from the piano and sitting in the middle of it. When she came to him he took her by the hand. "Did you know that you need a good spanking?"

Patricia felt her face grow very warm as he gently pulled her down across his lap.

"I understand that our own Detective Flagg generally tends to you." Anthony patted her bottom lightly through her clinging black Capri pants. "Is that correct?"

"Yes," she replied, suddenly breathless.

"He must spank you lightly, however," Anthony remarked, bestowing a few warm up smacks on her taut, upturned behind.

"Oh no!" she disagreed.

"Are you saying you receive proper discipline?"

"Well, yes!"

"Then why don't you have better manners?"

Patricia had no answer for a question which made her feel ashamed. Anthony gripped her firmly by the waist and spanked her vigorously for several minutes, warming the entire surface of her bottom through the thin woolen pants with the palm of his hand.

"This spanking is from me and every other celebrity you've ever plagued in your life," he told her, sliding her pants down over her hips to her knees. Patricia's perfect bottom was wrapped in sheer black briefs through which her peach skin blushed. "You do have a beautiful bottom," he praised her, while stroking it.

"I hope you won't be very severe with me," Patricia flirted, wriggling on his lap in such a way as to provoke him.

"Why shouldn't I be? You annoyed me, didn't you?" He pulled her panties down.

"Oh! I'm very sorry!" She tried to cover her bare bottom with her hand but he firmly pushed it away.

"Really? I don't think you're a bit sorry. Especially as now you're going to get what you want from me."

"I was brought up to believe that I should have whatever I want, whenever I want it."

"Then you were brought up very badly," he declared, proceeding to spank her soundly. Anthony's arm was tireless and he spanked her for a very long time, with increasing firmness, until a rosy glow suffused the entire surface of her exposed skin and Patricia began to feel the punishment.

"Anthony?" she presently stopped him.

"Yes, my love?" he said with unexpected warmth, enchanted by her reactions. He had seldom met a woman who arched her bottom up to be spanked in quite the way Patricia did, or parted her legs so prettily to reveal her bedewed pubic mound.

"Have we begun?" she asked.

Patricia was not in a position to observe whether her impertinent remark amused him, however, after a delay of about five seconds he deliberately renewed his grip on her waist and began to spank her again, significantly harder and faster than before.

Now there was no question of a disciplinary element entering into their game. He had no idea of how much really hard spanking Patricia could take but he estimated her capacity at no more than three minutes at the current tempo. Patricia broke down and begged for mercy in one.

"Oh God, please stop! I'm sorry for whatever it is you think I did!" she yielded.

"You call that an apology?" he paused to examine her bottom and found it tinged a deep, rosy red by his hand but scarcely marked. She was obviously seasoned to hard lickings.

When he released her she pulled her pants and panties back up in a moment, then gave her entire attention to hugging him hard enough to make his ribs creak.

"That was so good!" She wriggled her well spanked bottom on his lap as he held her and enjoyed her girlish warmth.

"Then why did you put your pants back on?" he asked, patting her bottom through the capris and for the first time cupping her firm, little bosom through her cropped dove grey cashmere polo sweater. She caught her breath and squirmed on his lap, encouraging him to slip his hand up under it to caress the satiny skin of her flat midriff.

"Should I not have put my pants back on?"

"That depends on what you want to happen now."

"What do you want, Mr. Newton?"

"I want to send Dennis home."

"Dennis!" Patricia was suddenly shocked to realize that the English boy was still in her bedroom below them arranging her closet. "But, what if he heard . . ."

"Oh, he's heard it all before," said Anthony with a smile, leaving her briefly to find and dismiss his driver for the evening. After his departure Patricia was thrilled to observe that Dennis had unpacked every box.

"Where did you find that boy? I'm in love." Patricia marveled at the organization.

"He was working as a valet in a London hotel when I found him about four years ago."

"But, doesn't he question the strange noises Mr. Newton makes with his lady friends?"

"I think he finds it fascinating," Anthony confessed. "And of course, he's a great favorite with the girls."

"He does know how to make himself useful. Should I tip him?"

"Sure. Let him give you a foot massage."

"Really? He'd enjoy that?"

"Take a look in your closet at the shoes. It's his specialty."

Patricia saw and was duly impressed by the meticulous arrangement of her hundred pair of shoes.

"So you keep a submissive man on your staff," Patricia observed with journalistic interest.

"He's just a kid," said Anthony, wickedly accepting a cigarette when she lit one for herself. They were sitting in the window seat overlooking the surf-beaten cove as the storm continued to pelt the light house.

"Most dominant men I've met have an aversion to submissive ones."

"But you'll have to admit it's a great quality in an employee."

"You're a funny one," she smiled at his lack of concern. "But I suppose it does come in handy to have someone around to do all those tedious things for lady friends they might ask you to do otherwise."

"You mean like setting up people's entire desktop publishing systems in 29 minutes?"

"I do mean to officially thank you for that," she replied with a blush.

"You mean Dennis isn't the only one to get tipped?"

"Anything. Just name it," she promised, ready to go down on her knees to him in an instant.

"Take your clothes off," he told her, still lazily enjoying his annual cigarette. Patricia stripped with alacrity, fully displaying her willowy body to him for the first time. "Come over here and turn around. Let me look at you. You are something though." Anthony was greatly aroused by her willingness to spread her legs and expose herself to him. "I think you must be the naughtiest girl I've ever met," he told her, inserting his middle finger into her wet pussy up to the knuckle.

Presently he made her kneel on the window seat to take his cock from behind. The entry was made smooth by her excitement, and the precision pistoning that followed conformed exactly to Patricia's notion of what a ravishment should be. She only had to whisper, "Take me hard and fast," once for Anthony to fasten his hands to her waist and plunge in to the hilt, for she was an accessible girl. He fucked her for a long time, during which she climaxed beautifully for him and he for her.

After the inevitable conclusion of the window seat engagement, Patricia stretched out face down on the rug in front of the fire to slowly come to her senses. He was calmly stuffing his still throbbing organ back into his pants when she lifted her head to cry, "We forgot to use a condom, damn it!"

Anthony was taken aback by her just accusation and flushed with shame at his own irresponsibility.

Being Patricia she sat up and panicked. What was it about being in Random Point that made her forget everything sensible she ever knew about sex?

"God knows how many people you fuck!" she exclaimed, anxiously lighting a cigarette and pulling on a smoky blue silk wrapper. "I mean, you're in the theatre world, which is absolutely teeming with homosexuals!"

"Sure, but I'm not one of them," he calmly replied.

"How do I know that? I mean, you're pretty kinky," she accused, remembering the male submissive employee.

"Patricia, relax."

"Have you or have you not fucked pretty boys?"

"Patricia, you're getting hysterical over nothing."

Patricia looked sullen.

"Look, you're just as much of a risk as I am," Anthony pointed out.

"Why do you say that?"

"Well, you've got a husband, an alley cat of a boyfriend and I understand you also play with Hugo Sands."

"Why do you say alley cat? Who has Michael been fucking besides Marguerite?"

"Around this time last year he had an affair with Susan."

"Susan?" Patricia drew a blank.

"Susan Ross. My girlfriend. Cute little blonde. You must have seen her at the Pandora orientation meeting."

"That must have happened just before I met him," mused Patricia, her face burning with indignation. How dare these men of nearly 40 disport themselves with college girls!

"You *did* know about Michael and Susan, didn't you?" Anthony harbored an unexpected relish for sexual gossip.

"No," she exhaled with resentment. "He never told me."

"I can see why. You're a bit volatile."

"You think so?"

"Borderline uncivilized," Anthony sadly replied. "First thing I'd do with you if I were Michael would be to teach you some manners."

"Oh? And how would you do that?"

"Constant correction by the rod, my dear."

"And I suppose this little Susan Ross has impeccable manners?" Patricia felt ill at the memory of running into Susan in New York during the first trip with Michael. If what Anthony said was true, Michael had already had the little brat and the two of them were dissembling outrageously as they stood there before her and pretended to be no more than acquaintances.

"Susan's manners are dreadful," Anthony replied, "But her intentions are good. And since she's only 22, she has something of an excuse. You, on the other hand, should know better."

"So, tell me, do they still see each other?"

"Oh, I shouldn't think so. She's been through two more boys and a girl since that adventure."

"And none of this bothers you?"

"Well, I've had one or two adventures of my own." He smiled.

"I hope you took better precautions than tonight."

"You won't believe me, but I generally do."

"So you and Michael have shared two women," she mused.

"Three if you count Marguerite."

"Oh? You've been on that ride too, have you?"

"Now, Patricia, there's no call for vulgarity," he admonished her.

"Damn it, I've never found myself surrounded by so much competition in my life."

"You ought to think of them as friends instead," he counseled mildly.

"Perhaps you should thrash me until I understand that," Patricia suggested mischievously.

"Since I'm a firm believer in my friends being friends with each other, whenever possible, perhaps I will."

Patricia found Anthony witty and warm and wanted very much to keep him with her all night, to which he had no objection. The following morning, while she was giving him coffee and they were waiting for Dennis to come by with the car, she climbed onto his lap to give him a hug.

"Do you like me just a little bit now?" she asked.

"I like you a lot now," he frankly replied. "And you can shoot my house any time you like. The one in New York too."

"I can?" she hugged him harder, thrilled by the unexpected bonus.

"Well, of course," he replied, adding with the modest gratitude of a satisfied male, "after all, you gave me everything last night."

"So I can count you as my friend now?"

"Now and forever."

This was a promise that Patricia Fairservis was very glad to have obtained approximately one month later, when in the last week of October, she was summoned to Boston by the publisher of *Cape Cod Style.*

Patricia wasn't sure what to expect as she drove into town on that wet, chilly day, but she knew that it wasn't going to be good. Randy had his secretary arrange the meeting and the language of her message had been terse.

Patricia had dressed exquisitely in a wasp-waisted suit that enhanced every elegant curve. Her shoulder length hair had never been more like that of Veronica Lake and her face would have seemed quite as lovely if not for the anxiety reflected there.

Anyone who has entered a grim, old, office building on Water Street, Boston, particularly in the rain, knows an existential desolation only to be found in the works of Franz Kafka. Patricia stayed away from the corporate offices as much as possible, usually managing to arrange meetings with her boss at Maison Robert. But today *he'd* sent for *her*.

As soon as she walked into Randy's 8th floor office, she knew that all the perfect suits in the world were not going to move him. He glowered at her from behind his massive desk, the color keys for this month's issue of *Cape Cod Style* spread out in front of him. She noticed the spread on the lighthouse on top, along with the full color ad for Hugo's shop. Now her heart contracted, for she knew exactly why she was here.

"What the hell is this?" Randy picked up the spread on the lighthouse and flung it across the desk at her. Randy Price was a sharp, calculating, young entrepreneur who had inherited a good deal of money and made even more on his own. One of his enterprises was the magazine that Patricia had been editing for the past three years. As a money maker it broke even, but he liked being a publisher with the unique power it brought. Randy was an arrogant Harvard Business School predator whose manners were far worse than Patricia's. A gangster could not have spoken to her with more contempt.

"It's a spread on the Random Point lighthouse. Why? Is there a problem with that?"

"Yes, there's a fucking problem. I hate William Random and everything that relates to him, and his name appears on every other line."

Patricia looked at him with amazement. "How could I have known that? I mean, he's an architect on the Cape, we do a magazine on the Cape; he has a great house, I photographed it. I was just doing my job."

"Doing your job, huh? Does that include living in his damned house, like you say here in the article?"

"Well, I've just left my husband and I needed a place to live."

"So you entered into some sort of sweetheart deal where you'd get the house and he'd get the publicity. Is that it?"

Patricia colored. "No, not at all. I'm paying rent to live there. And I honestly thought the spread would be nice for the magazine. Randy, how could I know you hated William? This isn't fair."

"Stop whining and explain this." He threw the ad for Hugo's shop across the desk.

"It's an ad," she slowly replied, trying desperately to think of a legitimate reason why it had ever found its way into the issue. By now she was so flushed with adrenaline that she could barely stand on her legs. She sat down to gaze at the color keys, numb with desolation at her probable fate.

"Yes, I know it's an ad. It's a goddamned full page color ad that hasn't been paid for. Now what's it doing in the issue?"

Patricia felt faint as her brain tried to work. She'd never expected him to personally review the advertising receivables for the magazine. But now that she was forced to think of the ad in terms of dollars and cents, she realized that if the magazine had gone to press she would have effectively robbed approximately five thousand dollars from her boss. What in the world could she have been thinking of—promising Hugo full pages color ads?

"Oh, the ad is paid for," she told him within three seconds that seemed like a month to her tortured nerves.

"Oh? So where's the check?"

"I . . . have it in my files."

"Why hasn't it been turned in?"

"I thought I had turned it in. I'll bring it in tomorrow," she promised hastily.

"And what about this?" he indicated the lighthouse spread. "You have something else to fill the space?"

"Anthony Newton's letting me shoot his house. It'll only take me a couple of days to do the photos," she replied shakily.

"Anthony Newton's house will do. Okay, you've got two days to get me some prints and the story. And you'd better produce that check for the ad at the same time. Otherwise, you're not only getting fired, but I'm going to have you prosecuted for accepting payola while in my employ. Now get the hell out of here."

Patricia had not been hit with a bag of oranges, as in *The Grifters*, she only felt that way as she stumbled back out of the building and found her car. Where was she going to get five thousand dollars to give Hugo in order to make him write the check to Randy? Michael was moonlighting just to make his bills. Patricia's soon to be ex-husband would have given her the money, but Professor Fairservis was a gregarious creature who loved to wine and dine his friends and consequently always ran in debt.

Patricia sobbed at the wheel half way back to Random Point as she reviewed all of the humiliating and nearly insurmountable tasks before her. First, she had to find five thousand dollars. Then she had to admit to Hugo Sands that her boss had demanded payment for the ad. Hugo would be furious and require the return of his costly furniture immediately. Then she had to go to William Random (to whom she had not yet paid her first month's rent) and admit that the spread on the lighthouse would never appear in *Cape Cod Style* because her boss appeared to hate him. Then she would have to quickly come up with some rent (and the rent was high for the tower duplex) to prove to William that she wasn't scamming him as well.

Hugo and William. Two painful interviews. And, of course, she would have to immediately get her cameraman out to Newton's house to shoot and rush the film back to Boston the next day, while writing the article overnight. And what a dreadful night that would be as she tried to think of what she could do to raise the money she needed to prove to Randy that the so-called sweetheart deal between herself and Hugo had been merely a figment of his imagination.

By the time she got back to Random Point Patricia was dry-eyed but still on the edge of tears whenever she thought of the ordeals she confronted. Choosing between the least of the evils before her, she went to see William first.

William, whom she found working at home, was astonished to learn that the publisher of Patricia's magazine was his old enemy Randy Price. He explained that he had been at odds with Randy since prep school. In recent years, Randy's unscrupulous business practices had led to the corruption of one of his most trusted employees, namely Damaris Perez Flagg.

"You mean Randy had dealings with Michael's ex-wife?" Patricia cried in astonishment.

"She was my secretary and I was very fond of her. But she had a drug problem at the time, and Randy tempted her to bring him information in exchange for payoffs. I asked Michael to help me trace the company leak and he, of course immediately discovered Damaris meeting Randy."

"So, Michael's ex-wife was bad. Really bad."

"She was bad," William smiled. "But she's been completely reformed for years."

"Michael is drawn to bad women," Patricia mused.

"Who isn't?"

"Well, what happened then?"

"Well, we were able to spoil Randy's last attempt on my company's job bids, to which he retaliated by seducing my wife."

"My friend Laura has had sex with Randy?" Now Patricia was astonished.

"It's kind of like a soap opera, isn't it? At any rate, the next time

Randy and I met, we commemorated the reunion with a fist fight. So you can see why he wasn't crazy about the idea of publicizing my lighthouse renovation in his magazine."

When Patricia intimated that she could lose her job over this, William was all concern, which charmed Patricia, who had a definite need to stall on the rent as long as she could now.

Hugo was far less compassionate as she tumbled the whole sordid mess out before him in his shop at closing time. Seeing she'd had a horrible day, he took her into his office and gave her a whiskey. She gulped it and gasped, then subsided on a leather sofa to await his reaction.

"So unless you get a check from me for the ad, Randy will know that you were lying and indeed on the take."

"Yes," she replied and hung her head, then lifted it to promise, "But if you save me this once, I swear I'll pay you the money back immediately!"

"How do you propose to do that?"

"I'll sell my car."

"You mean the Mercedes is actually yours to sell?"

"Well, more or less. I can get some dealer to pick up the notes and still clear five grand."

"That sounds a bit drastic. Don't you know anyone who can cover you?"

"No."

Hugo couldn't resist lecturing her. "Don't you see Patricia that this has been coming a long time? Luxury is an addiction. You're living above your means. Take a lesson from Emma Bovary. You've very nearly come to ruin today."

"Yes, sir," she agreed.

"I want every stick of furniture returned to my shop."

"I thought you would," she sighed.

"But I don't expect you to sell your car," he told her.

"I can't think of any other way to raise that much money."

"Why don't you try to persuade *me* to pay for the ad?" he dared her, with a certain tone to his voice that suddenly introduced sex into the equation of Patricia's professional disgrace.

"Could I?" She looked at him with sudden hope.

"Yes. You could agree to be my slave every Sunday for a month."

"Your slave, Hugo? What does that entail?"

"Oh, I have lots of things for you to do. I have a stock room that needs cleaning. Letters and articles to enter for my next issue. A mailing to stuff. A little writing. That should work off about half the debt."

"What about the other half?"

"For the other half you will serve dinner to a select party as my well behaved parlor maid. Then you will be given to my most awesome male dominant guest for his private use. Need I add that you will be severely whipped? Accept my terms and I'll give you the check for the ad and call it a good bargain."

"I accept," Patricia said before thinking.

As it turned out, Patricia had ample time to fulfill Hugo's requirement of the payment of the debt and didn't have to wait until Sundays. As soon as she came in with the check and the spread, she was summarily fired by Randy Price, who considered Patricia's relations with William Random as consorting with the enemy.

This was the second time she had driven back to Random Point from Boston in one week with tears in her eyes. Now she was off the hook with Randy. He wasn't about to put a contract out on her because the ad had been duly paid for. And things were pretty square with her and Hugo ever since she had agreed to his terms of reimbursement.

The fact that Hugo Sands had a heart did not escape her, and she would be grateful to him for the rest of her days for not exposing her to Randy's vengeance. William Random would wait a reasonable amount of time before throwing her out of the lighthouse since she would tell him she had lost her job as soon as she got back. Michael was bound to be completely unsympathetic, but at the very least, he'd feed her until she got another job or lined up freelance.

Michael was on the night shift for a few days and Patricia didn't bother to wake him with news like this. The next morning she awoke feeling wretchedly guilty and utterly at a loss as to what to do first. What she really needed was a thrashing, she thought, while having her morning bath, just to take her mind off the reality of what had happened and expiate her guilt. Since she was in a funk and had no focus, Patricia dressed in jeans, a flannel shirt and work boots and went directly to Hugo to report for work.

Hugo was fairly astonished to see Patricia first thing on a Friday morning in his shop and dressed like this. He'd never seen her in any outfit other than a smart business suit or cocktail dress and was charmed.

"I didn't have to wait until Sunday. Where's the stock room?"

As Hugo led her to the back, she confessed to him all that had happened since he'd given her the check. Hugo had seen her dismissal coming and said nothing. Instead he explained to her that some of the pieces got polish, while others needed only a rub with a rag. The floor, wall hangings and suspended pieces had to be thoroughly dusted. He expected every inch of the place to be gone over. He left her supplies and told her he'd come and get her when it was time for lunch.

Patricia began by sweeping the floor and there was a lot of it. She pushed all of the furniture to one side of the room first, and then back again to get both sides properly swept. This took about an hour and Patricia was nearly done when Hugo came back with coffee and saw her pushing the last piece, an enormous credenza, back into place.

"Patricia, what the hell are you doing?"

"I had to move everything to sweep."

"Don't tell me you've been dragging all this stuff around the floor?"

She stared at him.

"You didn't tell me not to move things," she protested helplessly as he took her by the wrist, found a convenient seat and turned her over his knee with exasperation.

"These items are delicate," he told her, warming the seat of her jeans with the palm of his hand. "You could have damaged something."

A hard spanking on the seat of her jeans was enough to make her tingle and think of nothing but sex until lunch.

The following day Michael brought back the furniture from the lighthouse in Hugo's truck. The youthful detective was not happy about spending his day off moving furniture, nor was he pleased at any of the recent developments in his girlfriend's career. Hugo was quick to notice the coolness in Michael's demeanor as he carted in merchandise.

"What's with Michael?" Hugo found Patricia in the small flagstone garden behind the shop having a smoke.

"Oh, he isn't talking to me," Patricia admitted unhappily. Hugo sat down beside her on the stone bench. "He says that my profligate lifestyle has led me to the brink of disaster."

"I could have told you that."

"You did. But you said it with a great deal more civility," Patricia squeezed Hugo's hand with affection.

"What else?"

"Oh, I got a pretty good lecture on a wide range of topics. For example, were you aware that influence peddling is a crime?"

"Is he upset with you for losing your job?"

"Yes," she hung her head.

"Don't worry, you'll get more freelance than you can handle. And in the meantime, you've got enough friends around here to see you through. The important thing is that you're with us."

"Hugo, what a nice thing to say!" Patricia felt a glow suffuse her entire body at his warmth. She hugged him briefly then ran back out front to help unload the rest of the furniture. Now she felt much better. Michael continued to glower, but she stopped noticing. Presently he finished the unloading and was about to walk home, when he decided to take Patricia aside and talk to her. They went back into the stock room.

"Patricia, I've been thinking," he said, making her heart strain for fear in her bosom. *"Am I getting the kiss off?"* she wondered.

"Yes, Michael? What have you been thinking?"

"That you'd better give up the lighthouse and come live with me to save expenses."

"Why Michael, that's vastly obliging of you, but considering what a perfect brute you've been today, the idea of being thrown on your charity is somewhat less than appealing. Excuse me." She stepped past him, picked up her rubbing rags and oil and attacked a hope chest zealously.

"You know Patricia, it was pride that brought you to this pass. Isn't it time you came down off your high horse?"

Patricia merely continued to polish furniture.

"Anyway, I'm not offering you charity. Just move in now and share expenses when you're able to."

"I would move in with you as a last resort only." She reflected bluntly.

"I see. Well don't do me any favors," he fumed, ready to leave.

"Okay," she returned pleasantly. Michael left in a black mood. He'd been worrying about her alone in the lighthouse with her mattress on the floor, but now he told himself he didn't give a damn. Fancy her calling him a brute when he hadn't even laid a finger on her. When he really should have gotten out his razor strop and tanned her backside for losing her job. He decided to teach her a well deserved lesson by not calling her for at least a week, or as long as he could hold out.

Meanwhile, Patricia, who rather enjoyed her mattress on the floor with the full view of the stars above her, had made a similar resolve. Besides, she was much too busy doing the editorial work which Hugo had given her to think about Michael. Happily, the few pieces of furniture she had brought with her still supported her computer system, and she was able to work undisturbed with the ocean before her.

The erotic material Hugo gave her to work on was a welcome change from dry, architectural writing and kept her in heat the entire week. As with the stock room reorganization, Patricia gave the editorial job her full attention and did an exemplary job for Hugo.

In the middle of the week, when she was halfway through her task, Anthony Newton stopped by and was shocked to note the absence of her furniture. He had walked in at about one in the afternoon on a chilly, rainy day, which called for the largest fire Patricia could build.

She had just finished transcribing a crude but effective spanking story and eagerly related the high points to Anthony, who found it impossible not to become infected with her enthusiasm immediately. Especially when Patricia confessed that she not only needed but deserved to be chastised severely for losing her job. No one had yet taken the time to do this properly, and she felt quite amazed that such a momentous error could go unpunished, considering that she was all but surrounded by dominants.

Never one to shirk a responsibility, Anthony hastened to occupy one of her two remaining straight-backed chairs to administer a very sharp correction to Patricia, dwelling with particular warmth on the ramifications of losing one's job in today's economy. Patricia took as long and hard a spanking as he could give and afterwards thanked him for his trouble in characteristic style. Now she felt Michael's absence even less and returned to her work with renewed energy.

Once the editorial work was turned in Patricia began to plan the final phase of her payment to Hugo, which was the execution of the dinner party. A glance at the guest list was enough to convince Patricia that the hardest task was before her, for Hugo had assembled to observe and enjoy her humiliation: Laura Random, Anthony Newton, Susan Ross, Marguerite Alexander and finally, the mystery dominant, Victor Kesselring.

Laura understood that Hugo was still determined to sell Victor that set of furniture he'd obtained for him and was now going to use Patricia as bait. Since Laura had botched the sale so badly the first time, she warned Patricia about Victor with much less trepidation than she felt for her friend. But she discovered to her relief that Patricia cared nothing for the whipping; her main concern was in the humiliation of having to wait on both Marguerite and Susan, both of whom she considered rivals for Michael's affections.

Patricia went to Anthony and asked to borrow Dennis for the night to help her cook and serve at Hugo's party. This favor was readily granted and Dennis was sent the day before the dinner to assist Patricia in the marketing.

Determined to make this an occasion of personal achievement rather than shame, Patricia bought the Chez Panisse cookbook and set out to prepare the ultimate meal.

Victor had been surprised to receive the message from Hugo promising a special treat the next time he passed through Random Point and made it his first stop on returning to the states. When he was told, over his first drink upon arrival, of the slim blonde with the high pain tolerance who was working off a penance to Hugo, Victor almost smiled with anticipation.

Patricia looked completely delectable in her formal maid's outfit, black seamed stockings and high heeled Mary Janes. She met no one's eyes but kept her eye on every dish, every glass of wine and water, expertly assisted by Dennis at every turn.

The dishes were very well received. So much so that no one thought of anything other than doing honor to them one by one. Patricia watched from the doorway with tension. The guest of honor, Victor, seemed to be enjoying his meal. Dennis knew what wines to fetch from Hugo's cellar to complement each course.

Marguerite chatted gaily the whole time to Victor, pausing at the outset to look at Patricia and pronounce the word, "Charming," as she took in every dainty aspect of her costume and demeanor. Susan stared at Patricia and blushed for her as she took away the dishes of the first course. Hugo had taken Susan and Laura aside before Victor's arrival and warned them about what they might see that evening.

"Now, I don't want any nonsense out of you two about Patricia," he warned them sternly. "She's doing this to pay off a large debt to me and she's fine with the whole thing. I know you two delight in obstructing justice, but tonight your intervention will not be necessary." He eyed both sisters with gravity.

"Yes, sir," said Susan.

Hugo looked at Laura.

"I won't interfere," she promised solemnly.

"And you, young lady," Hugo looked at Susan, "don't go falling in love with Patricia and offering to take her place or anything noble like that. As Laura can tell you, Victor is a martinet and Patricia is a lot better suited to his methods than either of you are."

"I won't say or do a thing," Susan promised meekly.

"So, what are we supposed to do, Hugo?" Laura ventured to ask.

"I know I'm asking the impossible, but just behave yourselves."

Between dessert and brandy Susan and Laura snuck out to the kitchen to congratulate Patricia on the splendid job Dennis and she had done.

"It was this darling boy," Patricia said candidly, locking her arms around the trim, aproned waist of the English boy and placing her fair head on his snowy collar. "He did 90% of the work." Dennis reddened deeply but looked quite pleased at the affectionate praise from this beautiful, poised lady who was for some lark playing the role of servant girl that evening.

Susan smiled at Dennis too, but for that moment he was only aware of Patricia. Susan and Laura exchanged a look. Meanwhile Patricia downed a glass of wine and took a good look at Susan Ross, wondering whether she knew that Anthony had been her lover as recently as three days before. Patricia had hardly eaten all day and the wine hit her fast.

"So," she asked Susan, "why are you involved with all these older men?"

Susan was not expecting this type of address and looked at Laura in surprise.

"All?" said Susan.

"I mean Anthony and . . . Michael."

Marguerite Alexander had entered the room in time to hear this last exchange and the statuesque redhead was less than pleased by it.

"Yes, Susan, do tell us why you must have *so many* of our men," Marguerite accepted a glass of wine from Patricia as she joined the group.

"Come to think of it," said Laura to her sister, "you *have* had them all!"

"Who else besides Michael and Anthony?" Patricia demanded.

"Well, my ex-husband William, our lawyer Sherman, and of course, our host, Hugo," Laura supplied the names while counting off fingers. "That's five that we know of."

"Tell you what, cutie," Patricia proposed flippantly, "Since you're only lacking one for six of the best, I'll let you have Victor for nothing."

"No thank you," said Susan, having received a complete description of Laura's night with Victor from her sister. Besides, even if she had known nothing at all about Victor, she didn't like the look of him and the way he never smiled. Patricia had been having these exact thoughts all through the dinner, for although she seemed to look at no one, she had looked long and hard at Victor Kesselring and had taken an instant dislike to him.

"Here," Laura handed Patricia something to smoke. "You'd better get your head straight before you go up."

"But don't drink too much more," said Marguerite, removing the wine bottle from Patricia's reach, as she was already on glass two. "If he puts you in bondage you'll be in trouble if you're drunk."

"Oh, have you played with him too?" Patricia looked at Marguerite with interest. Although the stunning, bespectacled book seller was Patricia's principal competitor, being near her like this Patricia felt somehow more excited than jealous, for a curious attraction had begun to operate on Patricia for Marguerite.

Certainly it was difficult for anyone who loved beauty to remove their eyes from the heavenly contours of Marguerite's body under the midnight blue crepe sheath, least of all Dennis who had been virtually paralyzed with adoration ever since Marguerite strode into the room on her 5-inch heels. Dennis had met Marguerite on several occasions over the years and her presence never failed to overwhelm him with the ardent desire to serve women forever.

"Victor can be a very difficult man to please," said Marguerite tactfully. "Are you sure you have to do this?"

"Honor demands it," said Patricia, touched by Marguerite's concern. "I was a very bad girl and ran up a big debt with Hugo. This is the last thing I have to do to pay it off."

"I wish you didn't have to," said Laura compassionately. "He's the most horrid man in the universe."

Patricia stared at her girlfriend with some alarm and would have eagerly continued the discussion of Victor with the three girls, but Anthony came to find them and bring them back.

"Victor's brought back some hardcore B&D videos from Europe and Hugo's going to put them on." Anthony announced, taking Susan out of the room.

"I'd better get back too," said Laura, kissing Patricia and squeezing her waist. "Just remember you *can* say mercy if it gets too rough."

"Marguerite, I'm getting scared. What should I do?" Patricia asked sincerely, smoking hard.

"Just seduce him as soon as you can," counseled the redhead wisely, embracing Patricia. "And by the way, you cinch magnificently." Then she too left. Patricia told Dennis to go in with the cognac while she freshened up.

"Oh God," she said, falling into a chair, "my feet hurt already! I hope he doesn't put me in stand-up bondage."

Dennis hesitated to leave her at these riveting words, but forced himself to do so. When he returned an eternity later, he was thrilled to see her still sitting and smoking and drinking another glass of wine. He immediately got to his knees before her and begged to be allowed to massage her poor, tired feet for a few minutes. Patricia was happy to allow him this liberty and watched with interest as he tenderly removed her shoes and began to massage her stockinged feet, which were narrow and elegant.

Patricia began to enjoy herself greatly under the English boy's skillful manipulations and decided to reward him by pulling up her skirt to mid-thigh and allowing him to admire her black stocking tops, lace suspenders and the milky white skin which surmounted them. Dennis grew dizzy with excitement at this mark of the lady's favor and blushed to the roots. Patricia found this charming and impulsively raised her skirt even higher to allow him a glimpse of her sheer black panties as he continued to massage her feet. It was at this interesting juncture that Hugo walked in. Patricia immediately pulled down her skirt and Dennis busied himself in strapping her back into her Mary Janes.

"Patricia, why don't you join us?"

"Like this, Hugo? Or should I change?"

"What have you got on under there?" Hugo asked, virtually ignoring Dennis, who swiftly completing his task, immediately busied himself at the sink.

"Why, a very sexy corset, of course," replied the slightly intoxicated blonde, who had been immensely cheered by the attentions of Anthony's young driver.

"Show me," said Hugo, folding his arms and waiting. Patricia pertly unbuttoned her uniform and let it drop to the floor, revealing a perfect black satin waist cinch that gave her a shape out of *Sweet Gwendolyn*. "My God, Patricia, have you been laced that tightly all night?" he walked up to her, turned her around and saw that she had her laces pulled to the utmost extreme.

Now that he mentioned it, mused Patricia, her back had begun to ache and she felt a bit faint, but all of the discomfort had been worth it when she remembered how no one could take their eyes from her swaying, wasp-waisted torso as she'd served.

Hugo quickly unlaced and slightly loosened her stays, then retied the laces. "There! That should feel a little better." Patricia took a slightly deeper breath than she had taken all evening and thanked him profusely. "You can go in like that."

Patricia entered the room where they all were. The lights had been dimmed and the focus was on the hard S&M video Victor had brought back from Germany. Hugo had told her that Victor's submissives were always required to kneel in his presence once the scene had begun, and she acknowledged that on entering the room, the scene had begun. So she went to her allotted place and knelt, aware of everyone's eyes on her exposed, corseted figure. Victor was pleased by the extreme slenderness of her frame, so greatly enhanced by the fully boned cinch. A sheer bra and scrap of panties revealed as much as they concealed and everyone could see that Patricia's cherry nipples were erect.

For a few moments Patricia became absorbed by the events being portrayed on the screen. She had never seen European videos before and was shocked. Patricia did not like the movies and wished she was back in the kitchen with Dennis. In fact, she had pretty much decided that she wanted to marry Dennis someday when Victor suddenly stood up and told her to go upstairs and wait for him in the room Hugo had set aside for his use.

After Victor and Patricia had gone upstairs, Susan and Laura volunteered to help Dennis clean up in the kitchen while Marguerite, Anthony and Hugo stayed where they were to watch the videos with decadent enjoyment.

"On your knees, girl," said Victor when he caught Patricia lounging in a chair in Hugo's splendid guest bedroom.

"Sorry, master," she replied without true repentance, getting into the required position. For her pertness she had her face promptly slapped. Although the blow wasn't hard enough to make her ears ring, it was more than a tap and the gesture brought tears to her eyes.

"Don't be flip with me," he told her, going into a cupboard for equipment and coming out with cuffs and a thin lashed flogger. Patricia held her hand to her cheek and stared resentfully at the floor. "And don't whimper," he told her, disdainfully taking her hand away from her face. Victor sat on a chair beside her and asked for her wrists, which he quickly cuffed. Patricia deliberately held her wrists taut to give herself some escape room. If Victor noticed he made no comment. She would hold her place with or without the cuffs. The bondage was merely a symbol of his control.

He then unceremoniously pulled her up to a standing position by the cuffs and from there to the edge of the big, richly covered bed, where he bent her over with her arms in front of her and her feet on the floor. Passing a rope through a loop in the wristlets, Victor pulled her arms taut and attached the end of the rope to a hook under the bedstead. Now she lay face down with her bottom thrust up over the edge of the bed. Going behind her, Victor roughly pulled her little panties down and off, separated her legs as far apart as they would go with a leg spreader bar and cuffed her ankles to it. Now she was bent over the bed with her bottom and pussy fully spread and exposed.

Victor took up the flogger and began to whip her bare bottom with slow, hard, deliberate strokes, stinging her with the lash tips each time. Patricia was prepared for the initial onslaught of whipping to be severe and refrained from screaming as best she could. But when she did not cry or sob, as he was used to girls doing, Victor increased the intensity of the whipping, swinging harder and faster and scoring her delicate skin with dark red lash marks each time his weapon descended to wrap her vulnerable hips.

"Mercy, master, that's too hard!" she cried, within moments of his beginning.

"Nonsense," he scowled, stopping momentarily to examine her already marked bottom and give it a slight rub.

"I swear it is!" she looked at him with trembling lips.

"Are you telling me how to discipline you?"

Patricia turned away from him and bit back the response which naturally sprang to her lips. He proceeded to whip her again, every bit as hard as before. She concentrated on submitting, trying to make sense of the pain by remembering how bad she had been to deserve this. She thought about what Randy might have done to her if Hugo hadn't bailed her out with the check and that helped for a second or two. But surely Hugo never meant for her to be beaten this violently.

"Master, please! I can't take it this hard!" she cried, turning her upper torso as much as she could to look at him. He paused to return her glance scornfully.

"I thought you'd agreed to submit to discipline tonight."

"Discipline yes, torture no!" she protested, still in shock from the white-hot pain of the whip on her bottom.

"Very well, if you can't take a proper whipping, we'll switch to something milder." He unbuckled his belt as he said this, drawing it out of his trouser loops, then doubling it and holding the buckle end in his hand. Patricia could only imagine his definition of the word mild, but subsided on the bed.

The moment he started to strap her Patricia realized that her disciplinarian was out of control. She remembered how much wine Dennis had poured for the guests during dinner and how the brandy had gone around twice in the den.

"Please sir, I beg for mercy!" she said again, after the first six strokes fell crosswise upon her well-whipped bottom. He seemed to be exerting the full strength of his arm and Patricia knew there was no need for this. Each stroke provoked a cry from her that was heard by all the company below.

Victor paused, as though to reward her with the mercy she sought. But the instant he saw the tension go from her shoulders, he treacherously stepped up behind her and gave her the end of the strap straight down the middle of her bottom, so that the very tip of it struck her spread sex. Now the scream that issued from Patricia was enough to cause the hair of everyone below to stand on end, especially that of Hugo's cat.

For Patricia it was all over. Without waiting to ask for permission she jerked her right wrist out of the leather cuff and then freed the other. Flipping over onto her back, with the leg spreader still attached to her ankles and a glare of bitter anger in her eyes, she trembled and sobbed her way into a sitting position and ripped off the ankle cuffs. Then she got to her feet, and dashing the tears from her eyes, first backhanded Victor across the face as hard as she could, then extended her hand for the strap.

"Give me that belt, you miserable coward," Patricia demanded, transfixing him with her gaze. He handed her the belt. "Take my position across the bed," she ordered, in a violent passion. "No! Pants down first, you despicable bully. I'm going to teach you a lesson you'll never forget!"

Victor got into position immediately, with a look of fascinated admiration on his cruel face that made Patricia angrier than before.

"How dare you strike me like that!" she asked and without waiting for an answer began to strap Victor's thighs and buttocks rapidly and with all of the strength in her arm. That the 46-year-old Genevan was toned and fairly well proportioned she noticed but hardly cared about. She didn't care how she aimed or what she hit either. Her only purpose was to hurt and humiliate him as much as he'd done her.

"You never strike a woman there, do you understand me, Victor?"

"Yes, mistress," he moaned as the leather cut into his flesh.

"Spread your legs," she commanded and returned the favor he had done to her with the end of the belt. He could hardly remain stoic when she struck his balls like this, but his reaction was muffled by the bedclothes in which he hid his face.

Now she returned to his buttocks and legs and whipped him from his hipbones to his calves.

"I don't know or care how you treat your European sluts, but you're in America now, and when you have the good fortune to be given a well-bred submissive to play with, you treat her with kid gloves! Do you understand me, you sad, pathetic excuse for a human being?" When she felt herself growing dizzy with the exertion she ordered him to get up.

"Unlace me. Now!" she snapped, turning her back on him with utter disdain.

"Yes, mistress," he replied, going to work with nimble fingers on her laces and finally freeing her from the corset. She meanwhile had undone the garters and was happy she had chosen stay-up stockings, for she had to lose the corset at once or faint.

Patricia did not let Victor know what a rapturous relief it was to be unlaced, but instead ordered him to hold her panties for her to step back into. Now garbed in her heels, sheer black hose, panties and bra, Patricia demanded the whip.

"Fold my corset properly and lay it on the dresser. Then I want you entirely naked with your arms around the bedpost. That shall serve as my whipping post and and I shall whip you until exhaustion overtakes me!"

When Victor complied with these instructions, unable to refrain from drinking in every inch of her newly sprung dominant beauty with his eyes, she cuffed him to the bedpost and attached his ankles to the spreader bar in the same way he'd done to her. Then Patricia stuck her head out of the room and in a loud, clear voice called, "Would someone send me Dennis? I want him!"

The three in the TV room who were still watching B&D videos did not hear Patricia's call, but the three in the kitchen did and Dennis looked at Laura and Susan for instructions.

"Go to Patricia if she wants you," Susan encouraged the handsome, blushing boy, who immediately ran up the stairs to the room where Patricia was. She met him in the hall and told him to go back downstairs and bring her the apron she had worn to serve dinner in and a tray of ice cubes.

"And when you come back, come directly in, my darling," Patricia told Dennis, briefly rumpling his neat brown hair. Dennis almost tumbled down the stairs to obey her strange commands, with the image of her remarkably beautiful body imprinted on his mind forever.

When he got back to the kitchen the girls were agog to hear what was going on. But Dennis couldn't stop to talk. He grabbed what she had asked for and ran back upstairs. Knocking discreetly at the door, then entering as he'd been bid, Dennis was completely unprepared for the sight meeting his gaze.

By now Victor had been blindfolded with his own handkerchief. Patricia stood by his side, holding the whip.

"Come in, Dennis. Oh, you brought the frilly apron. Good!" Patricia took the apron and tied it around Victor's waist, making a bow at the back. "I see you're shocked, young man. But never fear. You've only been brought up here for an object lesson. You see, our guest, Mr. K., is a very bad man. He entirely disrespects women and to prove it, he's abused three of the worthiest women you know: Laura Random, Marguerite Alexander and me."

Patricia allowed Dennis to watch in amazement as she flogged the aproned banker until his flesh was fully mottled purple, black and blue.

"And to think that he treated me so badly after we gave him such a wonderful dinner!" Patricia lamented, flashing Dennis an intimate smile. "Now that I think of it, Victor, you've yet to thank me for the beautiful dinner," Patricia said with some impatience.

"Thank you, mistress!"

"Comes a bit late. But just to show I have no hard feelings for your neglect, I've decided to give you a special treat! Ices for dessert!" Patricia broke the ice cubes into a bowl and flashing the wondering Dennis a grin, approached her victim.

"I have an entire bowl of ice here, Victor," she slide a cube over the surface of his buttocks, "enough to cool your ardor for tormenting women who are your superiors." She then proceeded to insert the ice cubes into his rectum any which way she could. If her intent had been to arouse him, she might have supplied herself with some lubricant to ease the way and stopped at three or four.

But her intent was to punish her persecutor, so she gave him the entire tray all at once while Dennis watched.

"That will be all, Dennis. Leave me alone with the ridiculous creature now."

Dennis was only too happy to be dismissed at the present moment, the situation becoming far too esoteric for an innocent instep worshipper like himself. Although the fact that Patricia had turned to him—Dennis—for assistance, in the very moment of her metamorphosis from submissive to dominant, was a delight to the sensitive boy.

As he went down to the kitchen Dennis reflected upon how much more exciting his life had become with the entrance of his mistress and her friends into his employer's life. Not that he ever imagined or expected to see anything like he'd seen tonight, a revelation he intended to share with no one.

"Hurt, Victor?" Patricia inquired, with a happy smile, as she swung a heavy wooden paddle against his bottom repeatedly. By now Victor was heavily marked and made distinctly uncomfortable by the ice she had forced into him. Patricia paused in the punishment to grab him by his very large, fully erect, uncut cock and squeeze it as though she were wringing out a sponge. "And to think I was actually prepared to let you put this in me!" she reflected with amazement. "I suppose that I should thank you for apprising me of your true nature before I made a fool of myself and treated you like a real man! Instead, I've made you my girl. Haven't I, darling?"

"Yes, mistress."

"Haven't I taken you? And am I not still doing so?" Patricia took up the paddle again and whacked his bottom vigorously, until he moaned from a combination of pain and cramping.

"Never have I been treated so roughly and rudely by a man in the scene," she continued to excoriate him, perspiring greatly with her exertions, yet still unsatisfied that he had sufficiently felt her wrath. "Do you find it enjoyable to frighten a woman out of her wits?"

"No, ma'am," Victor lied.

"Answer honestly," she said, smacking him so hard that he made a deep, animal noise in response.

"Yes, ma'am!" he croaked, his will now stronger than his flesh, which was past speckling.

"Your whipping is now concluded," she decided, throwing down the paddle and freeing his wrists. "Get down on your knees, take your cock in your hand and come for me. Yes, with your bottom still full."

Patricia gracefully disposed of her half nude body in an arm chair and directed him to kneel at her feet and masturbate. She'd watched several mistresses do this while visiting the Vault with Michael and remembered the lesson well. This would not be a scene until Victor came and she had three more minutes of patience left. And so resting the tip of her shoe beneath his scrotum, she helped the process none too gently along.

"That's right, Victor. I'm not done hurting you yet," she murmured, leaning forward to twist his nipple as hard as she could. Now it was all up for Victor. Patricia lurched back in time to miss being sprayed with the sadomasochist's milky benediction.

"Good boy, Victor!" she congratulated him, "You finally managed to do something right!"

Patricia drove home with renewed energy and quite pleased with herself. But she also felt inexplicably excited and hoped that there would be a message from Michael when she got home. There was something better than that. Michael himself was awaiting her arrival, having fallen asleep in front of her fireside on a handsome chaise lounge that hadn't been there when she'd left that morning.

As Patricia walked into the room and Michael woke up, she noticed many charming pieces of furniture that hadn't been there before. And yet these were not the items Hugo had previously lent her, but different antique pieces from various periods, all complementary.

Michael looked at his watch and saw that it was midnight.

"I finished my shift and decided to come by and see if you were here. I guess I fell asleep."

She sat down beside him and felt the fabric of the couch with appreciation.

"Where did all this stuff come from?"

"Apparently Anthony had it sent down from his house."

"How amazingly nice of him!"

"Remarkably nice," Michael observed cynically, causing Patricia to blush but instead of replying, put her head on his shoulder.

"Would you be jealous if Anthony liked me?"

"Does he?"

"I'm sure he likes me more than the man who marked me so badly tonight," said Patricia, pulling up her skirt and her panties aside to show Michael her bottom, which was heavily bruised.

"Patricia, what in the world have you been up to?"

"I was paying off a debt of honor to Hugo which involved playing with a man who wasn't very considerate. But don't worry, I fixed him good. He looks worse than me." Patricia climbed into his lap and hugged him hard.

"And is the debt of honor paid?"

"As far as I'm concerned it is."

Suddenly Michael did not feel like cuddling her and put her off his lap.

"I hope you're proud of yourself," he scolded, "a woman like you reduced to accepting hard whippings from strangers to pay off her debts! And all of this stuff from Anthony. Let me guess how you paid for it. And what about the rental on the lighthouse? You can't possibly afford this place now that you're out of work. Or do you plan to fuck William into letting you stay for free? Patricia, what are you becoming?"

Patricia, who did not normally color at accusations, felt her face grow warm at this one.

"Michael, I've already been thoroughly punished tonight, so please don't add insult to injury," she said, with some heat.

"Oh, sweetheart," he sighed, pulling her back into his arms. "I'm sorry. That wasn't a nice thing to say, especially after all you've gone through tonight. But who was this person who marked you? I can't imagine anyone having to hit you so hard. Should I go and arrest him?"

"Yes! That would be outstanding!" She jumped up and down. "You could bust him on a technicality when he's leaving town tomorrow, then we could get him handcuffed and hog tied in your dankest cell and I could fuck him senseless with a billy club!"

Michael raised an eyebrow at this, but soothed her with caresses.

"Actually, he would like that," she mused. Then she stretched out face down across his lap. "Oh Michael, won't you massage my bottom, please? It aches so! I heard it's better if you stimulate the circulation of blood to the injured area."

"I will but you realize I can't keep you in this position without spanking you a little, especially with you flaunting your infidelity the way you're doing."

"You can spank me a little. I want you to."

"I don't like the idea of you and Anthony Newton," Michael said, spanking her a little.

"You had *his* girlfriend. Why shouldn't he have yours?"

Michael said nothing as he stroked her bottom. Patricia wriggled and pressed against him.

"I saw *both* your girlfriends tonight," Patricia told him, "Susan and Marguerite."

"Oh? They were there while you were being whipped?" Michael was still adjusting to her knowing about Susan.

"Not in the same room, but they knew what was going on. Marguerite had played with Victor before and gave me prudent advice before I went upstairs. She complimented me when I needed bolstering and never once took advantage of my humble position tonight as I *cooked and served dinner* as Hugo's maid. I really liked her!"

Michael could hardly believe that the most jealous woman he'd ever dated now seemed to admire Marguerite. Especially when Patricia admitted, "Michael, I was *attracted* to Marguerite. She and the other girls being there to witness my so-called shame was what made tonight fun."

Michael continued to pet her without comment, attempting to envision Patricia waiting table for Marguerite and Susan.

"I wish I'd been invited," he commented.

"For some reason Hugo spared me that, bless him. Though I suspect it was only because we already had an even number of men."

"If you ever cook me dinner I promise not to whip you nearly as hard."

"On my newly reduced budget I expect to be cooking quite bit this winter," Patricia promised.

"That sounds like heaven," he told her, kissing her bruised bottom. Patricia wriggled at the ticklish attention and spread her smooth, slim thighs.

"Oh, Michael," she cried impulsively, "I've been so ill-used tonight! That bad man actually whipped my pussy!"

"Poor baby!" Michael examined the injured area with gentle fingers and much concern.

"If only you would kiss it and make it better!" she cried boldly.

"Darling, I'd be happy to," he assured her, turning her over and sliding her up a little on the sofa before kneeling between her white thighs. Now he would prove to Patricia that he was anything but a brute and could indeed give her pleasure gently. Patricia let him cup her silky bottom in his hands and gave herself up to his tongue. "Poor, little, punished girl," he soothed her, before making her come in a very few minutes.

Hugo Sands called on Patricia the following afternoon, natty, immaculate and bearing ivory roses.

"Got some furniture, I see," he commented with a smile, recognizing pieces from Anthony Newton's house. "You are an enterprising girl!"

"Anthony is my friend," Patricia proudly announced, in the tone of a clever girl.

"I am too," Hugo said, handing her a check for a thousand dollars.

"For me? Why?"

"It's your commission on the sale to Victor. This morning he finally bought the suite of colonial furniture I've been trying to sell him forever."

"But, I said nothing to him about furniture last night," she regarded the check with disbelief.

"You put him in a buying mood."

"Do you often sell furniture like that?" she asked, folding up the check with a smile.

"Most of the time it's done more conventionally, but with Victor I take advantage of the fact that he's also in the scene."

"So, you're saying he had a good time last night?" Patricia grinned.

"Why? Does that surprise you?"

"Well, he *was* very hard to please," Patricia equivocated, unwilling to give Victor's secret away even though he did not deserve the courtesy of discretion.

"But you pleased him greatly and me too all this last week. You made your little blunder up to me with integrity and genius."

Patricia was shocked to realize that she was blushing and

replied, "It was the least that I could do after you saved me from Randy."

"The least you could have done was much less than you did. I only hope that Victor didn't go too hard on you."

"Oh, I was able to call him to order after a while," Patricia smiled, for now her evening with Victor was but a strange memory. She had no desire to whip her own lover, but she was glad she had done it to Victor.

After Hugo left her, Patricia sat down at her desk overlooking the cove and wrote a note in fountain pen on her monogrammed ecru paper.

Dear Marguerite,

I wanted to write and thank you for your kindness to me last night.

It never occurred to me when Hugo arranged for you to come to dinner, that your presence would lighten my ordeal.

The pleasant recollection of your elegant person and charming manners remains uppermost in my thoughts.

I hope that you will come and visit me soon. Let me know in advance and we'll get Dennis to come and serve us lunch.

Yours truly,

Patricia

MARGUERITE AND MALCOLM

November 1,
Dear Ms. Alexander,

Thank you for responding to my ad in the **New Rod Quarterly**. You are certainly a seductive young woman. If Vargas ever drew a girl in glasses, she'd be you.

But your letter did not equally impress me. Frankly, you seem shallow, self-centered and vain. And for a submissive, highly demanding.

Your insistence on being "spoiled" also failed to charm me. Perhaps you should be advertising in the professionals section if this is such an important criteria for dating in the scene.

I apologize if my comments seem unduly harsh, but the practiced ease of your heavily perfumed note rankled somehow. In a way I still want to meet you, because you do look delectably spankable, but I expect the encounter would be a severe disappointment to us both.

I wish you luck in your future choice of playmates.

Sincerely,

Malcolm Branwell

P.S. Do you wish me to return your photo?

• • •

November 4,

Dear Mr. Branwell,

I don't think we have to meet for you to spank me. I think that you have already spanked me. And perhaps a bit harder than even I deserve.

You may keep my photo if you wish, as I still have yours to look at in the magazine. It was what first made me write you. I thought it very handsome at the time. Now I simply regard it as the portrait of a very stern gentleman.

I am bound to agree with your several observations on my character. Yet with your final conclusion I am compelled to differ: I don't think that our playing in person would be at all disappointing and the fact that you do only betrays your inexperience at dealing with a woman of parts.

I trust that your ad will draw a great response. Among your correspondents you are sure to find the milksop creature you seek and with her soon enjoy the exquisite pleasures our scene has to offer. I wish you luck in your search.

Yours truly,

Marguerite Alexander

November 7,

Dear Marguerite,

I had been regretting my rude letter to you when your return note arrived.

I owe you an apology for presuming to analyze your character on the basis of a flirtatious note. Your perception of my inexperience was entirely accurate. Could the privilege of playing with a woman like you be anything less than the thrill of a lifetime? But blundering beginner that I am, how would I know that?

I will be in Random Point opening one of my new book stores at the end of next week. Perhaps we could have lunch and I could attempt to convince you that I'm not as stupid as I seem. Please call me.

Malcolm

Marguerite handed her friend, Laura Random, Malcolm's letters with a sigh of irritation. "I appear to have developed a craving to play with a pompous, miserly prig who's about to put me out of business!"

"Branwell's Book Bag chain is his?" Laura considered Malcolm's photo in Hugo's magazine. She had studied it at length herself while laying the issue out for her lover and had been given several licks of the belt for fantasizing aloud about Malcolm B., who had posed stripped to baggy shorts on the deck of his boat looking young, rich and athletic. Malcolm was tall, with a lean physique and unlined skin. His ad said he was 31. Facially he reminded Marguerite of the 50's film star John Kerr, who once gave a spanking on an episode of *Rawhide*.

"What did you say in your letter to tame him so thoroughly?" Laura asked, comparing the language of his first letter with that of his second.

"Oh, I disarmed him by accepting his criticism with an air of humility then administered just enough of a scolding to let him know that for all his bluster he's a novice."

"Are you going to meet him?"

"I don't know." Marguerite sat down behind the polished wooden counter of her bookshop and put her chin on her hand. "He is very handsome, and apparently rich, but what good will it do me with his skinflintish attitude? I could bear to not be spoiled by a poor man. But for a wealthy lover to be close with his funds offends every instinct of chivalry."

"I completely agree," said Laura.

"And then again," mused Marguerite, "I've longed for a new lover for some time now and Malcolm does have the right look."

"He looks divinely virile," Laura commented.

"He's young, strong and barely used," Marguerite observed with a catlike grin. "And can't you see him in a well cut suit and a grey fedora?"

"Perfectly," Laura agreed. "He's leaning on the rail of a cruise ship and you're beside him in a white sundress, picture hat and gloves."

"Oh, Laura, what should I do? He really is terribly good looking, with those corded legs and so on, but is he mature enough for me?" In spite of her smooth, fresh looks, Marguerite was 34 and very worldly.

"I don't like that crack about your not being submissive enough."

"That bothered me too. I'm not about to put up with another Victor!"

"On the other hand, even though he's snotty, he seems fairly cultivated. I like that he apologizes for being unduly harsh. That shows that he has some gentlemanly instincts, even though he chooses to suppress them. Does Hugo know anything about him?"

"No. He's a new subscriber. If I'm not mistaken, he probably only discovered there's a scene as recently as a few months ago."

"You mean he may not have even played with anyone yet?"

"As anal retentive as he is, he's probably been holding his life-long desires in abeyance until now."

"Still, Marguerite, how could a man that firm looking not be able to give you a great scene? And for him to have gotten so far in business at his age surely indicates a streak of genius."

Marguerite agreed but decided that the pleasure of their first encounter would be increased by postponing it. So she wrote back promptly on her heavy book shop letterhead, inviting him to stop in at *her* bookstore on the day he came to town for a cup of tea by her fireside.

Malcolm Branwell was chagrined to realize that the woman he'd decided to pursue was the owner of a business whose business would greatly decrease when his business came to *her* town. But he was once again underestimating Marguerite, for there could be no chain store substitute for her enchanting shop with its gallery of rare erotica and all of the Edwardian ambiance with which she could infuse it. Marguerite's shop was the one the guide books mentioned. All of this Malcolm perceived in an instant on stepping into the fragrant and romantic book shop which filled most of the narrow, triple decker house.

It was a Saturday morning the week before Thanksgiving and Marguerite, in a tailored grey wool skirt and vest over a white blouse, was busy with a half dozen customers at once. Malcolm browsed for some time, going up into the galleries and collecting expensive books.

Until he emerged from behind the large stack of books he had placed on the counter, Marguerite did not even recognize her correspondent in the shop. Her green eyes opened wide behind her big, sexy glasses as she took Malcolm in appreciatively.

He was a broad-shouldered and ruddy-complected young man,

with crisp, short brown hair and the same color eyes. Add to this refined features and the benefits of a good tailor and the total equalled one new leading man.

"Why, hello." She extended a beautifully manicured hand to shake his blunt one. He was bewitched by the sound of her mellifluous voice, and needed a moment to recollect what he had been about to say.

"I've been all over your shop and I'm very impressed," he finally managed to blurt out, unwilling to relinquish her hand. "And even more ashamed of that horrible letter I wrote you."

"Yes," she smiled, "you should be."

"I'd like these books," he told her, throwing a credit card on top of the stack.

"Are you saying you don't stock these titles at Branwell's?" she teased.

"You know that we don't."

Marguerite began to write up the sale. The total exceeded five hundred dollars, but this seemed an inadequate consolation for having her business assailed by the corporate battering ram of Branwell's Book Bag. After the sale had been concluded he demanded the promised cup of tea and Marguerite obliged him by leading him over to the fireside where she always kept a pot on the grate. They sat at a small table enjoying the convenient lull in customer traffic.

"I suppose you can never forgive me for writing that first letter, can you?" he bluntly began. She inclined her head with an uninterpretable smile. "Well?"

"Well," she condescended to reply at last, "you *were* rather dreadful at first, but as you seem to regret your unkindness to me, I don't see why my *eventual* forgiveness should not be forthcoming."

"Oh, I do deeply regret it!" he swore, placing his hand lightly atop hers across the table. But she pulled it free at once and arched a slender eyebrow at him.

"I said forgiveness might be forthcoming, not hand holding, Mr. Branwell." Malcolm reddened. He had never felt so clumsy with a woman, and knew neither what to say or do to win her respect.

"May I take you to dinner?" he asked.

"I don't think so," she told him, not unkindly. "At least, not yet."

"Not yet? When then?"

"Frankly, Mr. Branwell, you're not ready to appreciate a woman like me yet. I suggest you let your ad run its course, play for a couple of months with a variety of young ladies, and if you still don't meet that perfect someone, call me again," she recommended with a degree of poise that unnerved him.

At this point a customer approached the counter and Marguerite jumped up to wait on him, leaving Malcolm in a state of acute frustration. Seeing Marguerite in person, hearing her voice and inhaling her perfume, was sufficient to convince him that he need never look any further for a playmate. But now she had imposed an intolerable penance on him for his initial rashness of address. He would be exiled for some months, during which time he had to force himself to play with women who were far her inferior.

He sat and drank tea, watching her conduct her business pleasantly and finding it impossible to leave, though it was evident that he had been dismissed. Finally when it became so busy in the shop that there was no further opportunity of attracting Marguerite's attention, Malcolm gathered up his books and left.

Resolved to accept and benefit from the practical lesson she had outlined, Malcolm refrained from attempting to contact Marguerite Alexander again for a period of six weeks. During this time he met every eligible woman in New England who had either answered his ad or ran one of her own in Hugo Sands' magazine. By Christmas week Malcolm had made contact with six different women and had played with them all.

They were nice girls, and thrilling to play with each in their way. But none of them possessed the polished womanliness of Marguerite. She seemed to tower above them all, not only in physical stature, but also in wit, beauty and accomplishment. And she had been completely right in her assessment that playing with others would increase his longing to obtain her special favors.

Meanwhile Marguerite seriously wondered whether the sanctimonious young millionaire should be made to *pay* for those favors after the insults that she had sustained at his pen. She did not hesitate to consult her original mentor, Hugo Sands on this matter when Malcolm's Christmas card arrived with an invitation to meet him for dinner in Boston and then attend the opera. The prospect of seeing a performance of *Mahagonny* was almost impossible to resist and she represented her desire to finally play with Malcolm just as strongly to Hugo.

"I say make him pay, baby. Your kind of glamour doesn't come cheap," the urbane publisher commented.

"I was thinking of making him get me a suite at the Copley Plaza for the night," Marguerite suggested modestly.

"Sweetheart, do you know how wealthy Malcolm Branwell is? Have you forgotten everything I've ever taught you? At the very least you should require a Christmas present."

Marguerite pouted momentarily, then flashed Hugo a mischievous look. "He'll be livid."

"So? He's got a big hard-on and a fat wallet. It's time he was punished for his impertinence," Hugo said, fondly taking Marguerite in his arms. Marguerite was his first real submissive and after ten years they still continued to enjoy an intimate friendship.

"But Hugo, then he'll think I'm as wantonly materialistic as he first suspected and write me off as a high priced call girl."

"Who cares what he thinks? He's an idiot," said Hugo with some feeling. Marguerite had all but forgiven Malcolm for his first letter, but Hugo would need years to get over the insult to his brilliant protégée. Some of what Malcolm had intimated was undoubtedly true, but Hugo had little respect for a wealthy man who would have let Marguerite slip through his fingers because she had a slight addiction to luxury.

"Should I tell him what I want or ask him to surprise me?"

"Ask him to surprise you and you'll wind up with a espresso maker." Hugo predicted.

"But Hugo, you saw his first letter. Malcolm's ethics are as rigid as my stiffest corset. If I ask him for something juicy he'll hate me."

"Marguerite, use your head. Haven't you already got one perfectly serviceable stud on tap who gives you no money?"

Marguerite smiled fondly at the thought of Michael Flagg, acknowledged Hugo's point and sent Malcolm an E-mail message that night.

December 28,
Dear Mr. Branwell,
If you would like me to come to Boston on New Year's Eve you may have to bribe me. There's an Art Deco jewelry shop on

Newbury Street named Damson's. I'm a good customer and they know my taste. A charming present might cause me to look upon your invitation with favor.

Your self-centered, vain, shallow and demanding friend in the scene, M.

Marguerite had correctly predicted Malcolm's reaction to her note. He felt such indignation boiling upon receipt of it that he could only work it off by going for a run in 30-degree weather. "Greedy little slut!" he thought, orbiting the Boston College reservoir. "I *should* buy her off, just for the satisfaction of giving her the thrashing she deserves!"

He visited Damson's that afternoon and asked to speak to the manager about obtaining a present for his friend, Marguerite Alexander. Marguerite had called ahead that morning to ask if the emerald and diamond bracelet from 1924 that she had admired the previous week was still available. She was told that it was still available with an attractive price tag of only forty-three hundred in cash out the door. Marguerite suggested the bracelet be put aside in case a friend of hers decided to stop in later. When Malcolm mentioned Marguerite's name, this was what he was shown.

He called her within an hour of making the purchase and tersely said, "Well, I've got the ransom. Where should we meet?"

She replied steadily, but with an aching, pounding heart, "A suite at the Copley Plaza would put us right across the street from the opera house."

"I'll see you there at six o'clock on New Year's Eve."

Two days later Malcolm dressed in a state of excited resentment for his first real date with Marguerite. Of all the women he had played with so far, not one besides Marguerite had asked for a bribe. But neither had their integrity, accessibility or breathless innocence seemed particularly compelling when compared to the sophisticated charms of Marguerite. Perhaps her particular radiance required some sort of extraordinary maintenance fees and this accounted for her apparent avarice.

Her approach actually made things a lot easier. Now he didn't have to feel awkward about taking the insolent girl across his knee.

They now had a financial arrangement. This was less than what he'd hoped for, but better than no relationship at all.

But he almost forgot how irritated he was when she arrived, punctually, in a peplum waisted, smoky blue silk suit under a full length sable (which he deplored), and four inch heels. They had to hurry to fit in dinner before the performance so there was little time to discuss the more important reason for their meeting.

During the overture he slipped the bracelet case into her hands and she momentarily opened it, then smiled and put it into her purse. He wanted to shake her then and there for the calm with which she accepted the bribe.

They were in a private box and as soon as the lights went down he took advantage of his presumed temporary ownership of Marguerite's person by placing his hand rather firmly on her thigh atop her skirt. Marguerite looked at him with some surprise and a flutter of her heart. This was sudden! As she didn't resist this liberty, he grew bolder and slipped his hand under her skirt to caress her leg from knee to stocking top.

Marguerite shifted on her seat. His hand went between her legs and his fingers probed the silken crotch of her panties. She was already damp! Now she pushed him away, shocked by this too rapid caress.

"Spread your legs and let me touch you," he ordered, pushing her thighs apart and attempting to reinsert his hand between them. Marguerite was appalled. Disengaging from him, she exited the box. He followed her out to the corridor and demanded an explanation.

Marguerite reached in her purse and retrieved the grey velvet jewel box.

"Here," she thrust it into his hand. "Did you think this meant you own me?"

"Well, what the hell does it mean?" he demanded, following her as she paced.

"Your hand on my thigh through the skirt was charming, but what is this spread-your-legs stuff? How dare you talk to me like that on such short acquaintance? Do you think that I'm some undiscriminating slave girl?"

Malcolm flushed so brightly that she thought he might overheat. But he forced himself to calmly consider the situation from every angle before replying. True, he may well have made a fool of himself just now, but if that was the case, why were her panties so damp? No, he suspected this gorgeous brat was almost as excited as he was by the prospect of playing for the first time.

With lowered eyes he apologized for taking a liberty with her and begged her forgiveness abjectly. After this she was easily persuaded to return to the box and the remainder of the opera was enjoyed by Marguerite without the slightest impropriety being visited on her luscious person.

Malcolm was grateful for the time the performance afforded him for deep reflection. It seemed as though he needed every moment of the succeeding two hours to plan his strategy for the rest of the evening. As he sat quietly reproaching himself for his ridiculously aggressive behavior, she covertly gazed at his cleanly chiseled profile and wondered whether she had managed to unman him completely or only temporarily destarch his collar.

Only once during the performance did she flash him a mischievous smile after catching him looking at her. But this was enough to banish his discouragement. In spite of all the setbacks he had suffered in the Marguerite campaign, her rebuffs did not so much bruise his ego as make him reevaluate his approach.

Thus, as they strolled back to the hotel after the performance, Malcolm plunged in with a bold, "You know, I *have* read your stories. We actually carry your books. I just didn't realize *Alma* was you until I talked to Hugo Sands the other day."

"You talked to Hugo about me?" Marguerite gave him her full attention.

"I'd just called to cancel my ad and I happened to mention that I had a date with a Marguerite Alexander and asked whether he knew anything about you."

"Oh my! What did he say?" She couldn't keep from smiling.

"He was rather curt with me. But he did say that you were *Alma* and that was all I needed to know."

"And was it?"

Discovering the previous week that Marguerite was an elegant author whose erotic prose had aroused him for years had shocked and embarrassed Malcolm. How he had misjudged her! But he wasn't about to let the cocky girl know how much he admired her descriptive powers.

"You certainly construct some Byzantine plots," he sidestepped her question.

"Actually they're quite straightforward and logical."

"All those complex motivations and subtle emotions. Do you honestly think the readers have the patience for all that?"

"Some do," Marguerite murmured.

"And I suppose you expect ordinary men to be as clairvoyant as your characters are when it comes to handling horrible girls?"

Marguerite simply smiled.

When they reached the Copley Plaza Malcolm asked her bluntly, "Am I going upstairs with you?"

"Didn't you intend to?" she replied, with flirtatious good humor.

"Yes, originally, but you sort of changed the arrangement at the theatre."

"We can discuss that," said Marguerite, preceding him into the lobby. When they arrived at the suite she found it very much to her liking. "Shall we have champagne?" she asked, picking up the phone to call room service.

"Anything you like," he told her, encouraged by her gaiety. As she went about examining the rooms, he followed her and looked at her. It was nerve-wracking not knowing exactly what to do and she wasn't helping him.

The champagne arrived and since a token sip was all Malcolm took, he soon had the advantage of her. Marguerite did love champagne and after two glasses became quite voluble.

"So you don't think that women ought to be spoiled," she opened her gambit lightly.

"It seems a sexist requirement."

"Well, really, Malcolm, what could be more sexist than turning a grown woman over your knee and spanking her as though she were a child?" she demanded.

"That would only be sexist if the woman wasn't into it," Malcolm pointed out.

"Look, I spoil men to death!" Marguerite attacked from a different angle.

"Oh. I see. I didn't realize that." He almost smiled.

"No and you still don't," she insisted. "And even though that darling bracelet would compliment my eyes, you'll hate me if I take it so I have to behave."

"Do you care what I think of you?" he sat next to her with sudden warmth.

"And not only that," she ignored his last remark, "but your wretched bookmarket thrashed my Christmas business."

"The fact that we're competitors is regrettable," he agreed cautiously.

"I should have known you'd be as circumspect as a lawyer," she declared disdainfully, pouring another glass of wine. "Do forgive me for whining."

"Maybe I can figure something out to help," he said, thinking hard. "I've got some influence with the distributors. Suppose I ask them to give you the same discounts we get? Would that enable you to match our prices?"

"Yes," she smiled ironically, mostly impressed at the speed with which he had thought of a way to help her at no cost to himself. Malcolm noticed her expression and felt as though she were laughing at him.

Seeing him at a loss for words she asked him to tell her about some of the girls he had met since seeing her last.

"That's right," he flushed, "you did *order* me to get some experience, didn't you?"

"I believe I may have made a good suggestion," she gently corrected him.

"I did meet a number of women," he admitted.

"And managed to play with them all?"

"Yes," he said, with a smile.

"I was wondering when I'd get to see you smile," she murmured. "You should do it more often. It makes you much more handsome."

Malcolm stopped smiling. "Yes, well at any rate, I don't feel at liberty to discuss my meetings in detail."

"Oh? Are you sure you want to miss this opportunity to tell me how much more exciting it would be to play with me?" she deliberately taunted him.

"You know, you're a very arrogant young lady," said Malcolm with sudden decision. There was no use putting this off any longer. Marguerite tried to jump to her feet a moment too late and he succeeded in seizing her by the elbow and turning her over his knee.

"No!" she cried, for form's sake.

"Yes!" he told her, shrugging off his jacket without relinquishing his grip on her waist. A muscular man, with vitamin-fortified strength infused into every unpolluted cell of his six-foot two-inch frame, he had no difficulty in restraining and nicely positioning the lithe redhead across his solid lap. He noted with some relief that she did not resist.

'What are you going to do?" she asked, somewhat impishly, with a full glance over her left shoulder at him.

"Give you a good spanking!" he declared, raising his right hand slightly and bringing it down briskly, once on either snugly skirted cheek of her bottom. He couldn't be sure, but he thought that Marguerite said, "Oooooh!" as she gave a little wriggle across his lap. Malcolm followed this with a series of six more smacks on either cheek. She caught her breath and ground against his thighs.

"You *do* deserve this," he told her, repeating the twelve count, but harder this time. She reacted with growing excitement. "You're not arguing," he commented, slowly smoothing out her skirt. "That must mean that you agree with me."

He continued to spank her, quite firmly now, for several minutes uninterrupted. Marguerite knew a good spanker when she met one. He spanked her hard and pressed her to his lap so firmly that she could feel his desire to possess her. His choice of spanking her over her skirt, rather than greedily baring her all at once, gained back for Malcolm points that he had lost in the opera box.

Malcolm continued spanking her until she could feel the heat radiating between her panties and lined skirt. She indicated that her ordeal across his lap was better extended than abbreviated, by arching to his hand.

"You've got a lot to answer for," he told her, "playing hard to get for two months!"

"I beg your pardon, but it's only been six weeks," she replied, reaching back to rub for the first time.

"But it felt like two months," he told her, removing her hand and continuing to spank her.

"Ouch!" she cried, the heat beginning to fully penetrate now. "You're lucky it wasn't six months," she boldly asserted.

"Oh, am I?" He did not find her impertinence amusing and applied the next six swats more vigorously. Now for the first time she kicked her legs and tried to break the position.

"Ow! That's too hard!" she objected.

"Where do you think you're going?" he pushed her back down and renewed his grip on her waist.

"But—." She twisted on his lap to force him to meet her big, green eyes. "Please don't spank me any harder!"

"Then don't say such naughty things," he admonished her, smoothing down her skirt again. Marguerite settled down across his lap again. "And say you're sorry," he added. She cordially ignored him. "Marguerite?" he patted her through her skirt ominously.

"Yes, sir?"

"Say you're sorry for being such a stuck up little brat!" He punctuated this command with six of the best. Marguerite cried out at each one but stubbornly refrained from answering him.

"Very well, I didn't want to have to have to humiliate you completely on our first date, but I'm finding your conceit intolerable. Lift up!"

"But, why?" she coyly asked him, reaching back to rub her bottom again.

"You know damn well why," he said, unzipping the back of her skirt and pulling it down and off. "You're getting it on the bare bottom." Suddenly her long, stunning legs appeared, gartered and hosed to perfection.

"No!"

"Yes, and immediately!" he declared, fingering the waist band of her pearl grey silk briefs.

"No!" she protested vehemently, refusing to be be deprived of a spanking on her panties first. "You mustn't pull them down yet. I forbid you to!" she cried imperiously, trying to slip out of his grasp.

"All right. Calm down," he ordered, stroking the panties. The silk was so papery thin that his calloused palm nearly snagged it.

"And anyway, I'm out of balance now," she protested.

"What does that mean?"

"My jacket should come off too," she suggested.

"If I let you up will you promise not to run away?"

"I promise," she said at once and slid off his lap. Kneeling gracefully on the carpet she unbuttoned her suit jacket and removed it to reveal a dainty bustier in the same color as the briefs. She sat on her heels and waited, looking up at him.

"Well? What are you waiting for?" he demanded.

"A kiss," she told him, removing her glasses and placing them on the coffee table. He leaned down with a fiercely pounding heart and taking her face between his hands, kissed her lips for the first time. Nor could he resist placing one chaste kiss on her ravishing bosom while cupping it for a moment through the lacy bustier. He grazed her exposed throat with his lips, causing her to sigh.

"Do you know that you're a wicked girl?" he asked.

She grabbed her champagne glass and downed its contents haughtily, forgetting for the moment that she was still on her knees to him.

He pulled her back across his lap.

"Hey, don't!"

"You're really going to get it now," he promised. Malcolm began to dust her panties vigorously with the palm of his hand, thinking of the frustrations he had suffered over the last six weeks. He principally remembered her request for the expensive present before agreeing to their New Year's Eve date and his indignation swelled. Malcolm held her fast and warmed her panties thoroughly.

"I don't know why you think you have to be spoiled. You're already more spoiled than any woman I know."

"Ouch!" Marguerite kicked her legs at the last series of smacks. "I deserve to be spoiled!"

"You deserve to be spanked. Imagine demanding a ransom before going out with me. I never heard of anything so outrageous in my life."

"Oh? You must lead a sequestered life," she replied.

"If you can still be so fresh I must not be doing this right," he remarked, increasing the severity with which he was bringing his palm down across her lushly padded bottom.

"Besides," she said, stopping him to rub, "I gave the bracelet back."

"Yes, you certainly did," he remembered her reaction to his touch in the opera box. "Embarrassing me as much as you possibly could in the process," he declared, tucking his thumbs into the waist band of her briefs and tugging them down over her hips and then to her knees. "There! That's better," he remarked, admiring her flawless, freshly pinkened bottom.

"No it isn't!" She attempted to pull her panties back up.

"No, you don't," he told her, taking her by the wrist and smacking her on the back of the hand before pushing it away and beginning the spanking all over again.

"Ow!" It stung more on the bare. "That really hurts!"

"I haven't heard an apology yet," he told her, pausing to rub.

"Mmmm," she said, burying her face in her arms.

"First you intimate that I can't have you unless I bribe you. Then you throw my present back in my face. Why the schizophrenia?" he interrogated her with more spanking.

"I simply changed my mind." She looked back over one shoulder to check the deepening color in her bottom, then subsided across his lap.

"And suppose I tell you to spread your legs now? Are you going to resist me again? Run away?"

"No," she softly replied, hiding her face again. Malcolm heard this shy avowal with great relief.

"Why did you balk in the theatre box?" he asked softly, gently separating her milky thighs and teasingly caressing their inner surface.

"Because you were being disrespectful," she replied, arching up to give him greater access.

"You don't like being given orders?"

"Not on such short acquaintance."

"Short acquaintance, huh?" He stopped stroking and started spanking again. "It's only been short because you put me off for so long. We could have been going out together for months now if you hadn't been so fussy."

"The only way to discipline a dominant male is to deprive him of one's company," Marguerite informed him, "and if anyone needed to be disciplined it was you!"

"Hmmph!" was his response, followed by several dozen hard smacks, which she held still for prettily. "You did admit that some of what I said was true," he pointed out, pausing to caress her again.

"That doesn't mean it was right for you to scold me in your first letter."

"Maybe you need someone to scold you," Malcolm bent his head to press his lips momentarily to her warm bottom. "And make you behave like a normal person."

"And how does my behavior differ from that of a normal person?" She pillowed her head on her arms and felt five or six more smacks before he stopped to answer and caress her again.

"Well, for one thing, a normal girl doesn't sell her favors."

"That really bothers you, doesn't it?" she wriggled on his lap, flaunting her bottom and legs.

"Shouldn't it?" he mused, once again returning to the satiny surface of her white inner thighs with his fingertips. How could anyone who looked so pure and virtually untouched be so worldly, he wondered, without letting it stop him from more widely dividing her thighs and slipping his palm in under her soft pubic curls. He pressed down on her bottom with his other hand, sandwiching her in a way which she found maddeningly sexy.

"I don't think so, Malcolm, seeing as I only play pure B&D," she replied, grinding against his hand, whose fingertips now pressed against her clit. At last, when her wetness was impossible to ignore an instant longer, he inserted one and then another finger up into her pussy.

"And what does that mean?"

"That means no sex."

"Oh? You didn't plan to give yourself to me tonight?"

"That would depend on how you handled me."

"And how do most men handle you?"

"Not nearly so well as you're doing now," she murmured, allowing him to masturbate her deeply as his other hand crept around to bare and fondle her breasts. Her body responded to his touch in a way that seemed to invite further liberties.

Malcolm released and rolled her over. "Look," he said, cradling her in his arms, "I'm not moralizing. Prostitution is a noble profession, I just don't like to think of my girlfriend as being a part of it."

Marguerite stiffened at the word he had used and decided he had enjoyed the weight of her body on his lap long enough.

"I'm sure you think you're very clever but I don't find such cynicism amusing," she icily replied, getting her panties back up, springing to her feet and looking down at him disdainfully.

"Marguerite, don't get offended, I'm just trying to understand you."

"Considering your lack of imagination, that would be impossible," she declared, marching into the bedroom and pulling a grey satin robe from the closet. In an instant all exposed flesh disappeared.

Malcolm paced the drawing room anxiously until she appeared in the doorway.

"Marguerite?" he appealed to her with eyes full of worried regret.

"Are you still here? I was hoping you would have gone." She aimed for coolness but her voice was full of emotion.

"You're dismissing me again?" Now he was equally agitated. "Because of one remark?"

Marguerite recklessly drained the last glass of champagne. "Do you think I had nothing better to do on New Year's Eve than be insulted by you? I might have been with my friends in Random Point tonight. It's time for you to leave."

"I really think you could forgive one comment, Marguerite, seeing as things were going so well."

"Yes, they were going well," she said, her eyes welling with tears. "But then you had to go and ruin the whole mood with your crudeness. And to think that I allowed you to touch me! I insist you wash your hands before you leave. I couldn't bear the thought of your taking any part of me away with you."

"Oh, Marguerite, I didn't mean to upset you like this. I didn't realize you were so sensitive about certain words."

"Well, why shouldn't I be, when they are patently untrue!" She had a high color by this time and without her glasses looked even more exciting.

He sighed, "I'm very sorry that I hurt your feelings and ruined your New Year's Eve." He picked up his hat and coat. "I hope you don't have a headache in the morning from all that champagne," he added. "I'll call you."

Marguerite made no reply and did not attempt to detain him. After he was gone she turned off all the lights and looked down on Copley Square, where it had just begun to snow. She saw him cross on foot and guessed that he lived in walking distance in Back Bay. Though walking distance to that man could be miles, she reflected.

How wrong she had been to give him a second chance! Marguerite blushed as she thought of the liberties she had allowed him. More than enough to pay for a hotel suite, she decided coolly.

How interesting it might have been to yield to that hard body in the moonlight! She felt a pang for the pleasures her pride had cost her. But no mere physical sensation was worth the degradation of being thought common by one's lover. Before he was through with her he would learn just how uncommon a woman she was.

She curled up on the bed and hugged a pillow to her bosom, disturbed by the memory of his very erect cock pressing through his trousers as he spanked her. And he had been such a splendid spanker too! But none of this signified if he remained so prejudiced. Victorian style worked wonderfully for corsetry and underground erotica, but with regard to her own sexuality, Marguerite was a child of the 60's with all the liberation that implied.

Even so, she began to regret that she had not let him stay, if only to give her pleasure. His skillful manipulations had been highly civilized. Marguerite brushed her wet curls with her hand under the robe. Sex might possibly be all that he would ever be good for. But was even the best sex in the world worth putting up with his unbearable attitudes? Now she gave a sob of frustration and rolled over on her tummy. Dreadful man!

For treating her like this on New Year's Eve he deserved the most stringent lesson any dominant had ever been taught by his lover. She resolved not to give herself to him until he pledged both his heart and his hand to her and she found him worthy to accept.

He came to call the next morning at eleven. Dressed in beige riding pants, cordovan boots and a fine white wool shirt, Marguerite was drinking her breakfast chocolate in the sitting room and reading *A Sentimental Journey* by Lawrence Sterne. He sat at her tea table in his overcoat, still red in the face from the biting cold outside and mightily embarrassed by the mess he had made of their evening. Marguerite looked composed as she turned down a page in her book and gave him her full attention.

"That looks old," he told her, eyeing the lean, courtly, 18th-century dandy taking the pulse of a beautiful lady on the cover.

"You're not familiar with the novel?" the book seller asked her highly successful competitor, somewhat ironically.

"No, why? Should I be?"

Marguerite merely smiled.

"Generally I don't bother to read any author who isn't alive to do a book signing," he explained.

"You don't know what you're missing," she gently reproved.

"I don't want to miss anything good. Why don't you draw up a book list for me to help me improve myself?"

"Be careful what you wish for."

"I'm serious."

"Very well then." She tore a sheet from her small spiral writing tablet with the Raphael angel on the cover and unscrewed her expensive fountain pen. "I'll write down five books I want you to read before I see you next."

"Wait a minute, I didn't agree to that!"

"You have no choice," she told him diabolically, writing neatly in her firm, round script and handing him the list. He looked at it and read aloud, "*The Brothers Karamazov, The Charterhouse of Parma, Pride and Prejudice, Camilla* and *Pamela.* How long are these?"

"Oh, four to nine hundred pages each," she replied with a winsome smile. "And in them you'll meet some of the best female characters in literature."

"I see I'm being disciplined again," he noted, pocketing the list.

"You'll have two, maybe three out of the five at your store. You'll have to go to a better store for the others. I'll write down the authors as you're too ignorant to know them."

"You know, I didn't get to go to brat school like you," he defended himself with some resentment. "I went to a community college and worked in my father's print shop."

"That sounds horribly bleak. No wonder you're so dour."

"Look, since it's going to be a least a month till I see you again, would you like to take a little walk with me this morning and see my place?"

Marguerite was extremely curious about where and how Malcolm lived and agreed at once to accompany him to upscale Marlborough Street, where he owned the top floor of an elegant old apartment building. Commanding extensive views of Back Bay and the Charles River, the loft had been decorated in the Italianate style, with walls washed in voluptuous Tuscan hues.

Each room held but a few pieces of furniture, clearly chosen by a talented decorator. A striped divan here, a highly rubbed writing desk there, a pretty cabinet against a far wall, all caught Marguerite's eye as Malcolm led her through the rooms.

"Who decorated for you?" she finally asked as they came to a stop at one of the bay windows overlooking the river. It was a frigid New Year's Day, very clear and bright.

"My ex-wife. But she took half the furniture with her when she left. That's why it seems so empty in here."

"How long ago was that?"

"About six months."

"Oh!"

"We weren't married long. I have wall calendars that outlasted my marriage."

"Why did you marry her?"

"She was decorating my apartment and we were spending a lot of time together choosing fabrics and so forth. She was pretty and flirtatious and seemed so eager to please that I mistook her for a potential submissive. In reality she was quite the opposite. And even though she pretended to think it was cute when I playfully spanked her during the courtship, once we were married she didn't have the slightest problem telling me that I'm disturbed."

"Oh no!" Marguerite felt so profoundly uneasy at the thought of Malcolm belonging to another woman that she wondered whether she wasn't already in love with him. "Thank goodness you discovered the scene!"

"It's nice of you to say so, even though you're mad at me," he remarked wistfully, never wanting so much to make a woman like him and never knowing so little about how to accomplish this.

Having disobeyed her passionate command about washing his hands, he had indeed retained her essence on his fingertips the previous night and this had painfully inflamed his desire for Marguerite. Severely tempted by her contours in the body molding outfit, Malcolm had to fight the urge to reach out and encircle her waist.

"I suppose you realize how badly I want you," he said with his chin on his hand.

Marguerite colored but replied rather daringly, "Lesser men than you have had me faster. You must be doing something wrong."

"Come over here, you brat." He grabbed her by the wrist as she walked past him and feeling the window seat behind his knees, sat down and pulled Marguerite across his lap. "I'll teach you to be so fresh."

"Malcolm, don't you dare!" she cried, attempting to wriggle out of his grasp. However, once her magnificent bottom was upturned in this position, she knew that there was no escaping another spanking.

"I love your riding pants," he told her, warming her up with a couple of dozen affectionate smacks. "You should never wear anything else."

"You can't do this," she protested, trying to cover her bottom with her hand. "I haven't agreed to play."

"But it's so pleasant having you like this," he told her passionately, holding her fast by the waist and squeezing her through the snug pants. She felt his large erection under her tummy again and wanted to grind against it, but forced herself to pull away from him and jump up from his lap. Her face was flushed and her heart pounding as she adjusted her glasses and walked away from him.

"Marguerite?" He jumped up and turned her around to face him. She let him kiss her once, then she pulled away, gazing at him thoughtfully. He seemed to be improving by the moment.

"You don't completely hate me, do you?"

"No, Malcolm. I don't hate you at all."

"But you won't let me make love to you."

Marguerite laughed at him. "Do you always wear your hard-on on your sleeve?"

"You were sopping wet last night and I'll bet you are now too," he accused coolly, causing her color to rise again.

"I suppose you've enjoyed the favors of *all* the women you've played with so far?" She deftly repelled his attack.

"All except the two married ones," he confessed candidly.

"Oh? You draw the line at adultery?"

"They did."

"And do you practice safe sex?"

"Of course."

Marguerite smiled and dismissed the entire matter, saying, "Now I'd better get back to the hotel and check out. I have a three o'clock train to catch."

"Let me drive you back to Random Point."

"Why?"

"I don't want our time together to end yet, since you're determined to exile me for who knows how long."

Marguerite compared the inconvenience of running for platforms to the comfort of leaning her head against Malcolm's sturdy shoulder all the way to the Cape and chose the cozier option.

They reached Random Point before dusk and Marguerite gave him tea before sending him away with the five required books from her shop.

He reluctantly returned to Boston. Once there he no longer had the heart to date others and amused himself solely by going to the gym and reading through his solitary meals.

Every night he would call Marguerite to talk about the books he had begun to read. After several weeks of this, Marguerite knew that Malcolm was in love with her and she with him, for her heart throbbed painfully each time the telephone rang.

Malcolm could not remember ever enjoying a more bracing romance. Of course he didn't mean to indulge Marguerite endlessly, but meanwhile he was finding her increasingly desirable as he learned about her tastes, ethics and passions though the books she had given him.

Pride and Prejudice made him feel the folly of giving vent to one's first impressions. How relevant this lesson seemed to him now, as he recalled how twelve careless sentences, composed in a frenzy of righteous indignation, had nearly lost him Marguerite.

Now they were in the third week of the new year. He happily read all of *Camilla* but threw *Pamela* against the wall, because there were limits to which even he, as besotted as he was, would not go to please the woman he loved.

"What about *Pamela*, Malcolm?" wondered Marguerite on the phone that night.

"*Pamela* can burn in hell for all I care. I'm coming to see you."

A dart pierced her tummy as she consented and they arranged to meet after the last working hour of her week.

It snowed all Saturday and traffic was light in the shop. But there was a sudden invasion of customers at five. Then Michael Flagg dropped in for a mug of hot mulled cider. This made Marguerite uneasy. She looked at the clock. It was twenty-five to six. Michael leaned against the counter to wait for her to finish with a customer who was writing a check. Time raced by as Michael chatted to several other customers. Everyone knew and liked Detective Flagg of the Random Point police department.

Now the last customer had departed and it was fifteen minutes to six. Marguerite looked at the clock with such desperation that Michael asked her whether something was wrong. She flushed and confessed, "I'm sorry, darling, but if a certain gentleman walks in within the next few minutes, I'm going to have to pretend that you're just an acquaintance of mine."

"Oh? And why is that?" Michael's heart contracted at these few simple words spoken so kindly to him by his occasional mistress.

"He's someone I've become serious about."

"Define serious."

"You know Michael, just because you never asked me to marry you, that doesn't mean no one ever will."

"I never thought you'd consider it for a minute," he admitted in great surprise.

"No?"

"This gentleman who's about to arrive, am I right in assuming he's some sort of rich genius?"

Marguerite smiled demurely. Michael smiled back at her.

"And handsome, no doubt?" he teased her. She again merely smiled.

"Enlightened?" he ventured hopefully.

"Decidedly not. He already thinks I'm a bad woman because I asked him for a bracelet."

"Though he could well afford it?"

"It's the principle of the thing."

"Self-righteous is he?"

"He was. I'm smartening him up."

"I don't know whether to feel jealous or sorry for him."

"I hope you'll feel a little jealous," she declared, unable to resist it when he leaned over the counter to kiss her on the mouth.

"Can I stick around to check him out?"

"Certainly not. In fact, you should go at once."

Marguerite walked Michael to the door and looked up and down snowy, cobblestoned Shadow Lane. All the little shops were pulling down their shades for the night and Malcolm was nowhere to be seen.

"I won't kiss you good-bye just in case he's around," Michael told her, "but don't forget I love you."

Marguerite watched him drive off, feeling warmth without regret. Then she looked at her watch and found it was six. The last thing she expected as she returned to the front counter to empty the cash drawer was to see Malcolm leaning against it, with folded arms and a cool expression.

"Malcolm!" she cried. "How long have you been here?"

"So you want to get married, do you?" he said, deliberately removing his jacket and rolling up his sleeves.

"Malcolm, what are you doing?" She backed away from him.

"Getting ready to teach my fiancée a good lesson!"

"But, why?" She felt the gallery steps behind her and ran up to the first level.

"Nice how you were planning to begin our relationship with a lie!" He ran up the stairs behind her as she ascended the second circular flight.

"What lie?"

"You were going to pretend you hardly knew that man, yet he's obviously your lover."

"I only wanted to avoid an awkward situation," she explained, still rapidly climbing the narrow staircase.

"Come back down here and take what you've got coming!" he advised as she scampered up to the third gallery in her impossibly high ankle straps. The view of her shapely bottom so snugly wrapped in a taupe wool pencil skirt was spectacular from behind and he appreciated it as much as any man could.

"No, I don't dare!" she confessed, seeking refuge among the most extensive collection of B&D erotica in New England. Malcolm joined her momentarily, pulled her out of the corner with an iron grip and looked around for something to sit on.

"So you're smartening me up, are you?" he demanded, dragging a straight-backed chair into the middle of the floor. Then grasping her by the elbow of her white cotton blouse, he pulled her straight across his lap. "I'll smarten you up, young lady!" He brought his palm down hard on either cheek through the skirt. Several dozen emphatic whacks descended on Marguerite's taut, upturned back-side before she began to whimper.

Marguerite desperately tried to remember her entire conversation with Michael for damning remarks. Suddenly the balance of power between them had been reversed and Marguerite no longer felt either sophisticated or in control. She darted a glance at him over her shoulder and was not surprised by the air of authority with which he stared her down.

"Tell me the truth about you and that man." He stopped spanking her to pull up her skirt. Finding it too tight, he stood her on her feet and looking straight into her eyes, deliberately unbuckled her chunky belt, unzipped the skirt and made her step out of it.

"He's someone I've been seeing on and off for a couple of years, but it's not serious," Marguerite replied, reaching back to examine her already pinkened bottom through her ivory silk panties.

"Not serious, huh?" He pulled her back across his lap, dazzled once again by her long, stunning legs. "What's his name?" He smacked her hard.

"Ow! Michael Flagg."

"He sounds as though he's already planning to cuckold me."

"Malcolm, you've misunderstood."

"You called him darling and let him kiss you."

"Oh, I let everyone kiss me!" she cried in some exasperation.

"Not like that I hope."

"Where were you to see so much?" she wondered indignantly.

"Hidden in the tiny alcove you've reserved for sensible books on money management. What did he mean by *enlightened*?"

"You know, Malcolm, cool."

"That's a pretty inarticulate answer coming from you. What the hell does that mean?"

Marguerite could not be compelled to answer until he spanked her repeatedly and much harder.

"I forgot the question," she finally cried.

"What did your friend mean when he wondered whether I was enlightened?"

"Not jealous and Victorian," she explained at last, reaching back to rub.

"I don't like him," Malcolm brooded, rolling her panties down to expose her completely.

"Malcolm, let me go. I haven't even locked the door downstairs."

"Oh, stop whining. I've been waiting for months to do this properly and I've even got a reason to this time."

Marguerite, who was fair and not frequently spanked, reddened deeply from his hand. The quick coloration might have restrained him had she not reacted to each smack in the prettiest possible way.

Had he really scolded her for not being submissive enough? Her little pants and whimpers as she took a very hard spanking excited him beyond compare. Everything about her was completely adorable to him now that he was certain she'd decided to be his.

"Why didn't you tell me about your boyfriend?" He stopped to stroke her bottom, which he'd spanked to a deep magenta and was radiant. He spread her creamy thighs and found her wet.

"You never asked me," she murmured, opening herself to his exploring fingers while grinding her muff against his thigh. "And besides, we haven't even started dating properly yet," she pointed out.

"Oh? And what is it we have been doing?"

"Flirting," she suggested mischievously. This got her twelve of the best from his very hard hand.

"When I undertake to read three thousand pages of literature to please a girl, I'm not flirting. Did you think that I was?"

"No, sir," she gratified him by saying meekly.

"And besides, you wouldn't be planning to marry someone you were only flirting with. So I've caught you in another lie." Another twelve of the best followed, making Marguerite cry out loud and begin to twist on his lap.

"I was simply considering possibilities," she explained.

"Well consider the possibility of being stood in the corner with your skirt up to your waist like a naughty school girl."

"Oh, please, don't make me do that," she appealed to him with her big, green eyes behind the sexy glasses.

"There is an alternative," he told her firmly, stroking the sting from her bottom again.

"What is it?"

"Agree to begin our honeymoon here and now, with you bent over the little wooden desk."

"Only if you go and lock the door!"

When he raced back up the stairs, Marguerite was still rubbing her bottom with her long red hair down her shoulders and the proper white blouse unbuttoned to her cleavage. He turned her to face him, unbuttoned the blouse all the way and pulled it off, and after this, her lacy bra. He then looked at her, as much as to say, have I really known you for almost three months without ever once seeing your bosom?

He took her large, luscious breasts in his hands and deeply sucked each nipple until Marguerite almost fainted from enjoyment in his arms. Then he bent her over the reading desk, and pressed her down until her tummy touched the blotter. She leaned up on her elbows to give him access to her breasts.

"You look irresistible in that position, Marguerite," he told her, pulling his belt out of his trouser loops. She flashed him a look over one shoulder as he shook out the strap and gave her a lick with the end.

"Ow!" she cried and pouted.

"Take off your glasses," he commanded.

"No!" she resisted pertly. He gave her two hard swats with the belt that made her catch her breath and she took off her glasses and lay them on the desk beside her.

"So you want to get married," he repeated.

"No!" she replied, still vexed that he had overheard her dreadful remark. He gave her a hard whack with the strap.

"Don't lie to me when I have you in this position," he scolded, laying on the belt five more times, and scoring her pink bottom with light marks. "This is too exhilarating!" he thought to himself, while maintaining a serious demeanor.

Marguerite thrilled to the sight of her handsome persecutor shaking out the strap, raising his arm and bringing it down. When he threw her a glance she felt her tummy contract. "He is too handsome!" she thought to herself.

"How do you think I felt listening to myself discussed as though I were a cheap trick!" he demanded.

"That's your interpretation!" she cried, starting up, but he pressed her back down with a hand in the small of her back.

"Where do you think you're going?"

"You're saying vile things again!" Marguerite cried passionately, instantly ready to burst into tears.

"Now, you listen to me young lady." He threw the belt down and smacked her hard with his hand. "I'm not going to put up with any more of your hyper-sensitive histrionics. Understand?" Smack!

"Yes!" she replied, breathlessly, her tummy fluttering again.

"I'm still getting over the fact that you interrupted our last session right in the middle just because I said something that offended you. Then I got my winter reading list. That was what I had to go through before I could claim the privilege of doing this to you again."

"A small enough price," she commented, reaching back to rub.

"No rubbing till I say so," he said, capturing both her wrists in his hand and pinning them to her waist. "You're right though, I did like the books. And now we have something to talk about besides your checkered past."

"Then why are you still spanking me?"

"Because I don't like my lady to discuss me with other men."

"But I haven't agreed to be your lady."

"Fine, I'll just keep doing this until you do," he promised, delivering a series of heavy, satisfying smacks to her glowing bottom. She reclaimed her wrists to bury her head in her arms as he warmed her thoroughly with the palm of his hand, then returned to the strap for twelve more.

"Well?"

Marguerite felt very sore when he stopped, but still wanted him to go on.

"I'm just surprised that you found it so difficult to conquer *Pamela*," she baited him, reminding him of the nine hundred pages he had finally plowed through to satisfy the letter of their agreement.

"Oh, I conquered *Pamela*, all right, and now I'm going to . . . capture you," he decided, drawing back his arm to really make her feel the next twelve. "This is exactly the sort of whipping Pamela should have been given for being so willful."

"I'm a good deal more willful than Pamela," Marguerite warned.

"Oh, really?" He brought the strap down hard now. Marguerite gripped the desk and gasped her way through many more strokes.

On another day, or in another mood, one fourth the strapping would have dissolved her in tears and cries for mercy, but this afternoon, being vigorously whipped felt somehow perfectly romantic.

When one final volley of six was all that flesh could bear, Marguerite cried out at last. Malcolm was relieved when she did, afraid that they were both becoming carried away with the passion of their first real session. He saw as he threw down the strap and unzipped his trousers that she had become shockingly marked with broad swatches of rose standing out against the paler pink that stained both cheeks.

He pushed her back down over the desk. "I don't think I've ever had a woman put me off as long as you have." Malcolm had a condom out of its package and on his fully erect penis in seconds. Then he spread her legs, pulled her up by the hips and guided his cock into her slick sex.

"Slowly, darling, please," she urged, looking prettily back at him over one soft shoulder. She gave a little shiver as he gripped her by the waist and began to penetrate her deeply. As he drove his large cock into her one insistent inch at a time, he leaned over to fondle her breasts, pinch her nipples and then her velvety ear lobes.

"You're damned right I'm unenlightened," he told her emphatically, driving into her pussy like an oiled piston. "So you're going to have to behave yourself from now on."

"I will never do that!" she cried.

"Oh yes you will, if we get married," he warned, smacking her on the thigh several times. She gave a little pant of excitement at this treatment, causing him to repeat it more firmly. Every time he did, a pre-climactic shiver rippled through her, bathing the deeply sheathed shaft of his cock with her affection. Malcolm was amused that she still seemed more than ready to endure additional smacks. She, who had the tenderest, whitest skin he had ever seen.

"You're being deliberately naughty," he told her, "and I can't in all good conscience spank you any more. You should see how marked you are."

These words of love were well received.

"I don't mind being marked by my fiancé," she murmured, succumbing at that moment to a rapturous climax. Immensely gratified, Malcolm then allowed himself to release the pent up emotion not only of the last three months, but of his entire life.

Their first sex act was complete. And Marguerite felt very glad that she had taken the time to choose the little desk and straight backed chair for her favorite gallery.

THE INDISCREET CHARM OF
MARGUERITE ALEXANDER

"TELL ME SOMETHING about Michael Flagg I don't know," Patricia Fairservis begged Marguerite Alexander Branwell over their first cappuccino together in the lighthouse.

Marguerite sat curled up in the window seat that raw March afternoon, a glorious new bride. They had already extensively discussed Malcolm, Marguerite's new mate, and were now on the topic of Michael Flagg, the good-looking detective whose favors had been shared between the girls for a time.

"Michael is a romantic at heart," Marguerite disclosed.

"Really? I haven't seen it," Patricia chortled, remembering the trip to the Combat Zone bookstore, plugged.

"I've always felt that Michael is just as disposed to worship women as to dominate them."

"He certainly isn't that way with me," Patricia confided, flipping back her straight blonde hair to light a cigarette.

"You know, I have *whipped* Michael, on several occasions," Marguerite let slip with something like a giggle. Patricia stared at her.

"Are you saying he's really submissive?" Patricia asked with sudden anxiety.

"Certainly not submissive, but perhaps a bit more of a sensualist than you thought," Marguerite explained. But Patricia was too new in the scene to understand such nuances and felt betrayed. Marguerite noted the change and was sorry she had spoken.

• • •

Marguerite was to regret her rash admission even more the following day when she was having lunch at the inn and Michael slid into the booth across from her with an expression that could not be described as cordial.

"Why Michael, how are you?"

"Not very well thanks to you, Marguerite."

"Me?"

"Thanks to you I no longer have a girlfriend," he reported gloomily, ordering coffee.

"Oh, my dear!" Marguerite remembered her conversation with Patricia the previous day. "You don't mean she minded what I told her?"

"She minded, Marguerite."

"But, how could she be so unenlightened?"

"How could you be so indiscreet?"

Marguerite couldn't meet his eyes and felt vexed enough to cry with self recrimination.

"I'll talk to her and make her understand," Marguerite offered.

"It's no use, she's lost all respect for me now," Michael said matter of factly. "She told me so."

"Then she's a little idiot!" Marguerite cried passionately. Michael sighed and looked at her.

"First you had to break my heart by getting married. Now you make it so I can't have Patricia either. What am I going to do with you, Marguerite?"

Marguerite blushed, surprised that he was not too upset to flirt.

"If I have to thrash her myself, I'll make her understand," vowed Marguerite.

"Marguerite?"

"Yes, Michael?"

"When may I expect satisfaction?"

"What?"

"I'm talking about me giving you the punishment you deserve for destroying my relationship with the Princess."

"Oh, Michael, darling, I'm afraid that won't be possible. You see, I've promised Malcolm that I wouldn't play with anyone else besides him."

"Who said anything about playing?"

– 277 –

"Michael, stop being horrid."

"Are you saying you refuse to submit to the strapping you have coming for breaking the first rule of the Scene?"

"I couldn't think of it. Malcolm would hate me if he found out."

"Like Patricia hates me?"

"Michael, please stop guilting me! It's not becoming in a man."

"I know. That's why I want to admonish you properly with my belt across your backside."

"No, it's out of the question. I'm very sorry about Patricia and I will intercede on your behalf. Now, if you'll excuse me . . ."

"You're getting that strapping, Marguerite, one way or another."

Much later that night, when Marguerite was driving home after a party at Anthony Newton's house on the cliff, she heard a siren behind her. Looking in her mirror she saw Michael put the portable light on top of his unmarked car. She pulled over and looked up at him when he came to the window.

"A siren, Michael?"

"Get out of the car," he told her tersely.

"What's the matter?"

Michael opened the door, pulled her out of the car, spun her around and cuffed her wrists behind her back.

"You're under arrest."

"But, why?"

"Speeding while under the influence."

"But Michael, really! It's four in the morning. There isn't a soul on the road and I've only had a couple of drinks."

"Shut up and get in the car," he snapped. Marguerite never remembered him taking this tone with her before and she felt a tear moisten the corner of her eye. He put her in the back seat of his car.

"Michael please don't take me to the station to do whatever it is you're planning. I couldn't bear it!"

"Afraid of it getting in the paper and Malcolm finding out?"

"Michael Flagg, if you go through with this insanity, I swear I'll never speak to you again!"

He looked at her in the rear view mirror as she curled up on the seat, cuffed and pouting, in her pearls, sable and evening dress, her russet hair rippling to her shoulders.

– 278 –

"There is an alternative to the station house," he suggested. "Come home with me and take what you've got coming like a woman."

Marguerite had never been blackmailed into playing before, but Malcolm was out of town until the following evening and she felt excited by the fantasy. Although Michael didn't need to know that.

"Very well," she agreed, rather proudly and refused to meet his eyes in the mirror for the rest of the ride.

Michael did not uncuff her until he had bent her over his spanking horse in his own playroom some five minutes later.

"Don't move," he warned her, pulling off her fur and smoothing down the back of her pearl grey velvet gown. She turned her head to see him unbuckle his belt.

The horrible part was that for once she'd actually done something that really merited a spanking, which was too humiliating to contemplate.

"You don't really deserve a warm up," he told her, pushing her skirt up to her waist to reveal a pair of pearl grey silk briefs that wrapped her like a present. "But I still love you, so you'll get the first fifty on your panties." He brought the belt down across her bottom with a snap.

Marguerite clamped her lips together and refused to make a sound. The strap came down ten or a dozen more times with a crisp, determined report. They were fifty she might have almost enjoyed had her mind not been filled with anxiety that she would be marked.

"Oh, Michael, please don't mark me!" she cried suddenly, before they had advanced to stroke twenty-five.

"Are you afraid of your husband, Marguerite?" He pulled down her panties to check for marks. She had already become deeply pinkened.

"Malcolm isn't free-wheeling like you. He'd never forgive me," she appealed to him with a melting look.

"I still don't understand why you get to demolish my relationship but I have to protect yours," Michael observed with perplexity, pulling her panties back up to finish the first set of fifty strokes.

"If only I'd known Patricia was so conventional!" Marguerite lamented.

"It surprised me too," Michael reflected. "Are you ready?"

"Yes."

"Now you're going to feel the way I strap Patricia," Michael warned her, then lay on the remaining strokes in two sets of twelve, hard enough to make Marguerite cry out at each whack.

Marguerite thought, "This Patricia is a heavy submissive!" But she liked the strapping. And it was very good to be with Michael again. However, when he bared her, she panicked.

"If you do the next set that hard I'll be marked," she stood up to examine her bottom, which was now a deep magenta in coloration and stinging from the strap. She rubbed it and went to a mirror. Michael folded his arms and waited.

"We can make a deal," he said, grabbing her when she returned to him and bending her back over the bench. He pulled her skirt up, made her step out of the panties and spread her legs. The next thing she heard was his zipper coming down.

A light, flaky snow began to fall at dawn, when Michael put Marguerite back into her car.

"I'm going to talk to her, Michael," Marguerite promised. He bent to kiss her good-bye.

"She can go to hell as far as I'm concerned," he said pleasantly. "Bye, honey."

"Bye, darling," said Marguerite, praying to the goddess not to let Malcolm return home early.

That afternoon Michael was shoveling snow off his front walk way when Patricia drove up. He gave her a look and said, "Oh, it's my fair-weather friend," then continued with his work.

"Michael, I've been thinking."

"I'll bet that was painful."

"I guess I over reacted about your being a switch."

"Look, Patricia, just because I let one woman whip me once a year—that doesn't make me a switch."

"Do you want me to whip you, Michael?"

Michael, who did not reply, was glad that snow shoveling required so much energy, otherwise he might have been tempted to wring her neck.

"Michael, I love you whatever you are," she assured him.

"You didn't seem to feel that way yesterday." He put the shovel away and they went inside. Patricia peeled off her coat. She was dressed in beige wool leggings and a white sweater and her hair was in a ponytail.

"I'm very sorry about the way I spoke to you yesterday," she said with some difficulty, for apologies did not come easily to her her lips.

"Okay," he said, "we'll forget it ever happened."

"Entirely?" she asked.

"I have no desire to go submissive to you, if that's what you're wondering about," he told her firmly.

"Well, but, do you accept my apology?"

"Sure."

"I don't know how I could have been so insensitive."

"You specialize in that."

Patricia hung her head. Her heart beat quickly as she wondered what would happen next. He came and sat next to her on the sofa and made her look at him. However she could not meet his eyes.

"What's the matter Patricia? Are you embarrassed?"

"Yes."

"Because you know you deserve a good spanking?" He drew her across his lap. Gripping her firmly about the waist, he brought his hand down a couple of dozen times in rapid succession across the nubby woolen seat of her heavy winter leggings. "You've been a disloyal playmate, haven't you?"

"Yes," she replied as he took down her pants and her silk tights to completely bare her creamy bottom.

"It's a good thing you had the sense to come over here and apologize," he told her, bringing his large palm down hard on her tender cheeks, which caused her to kick and cry. "I was never going to call you again."

The tone of indignation in Michael's voice caused Patricia's stomach to contract, but his hand coming down hurt too much to enjoy.

"Imagine being so narrow minded and judgmental!" he continued to scold her. "My own feelings aside, I should spank you very hard just for that one thing," he declared, putting additional force behind his swing.

"Ow!" she cried. "I'm sorry!"

"You know, Patricia, every time I think you've grown up and become a human being, you manage to disappoint me. Why is that?" He paused to stroke her deeply colored bottom.

"I don't know," she whimpered, really feeling sorry for herself now.

Michael delivered a final two dozen swats vigorously enough to make her wail like the spoiled child she was, then pushed her off his lap. She sat on the floor, rubbed her bottom and pouted until he kissed her.

"I'm glad that you decided not to desert me," he told her.

Marguerite's first marital infidelity greatly weakened her resolve to be faithful, especially with regard to Sloan Taylor, the handsome young man she had recently hired to manage her book shop.

Winter hung on tenaciously, lasting into the second week of April and depositing Frances in bed with the flu. This necessitated Marguerite returning to her shop to assist Sloan for eight days. Even before this convenient inconvenience occurred, Marguerite noticed that Wednesdays had become her favorite day of the week. This was Frances' day off and Marguerite customarily popped into the shop for the morning or afternoon to help.

It was during these long periods of being snowed or rained in with Sloan that Marguerite began to fully realize that her employee was uncommonly attractive and exquisitely sensitive.

It was not that Marguerite wanted to do anything like *play* with Sloan. Being his boss, she had no desire to go submissive to him and as he himself was apparently strictly dominant, there was no chance of her becoming his mistress. Marguerite's freshly sprung desire for her subordinate was straightforwardly sexual. She knew from looking at him that he was handsome. She knew from Frances that he had a large cock. She simply longed to feel it in her.

Marguerite desired Sloan. She had to fight the impulse to run her hands through his black hair and bite his white neck. The faint scent of his spicy aftershave drew her to him. Six-foot, two-inches and lean, he wore his good clothes well, and this entranced her. His thoughtfulness and warmth added affection to her desire.

She knew that what she was contemplating was not permissible. Even the fact that he shared her taste in literature to an uncanny degree could not excuse a blatant seduction.

And yet, with Marguerite, thinking was planning and planning was doing. She knew her own nature too well to try to resist her impulses for longer than two or three weeks. The only obstruction to her desire was the possibility of Malcolm finding out. Whether their marriage would weather her first deliberate infidelity was a question which preoccupied her.

Naturally she was more than fond of Malcolm. She had married him. But unfavorable comparisons between the aggressive businessman and the refined bibliophile were bound to arise while Marguerite worked side by side with Sloan.

Malcolm wanted to read more, but ultimately he preferred to fill his spare time with physical pursuits, some of which she happily participated in and some of which she left alone. A good example was the weekend he decided to enroll in a ski rescue school in Vermont. Marguerite applauded his noble endeavor, and packed a picnic basket for his drive, then happily spent Saturday in the shop with Sloan.

Malcolm was not due home till late Sunday night and she decided to use this weekend to accomplish her deed.

Sloan was not ignorant of the fact that something was about to happen between himself and Marguerite, he only hoped he had the patience and resolve to wait for her to initiate it. For when Marguerite liked someone as much as she did Sloan, she became as mischievously lovable as a kitten. No man in the commonwealth could have resisted her, least of all himself.

Yet Sloan wondered if the embarrassment and potential hurt to Frances and Malcolm would be justified in pursuit of a relationship which most certainly would not include spanking. He sensed this every time they flirted, during which she was always extremely careful to maintain her dignity, both as his boss and a goddess. It was very clear to Sloan that while he would most probably be permitted to make love to Aphrodite, he would not be permitted to chastise her. Considering the beauty, roundness and perfection of Marguerite's bottom and Sloan's secret desire to lavish every type of attention on it, this was a very sad state of affairs for the inflamed but well mannered young man.

Sometimes the absurdity of the situation frustrated Sloan, however, common sense told him to cut his own throat before laying disciplinary hands on the precious person of his employer.

Spanking Marguerite was positively out of the question. So naturally, this was what obsessed him. Her bottom was so lusciously ample. As a redhead, she would color so quickly and prettily. The very thought of taking her across his knee made him shudder with a surge of excitement. It was really too awkward.

Sloan had, of course, lied to Frankie when he declared that he did not think Mrs. Branwell the most provocative woman he had ever met, for he certainly did. But unlike Marguerite, who regarded Sloan as provided by the goddess for her amusement, Sloan had real respect for Marguerite and found the idea of seducing his employer to be extremely problematical.

In the end it was Sloan and not Marguerite who broke every rule, probably because his nerves were torn to pieces by the entire situation. They had just closed the door on Saturday night. Marguerite was pulling shades and Sloan was using an adding machine in his small back office to close out the day.

She was going around the shop collecting coffee cups when she entered his office. He didn't look up because he was adding. But as she leaned across his desk to grab a cup, her 24-inch waist caused Sloan to forget every rule of proper business etiquette and simply reach out to pull her down on his lap.

Marguerite gave a little gasp and looked at him in great surprise but did not attempt to repulse him.

"I'm sorry!" he immediately said. "But you're so irresistibly charming."

"I'm finding it rather difficult to resist you too," she smiled, locking her arms around his neck and kissing him.

"We shouldn't," he said several minutes later.

"Why not?" Marguerite was working on loosening his tie.

"Because you're married," he said, capturing her hands to kiss them.

"Oh, that," she said, while wriggling on his lap and allowing him to feel her bottom grinding against him.

"I'm sure your husband is insanely in love with you," said Sloan compassionately.

Marguerite felt somewhat vexed at Sloan for mentioning the uncomfortable subject of her marriage. "He doesn't have to find out," she firmly replied. They then resumed kissing. At length he suggested they retire to his apartment upstairs and Marguerite agreed.

She spent a few moments admiring the decorative improvements he had made since moving in. The more she touched and smelled and moved among his masculine things, the more eager to surrender to him she became. The fact the he was her employee now seemed completely irrelevant and she felt no more superior to him than Bertie Wooster did to Jeeves.

Meanwhile, every shred of his usual circumspection deserted Sloan as he watched her traverse his rooms in her crisp, tailored work outfit, a navy pencil skirt and matching wool vest over a white blouse, and medium-high ankle strap heels. She paused to admire a large, carved, Victorian box sofa, which had been sumptuously upholstered in honey beige brocade. "Is this new?" she asked, sitting down on it.

"Newly restored. The frame is from 1860. Do you like it?" Sloan came to sit next to her, handing her a glass of wine. She sipped with approval.

"It's wonderful. And large enough to do anything on."

"That was my thought."

"What would you like to do on it, Sloan?" Marguerite asked, causing him to color in such a way as to answer her question.

"Anything that would please you," he finally replied.

Marguerite laughed at him, which made him smile at her. "Many things please me," she elected to torture him.

"Tell me some of them."

"You've read my books."

"But they're all about B&D."

"Yes. Aren't they?" said Marguerite, virtually changing her mind about the tone of her relations with Sloan.

"Are you saying you'd be willing to play?"

"Do two people in the scene ever make love without playing first?"

"That depends upon whether they can agree on a definition for playing."

"Why don't you try something and see how I react?" Marguerite teased, delighted by his confusion.

"And what if you react badly?"

"Then I guess you could try something else," she suggested, her heart pounding in anticipation of the dynamic suddenly changing between them.

"What about role playing?" he asked, his color receding and his enthusiasm returning with a surge.

"That sounds like fun. I haven't done that in years."

"Any ideas?" he asked her.

"You decide," she encouraged him.

"Are you sure?"

"Quite sure."

"In that case, let's pretend that I'm your husband and I've just come home to discover that you've been unfaithful to me."

"That works," she cheerfully replied.

"My character is not unreasonable," Sloan rose in his animated way to paint the picture, "he understands that his wife is a free spirit. But there's also the issue of respect to be considered. Don't you agree?"

"Oh, undoubtedly. Cheating on one's husband is a sign of disrespect, if not to the man, at least to the institution of marriage," Marguerite helpfully replied.

"Naturally, he's distraught. He paces restlessly as he tries to decide how to deal with this startling revelation," Sloan continued, mesmerizing Marguerite with his pacing.

"Oh, he must forgive her!" cried Marguerite.

"Of course he must forgive her, dear girl, but not, I think, before administering a very sound spanking." Now that the word had been said it was her turn to blush. Her lips curved into a quiet, cat-like smile though she could not bring herself to meet his eyes.

He sat down beside her and very gently pulled her across his lap, causing her to admit to herself for the first time, that this was exactly what she'd had in mind when she had hired Sloan.

Sloan smoothed down her skirt, raised his strong right arm and brought his hand down twice, smacking her once on each cheek through the tight, wool skirt.

Marguerite settled in and closed her eyes. "You have a hard hand," she murmured, as he continued spanking her as firmly as he dared.

"It's just what you need," he told her, vigorously spanking every inch of her lush bottom several dozen times before pausing to let her catch her breath.

"I need whatever I want," she suggested pertly.

"Because you're a spoiled brat!" Sloan declared, starting all over again, but using a harder, faster stroke.

"Ow! That really stings!" she cried at length, reaching back to rub her bottom. Sloan pushed her hand away and stroked her himself. Then he very slowly pushed her skirt up to her waist to reveal a bottom snugly wrapped in a sheer nylon garter belt and panties and long legs in seamed stockings. Her fair skin was already darkly pinkened under the fresh white lingerie.

"I'm sorry," he told her, "but it's the only way you'll learn to take me seriously."

"I'm taking you very seriously, darling," she replied, grinding hard enough against his lap to feel his erection. Sloan's satisfaction in the moment was great. To pretend that he was Marguerite's husband enjoying the privilege of disciplining her was exotic beyond dreams. Her bottom arched to meet his hand now, in spite of the sting, convincing him that she was feeling more pleasure than discomfort.

"Didn't you realize that you had a jealous husband?" he asked, carefully tugging her panties down to bare her bottom.

Marguerite knew very well that she had a jealous husband. And it was pleasant to imagine that this was all that he would do if he ever did catch her cheating on him.

Even as Sloan spanked her bottom to a deep magenta, he thought, "I can leave it at this and prevent us both from committing a terrible error." Then he remembered that he was the one who had made the first move. By the rules of romance, to leave it at just a spanking would be an insult to Marguerite, not to mention the frustration it would cause them both.

A moment later, as he touched her intimately for the first time, he thought, "Who am I kidding? Doing this is just as bad as doing everything." Marguerite was very wet and had a scent like jungle flowers. Inserting his long middle finger into her sex to the knuckle, he pulled it out glistening and tasted her on his hand. The savor of her creamy essence ignited his partially Italian blood and every grain of resolve melted. He plunged two fingers back into her pussy to the hilt and began to possess her, still holding her down across lap, with his other hand on her radiant cheeks.

Marguerite was surprised at how deftly he plied her. This she really liked. She could almost come with his long fingers giving her pleasure while she still lay across his knee. But now that he'd aroused her to this pitch, she craved more spanking.

"Darling?" she said softly.

"Yes, Marguerite?" Sloan gently slid his fingers free.

"I feel my misdeed was most grave."

Sloan took this as his cue to unleash a more believable degree of husbandly indignation when he resumed the paddling. What bliss to be married to Marguerite and actually enjoy doing this on a regular basis. She seemed thoroughly content to lie across his lap and allow him to spank her as hard as he liked.

"I think that's enough," Sloan said at last, noticing some dark rose speckling under the deep pink his hand had left on her very fair skin.

"Are you sure I've been punished enough?" she asked brightly, growing very fond of his hand.

"I'm sure you're going to mark if I keep this up," he said, gently pulling her up and taking her in his arms.

"Perhaps we should do something else for awhile," she suggested, unknotting his tie.

Malcolm Branwell was made aware of his wife's infidelity with Sloan in a hideously unexpected way. Women being the intuitive individuals they are, and every woman in Random Point being a sort of witch by dint of simply residing there, Frances Wu guessed the moment she returned to work and saw her employer and her supervisor together; Sloan and Marguerite had had knowledge of each other in her absence. This suspicion was validated by the scent of Marguerite's perfume, lingering on Sloan's favorite vest and tie. She had gone through his closet with a nose like a cat.

Frances was both jealous and angry, seeing Sloan as a hypocrite for professing indifference to Marguerite, then seizing the first opportunity to seduce her. Sloan had long known of Frances' vindictive streak, but never guessed how far into mischief it would take her.

A few days after Frances' discovery, Malcolm received an anonymous letter telling him about the affair between Marguerite and Sloan. It was signed: A concerned on-looker. The letter arrived at the corporate offices in Boston on a Monday. It was the middle of the afternoon, and Malcolm had just gotten off the phone with Marguerite who was planning dinner. He'd intended to drive out to

Random Point in about an hour. He'd even made a shopping list of items to pick up on the way home. He crumpled it up and tossed it in the waste basket then stared bleakly at the wall as he decided what to do. Dully he dialed the phone.

"Marguerite? Me. Look, uh, something's just come up and I'm going to have to stay in town tonight." He hung up before his voice could betray his emotion. On the other end Marguerite looked at the receiver and suddenly knew that something was very wrong. As soon as she hung up, the phone rang again.

"Hello?"

"Marguerite?" It was Sloan and he sounded agitated.

"Yes, dear, is everything all right?"

"Not exactly. Frances has just given her notice. Apparently she figured out what happened between us and she's furious."

"How in the world did she?"

"She smelled your perfume on my clothes."

"Oh, Sloan, I'm so sorry!" Marguerite almost sobbed with vexation. "But tell me, do you think that Frances would be capable of betraying us to Malcolm?"

"In a heart beat."

"In that case, I've had a short and happy marriage."

"Oh, Marguerite, no! Mr. Branwell would never give you up over someone as unimportant as me."

"Look, darling, we've got to work on getting them back."

"I doubt there's any hope with Frances," he sighed. "She's gone back to Boston to stay with her parents for awhile. She says she couldn't bear to live in your guesthouse another day."

Marguerite was silent with worry and guilt. She had brought Frankie out to Random Point on a romantic whim and now appeared to be driving her away for the same reason.

"Oh, Sloan, what have I done?"

"Marguerite, don't blame yourself. I did make the first move," he gently reminded her. "Besides, Frances and I were never really compatible. And she was thinking of going to Europe with a knapsack in a couple of months anyway."

"Is this so?"

"Yes, she's been trying to get me to drop everything and go with her."

"But you don't want to?"

"Not at the moment."

"I regret causing anyone pain, but I don't regret becoming close to you," said Marguerite, hanging up.

It was raining when she left her house with an umbrella and walked the three village blocks to Hugo Sands' antiques shop. There were no customers in the store. Hugo emerged from his back office at the tinkle of the bell.

"Marguerite, what's the matter?" Hugo saw trouble in her face. Marguerite compulsively picked up and examined small objects while confessing all that had happened to Hugo.

"That little brat!" he declared angrily at the end of her recitation. "Someone ought to cane her senseless for doing that to you and Malcolm."

"Oh, Hugo, it isn't her fault. It's mine. You can't blame the girl for being jealous and bitter. Here I dragged her out to Random Point, made sure she fell in love with Sloan, then took him for a play toy myself. What I've done has been perfectly loathsome!"

"Oh, sweetie," Hugo took her in his arms and hugged her. "You can't help being attracted to good-looking men."

"Should I have not gotten married?"

"It was time you got a husband, Marguerite. Everyone knew that."

"He won't put up with this, Hugo. He's probably calling his divorce lawyer this very minute," she fretted, pacing up and down the narrow aisles of the shop.

"He's in the scene, Marguerite, you know what you have to do."

"What?" She looked up suspiciously.

"Why, prostrate yourself before him, of course, and humbly beg his forgiveness, preferably wearing something tight. If you're lucky you'll get off with a thrashing and probably have the best sex you've ever had afterwards."

"If only I could believe that."

"Trust me. Put on your grey jersey dress with the fringe tie scarf and four-inch heels. Get in the car and drive to Boston. Now."

As Marguerite walked back to her house she thought, "Hugo's never been wrong before." Before the dress went on she laced herself into her new pearl grey satin custom waist cinch and finished with a matching lace bra and G-string with seamed hose. Her new pumps were from Paris and the wool dress Hugo had suggested had a similar label.

Driving into Boston in the rain Marguerite made positive projections for the evening, envisioning a splendidly passionate scene and then forgiveness. Imagining the scene brought a radiance to her cheeks and she wondered whether she hadn't done what she had with Sloan partially to incite her husband.

"What's the fun of being married to a dominant male if you aren't going to try his patience now and then?" she wondered, finding it quite easy to rationalize her behavior from this point of view. This way what she did almost seemed innocent, a childish plea for attention. Would Malcolm go for that?

When she arrived at his rooftop duplex in Back Bay at around ten, Malcolm was not at home. She guessed he had gone to his gym, then to dinner and would be returning any moment.

Two minutes later she heard his key in the door and rushed out to the marbled and mirrored foyer to meet him. Malcolm was astonished to see her and flushed with a mixture of pain and excitement. He filled out his T-shirt and jeans as only a gym-rat can, and Marguerite longed to wrap her arms around his 28-inch waist very badly, but had no way of knowing just how angry he was and didn't dare get so close so soon.

"Hi, Malcolm, I hope you don't mind that I came."

"But, I told you I had something going on," he protested.

"Now, darling?"

"That's right," he said, "I have a late meeting tonight."

"Malcolm, you know that isn't true," Marguerite said softly.

"I'm sorry, Marguerite, but I think we need to spend a few days apart," he said decisively, strolling down the hall towards his bedroom. Marguerite's face became very warm as she realized that she had been dismissed. Pensively she walked down the hall to her own room and removed her hat and gloves. Then she lay on the bed face down, with her head pillowed on her arms, wondering what she should do. Hugo had counseled humility, but Malcolm hadn't stood still long enough for her to practice any.

Then he suddenly appeared in the doorway of her room, causing her to start up.

"It's true, isn't it? About you and Sloan Taylor, I mean."

"It's true that I was just a little bit naughty while you were away skiing," Marguerite admitted lightly.

"Is that how you see it?" Malcolm snapped.

"Yes."

"Well that isn't how I see it. And I won't be made a fool of."

"Oh, darling—"

"Don't darling me. I want an explanation of why you're running around seducing your employees when you're supposed to be married to me."

"Sheer self-indulgence," she replied in a properly regretful tone.

"Oh, is that so? Well, how would you feel if I indulged myself with every pretty girl who works for me?"

"I don't know how I'd feel, but I would try to understand."

"You know, I seem to remember you giving me your word on our wedding day that there would be no other men in your life from now on."

"I'm sorry," she meekly replied.

"Is that all you have to say after doing something like this?"

"I was bad," she admitted. "But I adore you."

Malcolm felt the tension leave his shoulders as he gazed at her open face. Now that she was here, most of the pain of the anonymous letter receded. He noticed how she'd dressed for him and was momentarily riveted by her impossibly small waist.

"Do you know that you need a good spanking?" he suddenly demanded, sitting next to her on the bed and pulling her across his lap. An oval, ebony hairbrush came easily into his hand from the dresser and he used it to administer twelve hard smacks to her skirted bottom. Marguerite caught her breath at each one but didn't cry out. A first punishment from an adored husband is a wildly erotic moment to any woman in the Scene.

"Imagine me having to do this," he scowled, "not three months into our marriage!" He smacked her hard with the brush ten more times, then put it down, pushed her soft jersey skirt up to her waist and renewed the spanking on her bare backside, now pink and luxuriantly framed by the hem of the corset and rosetted garter straps. Now he spanked her twenty times without pausing. She could no longer lie still or keep quiet and on stroke twenty attempted to break his hold on her waist. Each fair cheek was now brightly reddened and she twisted to avoid the brush with such urgency that Malcolm decided to toss it aside. "Calm down," he ordered.

Malcolm reached under the corset to grasp her G-string and pull it off. Then he separated her legs and slapped her bare inner thighs, just above her stocking tops, ten or twelve times each. Marguerite's soft skin was very sensitive in this area and Malcolm's hand was very hard. Tears sprung to her eyes immediately but she suppressed the accompanying sobs. She did, however, close her luscious thighs so tightly that he was compelled to pry them apart.

"I'm sorry," he told her firmly, "but you need this." This time he pulled her bottom cheeks apart and applied his palm sharply to her bottomhole. These smacks made her whimper, but she did not pull away or try to resist them, even when he spanked her hard.

The punishment was quickly becoming erotic, in spite Malcolm's resolve to simply teach her a lesson. However, it did seem to be working, both to relieve his lovesick anxiety and to make her wet. He had a throbbing erection and his anger was gone.

"Let's get this dress off," he told her, and quickly pulled it over her head while somehow managing to hold her in position. "And this can go as well," he said, unhooking her bra and tossing it aside. Now he adjusted her position so that she straddled one of his thighs with her slick, pink charms fully revealed.

"This is the naughtiest part of all," he told her, tapping her spread sex with his palm. Meanwhile, he reached under her bosom to lightly squeeze her breasts and pinch her nipples, which had grown stiff. But she refused to stay properly spread unless he held her that way, so he let go of her creamy bosom and devoted his full attention to her intoxicating pussy. He only patted her glistening labia, but each little spank went through her like a current of energy, swelling her dewy pink clit.

"Tell me that you're sorry," he ordered.

"I'm sorry!"

"Beg my forgiveness."

"Darling, please forgive me!" she appealed.

"Swear you'll never do it again."

"I swear I'll never do it again!"

He let her up. She pouted until he took her in his arms and buried his face in her hair. "But you're such a bad girl," he said sadly, pulling away from her, "and I'm so disappointed in you."

"Oh, Malcolm, please don't say that!" she pleaded, throwing her arms around his neck. He pulled them away and looked at her sternly.

"If you want me to love and respect you as a husband should, you'd better do some reforming—and fast. I won't have the patience to put up with too many incidents like this one," he told her firmly, then left her alone and returned to his bedroom.

Once there, he threw himself on his bed and stared at the ceiling, trying to decide how he felt. When all was said and done, he had no heart to punish her severely. But somehow she had to be made to feel that she had committed a very real error. And yet he lay there aching with love for Marguerite and knowing that nothing would be resolved until he possessed her again.

"I went to her once," he thought, "now she should come to me." He concentrated on willing her to come to him. Nothing happened. Then he sat up and strained his ears, wondering if she was crying herself to sleep. This notion renewed his hard-on and made it even more impossible to concentrate on anything but his beautiful wife. Suddenly the door opened and Marguerite entered in nothing but a peach silk dressing gown.

"Darling? May I come in?"

Malcolm nodded. She sat next to him and looked pensive.

"Well?" he growled.

"Don't I deserve to be comforted?" she asked.

"Do you?" His tone was cynical, but he took her in his arms immediately and dimmed the bedside lamp. "I suppose it's always going to be like this, isn't it?" he guessed.

"Darling, I went a long time before I decided to marry. I picked you because your rigidity made the perfect counterpoint to my fluidity. Does that tell you anything?"

"Yes, it tells me that you're going to make my life hell," he brooded.

"But, it doesn't change the way you feel about me, does it? What I mean is, if you don't like me now because of what I did, we should end it this moment." Marguerite sat up suddenly, as though considering this possibility for the first time.

"I like you all right," he conceded, pulling her back down. "I more than like you."

SHADOW LANE VI
PUT TO THE BLUSH

Phoebe and Pascal
Part One

Pascal Robbins, 36, was a photo journalist who had obtained a contract to shoot scenic Cape Cod for a coffee table book. His wife Phoebe Casper, 26, was an actress who'd signed on with the Woodbridge Repertory Theatre Group for the autumn season. They were subletting William Random's house in the cul-de-sac at the end of Shadow Lane.

The Robbins were an unusually attractive couple. Pascal was a lithe, angular, retro male, who wore trousers with pleats, shoes with laces and hats. Phoebe had become aware of him as he stared at her from the sixth row center two consecutive nights while she played Beatrice in *Much Ado About Nothing* the previous year in Boston.

Phoebe's sprightliness helped her land roles in the comedies of Goldoni and Molière, her scaled down voluptuousness showing to advantage in period costumes. Her mellifluous voice had seduced him, while her long, burnished hair and lambent eyes, all aglow in the footlights, worked a swift enchantment on Pascal.

The Robbins had been married for less than a year, barely knew each other, were passionately in love and quarreled whenever they met, which wasn't often. It had been a rocket year for Pascal, filled with international travel and spreads in important magazines, while Phoebe had spent the most uncomfortable winter of her life with a theatre group in Minneapolis, only seeing her new husband for a few days out of every month.

But now the coincidence of them both finding work in this idyllic location, during the most romantic season of the year, held Phoebe enthralled.

Each in their own way, Pascal and Phoebe were equivilantly difficult, willful, emotional, defensive, well-meaning and highly strung. Pascal was a meticulous planner, while Phoebe's methods often seemed as scattered as pick-up sticks.

The first time Pascal saw her turn a hotel suite into a yard sale simply by unpacking, he fancied he could feel his blood pressure rise. Luckily, whisky had the power to calm him, and he availed himself of its beneficial properties whenever he felt himself in danger of losing his temper with his adorable new wife.

Pascal had lived as a fussy bachelor for so long that making the adjustment to co-habitation with a bouncing, cheerful, suntea brewing, nonsmoking, nondrinking, decaffeinated, exercise conscious, Green Party crusading vegetarian was a tremendous challenge.

Unlike Pascal, Phoebe never suffered from anxiety, slept like a small, mossy stone and never awoke without a pink flush in her face and dazzlingly clear eye whites. All of this thrilled and annoyed him no end and he vacillated between feeling unworthy of her and repressing the urge to wring her smug little neck.

Often, over his first cup of coffee (that he himself ground, since she lacked all domestic skills) and cigarette of the day, he'd watch her flit around the charming old kitchen, leaving messes in her wake, and fantasize about forcing her to behave like a lady.

First he mentally replaced the T-shirt of his that was all that she wore, with a silk dressing gown and high-heeled slippers. Next, instead of yogurt and whole grain bread, he imagined her fixing them eggs Benedict and mimosas, without spilling or slopping or breaking anything. That was as far as the fantasy went but it always made him sigh with longing.

When Phoebe sat down and dug into her granola while casually turning the pages of *The Nation*, Pascal noticed for the first time how much like the hands of a twelve year old Phoebe's appeared.

"You bite your fingernails?" He took her small hand in his slim, graceful one and shook his head with disapproval.

"It's just a nervous habit," she confessed, hiding her free hand in her lap with a blush.

"You, nervous?"

"I guess I must be, huh?" Now she stopped eating and sat on both hands.

"Ever think of a manicure?"

"You mean put on toxic polish?"

"But crimson nails are so sexy," he replied, picking up *The New York Times*.

The organic Phoebe snorted in derision but the actress who enjoyed adopting new personae decided to obtain a manicure that afternoon.

That day magic happened for Phoebe Casper Robbins. First, the moment she arrived home, she received the call from the casting director telling her that she had been selected for the role of "Nora" in *A Doll's House*, the opening play of the season. This news caused Phoebe to perform cartwheels around the back garden.

Within the next half hour, as she wandered around the old house, allowing the thrill of popularity to wash through her, Phoebe made a discovery that relegated even Nora to the back of her mind momentarily.

She was in William Random's study when she came across an antique riding crop in the drawer of her landlord's desk.

Phoebe's heart began to pound as she examined it. She hadn't had a spanking fantasy in a long time, practically since she had gotten married, but the sight of the crop immediately recalled her secret passion. She wondered what Pascal would say when she showed it to him. Perhaps he'd turn her under his arm and use it on her for snooping!

Being an intuitive young lady, Phoebe was inclined to believe that the crop she held in her hand had not been used on a horse in some time. This in mind, she began to look more carefully into the cabinets and drawers, not only of the study, but of other rooms in the house. By the time Pascal got home, Phoebe felt she knew more about the sex life of William Random than she knew about her own.

"I found out some fascinating facts about the people who own this house," Phoebe confided to Pascal the moment he came in around tea time. He kissed her and began to de-camera in the handsome foyer.

"Really? Tell all," he encouraged her as she led him into the sitting room where she actually had the samovar heating. She had the flame turned up so high that the silver bottom had oxidized to black, but he was touched by the gesture. "You can't have this turned up so high, darling, you'll ruin the samovar," he told her gently, turning down the flame and wiping the bottom clean with a napkin.

"I'm sorry, but wait until you hear. Guess what I found in William Random's desk?" She carefully prepared a cup of tea for her husband, using a silver tea ball stuffed with real tea leaves from a tin on the sideboard. This genteel occupation suddenly brought back the real news of the day and she spilled half the tea as she turned in excitement to cry, "I can't believe I forgot, I'm to play Nora!"

"You're to play Nora?" Pascal took her in his arms. "Little you?"

"I'm just as shocked as you are," she confided, breaking from his embrace in order to cram a chocolate covered apricot into her mouth.

"*You're* eating chocolate?" Pascal was amazed.

"I have to start living and breathing Nora. Be prepared for a five pound weight gain in the coming days and weeks," Phoebe was philosophical.

"If we start corseting you right away, no one need ever notice," he teased her, pulling her down on his lap.

"I can't believe you mentioned corsets! That's just what I was coming to about the Randoms!"

"Don't tell me William Random corsets to achieve those rock-hard abs?" Pascal protested.

"Silly. His lover, that gorgeous Puerto Rican girl, has a world class collection of waist cinches in her wardrobe plus leather dresses, stiletto heels, opera gloves and velvet gowns for days. I tell you these people are serious fetishists!"

"Mr. Random's Significant Other is a very feminine creature," Pascal observed when Phoebe jumped off his lap to pour herself a cup of tea.

"You like that, don't you?" she accused with sudden excitement.

"You're very feminine, darling," he told her, taking the tea cup away and pulling her back down on his lap. She casually regarded her freshly enameled nails until he noticed them. "Phoebe, you followed my advice!" He was overwhelmed and kissed her hands.

"Nora is docile and obedient, always," Phoebe replied, with a serious gaze.

"Except for when she's doing exactly as she pleases," Pascal pointed out, squeezing her small waist.

"Nora trembles when her husband frowns," Phoebe insisted gravely.

"And you intend to follow suit?'

"Just for the next three weeks."

"Oh, I see," he smiled.

"Guess what else I found? Just wait until I show you!" Phoebe ran out of the room and reappeared in the sitting room a minute later, carrying a giant, chestnut leather album with peach cherubs carved into the cover. She lay it on the coffee table and sat down next to him.

"Now get ready for some racy stuff," she warned, beginning to turn the black pages, upon which a collection of artistic, black and white photos paraded. Some pictured pretty women in fetish attire, posing in studio settings or at what seemed to be rather gay parties. Some of the stills were of attractive couples, in fancy dress, striking poses that went beyond romance and into the realm of domination. Included were a number of spanking stills and others which involved more esoteric forms of corporal punishment. In every case, the dress, positioning and expressions were perfect. Phoebe watched Pascal's face closely as he turned the pages with an interest that was real but which fell far short of the fascination they had held for her.

Phoebe had spent a long time with the album, returning again and again to the six perfect, over the knee spanking portraits which appeared in the middle of the book. This pretty collection also caught Pascal's eye and he grinned at her.

"That's what you could use sometimes, a good spanking!"

This comment left her momentarily bereft of speech and she simply stared at him. "Do you really think so, darling?" she finally stammered, blushing hard.

"Just about three or four times a week," he reassured her,

pulling her towards him and kissing her. Then he let her go and began to turn the pages of the album again. She wondered that he could go through the beautiful photographs so rapidly.

"I wonder who she is," Pascal mused, as he came to a photo of a brunette who wasn't Damaris perched on William Random's lap towards the end of the album.

"Her name is Laura. She's his ex. Come with me!" Phoebe took him by the hand and led him upstairs to William's studio and unlocked the door.

"Phoebe, I don't remember William giving us the key to this room," Pascal said as he followed her inside. As the work space of an architect, this was one of the most beautiful rooms in the house. But the most interesting aspect of the decor was the gallery of framed illustrations which decorated the walls.

These drawings, mostly done in colored pencil or gouche, went beyond the photo album, which had been suggestive rather than explicit. The subject matter up here was hardcore B&D and all the illustrations were signed by Laura Random.

"Phoebe, where did you get the key to this room?" Pascal demanded.

"From William Random's desk," she replied, with a palpable flutter.

"And do you think he would have locked the room if he wanted us in here?"

"I don't know. Does it matter? He'll never know."

"Are you kidding? You can't look at a room without breaking or rearranging every object in it."

"You make me sound like 'Carrie'," she observed, not unflattered by his estimation of her powers.

"Come on, baby, give me the key."

"The key? But why do you want it?" Phoebe reluctantly dug the key out of the pocket of her khaki shorts and put it in his hand.

"To make sure you never come in here again. Now let's go," he told her, pulling her out the door and locking it behind them, then putting the key in his own pocket.

"Really, darling, you hardly even looked at the drawings!" Phoebe folded her arms and sulkily followed him downstairs again.

"Sweetheart, the owner left that door locked for a reason and I think we should respect it."

"But I'm sure it was only because of the drawings. They didn't want to shock us."

"Lock up the drawings but leave the photos out?"

"They just forgot about the photos. I know, because I found plenty of other stuff they did lock up!" said Phoebe triumphantly; but her glee evaporated as she noticed his frown.

"Phoebe, that's not nice," he declared, heading for the whiskey as soon as they reentered the sitting room. "We should respect the privacy of others."

"I'm sure they wouldn't mind," she replied intuitively.

"Phoebe, how can you say such a thing?"

"Because men who take photos like those don't get upset when women find them thrilling."

Pascal threw her a sharp look at this declaration. "Nevertheless, I want you to stay out of that studio from now on," he told her, lighting a cigarette.

"But I hadn't nearly finished looking at the beautiful drawings," Phoebe brooded, kicking her tiny work-booted foot against the delicately carved leg of a sofa.

"Phoebe, don't kick that sofa leg, it's an antique," Pascal scolded with some annoyance. Phoebe blushed and placed her tiny feet together and her hands in her lap. Imagining herself in one of Nora's corsets and gowns, she straightened her back and shoulders. "That's better," he immediately noticed, and rewarded her good posture with a kiss.

For a couple of days Phoebe was so busy with fittings and rehearsals that she forgot about the locked room, but she did not forget the photo album, or the additional cache of esoteric erotica she found in William Random's library. She had already memorized the faces of all the people in the six spanking stills, in case she should run into any of them in town.

Meanwhile, Pascal had begun his photographic odyssey with an inn and pub crawl from Random Point to Provincetown.

His first stop was The Dummy Up Club, which was all but hidden in the woods about two miles out of town. Rustic but luxe, the house included a piano bar, a billiards room and restaurant. He wanted to photograph the humidor.

The moment he entered he heard a voice he recognized, backed up by an accomplished pianist, rendering a Harold Arlen song that always gave him chills. As Pascal followed the enchanting sounds to their source he discovered his wife, gloriously clad in a pale blue portrait collar dress, sitting on the piano bench beside the musical composer Anthony Newton.

Pascal wandered over to the bar and ordered a scotch. Phoebe hadn't noticed him yet but this did not surprise him, considering her important quarry. He knew that Anthony Newton owned a house in Random Point, but never guessed he'd be accessible. No doubt he'd been playing when Phoebe arrived. (She'd never told him she was going to The Dummy Up Club after rehearsal!) And Phoebe had seized the opportunity to demonstrate the range of her classically trained voice to the handsome maestro.

Pascal sat at the bar, unnoticed by the performers, who had a small audience scattered throughout the lounge and adjoining dining room.

"I wonder who she is," said a young and naughty looking blonde in a white halter dress who slid onto the barstool beside Pascal.

"She's my wife," he told her, introducing himself.

"That name is familiar. Are you the couple who are renting William Random's house?" When Pascal confirmed that they were, she said, "I'm William's ex-sister-in-law, Susan Ross," and shook his hands with him vigorously. "And that's my boyfriend, Anthony Newton. Your wife is ravishing. Are you worrying right now?"

"I might be if I didn't have you as a hostage." He struck a match to light her cigarette. Susan tossed back two and half feet of silky, goldenrod hair with a smile.

"Wouldn't they make a glorious plate for your book?" she asked.

"Sensational, but I make it a policy never to torment celebrities."

"I'll go and ask permission!" Susan jumped off her stool without waiting for a reply. They had just finished the song and were about to start another when Susan appeared at Anthony's elbow.

"Hello."

Anthony introduced Phoebe.

"You know, you two look so picture perfect together that it

would be a shame not to let Mr. Robbins photograph you for his book," Susan suggested.

"Mr. Robbins?" Anthony asked.

"That handsome man at the bar, who also happens to be this lady's husband," Susan said, smiling brightly at Phoebe, who stared at Susan for a few seconds as though she recognized her, then suddenly did recognize her, then blushed deeply.

"I don't mind," said Anthony, waving at Pascal to come over. Another introduction was made. Pleased at his sudden fortune, Pascal rushed out to his car to get a couple of lights.

Phoebe wanted to communicate with her husband at once, but didn't dare abandon her precious seat on the bench beside the composer. An intimate portrait of herself and Anthony Newton would provide golden publicity for a girl whose objective was Broadway. Besides, Mr. Newton had magic. She felt it the moment she sat down beside him. And now that she had recognized Susan, a tinge of eroticism was added. Phoebe longed to know the details of Anthony Newton's relationship with the adorable 22-year-old blonde who had appeared so submissively in William Random's photo album.

Driving the short distance home down heavily wooded Shadow Lane, the tightness in Pascal's jawline alerted Phoebe that a lecture was coming.

"Is something the matter, darling?" she queried, receiving a glare for her pains.

"You bet something is the matter," he replied firmly, pulling into the driveway beside the Random house. Phoebe thought what a splendid Torvald her own husband would have made, had he only taken up the stage.

She locked the door behind them and followed him into the sitting room, where he immediately poured himself a scotch. She shuddered at the possible increase in husbandly belligerence this additional shot might spur, though she did admire his capacity. Alcohol did not agree with Phoebe, as she harshly rediscovered at least once a year.

"I just remembered, there's something I must show you!" Phoebe ran out of the room and returned a minute later with the photo album.

"Phoebe, I'm not in the mood," he snapped, lighting a cigarette. "What was the idea of swarming all over Anthony Newton tonight?"

"I beg your pardon?"

"I believe the term is, kissing up, unless you were all over that annoyingly wealthy and attractive man for some reason other than career advancement, in which case, I may well lose my temper."

"And what happens then?"

"You don't want to know," he promised, pouring another.

"We got a photo for the book, didn't we?" she cajoled, putting the album down.

"Yes," he admitted without pleasure. "But I still want to know why."

"Why what, darling?"

"Why you were practically sitting on Anthony Newton's lap all night."

"I was doing no such thing."

"You sang for ninety minutes. Fifteen would have been plenty. Then we lingered for two hours over a dinner we should have declined. On top of which, you simpered and cooed until I thought I would be sick."

"I thought I made a nice impression," said returned mildly, delighted by his jealousy.

"Not on me, you didn't."

"We got invited for tennis."

"Swell."

"Darling, don't you agree that this is about the best connection I'm ever likely to make?" Phoebe asked, sitting in front of the album again and casually opening it to the page with Susan's picture. Yes, it was the same girl, except in the photo she had a ponytail.

"Yes, I agree," he grudgingly admitted, "but that's no reason for you to throw yourself at him."

"I did no such thing!" she jumped to her feet and cried. "And you had better apologize for that remark."

"*Me* apologize?" he laughed contemptuously and again Phoebe thought what a shame it was the stage had missed Pascal, because he was as great a ham as she'd ever met.

"That's right," she haughtily replied, "and until you do, I will remain incommunicado!" With this she picked up the heavy album, tucked it under her arm and made her exit.

Pascal slammed his glass down and followed her. "Phoebe, don't you dare walk out on me while we're having an argument!" he stopped her half way up the staircase. "And why are you still dragging that around?" he gestured at the ubiquitous album, becoming somewhat annoyed at it's apparent fascination for his wife.

"What the *Necronomicon* was to Arkham, *this* book is to Random Point, and I must avail myself of its secret knowledge while I possess it," she announced bafflingly and quickly ran up the stairs to lock herself into a bedroom other than the one they'd been sharing. If she'd just begun speaking in tongues, Pascal could not have been more dumbfounded.

"Phoebe, open this door," he demanded, rapping smartly.

"No!" she said, curling up on a recamiere and opening the album to Susan's page again. Outside the door, Pascal took a deep breath and forced himself to think logically.

"Nora wouldn't lock the door on Torvald," he gravely observed. "At least not in Act I." Before he had lit a new cigarette the door opened. Pascal strode in, fairly crackling with masculine energy. "That's better," he commented.

"Remember," she warned him, "Nora turns everything around at the end of Act III."

"Phoebe, what the hell did that comment on the stairs mean?"

"Are you really ready to listen?"

"Sure," he flung himself into a wing chair.

"Do you recognize her?" she asked, showing him the photograph of Susan.

"She looks awfully familiar," he admitted.

"That's Susan Ross, the young lady we spent two hours with tonight."

"I suppose it is," he agreed, looking closely at the photograph. "But what of it? You heard her say that she was William Random's sister-in-law. Why shouldn't her photo show up in his album?"

"In this kind of album?"

"Why not?'

"I just find it extremely interesting," Phoebe insisted, turning over another page or two. Pascal found himself staring at the photos along with her, until one caught his eye.

"She looks familiar too," said Pascal, pointing to a still of a corseted blonde bound to a whipping post while a tall, Celtic god used a flogger on her bare backside.

"Does she? Where did you see her? Did you meet her in the village? Think!" Phoebe was wild with excitement.

"I know," he snapped his fingers. "Come with me," he said, taking her by the hand and pulling her after him down the hall, up a narrow wooden staircase and into a custom darkroom.

Inside he switched on the light to reveal a gallery of black and white stills clothespinned to a line. "Here she is!" he seized one of the stills. "It's the girl who's renting the light house I photographed yesterday. Her name is Patricia Fairservis." Pascal showed Phoebe the shot of a pouty blonde, sitting in the window seat of her lighthouse studio.

"Beginning to see a pattern?" she demanded.

"No."

"I believe that sooner or later we're going to meet everyone who shows up in this album, and in doing so uncover the best-heeled little B&D community in the commonwealth."

"The best-heeled little what?"

"Pascal, please don't tell me that you've never heard of B&D?" she sighed condescendingly.

"Sure I've heard of it," he said, flipping through the album as he desperately tried to recall what the letters stood for.

"Oh? So, tell me what you think it is."

"It's," he hesitated for a moment, but as he gazed at a photo in the album, his memory was jogged by the image of little Damaris Perez Flagg being buckled into a bondage collar while stretched across the lap of William Random and he triumphantly blurted out, "bondage and discipline!"

"Oh, so you do know," she replied, with some surprise.

"I suppose you see these nice perverts of Random Point as some sort of sadomasochistic coven grooming you for their sacrificial altar?" he ventured.

"No, of course not," she protested.

"Oh yes you do. I see what's happening here. It's the *Rosemary's Baby* Syndrome all over again. Fanciful actress senses dangerous conspiracy, sees herself as next ritual victim. Next thing you know, you'll be kidnapped, raped and impregnated by the head satyr, (Anthony Newton, no doubt), while I sell my soul to this one here," he indicated a sartorially elegant gentleman spanking Susan Ross in one of the photos.

"Let's see if any of your other photos match the ones in the album," Phoebe said, ignoring his hypothesis to scan the stills. "And yes, I've found another!" She pulled down a shot of several patrons sitting in the pub at The Bone and Feather Inn, one of whom appeared to be the same tow-headed monument of a man who'd wielded the whip in the photo of Patricia Fairservis. "Isn't this the fellow with the flogger?" she demanded.

"Looks similar," Pascal conceded.

"And here's another one!" she cried, pulling down a photo Pascal had taken of a stunning young woman on the gallery steps of the finest bookshop in the village. "Who is she, Pascal?"

"That's Marguerite Alexander, the owner of the bookshop I photographed two days ago," he told her, comparing the still he took with a shot in the album of this statuesque beauty in a spiderweb gown, using a martinet on a charming brunette, who was cuffed to an X-frame.

"You see what I'm telling you?" Phoebe demanded.

"I see that certain people in the village happened to attend a wild party at which some photographs were taken," he conceded, "but why do you know it wasn't some sort of Halloween hijinks?"

"Then what about the other photos in the album, the studio shots? How do you account for those?"

"William Random's hobby is erotic photography. What's so unusual about that?"

"Nothing, except for the quantity and quality of his models. Pascal. I really believe these are lifestylers," she insisted, riveted by the photo Pascal had taken of the man at the bar.

"Well, just don't go asking," he warned.

"But, why not?"

"Because besides being prurient, it's none of our business."

"I suppose you're right about that," she said, still studying her husband's photos. But no other remarkably attractive people were revealed.

"I still don't understand why you're so fixated on that album anyway," he said, leading her out of the dark room and closing the door behind them. "People have a right to be as kinky as they choose."

"Oh, I wholly agree!" she replied, linking arms with her husband as they returned together to the bedroom they'd been sharing.

"So why are you obsessing on them?"

"Because maybe I'm a little kinky myself," she answered slowly.

"Oh, are you?" he laughed affectionately for the first time that evening.

"Just a little," she blushed deeply as her heart began to race.

"Just a little, eh?" He folded his arms and looked her up and down. "Well then maybe I should turn you over my knee and give you just a little spanking for flirting with Anthony Newton all night!"

"But, I didn't flirt," she lamely replied, her wide eyes following his every movement as she unconsciously pressed her back against a dresser.

"Oh yes you did! Come over here, young lady," he commanded, seizing her by her slender wrist and pulling her over to the upholstered bench at the foot of the bed, whereupon he sat down and very easily pulled her across his lap.

Phoebe didn't utter the slightest protest as he fastened one hand to her waist and brought the other one down on her skirted backside a half dozen times rather firmly. He expected her to struggle and beg him to stop, but she merely gasped and whimpered, without making a move to escape.

If he was momentarily puzzled, the melting look she cast him over one bare shoulder cleared the mystery and he realized with a start that she really wanted this.

Carefully pushing her skirt up to her waist, he discovered that his wife was clad in a blue satin corset with garter straps and seamed hose. As Pascal was something of a fetishist himself, the sight of these exquisite undergarments stimulated him immensely and he stroked her small, but extremely well rounded bottom gently with the palm of his hand. A blue satin G-string afforded her a tiny measure of modesty, but her bottom was now effectively bare.

"I didn't know you owned a corset," he commented with approval.

"I don't. This one belongs to the girl who lives here," Phoebe admitted. "We're almost the same size."

"Phoebe!" Smack! Smack! Smack! "You can't borrow an intimate garment like a corset without permission." Now he delivered ten or a dozen more spanks to her satiny cheeks, which instantly pinkened deeply, for she was very fair.

"Ow!" she cried, at last. His hand felt very different on her bare skin. It really imparted a sting. But oh, how heavenly it felt to finally be in this position, held fast and properly spanked for the first time and by Pascal! Phoebe squirmed as her husband's hand came down hard again and again.

"I'll have it cleaned," she promised.

"I'll be happy to buy you some corsets," he told her, stopping to rub her pink cheeks. "But if I ever find out you've ransacked our landlady's closets again I'll take my razor strop to you." Pascal actually owned one. "Understand?"

"Yes, sir!" she immediately replied, causing him to smile. He seemed to have discovered an extremely important secret about his Phoebe.

"I'd expect that kind of behavior from a common sort of girl, but you're supposed to be a lady," he continued to scold her, reveling in the authority she had suddenly given him. Not to mention her reaction to the spanking. He thought he had seen her aroused before, but this sort of response made their wedding night look like a still life.

"You know, Phoebe, I've found you somewhat intractable in the past, but now I realize I've just been taking the wrong approach with you," he informed her, administering another volley of vigorous smacks to her bottom cheeks and upper thighs. "This is what I should have done whenever you were impossible. And this is what I will do from now on!"

When Pascal observed her not arguing, a splendid surge of power coursed through him, resolving itself into a large, pulsating erection. He spanked her until his arm began to tire, about fifteen minutes by the chiming mantle clock. When he finally released her, her bottom glowed magenta and was radiant from the tops of her thighs to the crest of her hips.

He had no idea of what had gone through her head during this procedure, but a good many sensations had passed through his own, from the thrill of mastery to the satisfaction of instilling some discipline into his exasperating beloved.

After letting her up he turned her around to undo her dress, which buttoned down the back. "Stand still," he told her as she fidgeted on her high heels. The dress fell to the floor and he turned her around to admire her dainty torso, so beautifully defined by the corset, which had a built-in brassiere to support her perfect bosom. "Let me look at you," he ordered as she blushed. "I've never seen you quite like this before, Phoebe, all flushed and fluttery. How do you account for it?" he demanded, while deliberately reaching into her bra and gently pinching each cherry nipple while she squirmed.

"I couldn't say," she replied, closing her eyes with a shiver as his hands traveled down to squeeze her nipped waist.

"Well, I'll tell you how I account for it," he said, suddenly standing up and deliberately bending her over the bench. "You've been waiting all this time for me to take control." He placed her palms on the seat of the bench, made her arch her back and separate her legs. "Now that I've started to do it," he said, smacking her hard on either cheek, "you're just a little bit scared. Am I right?"

"Yes, that's what makes it sexy," she thought to herself but instead shook her head in denial. Pascal laughed. Then she heard his zipper come down and felt him against her. In a moment he'd pulled the scrap of G-string aside and plunged his engorged cock inside her to the hilt. Pulling her up by the hips, he drove in even deeper, locking her against him with a hand pressed to her corseted abdomen. The placement of his palm directly atop her G-spot, in combination with the firm thrusts of his organ brought her to the edge of climax almost immediately, then promptly sent her crashing over it.

"Never!" she breathed, when he finally let her go, a few minutes later, having ejaculated deep inside her creamy core.

"Never what?" he wanted to know, helping her to stand again.

"Never have I felt anything so moving, so utterly cataclysmic!" she declared, throwing herself into his arms.

"Never have I felt you come so fast," he observed, as she went behind a wood-framed screen to slip into a silk nightgown.

"Do you know what I plan to do, darling?" Phoebe asked as she climbed into bed beside him a minute later.

"No, what?" He pulled her against him contentedly, ready to slip off to sleep.

"I'm going to spend the summer tracking down every person in the Random photo album and making them my friends."

"Good girl," he murmured drowsily. An instant later he sat up and stared at her. "What did you say?"

"I said I was going to find everyone in the album and introduce myself to them."

"But to what end?"

Phoebe thought, "Mine, actually," but chose not to share this bad joke as she noticed Pascal's growing unease. Instead she replied nonchalantly, as though she'd already lost interest in the subject, "Oh, they just seem like my kind of people."

"Phoebe, I don't like this," he said, lighting a cigarette.

"Don't like what?"

"Don't like the idea of you tracking down every B&D player in the village. What do you intend to do with them once you unearth them, eh?"

"I'd just like to get to know them. After all, we'll be spending three months in Random Point. Doesn't it make sense to socialize with the most sophisticated couples in town?"

"Are you sure you don't mean socialate?" he brooded.

"What does that mean?"

"What do you suppose is going to happen when you open Pandora's Box?"

"I don't know."

"But you want and expect something to happen, don't you?"

"I wouldn't mind getting invited to one of those parties."

"One of which parties?"

"The kind at which the album pictures were taken."

"I see." Crushing out the cigarette, Pascal laced his hands behind his head and stared out the window at the rustling trees and half moon.

"Pascal?"

"Yes?"

She burrowed against his side until he drew her into his arms. "You'll never know how much that meant to me," she confided, shuddering with the memory of the spanking and sex.

"And don't think that'll be the last time either," he warned her, hugging her closer. "Not with brainstorms like yours."

"I must admit, if there's any place a girl like me could get into trouble, it's Random Point," she mused.

"You know, unfaithful wives were pilloried in Random Point until 1797." Pascal informed her, "I looked that up in the town charter. The pillory still stands today. I intend to photograph it later in the summer. Just be careful I don't get a notion to lock my favorite actress into it when I do."

PHOEBE AND PASCAL
PART TWO

PHOEBE'S TORVALD WAS a tall, lanky, neatly bearded and rambunctiously jovial emoter, around her husband's age, who took to his new leading lady immediately. It was difficult to imagine such a big-hearted man portraying a stern, judgmental character like Torvald, but as soon as he stepped out on the stage he accomplished the metamorphosis ably.

One afternoon, as they were rehearsing their opening scene, where Torvald accuses Nora of eating chocolate macaroons, Phoebe happened to noticed a stranger in the back of the small theatre, walking around the perimeter.

"Who's that?" Phoebe asked the production manager, for she suddenly seemed to recognize the warrior king in natty tweeds across the rows of empty seats. It was the man in the photo album pictured flogging the blonde from the lighthouse.

"Oh, that's ex-detective Michael Flagg. He's installing a security system in the theatre this week," Todd replied.

As he heard his name mentioned, Michael waved at the little group on the stage.

"Don't mind me," he said, "I'm just taking some measurements."

Phoebe and Michael exchanged lingering smiles across the theatre. Then she suddenly turned to her co-star and said, "You know, Rene, I've had some thoughts about this chocolate moment."

"Share them with me," the actor encouraged her.

"Well, in the Julie Harris teleplay of *Doll's House* from the '50s, Nora gets a little slap on the hand. Remember?"

"I do," Rene replied.

"Do you know what I think would be even more provocative?" Phoebe asked.

"What? I can't wait to hear."

"Why, if Torvald turned Nora over on his knee and gave her a few spanks?"

Though she didn't dare to look at him, Phoebe noticed out of the corner of her eye that Michael Flagg had stopped measuring doorways.

"I like that," Rene approved the suggestion at once. "Makes it sexier, doesn't it?" the actor appealed to their director, Clara Harte.

"I'm not sure the scene's ever been done that way before," that fair young woman mused, "but I see nothing to oppose the interpretation. Especially since we've decided to stress the eroticism in the relationship."

As Phoebe and Rene began to block out the business she hoped that Pascal would choose any other afternoon than this to drop in. In fact, it would suit her very well if he didn't discover her on-stage spanking until opening night.

As she hoped and expected, Michael Flagg was waiting for her outside the theatre when she departed at dusk.

"Oh, Mr. Flagg, you're just the person I wanted to see," Phoebe confessed in a rush.

"Great," he replied enthusiastically, for he hadn't come up with any legitimate excuse for waiting for her and knew very well that she was married.

"I'm Phoebe Casper," she extended her hand to be shaken. "I understand you're an ex-officer of the law? I do have a valid reason for asking."

"Well, yes," he smiled.

"And you do security now?"

"Occasionally."

"In that case, I think I'd like to hire you for a consultation."

"Oh really? What about?"

"Stalking," she declared dramatically. "I am an actress, you know. And I suddenly realized that I don't know the first thing about dealing with stalkers."

"You could probably benefit from some security advice. Shall we make an appointment?"

"What about tomorrow afternoon? You could come to the house," she suggested, knowing that Pascal would be in Boston.

"You're staying at William Random's, aren't you?" Michael asked, making a note in a small book.

"I see you know all about me already," she said with surprise.

"I ran into William before he left for Europe and he told me," Michael explained, adding, "If I'm not mistaken, your husband photographed me at the pub last week."

"Yes, I believe he did."

"Does he know you're engaging me to counsel you on stalkers?"

"Why, no," Phoebe replied, flushing violently as his question reminded her of how naughty she was being. Michael merely smiled and told her he would see her the following day.

Phoebe had coffee ready for Michael Flagg's arrival. She served it in the sitting room, where they held their consultation.

"Oh, I never did ask you what you're going to charge me for this," she said pleasantly, carefully watching his reaction to her first pot of real coffee.

"Mmmm," he said. "Good." Phoebe smiled. "I wasn't going to charge you anything."

"Really? That's awfully nice of you."

"I can't wait to see you in the play," he confessed, unable to forget her pointed suggestion of adding a spanking to the business.

"I'll send you tickets for opening night."

"Thanks!"

"Michael, may I ask you something?" she asked suddenly, dragging the photo album over to him.

"Sure."

"Is this you?" Phoebe opened the album to the photo of Michael whipping Patricia.

"Yes, that's me," he replied immediately. "Let me see that, though." He took the album and flicked through some other pages.

"I guess you know everyone in there, huh?" she eagerly asked.

– 317 –

"I probably do," he replied, turning the pages with interest.

"Won't you tell me about them?" Phoebe brought Michael and the album back to the sofa, so they could turn the pages together.

"Sure. That's my ex-wife Damaris. She lives with William now, as you know. That's William's ex-wife Laura, she's Hugo Sands' girlfriend now. The four of them are vacationing in Europe together. Here's Hugo spanking Susan Ross, she's Laura's younger sister and Anthony Newton's girlfriend."

"I've met them!" she eagerly replied. "But there are no photos of Mr. Newton in this book. I suppose it would be too much to hope that he might be part of the group?"

"He's in it, all right, but he makes it a point not to get photographed doing anything scene-related because of his public image."

"Oh, I can imagine," Phoebe breathed reverently. "Do you think he would have minded me asking that question and you telling me the answer?"

"No," Michael replied with perfect confidence, "I'm sure he wouldn't. Now, this girl here is Marguerite Alexander," he returned to show and tell with the album. "She owns the bookshop. She's in and out of town because her husband's business is Boston-based. The young lady she's whipping is Diana Stratton; she's Susan's best friend. You'll probably meet her before too long. In fact, I'll make sure they all come to your opening night. The lady with me in this photo is my girlfriend, Patricia Fairservis. She lives in the lighthouse."

"She's glorious."

"Spoiled though."

"I'm surprised she has the nerve to be if you're her boyfriend."

"It isn't so much nerve as will."

"Well, thanks for filling me in. I've been looking at the photographs a good deal lately and wondering about all of you."

"What sort of things have you been wondering?"

"Mainly what it would take to become one of the clique," she answered frankly.

"What clique?"

"The B&D clique in the village."

"Why? Do you play?"

"I don't know. What does that mean?"

"This afternoon it meant getting Rene to spank you on stage, again and again. Quite an accomplishment for a novice. I was impressed."

"Did you enjoy watching us block out the scene?"

"You made him go through it ten times." Michael accurately recalled. "Three swats were given each time. And each time you encouraged Rene to smack you a little harder. Yes, I enjoyed watching that very much. Why do you think I waited for you afterwards?"

"I knew I recognized you from the book," she replied breathlessly.

"But tell me something, Phoebe, does Pascal share your interest in domestic discipline?"

"A little, I think. That is, although he never seemed the slightest bit inclined before we came to Random Point, now I think he may be a natural," she sagely reported.

"In that case, maybe we should return to the subject of security," Michael suddenly decided. "I installed an excellent system in this house myself. Let me show you how it works."

Michael led Phoebe through the house, showing her alarms and hidden cameras.

"Any room that has a TV or monitor is linked to the security camera system," Michael pointed out as they entered the master bedroom. He picked up the remote and tuned in to the security camera channel. Every few seconds, a different view of the outside of the house flashed across the screen. Then all four views would share the same screen for five more seconds before beginning again.

"See, Phoebe," Michael said, "this way you can tell if anyone has followed you home and is lurking around outside."

The camera facing the woods behind the house only showed a few squirrels. The cameras focused on the sides of the house were watching flowers grow. But the camera trained on the front door showed Pascal walking briskly up the walk to put his key in the lock.

"Oh dear," said Phoebe, her heart nearly stopping. "Let's go downstairs!" She preceded Michael out the door in a small flash.

Pascal registered immediate displeasure upon entering the house and encountering Michael Flagg descending the stairs with Phoebe.

"Hi, dear," Phoebe cried, rushing down to greet him. "You remember Michael Flagg, from the pub?"

"Sure. How are you?" Pascal put out his hand to shake Michael's and pretended he wasn't annoyed.

"Michael installed the security system in this house and he was showing me how everything works," Phoebe revealed brightly.

"Actually, we'd just finished, but I'd be happy to give you a quick run down as well," Michael offered.

"I'm sure Phoebe can explain it to me herself," Pascal said, staring pointedly at his trembling wife. "But will you stay for a drink?"

"No thanks, Phoebe gave me coffee. See you two soon, I hope," Michael pleasantly said, slipping out the door.

The instant it had closed Pascal turned an X-ray gaze on Phoebe and demanded, "What was he doing here?"

"Showing me the security system," she replied, less brightly than before.

"By your invitation?" he snapped.

"Well, yes," she timidly admitted, thoroughly cowed by the thunder cloud that had formed upon her husband's brow.

"I see!" Pascal strode into the sitting room to make himself a drink, not failing to notice and scowl at the coffee service that she had somehow managed to properly utilize for once.

Half a drink had already disappeared down his throat when she hesitantly followed him into the room, a blush of guilt suffusing her face.

"Phoebe, what have you been up to?" he asked, in a tone now slightly less overwrought, as the well known comfortable glow spread through every fiber.

"Nothing at all. Not the slightest thing," she assured him.

"What's this doing here?" Pascal gestured at the album.

"It's always here. This is the room it lives in," she replied truthfully.

"You quizzed him on the album, didn't you?"

Looking both sullen and guilty, Phoebe made no reply.

"You invited Michael Flagg over, ostensibly to find out about the security system, and wound up discussing B&D in Random Point. Is that the correct scenario?"

"Pretty much so. Only we hardly said two words about anything when you came home."

"Where did you run into him that you had the opportunity to invite him home with you?"

"Must you put it quite that way?" she bristled, biting off a large chunk of chocolate-covered macaroon for every swig of scotch he took.

"Where, Phoebe?"

"He happened to be at the theatre during today's rehearsal."

"And what were you two doing upstairs just now?"

"He was just showing me how the security cameras hook up to all the TV's in the house. That's all."

"I don't believe you."

"But, Pascal, it's the absolute truth."

"I don't trust you."

"I'm sorry." She hung her head.

"I was half way to Boston when I realized I'd arranged to shoot that leather bar in P-town this evening."

"Should I come and meet you there after rehearsal?"

"No. It's a gay bar. No one would want to pose for me if I dragged my frou-frou wife in there."

"Oh."

"I'm sure I'll be home before ten," he told her, finishing his drink then leaving her. Phoebe started after him in confusion, unable to define his mood. She followed him out to his car as he loaded in his lights.

"Darling? You're not angry at me, are you?" she caught his hand, brought it to her lips and kissed it. He melted instantly and pulled her into his arms to thoroughly kiss her.

"You'll find out when I get home tonight," he told her, letting her go abruptly.

"Maybe you'll cool off by then," she suggested as he got into his convertible.

"I want you to come home straight after rehearsal," he warned her sternly.

"I will, Pascal," she promised.

"I suppose you'd better stop in town for dinner first," he amended, "but come home right after that. Understand?"

"Yes, darling."

"And no male escorts."

"No, dear."

Pascal roared off in his sports car, leaving Phoebe trembling in the wake of his various orders and implied threats. He almost sounded as if he intended to *punish* her when he returned home that night!

After the rehearsal, Phoebe defied Pascal's orders and went out with some of the cast for dinner at The Bone and Feather. But she made sure to arrive home three minutes before ten.

It was nearly midnight before Pascal joined her there.

"Well," she declared, "the boys must have really liked you!"

"I got some great photos."

"I hope you didn't have to put out."

"Go ahead, add insult to injury," he warned her, opening the balcony doors and strolling out into the moonlight. She came out beside him and rubbed up against him in her slippery, cream satin pajamas.

"I've been waiting and waiting for you," she complained, squirming as he wound one hand in her hair and kissed her.

"I'm as inclined to beat you as kiss you," he scowled, pushing her away and lighting a cigarette.

"Well, darling, can't you do both?"

"Did you confide to Flagg what you're about?"

"I don't know what you mean, dear."

"You said you showed him the album, asked him questions. Didn't he wonder why?"

"I don't know."

"I can easily imagine why you'd invite that man over when you knew I was going to be away."

"My intentions were strictly honorable."

"That's what you always say, but I happen to know differently."

"Oh really?"

"When you want to get a man's attention you flirt!"

"If I wanted to get Mr. Flagg's attention it was only to discover more about the album in general rather than him in particular, and I assure you that I didn't flirt."

"And I suppose if he weren't the gym-hewn monolith that he is you'd have invited him home just as readily?" When Phoebe hesitated a moment in replying, he cried, "Right! You little baggage."

"I'm nothing of the sort," she replied with hauteur.

"Oh yes you are."

"Pascal, say you're not really upset with me."

"But I am upset," he replied stubbornly.

"I only asked him over to converse."

"Yeah, so you said."

Phoebe sighed and wandered back into the bedroom, unable to determine, as usual, what her husband's mood really was. She got into bed and pulled the covers up to her chin. In a minute he came in, dimmed the lights and began to undress.

"One more incident like this and you're going in that pillory," he promised before getting into bed.

A few days later Pascal was canvassing the village when he stumbled across Hugo Sands' antiques shop and discovered the remarkably beautiful young lady who was to become his favorite model.

Pamela Crane, who had been polishing an old clock, was thrilled to admit the photographer into the shop, especially when he promised to credit Sands' Antiques when his book came out. No sooner had Pascal taken a good look at Pamela than he decided to offer her a season of modeling work, which she enthusiastically accepted.

"You can quit worrying about the town stocks," Pascal informed Phoebe with ill-concealed excitement that evening over dinner at a pleasant Woodbridge roadhouse. "I've found a girl who'll go into them willingly, in Puritan dress, and she's willing to run up the costume herself." Then Pascal launched into a detailed description of the extraordinary creature he'd found in Random Point that afternoon.

"She must be 5'10", with hair like black silk and legs from here to heaven. And what a face, what style, what fashion sense. I tell you, I've made a discovery, and she's all mine," Pascal reported blithely to his smoulderingly jealous 5'3" spitfire. "I've decided to devote a complete section of the book to historical tableaux, with my girl Pamela in period attire."

"I look good in period attire. Can't I be in that portion of the book too?" Phoebe startled him by asking.

"Well, dear, you're already going to be in that handsome full page still with Anthony Newton," he explained.

"But this Pamela person is marvellous enough to have a whole section of tableaux just devoted to her?"

"Phoebe, don't be childish, she's a model, as I've told you. She's got the face and figure to plug into any fantasy. I see her as clay."

"Does that mean you'll be kneading and stretching her a lot?"

"Phoebe, don't start."

"Don't start what? And yes, I will have some wine," she declared, defiantly holding out her glass to be filled.

"Don't start throwing a jealous tantrum about one of my models."

"Oh, I'm not jealous of some vapid mannequin."

"This one isn't vapid. She's been to the best schools and has impeccable taste."

Phoebe regarded her own reflection in a mirror opposite. Her white and yellow sundress had a laced bodice and full cotton skirt. "You're getting better," Pascal told her, noticing her self-appraisal.

"Oh go to hell!" she snapped, infuriated by everything he had told her.

The next day Phoebe could not prevent herself from stopping by Hugo Sands' Antiques in order to meet and interview the young lady who had captivated Pascal the previous day. She found that his description of Pamela's grace and elegance had not been exaggerated; she was a classic model.

Phoebe was not ready to be disarmed by Pamela, but this was exactly what happened.

"I understand you're to be Nora and you're looking for a proper corset. Did you know there's a wonderful little corsetiere in P-town? I have a card." Pamela handed Phoebe a card for a Provincetown corset shop. "Bring a hundred and fifty dollars and you'll go home in heaven. You can teach your handsome husband how to lace you and be down to 22" by opening night."

"Gosh, that's a lot of money," said Phoebe doubtfully, at which Pamela stared.

"But it will last for years," the willowy one explained with reverence. "And I can't wait to see you cinched."

Phoebe glowed with vanity. She had never been stroked by another woman before and the approach suddenly turned her rival into a girlfriend.

"Pascal says you know a lot about outfits."

"Pascal says his wife's a tomboy," Pamela smiled, "but he wishes she weren't."

"Well, I'm an impoverished actress," Phoebe defended herself. "I wasn't even able to quit waitressing until I married Pascal, no less think about spending hundreds of dollars on lingerie at a time."

"An excellent corset is a basic piece of wardrobe equipment," Pamela informed her new friend firmly. "You'll learn. I'll help you. You're so gorgeous with just nothing, by the time I get through with you, you'll be a goddess."

"Really? In what way?"

"What I could do with braids, pearls and your hair," Pamela mused.

"Thanks, but you're the one who's amazing," Phoebe acknowledged, thoroughly tamed by her new friend. "And I understand you're also the one whose going to save me from the pillory."

Pamela smiled. "I've never walked by that pillory without thinking of being locked into it!"

"You mean with a sense of social outrage?" the actress queried casually.

"No, with a sense of arousal."

"You mean you're into discipline too?" Phoebe couldn't help but blurting out.

"Too?"

"Well, it seems there are a lot of people in Random Point who are into discipline."

"Oh, there are. Are you by any chance one of us, Phoebe?"

"I most ardently am!" Phoebe declared, finding this conversation even more satisfying than the one she'd had with Michael Flagg on the same subject.

"And your husband?" Pamela asked with great interest.

"Maybe," said Phoebe circumspectly. "I'm not really sure yet. Though he has spanked me once."

"I'm sure that was thrilling. Spanking is my favorite thing," the art school girl confessed.

"And how about you? Do you have a handsome husband who spanks you?"

"A fiancé," Pamela shyly replied, extending her slim, perfectly manicured hand to display a smart engagement ring. "And he is terribly handsome and wonderfully strict," she added, pulling Sloan's photo out of a small drawer.

"My, he is striking," Phoebe commented, of Pamela's logical counterpart.

"He works right across the street at the bookshop. You should go and introduce yourself. He worships Ibsen and we've already got our tickets for your opening night. Besides, I want him to see what a charming wife Pascal has. He's been a bit nervous since yesterday."

"But, you say this young man is your *dominant*?" Phoebe was intrigued and titillated as she stared at Sloan's photo. "How exciting it must be to be absolutely certain that your lover gets a thrill out of spanking you," Phoebe mused.

"I should think that anyone would get a thrill out of spanking you. Anyway, Pascal is certainly bossy enough," Pamela reflected.

"He intends to mold you. Like clay," Phoebe warned her new friend as she left to go across the street and visit the bookshop.

"Don't forget about the corset. Go tomorrow," Pamela called after her, then immediately dialed the bookshop.

"Alexander's Bookshop. Sloan speaking. May I be of some assistance?" Pamela's intended cheerfully replied.

"Sloan. Pamela. Pascal Robbins' wife is about to enter your shop. And guess what, Sloan, she's into it!"

"Into it?"

"You know what I mean. She just walked in. See her?"

"Thank you so much," Sloan said, hanging up in time to greet Phoebe.

Two afternoons later Pascal sat in the window seat of their bedroom and smoked as Pamela demonstrated how to lace a waist cinch. Phoebe, dressed only in a cream lace bra and panty combination, balanced on her highest ankle strap heels as Pamela deftly hooked the five steel clasps in the front of the boned garment to fasten it, attached each of the eight garter straps to her sheer stockings, then turned her around to lace her up the back. The waist cinch was of sand colored cotton reptide and handsome.

"Now, watch carefully," Pamela told Pascal, "because you're

going to have to do this for her the first four or five times, until she gets the knack of lacing herself."

"I'm all attention," said he, really riveted by the procedure of tightening the laces.

"Now then, your wife has a natural 24" waist. This corset will take her down four inches if she wears it a good deal and doesn't gain any weight. As it is, I can see her cinching comfortably to 22" in a few weeks. But let's start with a just an inch for now."

"It looks wonderful," he observed as Pamela pulled the laces, creating a classic, petite hourglass figure for Phoebe.

"Wear it just like that for an hour to two hours a day to start with," Pamela instructed. "After about a week you can tighten it up a bit and increase to three or four hours a day. I think you'll find the results remarkable."

But the next morning, when he was called upon to help Phoebe corset, Pascal was not in so mild a mood. For the previous night, at The Dummy Up Club, while Pascal had been photographing Pamela in a sophisticated evening gown, snipping a cigar between her satin gloved hands, Phoebe had been keeping Sloan company in the bar. And Pascal hadn't liked the way she did it. Sloan had only come along to keep his eye on Pamela, but now that the actress had learned what kind of man Sloan was, Phoebe was irresistibly drawn to him. Besides, he was such a natural tease that it was impossible not to fall under his spell. Pascal couldn't help but notice.

He was too tired from shooting all day to take it up with Phoebe when they got home, but the following morning, while he was lacing her into her corset, it all came back to him and with determination he began to pull the strings a good deal more tightly than Pamela had recommended.

"Hey!" Phoebe cried, "That's too tight!"

"Nonsense. That's the way it's supposed to be," he said, tightening the laces down from her nipped waist to her flared hips. "The two sides should meet in the back completely."

"Not right away!" she gasped. "Please, darling, loosen me up!"

"Not right away," he told her firmly, and instead pulled her down across his lap. She hadn't yet donned bra, panties or stockings and her round, creamy bottom looked more naked for the framing of the glove tight cinch.

"What are you doing?" She squirmed to get away for she felt severely restricted and her bottom seemed to swell in protest of the constriction at the hips.

"Giving you a good spanking for behaving so badly at the bar last night," he declared, wrapping one hand around her greatly reduced waist and bringing the other down on her satiny backside eight or ten times hard. His hand left a dark pink imprint on each cheek and caused her to squirm across his lap. "There!" he said, putting her back on her feet. "I hope you felt those."

"I did!" she replied, with a trembling underlip that softened him instantly.

"What's the matter?"

"Too tight and too hard," she sobbed, putting one hand back to rub her sore bottom.

"Oh, all right," he sighed, turning her around to loosen the laces with every evidence of annoyance, though his own heart pounded with excitement. There was something about lacing her more tightly than she liked that had given him a perverse thrill.

He loosened the laces a little. "How's that?" he asked, as though he didn't much care how she responded.

"Still very tight," she breathed, suddenly realizing that he had chosen this method to (dare she apply the sacred word?) discipline her! Something about lacing her aroused him. Just knowing this thrilled her. "But, I suppose it will teach me better self control," she ventured timidly.

"My thought entirely," he agreed, this time only patting her bare backside and even kissing her there. "Look how pink your bottom is, Phoebe," he told her. She looked over her shoulder into the wardrobe mirror to see.

After Pascal had gone, Phoebe got a tape measure and measured her waist. He'd gotten her down to 22" on her second day. No wonder she was gasping for breath! The corset changed her carriage and her gait. She couldn't take her eyes off her image in the many mirrors of the house after she'd donned her bra and panties and a beige cotton sundress, which now draped so loosely that she had to add a belt.

When she went into the village she noticed men looking at her differently than they had the previous day. But her back was beginning to hurt and she felt she hadn't taken a really good breath since Pascal had laced her. Therefore her first stop was the Antiques Shop, where she intended to have Pamela loosen her stays. But as she passed by the window she saw that she was foiled, because Pascal was inside, shooting one of the tableaux he'd spoken of, utilizing furnishings from the shop and a flawless Victorian costume Pamela had produced from her large and unusual wardrobe.

Now Phoebe was perplexed. It was too early to find anyone at the theatre and she simply couldn't stay another hour in the corset. Then she noticed Sloan in the window of the bookshop across the street and realized she was saved. She rushed over to the store, quite unaware that at the moment she slipped through the door, Pascal chanced to look up and spot her.

When Phoebe rushed in Sloan was alone shelving paperbacks.

"Hi Sloan," said Phoebe in a rush, "would you do me a giant favor?"

"Of course," he smiled as he noticed how charming she looked that day.

"Do you know how to loosen stays?"

"Loosen stays? You mean a corset?"

"Yes. I have one on and it's laced so tightly that I feel as though I'm going to faint."

"I'd be happy to help, but are you sure you don't want to go across the street and have Pamela do it?"

"That's the problem, Sloan. Pascal is there with her now and he's the one who laced me this morning. I don't want him to know I can't wear it this tight."

"Okay, come in the back for a second," he told her, leading the way into his office.

Back in Hugo Sands' Antiques shop, Pascal had abandoned his lights and 4 x 5 camera to stare out the street side windows as he waited impatiently for Phoebe to emerge from the bookstore. "I wonder what she's doing in there so long," he mused aloud, going to the phone on the counter and asking Pamela for the number. She told him, he dialed and the phone rang without being answered.

Sloan had just unbuttoned the back of Phoebe's dress and was sitting on a chair with the actress before him preparing to loosen her laces, when the phone rang. "Since we have to work fast, I won't answer that," he told her, untying the bow at the hem of the corset and carefully pulling the laces open without completely undoing the snugly interlacing network of restriction. "My, this is tight," he observed. "What was Pascal thinking?" Meanwhile the phone continued to ring.

Finally Pascal slammed the phone down and told Pamela, "I'll be right back." Then he marched out the door and across the street. As soon as he entered the bookstore, his heart began to pound violently. With an unerring sense of direction, Pascal ignored the aisles and rising galleries and walked straight into the back of the shop where the first office he came to yielded the pair he sought.

When Pascal entered Sloan's office the good looking store manager was just rebuttoning the last button at the top of Phoebe's dress.

"Pascal!" Phoebe cried, flushing scarlet.

"Phoebe, what's going on here?"

"Nothing, darling," she explained, stepping away from Sloan but no closer to Pascal, who looked furious.

"Phoebe's waist cinch was too tight and she asked me to loosen it," Sloan reported immediately.

"It's true, Pascal. That's the only reason I came in," she added meekly.

"I see," her husband replied. "Even though Pamela and I were right across the street and could have done it just as easily for you?"

"Well, this morning you seemed so intent on lacing me tightly that I didn't want to disappoint you by admitting defeat so soon."

"So instead you invite another man to perform this intimate service for you while I'm not 20 yards away!" the photographer reproached his wife with mounting anger. Unusually sensitive and overwrought, due to the stringent corseting, Phoebe's eyes overspilled with tears.

"I have to get back to the floor," Sloan explained, leaving them alone.

"Phoebe, is this the way you behave when I'm on the road?" Pascal demanded.

"No," she tremblingly replied, taking a step backward lest he be tempted to slap her.

"I don't believe you," he snapped. "And what's more, I think you're a horrible flirt."

"That's not true!" Phoebe cried, wiping her eyes with the back of her hand. He seemed to notice for the first time how upset she was.

"Phoebe, now look what you've done," he pulled her over to a mirror to show her how she'd smudged her mascara. The eye makeup was a new enhancement suggested by Pamela, and Phoebe was as unused to it as she was to her corset. Pascal dipped the edge of his clean white handkerchief in cold water and carefully removed the few specks of mascara she had displaced with her rubbing. "We can't have you going to rehearsal looking like a wreck," he told her firmly, unable then to keep his hands off her waist. "What am I going to do with you?" he murmured, suddenly intensely aroused by her dear femininity.

Phoebe took as deep a breath as she could as she put her arms around Pascal and hugged him hard. Then they kissed and kissed. Finally he let her go.

"Come on," he told her, pulling her out of the shop by the hand, "I'm taking you to the theatre myself so you don't get up to any more mischief." He put her in his car, drove her down the road and escorted her inside.

"Now remember, if you have to loosen those stays any more today, have one of the girls do it. Understand?" He held her hands as he gave her this command.

"Yes, darling."

"As soon as you get home tonight, we're going to have a long talk about how you let another man undress you," he warned firmly.

"We are?" She looked up at him in surprise, having nearly forgotten about Sloan.

"Phoebe, the fact that you went to Sloan today instead of Pamela and me is going to trouble me all day."

"But you seemed so unsympathetic when I asked you to loosen me up earlier," she protested. "And it really hurt!" she added, with a pout.

"Well, why didn't you say so?"

"But, I did and you ignored me."

"Nonsense. You never said it hurt."

"In the books I've been reading, when something hurts too much, the girl says 'mercy' and that way her—" Phoebe groped for the right word, "—dominant knows it's for real. Should I use that word next time?"

"Mercy!" he snorted. "That's what I've been showing too much of lately with you!" The next moment he was gone.

Phoebe had almost forgotten about the incident with Sloan when Pascal reminded her of it before bed. She had just come from her bath and was wearing a white cotton wrapper. Her hair nearly reached her waist in tight, glossy waves. He was sitting in the window seat smoking when she came to lean against him and stare out at the whispering trees. He put his arm around her waist and pulled her closer, but the feel of her tiny waist under his hand brought back the morning's events and instead of embracing her he crushed out his cigarette and seized her by her slender shoulders instead.

"I just remembered something," he told her, pulling her straight across his lap. "You were a very bad girl this morning!" he told her, bringing his palm down first on one cheek and then the other, sharply through her thin robe. "Letting Sloan unlace you! You deserve a good spanking for that," he declared, bringing his hand down again a resounding dozen times.

"Do you really think so?"

"I most certainly do!"

"I may have been indiscreet, but my intentions were honorable."

"That's what you always say."

"I only wanted him to loosen my stays."

"And you don't think that's provocative?" Smack! Smack! "You think a nice, young, married lady behaves like that?" Smack! Smack! The spanking continued. "You should have come and asked Pamela or me to loosen your stays. You realize that now, don't you, Phoebe?"

"Yes, completely!" His hand was really starting to sting her tender flesh and she wriggled on his lap to avoid it.

"Good!" He let her up. "Now get to bed," he ordered. "And don't ever let me catch you alone with Sloan Taylor again."

Phoebe climbed into bed with a pout as Pascal undressed. "Whereas you get to be alone with Pamela as much as you like," Phoebe muttered, pulling the covers up to her waist.

"That's different, darling," he told her, getting into bed and pulling her into his arms. "That's work."

"Ha!" Phoebe turned on her side and so did he, pulling her back against him and pressing his cock into the valley between her bottom cheeks. "No!" she cried, pulling away.

"Relax, I'm not going to," he told her, guiding his cock down between her thighs to nudge the proper portal. "But why I can't sodomize my wife now and then, I'd like to know."

"But it would hurt too much," she protested, very wet from the spanking and all too ready to take his cock.

"Don't you trust me?"

"After the way you laced me today?"

"Phoebe, you cut me to the quick," Pascal sounded hurt, but his cock was athrob, so she knew he was only teasing her. "I want you that way," he insisted, while plunging into her pussy to the depths. "And some day I'm just going to ignore your protests and take you that way," he promised in a tone that pierced her with a dart of painful pleasure.

Ten days passed, changing the weather from Indian Summer to pungent autumn. Phoebe began to lace herself and managed to reduce her waist to a comfortable 22" by opening night. Meanwhile, she received no additional spankings from Pascal and began to wonder, with an aching sense of frustration, if he'd forgotten completely about her intense interest in the subject.

Having become better friends with Pamela, she confided her anxieties to the willowy model as they walked in the woods together one chilly afternoon.

"A week or so ago, he seemed to understand what I needed," Phoebe mused, "but since then he's made no move in that direction. How can I get him to play with me without asking him directly?"

Pamela laughed, "Just do something to irritate him!"

"You mean be deliberately bad?"

"Why not?"

"I don't dare. He has a vile temper."

"I know, I've been working with him," Pamela smiled.

"Listen, couldn't you talk to him for me? Explain about the spanking thing?"

"I could, but wouldn't it be more fun to get him to do it naturally?"

"But I don't want Pascal to think badly of me."

"Oh, he won't."

"Well, what should I do?"

"What made him spank you the last time?"

"Didn't I tell you? It was when he found out I'd asked Sloan to loosen my stays."

"Oh, that's right." The girls emerged from the woods onto the thin, rocky strip of white beach. "Jealousy will no doubt always be the keynote in your scenarios," Pamela sagely predicted. "But as we've already gone on the Sloan ride, let's pick someone different to torment Pascal with this time. How about your attractive leading man, Rene?"

"Rene's a married man."

"Excellent, makes you seem even naughtier. Now, let's think of some subtle way we can place the thought of Rene in Pascal's head."

"No, Pamela, let's think of something else. This idea is too dangerous. What if Pascal really thinks Rene is making a play for me and tells him off, or worse?"

"Just leave it to me," said Pamela.

On the following Saturday, Pamela and Pascal shot at The Murderer's Clock Inn, an old hotel with a fine pub. In between setups they drank Irish coffees at one of the tables and Pamela leafed through the local entertainment papers until she came to a full page ad for the upcoming run of *A Doll's House*. The ad featured Phoebe most prominently, with Rene in the background, but this was enough for Pamela to work with.

"That Rene Whitfield is certainly a fine figure of a man," she commented. "He must be all of 6'4"!"

"You really like beards?" Pascal looked at the photograph critically, having never thought of his wife's leading man as being particularly striking.

"Not just any beard, of course," Pamela remarked, "but this man has the head of a Greek coin. We really ought to get him for one of our tableaux, Pascal."

"Yes, I suppose you're right," the photographer replied, looking at the ad again.

"I'll bet Phoebe has a powerful crush on him," Pamela remarked. Pascal looked at her sharply.

"What?"

"She's so romantic and he's so heroic."

"Oh, nonsense," Pascal snapped, but the few words were enough.

• • •

Phoebe's opening night went beautifully. The play was enthusiastically received and afterwards Anthony Newton threw a party for the cast at his house on the cliff. Rene's wife, a large, sweet, New England craftswoman, had no love of crowds and spent the greater part of the evening wandering around the mansion and admiring the art which decorated the halls and rooms. Her absence from her husband's side at his moment of triumph displeased Pascal more than it did Rene, who was used to the retiring ways of his beloved.

That was not the only annoyance suffered by Pascal, who was still in knots over Nora's opening scene, which had included the little spanking over the chocolate macaroons. He didn't remember any spanking in *A Doll's House,* therefore it must have been at Phoebe's suggestion that the business got added in. This notion seemed to make Pascal's blood pressure rise.

It wasn't only the idea of another man laying hands on her that upset him, it was the thought of how many times she might have insisted the scene be rehearsed. He knew Phoebe's passionate nature and had already observed the effects of a spanking upon it. He knew he could rely on her faithfulness, but only up to a point. For example, he guessed that his wife would permit any man she allowed to spank her, to also embrace and possibly even kiss her. And perhaps it had already gotten that far with the beard.

Meanwhile, it was maddening not to be able to go up to Phoebe and shake the truth out of her, but there was no chance of that with this crowd surrounding them.

Finally Pascal was able to catch Phoebe as she ran downstairs, holding the skirt of her new party dress above her ankles with both hands.

"Phoebe!" He grabbed her bare elbow. "I want to talk to you!" He pulled her back up to the second floor landing and over to an upholstered bench in the hall.

"Oh, Pascal, I'm having the most wonderful night of my life!" she breathed joyfully, throwing her arms around his slim torso and pressing her cheek against his face.

"Never mind that," he snapped, holding her at arm's length, "What about that first act?"

"First act?" Phoebe was baffled.

"The spanking business in the first act. You didn't tell me about that."

"But, darling, there was nothing to tell," Phoebe protested, blushing instantly.

"There's never been a spanking in *A Doll's House* before. Why is there one now?"

Phoebe tried to think of an answer that would satisfy him.

"Well? You initiated that business, didn't you, Phoebe?"

"Well, what if I did? It worked," she replied confidently.

"I can't believe you thought up a thing like that just to get a thrill."

"Pascal, I didn't!" she protested, shocked to hear it put that way.

"And with a man who isn't your husband. In front of an audience, no less!" Pascal got up and paced.

"Really, darling, it was in the context of the play, after all."

"And what an audience. You must have realized you were turning half of them on," he accused, remembering all the players from the album who had been in attendance that night.

"The theatre is supposed to excite the senses," Phoebe declared firmly. "My director permitted my input because she agreed that it worked. She didn't accuse me of pandering!"

"That's just because she doesn't know your true leanings."

At that moment a tremendous voice booming *Old Man River* began to issue from the music room, accompanied by Anthony Newton on piano.

"I'll bet that's Rene," Phoebe fondly remarked, "he's got the most marvellous voice."

"You used to say I had the most marvellous voice," Pascal brooded.

"Oh, darling, but you do! It's practically the most thrilling thing about you!" Phoebe hugged him sincerely.

"Do you know that you're maddening?" He shook her by the shoulders.

"Pascal, you're not jealous of Rene?" she demanded gleefully. Pascal merely glared at her.

"This party has to end sometime, and when it does, we're going home and you're going to be sorry you ever looked at a beard," Pascal threatened before abandoning her to stalk off in search of a drink.

Finding a full wet bar in the billiards room, Pascal set about preparing a drink before he realized that an intimate grouping of Susan, Diana and Sloan were audibly discussing himself and Phoebe, as they lounged upon a set of high backed leather furniture off to one side of the pool table.

"So, are they into it or not?" Diana wanted to know.

"Phoebe is for certain. Not sure about Pascal," said Sloan.

"How do you know she is?" asked Susan, while Pascal also strained to hear the answer with mounting indignation.

"She told Pamela, " Sloan replied.

"God, he's handsome," Susan mused, which pleased Pascal no end but reminded him that he ought to withdraw before he was noticed. And yet he longed to hear more about Phoebe. "Why don't we kidnap him for a couple of hours and use him for our pleasure?" the mischievous little blonde suggested to her dark-haired friend. Diana laughed while Pascal bristled.

"Susan, behave yourself," Sloan scolded. "They're practically newlyweds and madly jealous of each other."

Pascal couldn't disagree with this assessment, but disliked being discussed in this way. Besides, the idea of being swarmed over by the two perfect New York beauties was not an unpleasant one. He wished Sloan would not discourage the girls quite so firmly.

Slipping back out of the room, Pascal went out to his car for his camera and began to traverse the mansion, snapping candid portraits of the *Doll's House* cast and Anthony Newton's guests.

Isolating Susan and Diana in a private room was not difficult, for they were excited by the idea of modeling for Pascal. Susan wore a black velvet suit and Diana a fitted dress of white winter wool, her shiny sable page boy counterpointed by Susan's waist length blonde mane. They playfully posed in each other's arms. While Pascal was reloading the girls began to question and tease him.

"Your wife is glorious," Diana told him, "is she by any chance bi?"

"I never asked her," he coolly replied, a bit surprised. "Why? Are you?"

"Oh no!" Diana replied, pillowing her head against Susan's small rounded bosom and locking her arms around her blonde friend's tiny waist.

"Isn't she bad?" Susan asked Pascal as she arranged the folds of Diana's dress to expose more stockinged leg for the camera.

"You're both bad," he declared, taking several shots of the new pose from different focal lengths. Susan and Diana exchanged a look. Now Susan pulled Diana closer against her and pulled up her skirt in back to reveal the brunette's stocking tops, white lace garter belt and panties.

"That's perfect," he told them. "But don't move until I tell you to."

"Too bad we didn't get to see any of Phoebe's underpinnings when she got her spanking on stage," Susan casually lamented. "But it was an exquisite moment all the same."

Pascal merely grunted in response, then said, "Okay, new pose."

Susan repositioned Diana on her knees on the loveseat, her back to Pascal, then made her lean on her elbows, and look over one shoulder with her bottom thrust out. Susan pulled up Diana's skirt again to expose her submissive's pantied bottom completely, then took the brunette by the waist as though she might either spank or caress her bottom.

"How's this, Mr. Robbins?" asked Susan ingenuously.

"Great." He took a few shots. "Okay, now take her by the earlobe," he instructed, because this was what he felt like doing to his annoying wife. The pretty posing continued until Pascal had shot another role.

"Thanks, girls," he told them, while Diana lit both his and Susan's cigarettes.

"May we see the proof sheets when they're ready?" Susan asked.

"Please do."

"And now you have to drink with us," said Susan before ordering Diana to go and bring them champagne.

Susan and Diana were equally captivated by Pascal, who to them represented all that was adorable in the thirty-something male. They began to ply him with intimate questions.

"Do you spank you wife?" asked Susan.

"Only when I think of it," he replied quite honestly.

"Will you think of it tonight?" Diana asked.

"Well, what would you do?" he asked them, "After the liberties she granted that baked ham!"

"Ah ha!" cried Susan. "The spanking in the first act surprised you too?"

"I reeled," he declared, becoming carried away by the dramatic moment on top of all the drinking he'd done.

Pamela had just entered the room looking for Sloan. Unnoticed by the group on the sofa, the graceful brunette hovered for only a moment until she identified all three voices as well as the topic under discussion, then disappeared uneasily.

Going immediately to the music room, Pamela waited for a pause in the singing to take Phoebe aside and counsel her to seek out Pascal.

"But I was about to sing some more with Anthony," Phoebe protested.

"Do you want the two cutest girls here to devour your husband alive?" Pamela demanded, unable to forget, despite a friendly acquaintanceship with Susan Ross, how that young lady had nearly annexed Sloan earlier in the year.

"What do you mean, Pamela?"

The girls went out into the hall and Pamela quickly recounted the conversation she'd overheard.

"But, what should I do?" Phoebe asked her worldly counselor.

"Get Rene to take you for a stroll through the gallery. Laugh and talk gaily as you pass the billiards room. Pascal will notice."

Five minutes later, while Pascal was being charmed by the naughty girls from Manhattan, his wife passed the billiards room arm in arm with Rene. Pascal rushed into the hall as they passed and called to Phoebe from the doorway.

"So there you are," he said.

"Here we are," said Phoebe.

"Why not come in here?" he asked, gesturing into the room with a bottle of champagne. Rene followed Phoebe in and was introduced to the girls, who immediately overwhelmed him with praise of his performance. This left Phoebe free to contend with her husband.

"Ready to go home now, Phoebe?"

"So soon?" she asked, with a flutter.

"It's almost one. And you must be feeling the strain of your big night by now."

"No, I feel wonderful."

"You'll feel even better once we get you out of that corset."

"Oh, I changed out of that right after the play," she smiled, thrilled that her waist had become reduced enough to appear corseted when it was not.

"Anyway, let's go home," he insisted.

"But wouldn't that seem rude to Mr. Newton?"

"Mr. Newton will understand perfectly."

"I should at least go and say good-bye," she decided, turning to leave. Pascal caught her by the arm.

"No, you shouldn't," he told her, leading her from the room. "Bye, girls."

"I really think I ought to thank Anthony," she declared, starting in the direction of the music room. Pascal yanked her back by her smooth forearm.

"You've done enough showing off for one night. We're going home now," he told her coldly, escorting her out of the house.

"Showing off?" She stopped on the stairs. "I beg your pardon! I happened to have starred in a play tonight."

"You sure did." He again caught her hand and pulled her after him.

Phoebe was about to begin arguing reflexively when she suddenly noticed him eyeing her as a cat eyes a sparrow.

"You just wait till I get you home, young lady," he promised, throwing her into the car.

"But, what did I do?" she demanded with a pounding heart.

"That's what I'd like to know. What exactly *did* you do with Rene on the days you rehearsed Act One?"

"I'm sure I don't know what you mean!"

Pascal merely sped home.

"I suppose you never thought of *this* happening," Phoebe cried triumphantly while buttoning herself into a quilted dressing gown and actually accepting a brandy from Pascal.

"What happening?"

"Me becoming someone!"

"What's this you're saying?"

"That you never expected me to be taken up by a VIP."

"And is that what's happened?"

"I should say it has. Why, only tonight Anthony Newton told me he's working on a play that has a fine part for me."

"I hope you're not getting a crush on that rich, attractive genius."

"Certainly not, my angel." Phoebe embraced her husband, but he took her by the shoulders and gave her a shake.

"Don't give me that." He took her over to the first armless chair he saw and turned her over his knee. "This is to remind you that you're married to me!" He pushed her light blue satin robe up to her waist to expose her bottom then brought his palm down hard and repeatedly upon its equally satiny surface. "I overheard your friends speculating about us tonight," he revealed between spates of smacks.

"What friends? What did they say?"

"Pamela, Sloan and those two brats from New York. They said it was a shame you didn't show your devoted husband more respect."

"Oh, darling!" she sighed.

"Hold still."

"But it hurts!"

"Oh, I'm sorry!" he exclaimed insincerely, while quickening the pace of his descending palm and pinkening the entire surface of her alabaster bottom. "Now, get to bed," he ordered, pushing her off his lap, "and be prepared for anything!"

"What does that mean?" she wondered, shyly sitting on the edge of the bed.

"It means that I am going to look for the KY and bad luck for you if there is none."

When he returned, properly equipped, Phoebe was hiding behind a fort of Ralph Lauren pillows. "Pascal, I'm not ready for that!" she insisted, with an edge to her voice.

"Oh yes you are," he told her, closing in on Phoebe while she darted from one side of the bed to the other, still shielded by the pillows.

"Pascal, stop, you're scaring me!" she cried, as he grabbed her by the wrist and pulled her into swatting reach.

"Phoebe dear, get over the pillows," he told her firmly.

"No!"

"All right, I didn't want to have to do this, but you've forced me to take drastic measures," he told her before disappearing out of the room. Phoebe gazed after him in wonderment. When he returned an instant later, he was carrying the much caressed Random photo album. He sat on the bed beside her and throwing her one cool look first, leafed through the heavy black pages until he came to the photo of Marguerite Alexander whipping Diana Stratton.

"See her?" Pascal pointed to the enchanting twenty-one-year-old Diana.

"Yes," Phoebe replied cautiously.

"And her?" Pascal turned to the photo of dewy, blonde Susan Ross across the knee of Hugo Sands.

"Yes," Phoebe replied.

"You know who they are?"

"Yes, Susan and Diana, Anthony Newton's protégeés from New York."

"Oh yeah?" He put the album on the marble dresser, "I say they're the protégées of anyone who orders either one of them to bend over in the right tone of voice."

"What are you saying?"

"I'm saying I overheard these two talking about how much they wanted to kidnap me and use me for their pleasure," Pascal reported with perfect veracity.

"You did?" Phoebe felt her heart lurch painfully.

"I'll bet they love being sodomized," he speculated.

"Pascal!"

"I could find out," he calmly threatened, "or you could obey me for once."

Phoebe glared at him momentarily, then gracefully disposed herself across the pillows, with her bottom uppermost.

"If it will help, you might imagine that I'm Anthony Newton about to give you a part, provided that you please me."

"How dare you! Mr. Newton isn't like that and neither am I!" she sprung up but he pushed her back into position.

"Oh, save your indignation for the stage and just do what you're told," he ordered, smacking her upturned bottom until she became breathless. "Rebellion over?" he asked.

"Yes," she mumbled.

"Technically, if you like being spanked, you ought to enjoy

– 342 –

being sodomized," he mentioned, spreading her pink cheeks to expose her tiny, stubbornly compressed bottomhole. "Are you going to relax?" he asked in a warning tone.

"How can I?"

"I'll show you how," he returned, spreading her and spanking her anus. This treatment caused her to whimper without trying to squirm away. "Look how wet you are!" he charged, spanking her pussy as well. Unconsciously, she tilted up and opened up to him. The only word she said was, "Oh!" but she said it many times. Now he went to work spanking her smooth inner thighs and even the backs of her muscular calves, until she was the same shade of pink everywhere he spanked her. Phoebe thrashed, moaned and panted, taking every smack with mounting excitement.

Finally, when the heat was a tangible entity and her soft skin began to recoil from his unremitting hand, she cried out with some urgency, "I'm ready now!"

The sensations and lubricity produced by the spanking eased the shock of penetration. As an afterthought, he held one wrist behind her back as he took her bottom and this slight act of mastery seemed to affect her in a wonderful way. While her body felt stroked, filled and loved, her mind told her she was his personal whipping girl, with no choice but to submit to this humiliating and invasive *punishment*.

Normal, well-adjusted, guiltless Phoebe had no idea of why, in her innermost heart, she longed to be treated as the chattel of an insolent master, but this did not stop her from luxuriating in the pleasure the treatment provided. She gave up a climax in two minutes, the violent contractions of which soon wrung an explosive orgasm from his deeply lodged organ.

"Was it all that you expected?" she shyly asked, after they had disengaged and lay in each other's arms.

"I never felt closer to any woman before," he confided. "How about you?"

"I feel as though this were our true wedding night," she replied.

"We're in agreement for once." He tightened his arms around her.

"I wish we never had to leave Random Point."

SHADOW LANE VII
HOW CUTE IS THAT?

How Cute Is That

Even though he had been teaching at Hollywood High for twelve years, and had been robbed so often that he now held a gun permit, David Lawrence had not lost his optimism. He was an amiable, youthful thirty-seven, amusing and well liked by his associates, especially the female ones.

Living in the *Blade Runner* world of modern Los Angeles, he accepted his grim wages, the fact that his marriage had failed and the continuous dangers of his thankless profession without repining. Blessed by nature with wit, remarkably good looks, a cheerful disposition and a propensity for indulging his senses, David found ways to enjoy himself every day.

Meeting women was not a problem, but finding a girl who shared his interest in *spanking* was. It wasn't enough just to find a woman who would take a spanking. What he really craved was a female counterpart, a fabulous fetishist, who thought about spanking as much as he did.

"It wouldn't have to be someone like Babydoll," he mused, looking out his classroom window, three stories above the intersection of Sunset and Highland, where every day at 3:45, for the last week, the most heavenly little blonde with wavy hair to her waist in a halter top and snug knee pants, on rollerblades, flew down Sunset on the south side of the street, urgently transporting a bag of take-out food.

On day five David made it his business to be out on the street at 3:45. Sure enough, Babydoll passed, this time carrying her take-out in a glossy shopping bag with Clark Gable's photograph on the side. She gave David a quick, little smile as she skated past him, and actually said, "How cute are you?" An instant later, she blushed as she realized that she hadn't meant to say that aloud.

Meanwhile, David was bowled over by his first closeup look at Babydoll. First of all, she was a radiantly beautiful young lady, in her early to middle twenties, whose only business on Sunset Boulevard ought to have been in decorating a billboard. She was in fact, astonishingly beautiful as she turned the corner at La Brea and disappeared.

"I must have imagined I heard that," David mused as he strolled to his favorite coffee bar. He chose a window booth and opened a copy of the *L.A. Free Press* inside of his *L.A. Weekly* in order to daydream about visiting one of the B&D salons that advertised in the former.

David didn't bother to go up the counter and order because Brooke Neuman began to prepare his regular double cappuccino as soon as he sat down.

Brooke was the brightest student in David's World Literature class. Her single parent was a subsistence-level stand-up comic and Brooke had to maintain several part-time jobs in order to supply herself with an allowance. David had conversed with her many times and found her both original and charming.

Brooke's graceful form, fine complexion and dark, silky hair barely registered on David because he never thought about his students in that way, although he couldn't fail to notice that she was perhaps the only student at Hollywood High who wasn't either radically pierced or in some way tattooed, and whose hair was all one color.

Brooke's boyfriend, a sardonic German boy named Willie Kronenberg, was the only other brilliant student in the class, but David didn't care for Willie's captious personality and wondered what Brooke saw in him besides his good looks and outstanding grade point average.

Sublimely unaware of the magnitude of crush Brooke had on him, David didn't even bother to close the adult newspaper when she brought his coffee over. He couldn't have closed it at that moment if he wanted to, for he had just seen a photograph that riveted him. In the middle of a two-page spread on a well-bred B&D club called The Keep, there was Babydoll! The girl he had seen on the in-line skates just minutes before and had watched from his window for a week, was billed as a *submissive* and displayed in a leather halter dress, perched naughtily on a bench with a paddle close by. David's heart leapt so high he nearly choked.

Babydoll available for sessions! His Babydoll. Right here in Hollywood. The ad called her Hope and as both a student of language and a dreamer he took note.

"I can't wait until *I'm* old enough to work in a B&D club," Brooke remarked to her mentor casually. David gave her a look and smiled, used to her cynical humor. "And that one in particular," she added, beginning to shock him. "I've been staring at their ads for two years."

"Why this one?" he returned off-handedly, wondering whether she was as intuitive as she was precocious.

"The mistress of course," said Brooke. "I love the way she never takes her glasses off. I've written her several letters, but she's firm that I can't even come and visit until I'm eighteen."

"Brooke, you astonish me," David nearly gasped at her temerity. Meanwhile, he thought to himself, "That does it, I'm visiting The Keep today!"

Brooke left him to wait on another customer while David smoked and looked out the window. Finally he got up and went to the phone in the back of the cafe and dialed the number of The Keep. The phone was answered on the first ring.

"Hello!" a euphonious female voice replied.

"Hello," he replied, in his own dulcet tones. "I've been looking at your ad in the *Free Press* and was wondering what was involved in a visit?"

"Well, what exactly are you looking for?"

"A spanking session."

"Giving or receiving?"

"Giving."

"Well, a half hour session is a hundred, an hour one sixty. Today we have Cherry and Hope available for spankings."

"I'd like to see Hope if I may," said David, throbbing with excitement at his perfect luck.

"She's free right now," the young woman said pleasantly.

"Where are you located?"

The mistress of the house gave David a residential street address not four blocks from where he stood. David promised to arrive within fifteen minutes and went to the counter to pay his bill.

Brooke, who had seemed to be busy the whole time he was on the phone, had none the less noted his every expression and attached great significance to the fact that he had left his paper open to the spread on The Keep before making his call. On his way out he scooped up both his newspapers and departed with an urgency she'd not observed before.

Rushing back to the phone she inserted a quarter in the slot and pressed the redial button. The same mellifluous voice answered, causing Brooke to hesitate a moment before replying, "Mistress Hildegarde?"

"Yes." The voice grew even warmer.

"It's me, Brooke Neuman. Remember? The girl who wrote you the letters?"

"Of course I remember, darling. But do you remember that I told you I couldn't even talk to you until you turned eighteen?" Hildegarde sounded only mildly annoyed.

"I'm sorry," Brooke meekly replied and immediately hung up. Then she ran outside to see whether Mr. Lawrence was still on the street. Luck was with Brooke and she spotted her teacher across the street at an ATM. "Wow, he's really doing it!" she said to herself, racing back inside to tell her boss, Oscar, that she needed an hour to take care of an errand. Then grabbing her camcorder, which she never went anywhere important without, she ran out the door.

Mr. Lawrence had just begun to walk briskly up Sunset. Brooke followed at a distance, filming kids on the street as she went. She had decided to be a filmmaker at age 11 and since then had devoted every leisure moment to watching films, shooting footage and writing scripts.

Mr. Lawrence was easily tracked to the quiet, shabby-genteel side street on which the white wooden house that lodged The Keep was situated. She was even able to video Mr. Lawrence knocking on the door and being given admittance by a gloriously beautiful blonde.

In the office of the club, the tobacco-marinated bouncer Rusty watched the closed circuit television monitors which pictured the street with mounting unease. As soon as Mistress Hildegarde came out of session he intended to make her aware of the girl who was taping everyone going in and out of the club.

Meanwhile, David had been taken by Hope up to the blue dungeon.

Since returning to the club and being told that a spanking session was on his way, Hope had changed into a gauzy white party dress and put her hair in a ponytail with a blue satin bow. The dress was new and matched to white pumps.

"We can pretend I'm Carol Linley, circa 1959," she said, when he admired her outfit, for her hobby was the history of glamour and she enjoyed identifying with various periods and looks.

"What's that?" he asked, regarding a form on a clip board she was preparing to fill out.

"Just your membership application," she explained, handing it to him. "We'll just need you to write your name and address in the blank spaces there."

"Must I? I'm a high school teacher and I'd really rather not."

"You can make up a name, you know. And don't you have a P.O. Box?"

"As a matter of fact, I do."

"I'm sure!" Hope laughed, then observed cleverly, "How else could you receive naughty things through the mail?" Then she looked at him closely. "Do I know you?"

"I work in the neighborhood. Perhaps we've eaten in the same restaurants," he ventured, delighted that she remembered him from their brief eye contact on the street earlier.

"If I'd had teachers as handsome as you I never would have dropped out of college," she confided flirtatiously.

"Dropped out of college, did you?"

"I suppose you don't approve of that."

"You bet I don't."

"Would you like to give me the allowance now so I can take it downstairs and have them start us?"

"Certainly."

David handed her the money and watched her slip out of the room. While she was gone he noticed that someone had placed a paddle, a hair brush, a strap and a small flogger on a leather

– 351 –

padded bench. The thought of Hope collecting these items for use on her own (no doubt) flawless bottom was sheer heaven.

But oddly, just before she returned to him, the image of Brooke Neuman flashed into his mind. Why would a quiet, thoughtful girl like Brooke dream of working in a place like this?

He paced the room, examined the equipment, lit a cigarette, then pulled the heavy velvet drapes aside to look out the window. What he saw on the street below caused his heart to lurch painfully. There was Brooke Neuman, on the sidewalk opposite The Keep, with her camcorder on her shoulder, blithely taping as she walked up and down. He let the curtain fall back into place and rushed for the door. Then he forced himself to pause and wait for Hope's return.

When Hope came back with a serene smile on her face he allowed himself one moment to appreciate her loveliness before panicking.

"Come here," he said, pulling back the curtain slightly. "Look out there. Do you see anyone across the street?"

"Yes, there's a girl with a camcorder on her shoulder. God, is she taping our front door?" Hope looked at David in alarm.

"That's my favorite student. She must have followed me over here."

"Does she know what kind of place this is?"

"Does she! She wants to work here."

"Oh! Well, she's certainly gorgeous," Hope breathed sincere admiration. "She'd make a fortune."

"She's only seventeen at the moment."

"Ooops. But why is she taping the house?"

"She tapes everything. She wants to make movies."

"I admire her initiative, but we'd better get her to stop filming, before she alarms everyone in the house," Hope said sensibly. "Do you want to go out there and talk to her?"

"Me? God, no!" David protested. "I could probably lose my job for talking to her under these circumstances."

"Is that really true?"

"I have no idea and I don't think I'll ask."

"I'd better go and explain the situation to Mistress. Just wait here. And don't worry."

After Hope's departure David continued to monitor Brooke out the window. In a moment craggy old Rusty crossed the street to confront Brooke, never taking his cigarette out of his mouth or his hands out of his jeans' pockets. No more than two sentences were exchanged before Brooke quickly marched away. Rusty then ambled back to the house and Hope returned to the dungeon.

"It's all taken care of," she reported sunnily.

"What did that man say to her?" David asked with some concern.

"Just that you need a permit to film on the streets of Hollywood."

"Smart!" David was all admiration for Rusty.

"I hope this hasn't put you off playing."

"Oh, no," he replied candidly, hanging his jacket on a peg. Hope gasped as he turned to see the reflection of his gun and shoulder holster in the mirrored wall opposite.

"I thought you said you were a teacher!" she cried with some alarm. "Are you a vice cop? Was that chick your back up? Is this a bust?"

"Not at all. And do calm down. Honestly, I'm just a high school teacher whose been beaten up enough times that they finally gave me a permit to carry a gun." David showed her the permit, his driver's license and teachers' union card. Hope was still skeptical and looked as though she might burst into tears of frustration, for she had been looking forward to playing with him. "Take these to your Mistress," he said with a sigh, thrusting his I.D.s into her hands. "I'll be here."

Hope disappeared yet again, only to return a few moments later, wreathed in smiles. "Hildegarde says I should ask you some questions to make sure you're on the level."

"Oh? What kind of questions?"

"You say you're into spanking, right?"

"Why, yes."

"Prove it."

"How do you mean, prove it?"

"Tell me some things about spanking that you like." Hope sat beside him on the leather covered bondage bed, stretching out her legs to admire the white grosgrain bows that tied across the insteps of her shoes.

"That would take some time," he smiled.

"You haven't proven anything yet."

"Say, how old are you anyway?" he asked her suddenly.

"How old do you think I am?" she laughed.

"Twenty?"

"Thanks! If you are a cop, you're a gallant one. I'm 25."

"That's a relief anyway."

"Oh? You wouldn't rather be spanking your adorable pet with the camera?"

"I'm not interested in my students."

"If that really was your student, I'm sure she has a giant crush on you."

"That's true, girls do get crushes on me from time to time. But she has more common sense than that."

"Then why follow you here?"

"Oh, we had a conversation in the cafe where she works about an hour ago during which she revealed that she's been dreaming about working at this very club for two years. I was indiscreet about telephoning and she was smart enough to follow me."

"So she's brilliant, beautiful, has a crush on her dominant male teacher, and wants to work in B&D. How cute is that?"

"I think one of the things we're going to discuss if we ever do get to play is this NewSpeak you kids talk. You, for example, seem smart enough to form more original expressions."

"Now I know you're a teacher!" Hope declared, with an irrepressible grin. Then she hit the intercom button and told Rusty to call them in a half hour.

Except for the nagging sensation of impending doom which set in every time he allowed himself to ponder the notion of Brooke and what she now knew about him, David felt divinely satisfied by his first trip to The Keep.

Spanking the vivacious yet compliant Hope had surpassed all his expectations of sublime erotic pleasure. The way she ground against his lap, the way her alabaster skin had pinkened under his hand, the delicious little gasps she gave as he stroked her in between smacks, all confirmed his long held theory that some women did really enjoy being paddled.

Hope had been all high spirits and ingenuity. She seemed as

interested in him as he was in her and made such incisive comments on his favorite subject that he felt as though he was out on the most agreeable date of his life.

When the session ended she had sat on his lap the right way around and given him a tremendous hug, telling him she hoped that he would visit her often. He vowed he would never visit anyone else and pressed a twenty dollar tip into her hand, wishing it could be more.

Toward Brooke, David's feelings were a mixture of resentment, distrust and uneasy admiration. He felt in his heart of hearts that Brooke would do nothing to hurt him. Not even if he gave her the spanking she deserved for following him to The Keep and setting everyone's nerves ajangle! But given the current climate, he wondered if instead he ought to consult a lawyer before even talking to his student again.

Brooke suffered torments all weekend, wondering whether Mr. Lawrence had been informed by the walking tobacco stick that she'd been outside The Keep with her camera. World Lit was her Monday second period class and the moment he walked in and slammed his briefcase down on the desk she no longer had to wonder.

Normally, Brooke was the first person her instructor smiled at. Today he never glanced her way unless he had to. Of course he had to eventually, because she always raised her hand. Even today, when she wanted very badly not to, pride forced her to do so. They were reading *Madame Bovary* and she was full of opinions on it.

Willie, who sat directly behind Brooke and noticed everything which pertained to that young lady, marked a difference in their teacher's attitude toward his girlfriend which puzzled the observant boy.

As they left class he demanded an explanation in his usual overbearing style. "How come Mr. Lawrence was ignoring you today?"

"Mr. Lawrence called on me several times," Brooke pointed out, unwilling to be roused from her bittersweet meditations on her idol by her tiresome contemporary.

"Yes, but he didn't commend your responses with his usual enthusiasm. In short, he seemed much less than charmed with you today. What's going on?"

"I don't know. Maybe he's gone off me."

"Aren't you concerned?"

"Why should I be concerned?"

"Weren't you counting on him for your college references?"

"I'm sure he'll give me the references I deserve."

"You know more than you're letting on," Willie accused. But the commencement of their third period American History class cut short the conversation.

Brooke had been going out with Willie since their sophomore year. He was her first lover and she his. Early on she had confessed her spanking fetish. Being a German male, naturally dominant and sexually playful, Willie had given Brooke a spanking on their first date.

They had driven up to the restaurant Yamashiro, which sat atop a Hollywood hill. Brooke had attempted to order wine with dinner, though she only just turned 16. Willie told her, "Behave, or I'll spank you," in front of the waiter.

"They weren't going to proof us," Brooke protested, for it was her birthday and this was her first real restaurant date.

"You need a spanking anyway," Willie told her firmly, causing Brooke to fall instantly in love.

After dinner, while they were waiting for the car to be brought up, they leaned over the parapet to view the magnificent city lights stretching below.

"That reminds me," said Willie, locking one arm around her waist, "you needed a spanking." And briskly he brought his hand down on the seat of her skirt six or eight times, letting her up the very instant the valet drove up with the car.

Brooke shuddered with excitement all the way home. Since it was a night when her father was emceeing at The Star Strip until three a.m., she invited Willie in and her first love affair was begun.

As it later turned out, Willie spanked more out of an innate feeling of male superiority than a desire to arouse her, and this was not an attitude that Brooke was prepared to tolerate much beyond graduation.

David now avoided the coffee bar where Brooke worked. He never addressed a remark to her that wasn't relevant to a lesson or walked with her down the hall chatting. In short, an arctic floe separated them until graduation and well beyond.

Of course David wrote outstanding recommendations for

Brooke. By early spring she'd received all her acceptances. She might have gone to Yale if she'd chosen to do so. Instead she picked the U.C.L.A. film school and decided to save on expenses by living at home. She had more than one reason for selecting this option.

Towards the end of the school year, when everyone was discussing their college plans, David's resolve never to speak to Brooke again began to weaken. Some months had passed since the incident at The Keep and David was virtually positive that Brooke did not intend to expose him. But there was still the problem of her being underage dynamite. He couldn't risk igniting her with so much as a smile. Even on graduation day, David remained remote.

Brooke felt that she was being cruelly punished, but the firmness of her handsome teacher thrilled her.

Meanwhile, David went to visit Hope once a week, whether or not he could afford it. She was an exquisite addiction.

Then, one Friday afternoon in late September, David arrived at The Keep for his usual appointment and was told that Hope had quit!

"She's going to do lots and lots of movies," Hildegarde informed the stunned David. "Don't despair, darling, she was determined that I give you and you alone her number," the pretty mistress told him, writing down the number. "She said she couldn't live without her favorite spanker." David's heart contracted at these soothing words.

"I don't suppose you'll ever find another sub of her quality," he mused.

"I wouldn't be too sure," Hildegarde smiled. "I've got a brilliant little college girl coming to me in October, as soon as she turns eighteen."

"You're not talking about my Brooke?" he snapped back at once.

"Is she your Brooke already?" Hildegarde shook her head with disapproval.

"No, certainly not. In fact, I haven't even talked to her since that incident back in March."

"Neither have I, but I feel certain we'll be welcoming her shortly. In fact, if I were you, I wouldn't miss our Halloween party. October 31st is her birthday."

•••

– 357 –

Not even a large earthquake could have kept David away from The Keep on Halloween. He arrived at eight, in a medium grey pin-striped suit, bearing a large bouquet of red and white autumn roses, which he had cut from the bushes outside his tiny cottage in Laurel Canyon. Hildegarde was gratified but not surprised by the perfect buds. David's funds were limited but his thoughtfulness was not. In the short time she had known him, he did her many kindnesses, from driving girls home to editing her advertising copy.

Hildegarde was pouring David a glass of wine in the kitchen when Hope arrived, in a black velvet gown and cape. The blonde girl put one arm around David's waist as she held out her wine glass to be filled.

"Darling, I'm so glad you came," said Hildegarde, who was exactly the same age as her ex-employee and had missed her favorite this last month. "Are you going to play?"

"I think I should. Don't you?" Hope grinned at David, for she knew that he rather enjoyed spanking her after she'd already been spanked hard. "Is she here yet?" asked Hope.

"Not yet," Hildegarde replied.

"She probably forgot all about it by now," David stated with conviction.

"Darling, a girl who's been dreaming B&D for years and who lives ten minutes away from me, is not going to forget about it," Hildegarde declared as the bell rang. "Excuse me," she said, kissing Hope's white throat as she exited.

"What are you going to do and say?" Hope demanded, smiling up at him.

"What do you mean?"

"When she comes in?"

"She isn't coming. But if she does, I don't know."

"You've never been at a loss for words with me," Hope teased him.

A glance upward at the kitchen security camera monitor showed them a leggy young brunette in a black PVC slip dress.

"That's her," David breathed. Hope squeezed his hand.

Brooke was conscious only of a blur of faces as Hildegarde ush-ered her into the main parlor and relocated a gentleman or two so that they might sit down together on a sofa.

"Mistress Hildegarde, I'm the girl who wrote you those letters this summer," Brooke confided, momentarily riveted by the milky perfection of the club owner's bosom, displayed in a midnight blue velvet bustier gown. "I hope it's all right that I came by tonight," Brooke continued, producing her driver's license and passport for inspection.

"I've been expecting you," Hildegarde told her, handing her identification papers back with a smile. "And so has someone else."

"You mean he's here?" Brooke looked around with a sudden thrill and saw David in the doorway. She thought him more striking than ever and felt her face grow warm as his gaze fell upon her lissome body in the shiny cocktail dress. He approached her with a smile too faint to please her and she wondered whether David was still angry with her for taping him going into the club the previous spring.

"Hello, Brooke. How are you?"

"Is that all you can say to me on the occasion of my 18th birthday and my first visit to The Keep?" Brooke jumped up and impulsively kissed David on the lips. "Please forgive me, Mr. Lawrence, but I've been wanting to do that for several years now," Brooke explained, intoxicated with joy at the coincidence of him being at The Keep on this of all nights.

"Really, Brooke, I would have thought you had more common sense," David scolded, while inwardly aglow. Normally he wasn't attracted to college girls, but Brooke was so sophisticated for her age. The very fact that the little go-getter didn't seem to need him to accomplish her fantasies raised her to a level of experience he'd not met in women twice her age. Now that it was legal to admire Brooke, he did, though he wasn't about to let her know it.

"Mr. Lawrence, may I ask you a question I've been dying to know the answer to ever since that day I followed you here?"

"You certainly may not," he growled, but then smiled as Hope brought him a glass of wine.

"Hello," said Brooke to Hope.

"Hi. How cute are you?" Hope complimented Brooke.

"Hope, what did I tell you about that mindless incantation?" David demanded with real annoyance.

Hope looked at David with surprise, then, in her usual quick way, realized that David's most intelligent ex-student might not think too well of Valspeak. Now Hope blushed deeply as only a natural blonde can, for she was in love with David herself and wanted always to be thought well of by him.

"I'd better escape while I can then," Hope smiled with perfect grace at Brooke and avoided David's eyes entirely as she slipped out of the room and ran upstairs to join a friend in a dungeon.

Meanwhile, Brooke had mentally recorded the little scene for all eternity and was moved almost to tears by the pathos of her ravishing rival's humiliation. So this was David's favorite, a heavenly creature as sensitive as she was kind. But David didn't value her, thought Brooke, not nearly as he should.

Brooke was aflame with excitement. Everything was glamorous tonight. To think that the male she worshiped had his own fairy creature to punish and pet was past exotic. She had never seriously thought Mr. Lawrence submissive, but there was always the possibility. Until now, when he had made his attitude so clearly known. Whether in the classroom or the dungeon, Mr. Lawrence remained the instructor.

"Now see here, young lady, you don't seriously mean to come work here?" They sat down in the parlor.

"Why not? It seems to have the nicest clientele," Brooke teased.

"Does your father know you're here?"

"My father knows and approves of everything I do," she returned haughtily, which gave David a start and caused Hildegarde to beam. "You don't think he wants me to graduate college sixty thousand dollars in debt, do you?" the eighteen year old replied sensibly.

"Well, no but—" David stammered.

"My job at the cafe paid seven dollars an hour."

"But a girl like you in a place like this?"

"Don't be disrespectful, Mr. Lawrence," Brooke replied, "after all, Mistress Hildegarde is here."

"Yes, well I'm sure she agrees with me that there are better places for you than in a dungeon," David said with a conviction Hildegarde didn't share.

"David," Hildegarde said, "one of my best girlfriends put herself through law school working for me."

"I never realized you were so stuffy, Mr. Lawrence," Brooke

baited him, while looking around the room for the first time at the waiting clients.

"Let's go somewhere and talk," said David impatiently.

"You mean leave now?"

"I do."

"But I just got here."

"Surely you didn't intend to start working tonight?"

"David may have a point, darling," said Hildegarde, cognizant of the hostile looks being tossed in Brooke's direction by several of her other girls. "I've got a full house tonight of both staff and clients and it's unlikely I'll be able to give you a complete tour."

"But I was counting on at least one birthday spanking," said Brooke.

"Is it your birthday?" a plain, conservative looking, fifty-year-old male asked with some excitement from a nearby loveseat.

"Yes. I turned eighteen today," Brooke replied.

"God, I'd love to do a session with you," the gentleman vowed. "What's your name?"

"Yes, darling, what is your *play* name?" Hildegarde ignored David's glower to murmur.

"Do I have to have one?"

"Everyone does."

"I've always liked the name Alison."

"Excellent. Well, Alison, may I present Paul, who is very much into spanking. Why don't you let him know what days you'll be coming to us and he can plan his next visit accordingly," suggested Hildegarde pleasantly.

"Friday and Saturday nights for sure," mused Brooke, upsetting David. "And probably a weekday afternoon or two as well."

"I'll definitely be in," Paul promised.

"Meanwhile, Cherry is here and I have Hope visiting for the entire night," Hildegarde consoled the spanker before jumping up to answer the door.

"Can we go now?" David demanded, causing a shudder to run through Brooke.

"Are you going to buy me dinner?"

"Dinner? Sure. Of course." He was taken aback by her complete lack of embarrassment at the entire situation and found himself continually readjusting his attitude toward his ex-student.

"And what about my birthday spanking?" she asked as he led her out the door.

"Don't worry about that!" David promised.

Because he hadn't spent any money at the club David took Brooke to an expensive French restaurant, where she was served wine without question. With her tall, elegant carriage, sophisticated dress and high heels, she might have passed for twenty-one.

Brooke was as happy as love, success and promise could make a girl. Her guiltless exuberance was attractive yet frightening to David.

"Tell me about you and that fairy princess at the club," Brooke demanded over dessert.

"If I give you my cake, can I avoid answering that question?" David asked, pushing a chocolate lacquered pyramid across the table to her.

"I want to know about my rival."

"Your what?"

"My competitor."

"Brooke, what's gotten into you?"

"Nothing. I'm just staking my claim."

"That wine must be going to your head," he declared, amazed at her boldness.

"What's the matter, Mr. Lawrence, don't you want Betty and Veronica fighting over you?"

"Certainly not."

"We don't have to fight. We can do a split shift."

"You're talking out of turn, young lady," he growled, both shocked and aroused by her self-confidence.

"Oh, yeah? What are you going to do about it?"

"I think there's only one thing to do—take you home and spank you."

Brooke had not the slightest hesitation about being alone with her ex-teacher, who took her home to a pleasant guest house on Amor Drive. In fact, she longed to surrender to him as soon as possible. But as he locked the door, adjusted the lights and gave her a long, cool look, she suddenly remembered the remarks she had made at dinner and wondered if he thought her very rude.

"I suppose I did speak out of turn," she confessed shyly.

"Having second thoughts about coming?"

"Oh, no. Never. You must have figured out how much I care."

"I did nothing of the sort. You think I sit around daydreaming about my students?"

"No, but after the incident last Spring . . ."

"Oh, that. I see your point. Well, yes, I admit I did think about you quite a bit after that, but only in the context of my job being jeopardized by your infernal snooping and video taping."

"Oh, I see, you're too pure and noble to ever think about a girl student, is that it?"

"No, that is not it, you fresh brat. I never claimed to be either pure or noble. Far from it. I'm just not attracted to teenaged girls. Now, I know that may come as a shock to you, but it happens to be a very good trait in a high school teacher."

"I see. I have to get older before I can become interesting to you."

"I didn't say that. You may be the exception." David smiled. "You certainly don't act like any teenaged girl I've ever met before."

"Thanks!"

David's house was decorated in the pastel-hued, spare, uncomfortable Southwestern style. Thus, Brooke was led into a nook with peach washed walls, which contained a distressed plank table and four sturdy, wooden chairs. One of these was pulled out and David sat. He then pulled her down across his lap.

"Tell me what kind of spanking you've been thinking about," he demanded, smoothing her short, shiny skirt down and running his palm across her slim, upper thighs.

"The silver screen kind."

"You mean, just over your skirt?"

"For starters."

"How many smacks?"

"You're asking me?"

"How hard?"

"You decide."

"I don't want to hurt you."

"You won't."

"Oh? You mean someone has done this before?"

"Willie has spanked me," she admitted.

"Willie!" David didn't have to pretend indignation. "You granted that callous youth the divine privilege of turning you over his knee?" Smack! David's hand came down. Smack! Now on the other cheek. "I'm appalled," he added, unleashing a stinging volley of spanks that caused Brooke to yip.

"But, he was my boyfriend," Brooke pointed out. "Ouch! You have a hard hand, Mr. Lawrence," she added, without rancor. When she reached back to rub he caught it and pinned it to her side before continuing the spanking.

"If you want to work for Hildegarde you're going to have to learn to take much harder spankings than this without making a fuss," he informed her, rapidly warming the back of her skirt with sharp, measured smacks.

"I wasn't complaining," she hastened to explain.

"You'd better not complain, after the anxiety you've put me through!" Now David began to fully express his resentment against Brooke for tracking him down at The Keep seven months before. He pulled up her PVC skirt, carefully tugged down her expensive seamed pantyhose and snapped the black satin G-string she had on underneath. "Lesson #1," he told her, slapping her hard after every remark for emphasis, once on each cheek, "you don't go out to play with a spanking person in pantyhose and a G-string!"

"But this skirt is too short for a garter belt," she confessed after catching her breath, for his hand felt much harder on her bare bottom. Now he yanked her g-string down and spanked her several dozen times more.

"Then the skirt is too short to go out in," he declared. "You want to be mistaken for a hooker?"

"I got this jumper at the hottest shop on Melrose," she protested, wriggling on his lap.

"I say the dress is too short. Are you arguing with me?" he demanded.

"No," she replied.

"And wear regular panties next time," he ordered.

"Is there going to be a next time?"

"I mean next time you go out with a spanking person," he replied coolly.

"Oh."

"That reminds me." He renewed his grip on her waist and brought his hand down hard on her already pinkened, peaches and creamy bottom, "I didn't like that fresh remark you made about staking your claim." Now he spanked her even more emphatically. Brooke took it as long as she could, but finally burst into sobs.

"What are you doing?" he stopped spanking her and looked at her face. He'd never spanked a girl to tears before and it gave him a terrible thrill.

"I'm not sorry I did that," he told her, lifting her off his lap and helping her to set her clothes to rights. "You had a real one coming for all sorts of reasons."

"I know," she replied, as meekly as it was possible for her to be.

"Naturally, I never meant to make you cry," he added, searching her face for a clue to her real state of mind.

She merely rubbed her bottom and returned his gaze wide-eyed.

"You see how disagreeable I can be when someone irritates me," David tossed off casually as he lit a cigarette.

"I don't blame you," she told him.

"No?"

"Oh, no. You have every right to be annoyed with me. Because I'm such an egotist, I never considered the fact that you might be truly indifferent to me. I apologize."

"Come off it, Brooke, I hate false humility. I've never been indifferent to you for a second and you know it."

"Then how do you feel about me?"

"You scare the hell out of me."

"I'm really harmless," she assured him with a smile.

"Yeah?" he laughed.

"May I have a cigarette?"

"You don't smoke."

"I started."

"You ought to know better," he observed, lighting her a cigarette.

"So, are we going to play again?" she asked shyly.

"I don't know. I want to talk to a lawyer first."

"But I'm eighteen now."

"You're also a recent ex-student of mine, which could damage my reputation, and possibly lead to my dismissal. And what kind of references could I expect if I were fired under those circumstances?"

"I see that I'm getting the brush-off," she commented.

"Honey, it's not like that. But a man in my position has to be more careful than the average player in the scene."

"I see. The man I worshiped has no backbone!" Brooke said angrily.

"You must want another spanking," he replied, unruffled.

"I might as well, since it's the last time I'll be seeing you."

"Look," he told her, taking her by her forearm and pulling her against him, "you'll see me whenever I tell you to come over here. Understand?" Then he kissed her.

The next day was Saturday and as on most recent Saturdays, David's first order of business was calling on Hope at her tiny, fifth floor apartment on Franklin Street, Hollywood, to see if she needed help with any errands. He found her in her favorite position, in front of her mirror, planning her morning outfit. She was in a robe of white merino wool, her small feet thrust into matching slippers with embroidered toes. Next to her was fresh ground coffee. Propped up against the mirror was *Elle*. Laid out on a nearby chair was a short denim jumper and white T-shirt. It was a warm day for November and Hope planned to do some shopping. She was deciding between well behaved flats and open-toed, sling back, 4" pumps when David entered with his usual offering of rose buds.

"I didn't expect to see you for some time!" Hope cried, jumping up to throw her arms around his neck.

"Why not?" He looked puzzled.

"Well, you did leave with Brooke last night," Hope pouted.

"Well, it was her birthday."

"And I suppose she got her birthday spanking?"

"Yes."

"And what else?"

"A kiss. She's only eighteen, you know."

"Whereas I'm all of twenty-five," Hope said, sitting on his lap and nuzzling his ear. "You need have no reservations with me, my darling."

"Thanks," he tightened his arms around her waist.

"You know, we haven't played since I left The Keep," she reminded him, squirming on his lap in a way that aroused him acutely.

"I know. But I did bring allowance today," he told her.

"That's nice, but not necessary. In fact, I'd almost rather hand you money now and then, you dear, underpaid public servant. "

"That arrangement wouldn't suit me, my little working girl," he told her firmly, divesting himself of his jacket and moving a good armless chair into the center of her studio.

David took Hope over his knee and spanked her as he always did at The Keep. He began over her robe and gave her a good warm up, then pulled it up to discover that she had nothing on underneath.

As usual, her silken skin colored quickly under his hand. And as usual, fifteen minutes into the session, Hope began to reveal her accessibility and excitement. But as usual, when she arched to his hand, he ignored the invitation, refusing to touch her intimately. And with her usual frustration, Hope wondered why.

"David?"

"Yes, dear?" He paused to rub away the sting.

"Don't you like girls?'

"What?"

"Don't you like me?"

"What a question. You're one of my favorite things in life."

"Then why do you always spank me so prudishly?" Hope sprang off his lap. "Are you not into sex?"

David flushed. "Of course I'm into sex. But not with someone I'm paying for a session."

First she gasped with indignation, then hot tears filled her eyes. Drawing herself up to her full five feet and five inches of lithe femininity, Hope deliberately slapped him, albeit very lightly, across the face.

"Is that all you think of me?" she cried.

"I think the world of you, that's why I wouldn't insult you by expecting your favors for a hundred bucks," he replied angrily, for he also had a quick temper and disliked being slapped, even lightly.

"Insult me? Don't you think you insult me every time I invite you to touch me and you ignore me?"

"I was attempting to behave respectfully," David frostily replied.

"It's a safe sex thing, isn't it? You think I'm some sort of high risk slut, don't you?"

"Certainly not. Everyone knows you're a princess."

"They do?" Hope smiled briefly with relief.

"I'm probably a lot more of a slut than you are," David tantalized her. "Anyway, I always use a rubber, so that's not the point."

"Well, what is? You're not in love with Brooke, are you?"

"Of course not. She's even less suitable than you are."

"Don't tell me you only go out with other academics," Hope protested.

"Not exactly."

"You don't think I'm smart enough for you!"

"You're plenty smart, but you're also a B&D call girl. You think I want my girlfriend running out at all hours to do sessions with strange men? Or making fetish videos?"

Hope began to cheer up when she realized he had given this some consideration before deciding to act like an idiot.

"Why not? You often told me at the club that you liked to spank me after two or three other men had warmed me up. Now you're playing the Puritan," she reminded him.

"That's a good point," he granted.

"If you wanted to keep things impersonal between us, you shouldn't have begun coming to see me like this. Why, the way you're always offering to perform chores and do favors for me, is it any wonder I got the wrong idea about your intentions?" she demanded haughtily, shrewdly targeting the one area in which he was genuinely culpable.

"Look, isn't there some way we could still be friends and play without getting involved? I mean, I thought that was the beauty of doing sessions," he protested weakly.

"Oh, you make me sick. Get out. And don't come back!" she ordered, throwing the allowance at him. "You stupid, conventional, hung-up, impotent, high school teacher!"

David stared at her for a moment, more impressed by her ability to tell him off so succinctly than hurt by her accusations.

"All right," he snapped, "you asked for it. Get over here!" He took her in his arms and kissed her on the mouth for the first time. She went limp, then clung to him, astonished at the depth of his kiss.

Then David pulled her robe off and looked at her completely nude body for the first time. "Slap my face, will you?" He gave her a shake, wound his hand in her hair and kissed her again. Then, because she weighed nearly nothing, he picked her up and carried her to the day bed.

"Face down," he told her, taking off his belt. "You're getting six of the best for that smack in the face."

"You deserved it," she replied defiantly.

"I said face down."

Hope obeyed with a pout. The belt came down hard and fast across her bare bottom six times. She hardly had a chance to gasp between each whack. Number three brought tears to her eyes and by six she was sobbing. When he was finished he threw his belt aside and pulled her around to face him.

"I've got a better way to punish you for that crack about impotence," he told her coolly, but wiped her face dry with his handkerchief. Then he took her over to a green leather spanking horse, which was the only piece of B&D equipment in the tiny flat, and bent her over one end.

She turned to him and asked, "Are you telling me you have a rubber in your pocket this instant?"

"Worried?" he asked insolently, pushing her head back down. "Just behave yourself like the submissive you're supposed to be."

Hope gave a murmur of surrender at the new tone in his voice. She turned to see a zipper come down, a large cock emerge and a rubber come out. Once the truncheon was properly sheathed, he let it rest between her cheeks and reached around to capture and lightly squeeze her breast. She ground back against him with her bottom and arched her sex up.

"Since you're so impatient . . ." he spread her and nudged into her lightly, but she was extremely small and he pulled away. "You're not nearly wet enough," he told her, spanking her bottom and fingering her pussy until she was. He had never touched her like this before and she could only whimper and pant her encouragement. "How aggressive you were today," he scolded. "My little Princess demanding sex!" He slapped her inner thighs until she squirmed. "Is that the way a perfect submissive is supposed to behave?"

"I suppose not," she conceded. Her soft response was rewarded by five or six light, sharp smacks on her parted sex. She arched up a little more to show him how agreeable this felt. He went around

to one side of her, tucked one arm under her waist, lifted her off
the horse an inch or two and spanked her damp pubic mound and
labia even more firmly.

"You couldn't wait for our romance to take its course and for me
to approach you in the proper way at the proper time, could you?"

"I'm sorry," she murmured as he let her back down and went
around behind her again.

"Did it ever occur to you that you may have opened Pandora's
Box?" he suggested, penetrating her slowly, with his hands fastened to her waist.

"What do you mean?" She gasped as he thoroughly filled her.

"Now that I've had you like this, do you think I'm going to be
satisfied just to spank you and lace your corsets?"

"I hope not, my darling," she breathed.

"Got any lube?"

"What for?" she turned her head.

"What do you think?"

"Isn't this a little sudden?" she squeaked, barely able to accommodate him in the proper place.

"Not to me; I've been daydreaming about sodomizing you for
six months," he confessed, spreading and examining her bottom.

"Can't I have six months to dream about it too?"

"You can have six minutes," he told her, withdrawing to
abandon her and search for the lube. "And don't move, unless you
want the strap again," he warned her.

Upon his return he found her pacing and nervously smoking one
of his cigarettes. He relieved her of it with a smile. "Worried?"
Now he bent her back over the horse and went to work with the
lube, fingering her deeply in both places until she sighed and
ground against the leather. Then he only fingered her bottom and
slapped it in the middle of it. "Your six minutes are up, bad girl."
When Hope only whimpered in reply he spread her and took her,
like an expert in the tricky art of sodomy, giving them both an
orgasm in a matter of a few short minutes.

"You brute," she whimpered, for form's sake. "No one's ever
done that to me before."

"Really?"

As she turned to see him smile there came a knock on the door.

"You expecting some one?" He unceremoniously extracted his

still throbbing cock from her tighter than ever sheath and disappeared into the bathroom to dispose of the evidence and put himself back together.

"Only Brooke," Hope replied, pulling her robe back on and answering the door without concern.

"Brooke! What are you doing here?" David demanded as Hope let her in.

"We're going shopping on Melrose. Didn't I tell you?" Hope linked arms with the willowy brunette, who smiled down at her and then across at David.

"So you're going through with this, are you?" David frowned at his ex-student.

"Through with what?" Brooke replied.

"The Betty and Veronica thing."

"Nonsense, Mr. Lawrence, we've simply realized how much we have in common," Brooke explained.

"And think of the impact we'll make as a tag team," Hope suggested blithely, squeezing Brooke's long waist. David did and it made him shudder.

"I'll just jump into these," Hope reported, taking her pre-selected outfit into the bathroom to dress.

Alone with David, Brooke wasn't quite so cocky and indeed avoided his gaze.

"I still say you're too young for any of this," he grouched.

"And I still say I'm into B&D and always have been."

"Well, if something awful happens, don't say I didn't warn you."

"Something awful could have happened to you when I discovered your secret life. But it didn't."

"Your point being?"

"My point being, preach what you practice, Mr. Lawrence."

"Don't be smart," he snapped and Brooke had the grace to blush. Still annoyed at the interruption of his first sexual tryst with Hope, he frowned at Hildegarde's newest protégée. Then he put his jacket on and crammed his grey fedora down on his head. "I'll be going now," he announced as Hope emerged fully dressed.

"You don't want to take us to brunch?" Hope asked, astonished at his eagerness to deprive himself of their company.

"No, I do not want to take you to brunch," he returned, with an edge to his voice that made the girls stare at each other.

"Good-bye!" was his final word to them before clattering down the five flights of stairs.

"What did we do?" Hope wondered.

"Maybe it's a sensory overload thing," Brooke speculated as they leaned over the railing to follow the descending fedora.

"You're probably right," Hope agreed. "In the past twenty-four hours he's spanked you for the first time, had me for the first time and now he's just found out we're determined to be friends. No wonder he's confused."

"He seemed more hostile than confused," Brooke observed.

"Well, that's to his credit. Could you respect a man who wasn't slightly unnerved by a situation like this?"

"Still, he might at least have offered us a ride to Melrose."

"Never mind, he brought me plenty of allowance. We can take cabs, have lunch and even buy stockings."

"And let's not forget a present for Mr. Lawrence," Brooke suggested, training her video lens on Hope's radiance for the first time.

"Mr. Lawrence doesn't accept presents from ladies," Hope declared, establishing an immediate relationship with Brooke's camera.

"Nor apparently does he take them to brunch."

"It's better this way," said Hope, "we can talk about him all afternoon." They ran downstairs and followed David out into the brilliant sunlight.

The Attemped Taming of Marguerite Alexander

DETERMINING TO SEPARATE Marguerite from all temptations, Malcolm Branwell forbid his wife ever to set foot in her bookshop again while Sloan Taylor was its manager. Then he caused her to shut up the house in Random Point and took her back to Boston where he retained a handsome residence.

And this was the reason Marguerite had still not met Hope Spencer Lawrence, the new beauty of Random Point whom Sloan had hired as a clerk at the shop. Hope was being talked of as a jewel and Marguerite was eager to appraise her new employee. But Malcolm cared more about keeping her away from every man in the small Cape Cod village who had enjoyed her favors.

Even so, he continued to brood. Kisses, hugs and smiles became dim memories, conversation minimalistic. Sex was hard-driving, deliberate and initiated wordlessly, foreplay consisting of Malcolm bending Marguerite over some conveniently curved piece of furniture, pulling her panties off roughly and slapping her hard.

But even sex out of an Ayn Rand novel was not enough to make up for the sudden lack of approbation in Marguerite's life. Having cut her off from everyone—he also pointedly withheld his own affection. This situation had prevailed for several weeks when the neglected redhead thought of rebelling.

Marguerite had invited Laura Random to Boston for the weekend so her best friend could observe how she suffered. This picture of domestic strife was thoroughly analyzed by Laura, Patricia Fairservis and Laura's sister, Susan Ross as they lunched one afternoon shortly thereafter at The Golden Owl Inn in Woodbridge.

"He barely speaks to her, except sarcastically, uses no endearments, never touches her, except to take her—roughly mind you—" Laura revealed indignantly.

"Yum," Susan cut Laura off.

"—and afterwards he just zips up and walks away," the brunette hotly concluded.

"I can't believe Malcolm Branwell capable of such Gothic behavior," cried Patricia, who now headed the P.R. department of Malcolm's Boston-based bookstore chain.

"I wonder how long he can keep it up," Susan mused. "It sounds kind of sexy."

"You don't know Marguerite if you can say that," Laura corrected her younger sister. "She needs to be adored."

"Then she shouldn't have picked Malcolm," Susan observed.

"Susan, you're not being helpful," Laura chided. "If you could have seen how miserable Marguerite was, trying to please Malcolm in every way, while he ignored her, it would have infuriated you."

"And then he all but rapes her, does he?" Patricia marveled.

"Yes, well he has to do something to hold her attention," Laura pointed out.

"If he was thoroughly disenchanted with Marguerite he would have just walked out," posited Susan. "His staying on to punish her must mean that he still cares deeply for our friend."

"We should think of some brilliant way to teach him a lesson and at the same time restore him to Marguerite's ample bosom," suggested Patricia.

"There are three of us here, let's concentrate," said Laura. Each of them stirred their tea.

Susan said, "If he's tempted to cheat on her, then they'll be even and he won't be able to feel superior."

"Good idea!" Laura approved.

"So, does anyone here want to volunteer?" Susan asked.

"I'd do it in a heartbeat," said Patricia, "if I didn't work for Malcolm and date Marguerite's ex-boyfriend."

"You're right," agreed Laura, "it would look like you're only interested in Marguerite's men."

"He is the body beautiful though," Patricia fondly mused.

"I'd volunteer if I wasn't so furious at the way he's treating Marguerite," Susan admitted, "but I'm sure my hostility would surface and he'd catch on to our plan."

"Me too. After the way I've seen him behave, I'm more inclined to slap him than let him slap me," Laura replied resolutely.

"What if we were to engage someone else to do it?" Laura suggested.

"Anyone in mind?" Patricia asked.

"Actually, the girl who's working in the bookstore now with Sloan would be perfect."

"Of course," Susan cried, "the glorious Hope Spencer Lawrence. I first met her that time Diana and I went out to Hollywood to play at the B&D club. She's ideal. No man could possibly resist her."

"But would she do it?" Patricia asked, making a mental note to keep Michael Flagg out of the bookstore for the next few years.

"We could try to bribe her. She makes nothing at the bookstore and her husband earns a teacher's salary. She's already seen Anthony a few times for allowance," Susan informed them.

"But this wouldn't be a straight-forward session. Subterfuge would be involved," Patricia pointed out, "not to mention actual closure."

"You know, that's true," Laura agreed, "and Hope is a newlywed. With a divine husband who's a little bit strict. She might not be willing to seduce a stranger."

"We can ask her anyway. She might enjoy the challenge. And I know she'd appreciate that her sacrifice was in a good cause," Susan declared. "She has a generous spirit. And she's read all of Marguerite's novels. Let me lay the proposition before her."

"Show me the man's photograph," said Hope after Susan unfolded the plan to her over the coffee bar at Marguerite Alexander's book-shop the following day.

"No problem," said Susan, running upstairs to the third floor gallery which housed the most extensive collection of fetish literature in New England. There she found a set of Hugo Sands' *New Rod Quarterlies* going back several years. She grabbed the relevant issue and ran back down the spiral staircase.

"Here's his picture, with the personal ad that Marguerite first answered." Susan opened to the page with Malcolm's photo, showing him stripped to khaki shorts on the deck of his boat.

"I've ogled that ad before," Hope admitted.

"Good player too."

"If I accept the assignment it can't be for money. It can only be to help Marguerite," stipulated Hope. "After all, I have a soul."

"As you know," said Susan, "Marguerite created this wonderful shop and she's passionately attached to it. Malcolm is extremely ungrateful in keeping her away from here, seeing as even he had Marguerite for the very first time upstairs in the third gallery," Susan revealed.

"I suppose that a good deal of sex has been had in the shop," Hope mused as she gazed across the floor to where her handsome young supervisor Sloan Taylor was ringing up sales.

"Yes, the shop has magic," Susan asserted.

"Then this is where I should attempt the seduction," Hope decided.

"Bringing him full circle," Susan eagerly agreed.

"And proving to him that the shop's influence is impossible to withstand if you've a drop of blood in your veins."

"If he succumbs to you here, he will then comprehend with crystal clarity how Marguerite managed to succumb to Sloan," Susan thrilled to the plan's symmetry.

"All right. I never come on to men, but I'll make an exception this once, for the sake of my dear boss whom I've never met. But how are we going to get him in here?"

"We'll start by visualizing the event," Susan decided, "That always helps to actuate sex."

Coincidentally Malcolm's spell of bad temper had just about run its course. One morning, a few days after Susan's discussion with Hope, he looked across the breakfast table and realized that he was forcing himself not to smile at his adorable wife. His dark eyes briefly flickered towards her green ones, remembering with a pang that he'd been mean to her for weeks. He cleared his throat and turned a page of the *Wall Street Journal*, attempting to ignore the nagging guilt which suddenly seemed to choke him.

"I suppose you're just dying to go to Random Point," he said disinterestedly.

"It has been forever," she admitted.

"Want to go for the weekend?"

"That would be lovely!"

No sooner was he out the door than Marguerite was on the phone to Laura.

"Is he still being frigid though?" Laura asked.

"Arctic, as opposed to Antarctic. I seemed to feel a warming trend today."

"Do me a favor. Send Malcolm over to the shop around closing time on Saturday evening. Tell him Sloan won't be there, just the new employee, Hope Lawrence. Ask him to check her out for you to make sure she fits in with the image of the shop."

"But, to what end? I know that Hope is perfectly suited to the shop right now."

"Never mind. Four women put their energy into this scheme, so have faith."

Saturday was filled with chores as Marguerite had been away from home for weeks. Towards the middle of that stormy afternoon Malcolm walked into the kitchen, where his wife was painstakingly rolling out a pie crust.

"What are you doing?"

"I'm baking us a shepherd's pie for dinner."

"You seem to be going to a lot of trouble," he commented. "Is there anything I can bring you or errands I can run?"

He seemed so genuinely friendly all at once that she beamed. "I do have a shopping list." She handed him a long one. "And you might buy some flowers and wine. Then, if you can possibly get there before six, I'd love for you to drop those pictures off at the shop." Marguerite indicated an open crate containing six gilt-edged literary portraits. "Sloan's out of town this weekend, but the new girl will be there," Marguerite added, seeing Malcolm's splendid shoulders stiffen, "and I'd love to hear a report of her."

"Okay," he agreed, grabbing the crate and walking out.

At around ten of six, when Hope had nearly given up on Malcolm visiting, he entered the bookstore with the crate.

"Oh, hello!" she cried, coming forward to meet him. "Aren't you Mr. Branwell?"

Malcolm was astonished to be recognized but even more surprised by the physical perfection of the shop's new clerk. He'd never expected Sloan Taylor, whom he deemed an unprincipled wolf, to hire an unattractive assistant, but Hope Spencer Lawrence was so far at the other end of the spectrum that he was momentarily bereft of speech. Attempting not to stare too lingeringly at the California-bred Aphrodite, with her two feet of flaxen hair and heavenly waist, he gazed instead into her wide blue eyes and found himself in even greater danger of becoming enthralled. He slid the crate onto a countertop and extended his hand. "You must be Hope Lawrence?"

She warmly shook his hand. "Your photo didn't do you justice, Mr. Branwell."

"Photo?"

"In the magazine."

Malcolm tried to remember the last time his photo had been published. As the youthful CEO of the Branwell's Book Bag chain he had been profiled a number of times, but not in any publication he would have expected Hope to have read.

"Hugo Sands' magazine," she reminded him helpfully.

"Oh!" He colored as he suddenly remembered that Hope was in the scene. Marguerite had mentioned this at a moment when Malcolm had entertained only feelings of resentment towards the shop and the scene and he recalled being more annoyed than intrigued at the time.

"What were you doing reading that?"

"Well, we do carry it here in the shop," she explained, examining the literary portraits in the crate with a racing pulse. She had never seduced a man and hadn't the faintest notion of how to begin. "I've read every issue from cover to cover," she added, so there could be no doubt as to her own orientation. "These portraits are charming. Would you hang them for me?" she asked casually.

"Do you know where you want them?" Malcolm was relieved to get away from the topic of Hugo Sands' magazine and once again shouldered the crate.

"Yes, I think I'll put them in the third gallery!" Hope cried, inspired. "I'll get a hammer and nails and meet you up there!"

Malcolm watched her lock the door and put out the Closed sign before disappearing into the office, then he climbed the spiral staircase to the third floor. He remembered the last time he'd been up there. It had been tremendous finally having Marguerite. But he hadn't forgotten that only minutes before he took his wife-to-be for the very first time—Michael Flagg had been flirting with her on the lower level!

Hope joined him as he lay the pictures on the reading desk. The gallery walls were painted dark green, against which the gold framed portraits would show richly. Grateful for the time it gave her to think, she carefully directed him as to the placement of the pictures.

"How charming," Hope commented, as the portrait of Charlotte Lennox went up. "Your wife has such exquisite taste!" Malcolm couldn't quite smile in acknowledgement. "How I long to meet her!" Now he positively frowned.

"Which one next?"

"Frances Burney. Right here," Hope indicated a spot. "Why doesn't she ever visit the shop? She and I seem to have so much in common."

"Hmph," he grunted, thinking, *"If that's true I feel sorry for your husband!"*

"I think it's marvelously romantic the way you met through your personal ad."

"Really!" he pronounced the word ironically.

"I think it's the height of good breeding to meet through a correspondence. My husband was compelled to beat a much cruder path to my door," Hope revealed.

"Oh?"

"He found me working in a B&D club in Hollywood."

"So, was that your last position before coming here?" Malcolm was scandalized.

"No. Just prior to coming back East I was doing video work. Then David got offered the teaching post at Braemar and invited me to accompany him here as his wife. Wasn't that romantic?"

"Which one's next?" Malcolm asked, hammer and nail fixture in hand.

"Elizabeth Inchbald. Place her just to the right of Frances Burney, please," Hope directed, stepping back to study the effect. "I understand you're practically a newlywed yourself?"

"Practically," he replied in a tone devoid of warmth.

"Better move that one over to the left another inch."

"Are you sure?"

"Uh-huh," murmured Hope, studying the dramatic "V" formation of his shoulders and waist when he turned to hammer the nail. While she was growing fonder of his physique by the moment, she felt increasingly self-conscious about initiating the planned mischief. Damn him for his polite indifference to her brilliant pheramones.

"You must have received dozens of answers to your ad," she returned to the subject of Malcolm with renewed zest. She had thought of her assignment as simply doing a good deed for a goddess but now it had become an artistic challenge. Unlike her alley cat of a husband, this modest and sincere married male would never be the first to make a move.

"I got a few."

"I'll bet your heart nearly stopped when Marguerite's was one of them," Hope guessed ingenuously.

"Now look," he suddenly snapped, causing her heart to contract, "I'm sure you're a very nice person and mean no harm, but you've been asking some very impertinent questions and I think you'd better stop."

"I'm sorry!"

"Who's next?" he gestured at the art.

"Oh, Maria Edgeworth. Line her up about three inches below Charlotte Lennox, please." Hope paced as he hammered the nail. The pictures were going up fast and she was no nearer to winning him over. Just the opposite! He seemed irritated with her. "Please forgive me if I offended you," she murmured.

"You didn't offend me."

"If I seemed too familiar it's only because I know that you're in the scene. Just that one fact seems to promote intimacy. I guess you don't agree?"

"I never thought about it."

"That's your problem," she blurted out.

"I beg your pardon?"

"Never mind."

"I want to know what you meant by that remark," he persisted.

"I can't elaborate without being even more impertinent."

Malcolm straightened Maria Edgeworth's portrait with a critical eye. "My wife forced me to read a book by her once," he admitted mildly. "Not bad."

"I like your wife!" cried Hope enthusiastically. "Oh, how I wish you'd let her be my friend!"

Malcolm felt himself becoming angry. Unaware of how rapidly information could be disseminated within a clique, he was astonished that this shop girl, a total stranger to him until minutes ago, should know so much about his relationship with Marguerite. It was also humiliating to be reproached for what even he was beginning to consider his unfair repression of his wife by this infuriating brat.

"And oh, how I wish I had the authority to fire you for your utter lack of tact and total rudeness!" he declared.

Hope went pale and red by degrees. Suddenly she also felt angry. She was about to retort but tears filled her eyes and she turned her back on him to compose herself. When he noticed the shoulders of her dove grey cardigan tremble he felt an unpleasant spasm of guilt.

"Sensitive, aren't you?" he brusquely observed.

"I'll be happy to resign," she whimpered, wounded nearly beyond words.

"Oh, don't be silly."

"You don't know me and I was forward with you," Hope excoriated herself.

He suddenly felt a cad. "Look, I didn't mean what I said. I'm sure the shop is lucky to have you. Will you forgive me for upsetting you? Please?"

Hope turned to him and smiled. "Yes, thank you." Then she ingeniously added, "Will you show me that you forgive me too by giving me a hug?" Without allowing him to decide, she threw her arms around his slim waist and pressed her fair head to his chest, breathing a sigh of contentment. Malcolm felt it was very wrong, but couldn't help locking his own arms around the bewitching beauty, who did not seem inclined to release him for some moments. When she pulled back it was to look up into his eyes with frank admiration. "I love when I can feel a man's rib cage."

"That's nice but I think you'd better stop now," he advised, pulling her hands away. However, he could not bring himself to relinquish them at once. "You know, I'm beginning to think that you're a very naughty girl." He let her go and went back to hanging the remaining two portraits. "I assume Jane Austen is next?"

"Yes, please."

"I wonder what your husband would say if he knew that you went around fondling other men's rib cages."

Hope laughed, "He wouldn't *say* anything."

"Right!"

"That looks good. Now put Anne Brontë up just to her right."

"Suppose the situation were reversed and I squeezed *your* waist? Would you consider that acceptable behavior?"

"Highly!" she readily assented, bringing up his color again. "But why stop there?"

"Mrs. Lawrence, I'm beginning to get the impression that you're flirting with me," Malcolm pronounced disapprovingly.

"Is that so terrible?"

"Considering we're both married, yes."

"Aren't you ever spontaneous?"

"If I did what I really feel like doing right now you wouldn't like it," he asserted bluntly, putting the last picture up.

"You mean fire me?"

"No, turn you over my knee!"

"Oh!" Hope blushed, having almost forgotten that option in her unadulterated lust for his athletic body.

"However, I don't chastise other men's wives," he told her, standing back from the portrait to judge his job.

"You know, you're impossibly stuffy! It's really hard for me to believe that you're even in the scene, no less husband to the divine Marguerite Alexander. I've heard about straight-laced New Englanders but always thought they were a Hollywood cliche. Don't you realize the millennium is here?"

Malcolm regarded her for a long moment. "God, I'd enjoy spanking you for your insolence!"

"But you just don't dare, do you?" she mocked him, weary of attempting to seduce him. "Because then you would have *touched* a girl and you couldn't lord it over Marguerite that you were so pure and she so abandoned!"

Malcolm thought of slapping her face but good manners held him in check. "I just realized something," he murmured, "you're stuck on my wife!"

"Really, Mr. Branwell, what a thing to say," she weakly protested, cursing herself for blurting the recrimination out.

"You just used the word *abandoned* with regard to Marguerite. Thank you for opening my eyes. Compared to you, she's a Catholic saint. At least she has to know a man three or four weeks before committing adultery."

She calmly swept the hammer and nails into a drawer in the reading table, then sat on the table to look at the job he had done. "I can't believe how fast you put those up," she remarked, feeling her face begin to burn with embarrassment at the way she had failed in her task. She had never in her life had so little effect on a healthy male.

"As I said, you do need a good spanking, but I'm going to let your husband give it to you," Malcolm announced with resolve.

"My husband? What do you mean?" Hope cried, her heart contracting.

"Do you know what this shop is, Hope? It's a breeding ground for marital infidelity. But you and I are going to break the cycle!"

"Yes, of course, but what did you mean when you mentioned my husband?"

"At least I'm going to break the cycle," he amended, remembering that that unprincipled seducer of married women, Sloan Taylor, still ran the shop and was Hope's superior. "You've probably already been down on your knees to your boss," he accused with cruel derision.

"Nothing of the sort," she replied unsteadily, "but what did you mean about my husband? You did mention him just now."

"I intend to send him a letter informing him of his wife's outlandish behavior."

"You're joking."

Hope followed Malcolm downstairs, turning out lights behind them as they went, her knees rubbery. "You really don't intend to do that, Mr. Branwell, do you?"

"You're afraid of your husband, I see. Good! I hope he beats the daylights out of you."

"Mr. Branwell, you can't mean that!" she nearly sobbed. "I mean, think of his feelings. Be a sport."

This exhortation weakened his resolve, but he was enjoying her humility and pleading far too much to let her know she'd gained an edge.

"Good night, Mrs. Lawrence," Malcolm said, striding out the front door, whereupon Hope immediately burst into tears. Not only had she failed in her mission, but now she was going to have a note written home to David!

"Well, you may or may not be happy to know that you've got a 100% bona fide tart working for you at the bookstore," Malcolm matter of factly announced to Marguerite as he unpacked groceries in the kitchen of her house on the tip of Random Point several minutes later. Marguerite turned to him as she gingerly removed the shepherd's pie from the oven, steam rising from the punctures in the crust.

"What do you mean?"

"I mean that Hope Spencer Lawrence is an unrepentant thrill-seeker with no more respect for her own marriage vows than anyone else's, least of all yours."

"I don't understand."

"I hadn't been in the shop ten minutes before she began coming on to me."

"Coming on to you?"

"As I was putting up the pictures she began to needle me."

"Needle you about what?"

"Our relationship!" he coldly returned. "She's pretty well informed about it."

Marguerite changed the subject. "Is she as attractive as I've heard?"

"Stunning. But of course she'd have to be to get away with half her nonsense."

"Tell me more about what happened."

"Well, after she got a good rise out of me and I responded by telling her off, she proceeded to squeeze out a couple of tears, which of course turned me to butter. During the consolation stage she heavily turned on the charm, giving me to understand that spontaneity was her god. There wasn't a doubt in my mind that I could have had her then and there. I tell you, it made me so mad, I almost spanked her."

"Almost? That doesn't sound like you."

"Marguerite! You're just as bad as she is. In fact, you really are two of a kind!" he declared, pacing with his hands in the pockets of his khakis. "Oh, and by the way, she worships you. Worships you and yet feels no compunction about putting the make on your husband! Can you even begin to comprehend such a twisted mentality?"

"Worships me?" Marguerite smiled.

"You don't even care that she came on to me, do you?"

"If she couldn't help herself."

"How could she not help herself? I'm a married man. She's a married woman. We'd met two minutes before in a semi-public place. How could she not help herself?"

"If she found you so attractive as to be irresistible."

"Are you saying that you wouldn't be upset, disturbed or in the least bit jealous if I were to make love to another woman? And a beauty at that?"

"I'm saying nothing of the kind. I'm sure I would be jealous if I thought you did make love to her, especially if she's as glorious as everyone says she is. But not if you just spanked the naughty flirt."

"Hmph!"

"You really should have spanked her. I'm sure that's what she wanted."

"And how do you think her husband would feel if he found out about it?"

"Perhaps he's the liberal type."

"We'll see how liberal he is after he's been apprised of the situation."

"Malcolm, you aren't going to tell him!"

"Maybe after she's had a sharp lesson from her husband she'll think twice before accosting strangers as she did me."

"Malcolm you couldn't possibly be so cruel as to report her misbehavior to her husband. He might be terribly hurt."

"Better now than later, after she's trampled on every marriage vow she ever made."

"But, Malcolm, this isn't funny. We have no idea of what Mr. Lawrence may be like. He could really be the violent type. You don't want to be responsible for Hope getting a black eye, do you?"

"Oh, Marguerite, don't be ridiculous. Hope's a willful, arrogant, spoiled rotten, little slut."

"Still, why not think it over a couple of days before you do something rash?" Marguerite urged, cutting him a slice of pie.

"I can't understand why you have the slightest degree of sympathy for that brat. Mm, this is good. It tastes very rich though," he commented with disapproval.

"You can indulge yourself slightly for once," she fondly observed, pouring his tea. "Surely you used up your daily ration of puritanical self-denial in refusing to enjoy Hope Spencer's charms?"

"There must be a thousand calories in one slice of this," he speculated.

The small seed of lust which Hope had planted in Malcolm's brain germinated overnight to the point that he awoke the following morning with a raging erection, having dreamt of her cornsilk hair. It was another rainy day. Marguerite was already downstairs brewing coffee as he sat up with a start and tried in vain to recapture the elusive wisps of dream that were quickly floating out of his mind.

He showered and dressed in confusion, wanting nothing more than to stroll directly over to the bookshop and immediately claim all that had been so casually offered to him the previous day.

"I think I'll go out for some bagels," he told Marguerite on his way out the door.

"Okay, dear," she called from the kitchen.

Malcolm walked through the village under a big, black umbrella, hoping that Sloan would still be out of town and Hope manning the store. He found her alone in the shop, dressed in a white shirt and jeans under her cranberry apron, polishing the antique espresso maker while humming along to the 1924 cast album of *Funny Face* playing on a victrola in the corner.

"Mr. Branwell!" she cried with a blush as he walked in the door.

"Anyone here?" he asked, looking around.

"No."

"In that case we're closed for lunch," he told her, turning the sign in the front window around and locking the door. Then he strode over to the cappuccino bar and pulled her out from behind it by the wrist. "We have unfinished business," he told her, dragging her to the back of the shop, behind the back counter and into the office where he deposited her on the leather sofa before locking the door.

"Mr. Branwell, what in the world are you about?" she cried, jumping up. But he pushed her down again and sat down too. "I thought over everything you said and decided that it would be madness to repress my urge to spank you for a moment longer." And in so saying he took her by the arm and pulled her straight across his lap. The dark red apron strings framed her bottom in the jeans as cutely as could be, but the roundness of her cheeks had to be squeezed to be fully appreciated.

"Mr. Branwell, you're so different today!" she exclaimed, inwardly rejoicing at having worn her newest, darkest blue jeans, against which the sweep of her long fair hair looked particularly handsome as she lay across his powerful thighs.

He began to spank her with short, fast, warm-up smacks that were hard enough to elicit whimpers from Hope.

"I thought it over and realized that you deserve many spankings, not just ones from your husband. So in a sense I'm helping."

Now the spanks came slower and harder. The jeans kept in the heat, but he could feel it coming through them. An experienced submissive, Hope rapidly fell under the hypnotic spell of the falling smacks and ceased to whimper.

"Lift up," he ordered and when she did, he unbuttoned and unzipped her jeans and deftly slipped his hand into her panties to capture her sex in his palm. Then pressing his hand against her Venus mound and slit, he continued with the spanking though her jeans.

"My God, what are you doing?"

"I just want to feel you get wet."

"Oh! How dare you!" She tried to wriggle away from his hand but he held her fast. Five or six more smacks fell on her snugly denimed backside.

"Hold still, you. It's a bit late to start playing the prude."

Hope didn't know whether to say "Ow!" or "Oooooh!" as he lightly entwined his finger tips in her dewy pubic curls while simultaneously smacking her bottom ever more resoundingly. Harder and faster he spanked her while holding her sex in the palm of his hand. Finally he allowed one slender finger to slip up into her vaginal canal, which instantly clung like a wet, velvet sheath. At the same time he yanked her jeans down, along with her thin white cotton panties, to bare her silken pink-on-cream cheeks.

Ceasing to masturbate her, he held her fast around the waist and continued the spanking resolutely, covering her small, round bottom with score upon score of sharp smacks.

Hope passively submitted, transported by his firm but sensual techniques. She enjoyed the way he reached under her and deliberately divided her labia before pressing her back down against his olive twill trousers.

Then he took her one step further, by deliberately spreading her pinkened cheeks and spanking in between them.

Hope couldn't help but gasp when he spanked her anus.

"I couldn't stop thinking of you the entire night," he reported at length.

She shifted and the tiny target disappeared. She squirmed and twisted, broke his hold and seated herself upright on his lap.

"You thought of me?" she cried, wrapping her arms around his neck and nuzzling his throat with her cheek. "Thank you for telling me that! I thought you despised me when you walked out of here yesterday."

"I just wanted to wring your neck."

"You wanted to tell my husband how I had outraged your decency," she smiled, jumping off his lap to pull up her jeans.

"Oh, I never really meant to do that."

"Really? I was so certain that you would that I went home and made a full confession to David."

"I'm sure you did not such thing!"

"You shouldn't be so sure of everything. I would have told him anyway. It might have been a day, it might have been a week. But I'd have blurted it out."

"And what happened?"

"I don't think I'll tell you."

"No, really, how did he take it? I'm curious about how other men react to such behavior."

Hope straightened her apron and hair in the Art Deco mirror. "Well, unlike you, David has a sense of humor. Though he said it served me right for thinking I was irresistible to men."

"Is that all he said or did?"

"Must I really reveal how I was punished by my husband?" She pouted so deliciously that he could no longer resist the impulse to take her in his arms and kiss her full, red mouth.

Hope gasped when Malcolm finally let her go.

"You're a sweet girl. I'm sorry I didn't realize that yesterday. I hope you didn't get in too much trouble."

"Oh, David doesn't take things too seriously," Hope disclosed.

"Good," said Malcolm, pulling her back into his arms to kiss her again.

"What's going on?" she asked, in a daze from his bruising kisses. "You changed."

"Just consider yourself lucky you're not wearing a skirt," he warned her, fondling her waist as well as her firm, little, apple-round bosom through the apron and shirt. "I could bend you over and be in you in a second." He pulled her hard against him again, breathed in the faint perfume of her hair and squeezed her bottom through the jeans with both hands while fastening his lips to her throat. She luxuriated in his deep kisses for several minutes, feeling like the cover of a bodice-ripper.

"I could kneel and give you head," she suggested, "And you could correct me with your belt."

Malcolm sat on the leather sofa and she knelt between his legs to watch him unbuckle his belt and pull it free. Doubling it he motioned for her to unzip his trousers. Hope did this without hesitation for her animal spirits were running high and she'd dreamt of Malcolm all night. His erection sprang into her hand.

"What a beautiful cock," she murmured. "Now I really wish I'd worn a skirt too." For she hated the thought of being bent over and taken with her jeans inelegantly around her ankles, nor could she see herself stripping in Sloan's office in the middle of a work day for a romp on the leather sofa with the owner's husband.

"That's why you're being punished." He began to strap her lightly, not too certain it was safe to do otherwise with his organ between her teeth.

"Mm, a little harder would teach me a better lesson," she prettily begged, for the strap felt divine through her jeans and made the act of servicing him while fully dressed exquisitely submissive.

Five minutes of this and he was ready to relinquish all claim the moral high ground in his marriage and discharge passionately. Hope sensed the subtle indications of the coming deluge and pulled away just in time to miss being choked or drenched by Malcolm's liquid tribute as it harmlessly fell on the soil of a potted palm several feet away.

"You little darling," he told her, kissing her head before pulling her to her feet.

"You big bruiser," she teased fondly.

He took her in his arms and held her close, all his resentment and confusion about Random Point evaporating into the cedar scented atmosphere of Sloan's office.

Hope was pleased, feeling she'd done good to her boss and the scene. But late that afternoon, her husband strode into the shop with a look on his face that told her she'd outsmarted herself.

Without much preamble, David took Hope by the ear and dragged her into the back of the store, where he threw her into the first open doorway he came to, which was Sloan Taylor's office, where she'd given Malcolm Branwell such a thrill earlier that day.

Accusations issued from her husband's handsome mouth as concisely as might be expected from a prep school English teacher. It seemed he'd made one of his rare visits to the gym in search of a game of squash. There he encountered Malcolm Branwell, who introduced himself to David and accepted the challenge. David presently discovered that Malcolm was the husband of the owner of the book shop where Hope worked. David then revealed to Malcolm that he was the husband of Marguerite's employee, Hope. Hearing this, Malcolm Branwell was at first flustered, then confiding.

Naturally, David was not surprised to be complimented on his bride, to hear her looks compared to those of the young Grace Kelly and her manners described as charming. What disturbed him was when Malcolm said how much he admired David for "being so evolved about Hope, and her unabashed availability." This statement leaving David speechless, Malcolm added quickly that Hope had explained about how she shared everything with her husband, or he never would have said a word. Indeed, he would have felt extraordinarily uncomfortable even confronting David.

Playing along, David had agreed that it was wonderful how Hope told him everything, while Malcolm lamented the fact that his wife told him nothing. David said perhaps there was nothing to tell, which made Malcolm laugh. Then Malcolm beat David at squash and they parted on a friendly note, after which David had come directly to the book store.

David sat on the edge of Sloan's desk and crooked his finger at his wife, who blushed and hung back. But the office was small enough for him to reach out for her wrist and yank her straight across his knee.

"Hope, what does Malcolm Branwell think you told me?"

"You want to converse with me like this?"

Smack! Smack! Smack! "Answer the question, Hope."

"No. Let me go! I will not be interrogated like this! And David, the store is still open for business. What if a customer came in?"

"If a customer comes in, we'll hear the bell and I'll let you go."

"How can we hear the tiny tinkle of the bell with you whacking away at me with all your might?"

"What did Malcolm mean when he used the term 'unabashed availability' with regard to my dear wife?"

"I suppose it was just something he inferred from my conversation," Hope suggested, trying for a more comfortable position as she dangled in mid-air. David resumed spanking her in a most unpleasant style.

"Hope, did you come on to Malcolm?"

She was momentarily reprieved by the tinkle of the bell. "I may have flirted a little," she blushingly revealed before running out to attend to the customer.

The shop was closing in fifteen minutes. Hope busied herself with all the usual chores while David paced the aisles impatiently.

When six o'clock struck he himself ushered the lone browser out and locked the door.

Hope was not so easily corralled this time and he had to chase her around the first floor and up the stairs before finally catching her on the third gallery landing. Hope attempted to marshal her thoughts as David seized her by the forearm and thrust her down across the reading table, pinning her by the waist and using his other hand to renew the warmth in her jeans.

"You're not supposed to be flirting," he advised her, bringing his palm down hard across either cheek repeatedly. "You're a married woman now. Remember?"

"Of course, David. Naturally. I think about it all the time."

"Then why approach your boss's husband?" David stopped spanking her to let her reply.

"It's a long and complicated story," Hope explained, reaching back to rub her bottom.

"I've got time."

"But we have to get home. I have to cook dinner and—"

"I want to hear the long and complicated story," David told her, reaching under her to unbuckle her belt and lower her zipper. Like the proper submissive she was, Hope sighed and stayed in position as he pulled down her blue jeans and panties to mid-thigh. He found her stunning bottom already creamy pink from his hand. Pressing her against the table hard he began to loudly smack her and stain her cheeks magenta with his punishing palm.

Hope sighed again. When he pressed her down against the table a thrill rippled through her that nearly triggered an actual climax, but the pain of the slaps that followed all but blocked the sexual charge. Hope cried out but he ignored her, renewing his grip on her waist.

Becoming more accustomed to the rhythm of his arm she succumbed to its seductive power and began to experience spasms of pleasure in spite of the pain. Somehow being *held down* for a spanking, in just the right way, sent her into transports. She communicated the effect he was having upon her with whimpers and pants.

No man ever being proof against Hope in a state of excitement, least of all her husband, David relented and let her up, drawing her into his arms. Kissing and fingering her he determined she was ready and wet.

Bending her over the desk, David entered Hope from behind. The indignity of being taken with her jeans around her ankles did not please her but the throbbing in her clitoris cried out for appeasement.

"I can't believe you flirt with other men!" He drove into her hard and spanked her for good measure. Hope could only sob with sexual emotion and grip the edge of the desk as he took her with abandon.

"It was for a very good cause," she explained, some minutes later, as they set their clothes to rights, counting herself lucky to get off so easily, having been so very wayward that day.